SNOW PLACE
Like Home

SNOW PLACE
Like Home

We Three Kings
Book One

RACHEL THORNE

Romances by Rachel Thorne

CLOSED DOOR ROMANCE
We Three Kings
Snow Place Like Home
Snow Hard Feelings
(October 2026)

Romances by Denise Grover Swank

Asheville Brewing
Any Luck at All
Better Luck Next Time
Getting Lucky
Bad Luck Club

Bad Luck Club
Love at First Hate
Jingle Bell Hell
Fraudulently Ever After
Matchmaking Mischief

SPICY ROMANCE
The Wedding Pact
The Substitute
The Player
The Gambler

Chapter One

Finley

"Barb, I need to go," I tell my seventy-eight-year-old neighbor on my phone screen, cursing the day she learned how to make video calls. I'm hiding in the backroom of the coffee shop where I work, because Barb has called me five times in less than two minutes and I was sure that this time it's an emergency.

It is not.

"But you didn't tell me if your hospital gives out free condoms," she pouts. "Shirley insists they do."

"I've never seen free condoms lying around," I say with a tight smile, "but I can ask around tonight at work, if you want." I have no intention of doing so, but what she doesn't know, won't hurt her. Most nights I'm too busy running around the hospital drawing blood, and even if I had time to look, I wouldn't. But if push comes to shove, I'll buy a ginormous box and bring it home, telling her they were free.

"Shirley says I need to use condoms because senior citizens have a high rate of getting the clap."

I bite my bottom lip to keep from laughing. Now I'm *definitely* picking up the box. While I know Barb has an active sex life, it's never occurred to me to ask if she was using condoms. Then again, safe-sex talks with my neighbor old enough to be my grandmother wasn't exactly on my bingo card. Now I realize I need to rethink that. "Shirley's right. I'll make sure you get some."

She frowns, her face filling the screen. "What if—"

"Finley!" my boss, Maggie, shouts from the front. "We've got a rush comin' in."

"Barb," I say, already walking to the door, "I really have to go. I'll find out about the condoms and let you know." Then I hang up before she can find another reason to keep me on the call.

I shove my phone into the pocket of my red apron, take a deep breath, and push through the swinging door.

Maggie's right. At least fifteen people are in line, and my coworker, Bethany, already looks haggard trying to keep up.

I flash Bethany an apologetic smile and slide into my position behind the espresso machine.

Most Beans to Go customers work on one of the forty-two floors above us, and right now they all look desperate for caffeine. We're always busy in the mornings, but the past couple of weeks have been next-level since it's the holiday season and Christmas is less than two weeks away. Between shopping, decorating, parties, and everything else, our customers need IV drips of energy. Since we're not qualified to offer those, we sell them caffeinated beverages instead.

"What did Barb want this time?" Bethany asks with a laugh.

She's heating up a pastry, so I lean closer and lower my voice. "She wanted to know if the hospital gives out free condoms. One of our neighbors told her that seniors have a higher incidence of STDs."

Bethany's eyes go wide. "You're kidding!"

"Kiddin' about what?" Maggie asks, as she scribbles a name on a cup and sets it on the counter beside me.

I take a quick glance at the name and confirm that Constance from the twenty-fourth floor hasn't gotten a wild hair up her butt and changed her usual order. It's the same caramel latte with skim milk she gets every day. I know most of the regular's names and drinks, and while some switch it up, most stick to their usual.

"That old people get a lot of STDs," Bethany says.

Constance pays and moves along the counter toward the espresso machine. "It's true," she says with a prim nod. "My aunt caught syphilis when she moved into a retirement community."

Bethany gets a wicked gleam in her eye. "Don't *you* live in a retirement community, Finley?"

I laugh as I steam Constance's milk. "I live in an apartment complex for seniors, which is *very* different than a retirement community." The rent is about three times cheaper, and the only amenity is a laundry room that sometimes has all five washing machines in working order. "But I have to admit that some of my neighbors have *very* active love lives."

"Unlike you," Maggie pipes up, jotting the next name on a cup.

Mike from the sixteenth floor—recently divorced and has two teenage boys who play baseball. His usual drink is a medium Americano.

I grin. "I'm not into men three times my age."

Mike taps his phone to pay, shooting me a sidelong glance.

I quickly add, "And even if I was, I don't have time for a love life." It's not a lie, even though I said it loud enough for Mike to hear. I've seen the interest in his eyes lately. The last thing I want is to risk offending him when I inevitably turn him down.

"You need to live a little, Fin," Maggie says. "Life is more than work and school. You need to have *fun*."

"There'll be plenty of time for fun once I graduate."

But her words scrape an open wound. The anniversary of my mother's death is coming in a few weeks, and I've been thinking about the promises she dragged out of me on her deathbed. I haven't lived up to them, and I can't help thinking she'd be disappointed. Every year I tell myself that I'll keep my promise once I'm more financially stable. Get a little farther in school. When my life's more stable. But I can hear her voice in my head—the one from when she was strong and cancer free—telling me I'm making excuses and letting her down.

Again.

But I don't have time to dwell on sad things. Lord knows I'll have plenty of time over Christmas. Alone in my one-bedroom apartment, splurging on a steak and baked potato and watching

While You Were Sleeping with my grumpy, long-haired cat Maybelle.

The next half hour flies by. Maggie, Bethany, and I work like a well-oiled machine until the line dwindles down to just a few customers.

I'm wiping down the espresso machine when Lauren, a legal assistant from the twenty-ninth floor says, "Oh, my *word*, Maggie! The Christmas decorations are even better than last year!"

"That's all Finley," Maggie brags. "She's chock-full of Christmas spirit!"

"Finley decorated all this?" Lauren asks, glancing around the store.

"She sure did!" Bethany pipes up. "She's decorated the place for the past three Christmases and adds to it every year. Isn't it something?"

"The owner gives me money each year to add to it," I admit, blushing.

"She loves Christmas," Maggie says. "Like *looooves* it."

"It's true." My face heats even more. "It's my favorite holiday."

"Understatement of the year," Bethany says.

I shrug as I take Lauren's cup from Maggie. I'm surprised my coworkers don't expand on why I love Christmas, but I'm grateful. My heart feels more tender than usual today.

"She makes a lot of this stuff," Maggie says. "Isn't she talented?"

"I also thrift a lot of it," I add, starting Lauren's peppermint mocha.

Thrifting helps stretch the meager budget I'm given each year. When I first started working here, the decorations were sad —tired tinsel and cheap stockings with our names in glue and glitter. I asked for a couple hundred dollars to fix it up, convincing the owner it would be good for business. She'd been so pleased that she's given me a few hundred dollars every year since. The past two years, the decorations have drawn foot traffic.

Passersby spot them through the street windows and come in to admire the display, usually purchasing a drink and sometimes a pastry.

Now the dining room has two full-sized artificial trees, chock full of ornaments in different themes, several smaller trees scattered around, snowmen and Santa figurines, a working train, multiple reindeer, and a whole host of other decorations. I even paint holly and snowmen on the windows. I do it all on my own time—which Maggie thinks is unfair—but I don't mind.

From early November to mid-January, it makes me feel a little closer to my mother.

But now I'm thinking about Mom again. Our Christmases were always meager, but we still decorated, even if it was just homemade ornaments. It was our favorite holiday, and her most fervent wish was to go north for a real white Christmas with all the trimmings.

But money is always tight for a single mother, so we never made it happen. We kept putting it off to "someday." Then Mom was diagnosed with stage four breast cancer at the start of my senior year. The treatments and hospital visits whittled what little we had and left me with a debt so enormous it's taken me six years to crawl out.

Promise me you'll live, Finley. Promise me you'll take chances and have fun.

Taking chances has been impossible while holding down two jobs and community college part time. And having fun? My sweet neighbors count, but I know that's not what she meant. Still, there's a light at the end of the tunnel. In a few more months I'll have the debt paid off, and maybe I can finally breathe.

Then I can have fun.

Who am I kidding? I still have two years of college, and after years of juggling credit payments, I swore I'd never be in debt again. I've only taken the community classes I could afford to pay outright, but most community colleges don't offer bachelor's degrees in nursing. Tuition will take a leap, and since I refuse to get student loans, unless I get the Freeman Scholarship, I might not even go.

I hand Lauren her drink and glance up to check the line. And that's when I see him.

Alex from the twenty-eighth floor.

He's with his business partner, Roland. They rarely come in together, and both are usually in earlier, so they must be on their way back from a meeting. Roland's a huge flirt, and Alex...

Alex is a conundrum.

I'm immune to most men's charms, but he gives me butter-flies. Tall, dark, and handsome, sure—but there's something else about him. Something I can't figure out.

Not that anything will ever come from it. For one, I refuse to date customers—too messy if things don't work out. And two, I don't have time. I've tried dating over the past few years, but most men want more—more than I'm willing or even capable of giving. So, I've decided to stay single until I get my life together.

Which means I might spend the rest of my life alone.

But I'm strangely okay with that. I have my neighbors. I have my cat. I have my memories of my mother.

That's enough. Right?

Chapter Two

Eloise is coming for Christmas! Suck it, bro!

"Grant, you damn bastard," I mutter under my breath.

I'm in line at the Beans to Go, the coffee shop on the ground floor of my Atlanta office building, with my business partner Roland Greer at my side. He's scrolling through his phone as are most of the people in the line in front and behind me.

Festive holiday music is playing on the overhead speakers. The shop has floor-to-ceiling windows on two of the walls. One faces the street, and through the painted glass I see people hurrying to wherever they seem to be heading. The other glass wall looks into the three-story lobby. A giant fifteen-foot glass bobble chandelier hangs in the lobby, making the dark marble floor gleam.

The coffee shop is always bright and cheerful, with live plants and comfortable furniture. But from November to January, when it's decorated for the holidays, the place transforms into a holiday wonderland. It reminds me of Christmas at home, so some days I'm down here twice, even if lately it makes me more homesick than usual.

But I'm going home in five days—a trip I'm equally excited for and dreading. And now that Eloise is coming, dread is winning out.

The woman in front of me must have heard me swear, because she glances over her shoulder, giving me a dead-eyed stare.

Clearly, someone needs her caffeine fix.

I'm about to ignore her, but she looks so much like my Aunt Sylvia—from her widow's peak hairline, the bump at the bridge of her nose, and the way her eyebrows seem sunken over her eyelids—that it's damn spooky, and there's no way I'd blow off my aunt. So, I cringe and say, "Sorry, ma'am. I just got some bad news."

She turns to face me, her irritation replaced by concern. "And at Christmas time too, you poor thing." She shakes her head. "What happened? Did you lose your house? Your job?"

"No, ma'am."

"Did Grant run over your dog?"

I'm taken back that she knows my brother's name, then remember I used it when I swore. "What? No, nothing like that." I take a breath, trying to figure out the shortest way to explain it. "Grant stole my bed."

Her eyes widen, and she eyes me up and down, clearly appraising me. I'm used to it from women of all ages, but they're usually more sly about it. Finally, she tilts her head and narrows her eyes with a venom I don't expect. "Grant could do worse, so you must be a downright bastard yourself if he left you." Then she turns around and begins whispering to the older woman next to her.

Roland bursts out laughing. "She thinks you're gay."

"No shit," I grumble. "I got that."

I'm not irritated that she thinks I'm gay. Curtis, one of my best friends from high school, is gay, and if I swung that way, he'd be the first man I'd hit on. But I'm still pissed at Grant, and becoming more so by the second.

"So, Eloise is coming to Christmas after all?" Roland asks, still chuckling.

Given his narcissism, I'm surprised he figured that out without me spelling it out.

"I'm so glad you find this amusing." I give him a dark look. "You're not the one who's going to end up sleeping on a sofa bed for eleven days. And on top of that, my mother said my Aunt Jean is coming this year and bringing her three grandchildren." I narrow my eyes. "Who are sleeping in the rec room." I level my gaze. "Where the sofa bed resides."

The line moves forward, and Roland breaks out into another fit of laughter. My Aunt Sylvia doppelganger has reached the register, and she and her friend are placing their order, some complicated mash up of syrups.

Roland can't seem to let this go. "You're bunking with three little kids? Dude, that's insane. Just get a room at a hotel or rent an Airbnb."

"Have you ever been to Hollybrook, Vermont, at Christmastime?" I ask. "It's like a Christmas Hallmark movie. Hotels and Airbnbs sell out by February for the next year. And even if I *wanted* to stay somewhere else, my mother would have a fit. She insists we all stay in the same house, especially since it's the only time she can see some of us." Last time she said it, she'd looked me dead in the eye.

Guilty as charged, though. I don't see them enough. The start-up takes nearly all my time and attention. But that's an excuse, and I know it.

"So don't go home," Roland says.

Don't go home. Part of me leaps at the thought. Another part panics. As much as I've hated going home the past six years, I'm somehow even more homesick than ever. Still, fear they'll discover my secret outweighs everything else—even my longing to be there.

Fake Aunt Sylvia hands her credit card to Maggie, the woman who's working the register. Sometimes Maggie makes drinks, but during the morning rush, Finley or Bethany usually work the espresso machine.

Yeah, I know all the employees by name and where they usually work. That doesn't make me a stalker—it makes me observant. At least, that's what I tell myself when really, I'm looking for one employee in particular. Watching everyone else makes it less creepy.

Today, Finley's making drinks. Her mouth is twisted to the

side as she concentrates on making Fake Aunt Sylvia's complicated diabetes in a cup. Her long dark hair is pulled into a high ponytail that she's doubled up into a messy bun with a red and white scrunchie. All week she's been wearing a vintage-looking gold reindeer pin which has a red stone for the nose. The reindeer pin's clipped to her red apron, the one with a snowman over her chest and her name tag above it. Maggie and Bethany wear the standard brown aprons with the Beans to Go logo, so she must've brought hers from home. Her cheeks are flushed from the cranked-up heat to fight Atlanta's so-called cold spell—mid-thirties. Please. That's light jacket weather in Vermont. Finley's layered in a black, long-sleeve shirt under a kelly green, short-sleeve shirt.

"Tell your mom you're too busy with work." Roland barely glances up from his phone. "Which is true. It's a critical time and we need all hands on deck to get this project ready to launch at the end of January."

He has a point. It's a bad time to disappear, but I've skipped the last two years. My mother had been understandably upset when I'd cancelled a week before Christmas last year. We'd hit a snag that demanded my full attention, but the disappointment in her voice nearly broke me, so I'd promised I'd stay at least a week, maybe longer, this year. Roland had agreed to it at the time, but now that the trip is looming, he's been trying to convince me to cancel.

If I'm looking for a reason, this is a good one.

But I can't disappoint my mom again. I hate when I make her unhappy—which has unfortunately become something of a habit. Still, why had I told her I'd come for eleven days? A year ago, this Christmas had seemed so far away.

Now I want to strangle Past Alex.

The truth is, I love my family. Despite my reluctance to go home, I miss them. Even my damn bastard brother Grant. Roland, on the other hand, can't stand his brother and sister and barely tolerates his parents. His idea of skipping a family Christmas is equivalent to a reprieve from a prison sentence. He doesn't understand why I *want* to see my family, and after three years together as business partners, it's a waste of time and breath to try to explain it to him.

My seesaw of dread and excitement had finally found a balance, but now dread is winning by a landslide. Ten nights of sleepless nights on a saggy, two-inch mattress, springs poking my back and ass, kids screaming in my ear while I'm trying to sleep.

It's almost enough to risk my mother's disappointment and my brothers' guaranteed texts calling me an asshole for disappointing her again. Which, I'm sure, is exactly what Roland wants.

"We had a deal, Roland," I mutter, but the intensity of my voice leaves no room for doubt. Part of me can't believe after putting so much effort into staying away, that I'm now fighting to go.

He gives me a long look, one that makes me nervous before he says, "Okay, so you want to see your family and have your Hallmark Christmas. Tell me again why Grant bringing his girlfriend means *you* have to sleep on the sofa bed."

"It's simple. When we go home, we stay in our childhood bedrooms. Grant and I shared a room, but if one of us has a girlfriend, the other gets banished to the rec room."

"And if you *both* bring a girlfriend?"

"The oldest gets the room. I'm eleven months older, so it's mine."

"That's diabolical," Roland says with a wicked gleam. "I love it." Not a surprise. But I've seen that look before, usually right before one of his big ideas. Which means I should be terrified, because clearly this one involves me. "Sounds like you need a girlfriend."

And there it is.

I laugh. "You realize I'm leaving in *five* days."

"Look at you," he says, gesturing at my ... everything. "You could have a girlfriend by tonight if you wanted."

I'm not sure about getting a girlfriend, but yeah, I could probably find a woman to sleep with me. Finding a woman willing to fly to Vermont over the holidays would take more effort, but I might be able to pull it off. I can't help that I've been blessed with great genetics; I hit the gym to burn off my stress; and I know how to say things women like to hear. So yeah, there's a chance I could find a woman who'd go along with a crazy scheme.

But just because I *can* do it doesn't mean I *will.*

No way am I bringing a stranger home to my family—and any woman who'd say yes to that kind of a crazy scheme probably isn't the kind of woman I'd ever introduce to my mother.

Fake Aunt Sylvia finally moves to the side, opening up the register.

Roland and I step up to the counter. Maggie flashes me a mischievous grin. "Lookin' for a girlfriend, Alex? Because I can set you up with someone *amazing*." Her eyebrows dance over her eyes.

Roland stares, fascinated. "I didn't know eyebrows could do that."

While I'm also impressed with her eyebrow skills, I'm dumbfounded at her question. Maggie's an attractive woman, but I'd put her in her mid-forties. Nearly twenty years older than me. Never once in the year and a half that I've known her have I gotten the impression she's interested in me. "Uh..."

She laughs. "Calm down, lover boy. Not with *me*. As if you could handle this." She sweeps her hand up and down her body, then holds up her left hand, wiggling her fingers to show off the small diamond on her wedding band set. "Besides, I'm *very* happily married and my husband's quite good at handling *me*." She winks. "If you catch my drift."

Imagining Maggie's husband handling her wasn't on today's to-do list. "Uh. Yeah."

"Okay, then." She nods to her right. "I'm talkin' about *Finley.*"

Finley.

I swallow hard. Never in a million years would I date her.

Sure, I'm fascinated—but only because she's nothing like the women I usually date. Sweet. Kind. Always cheerful. She's sunshine in a bottle. She knows all the regulars by name, their drinks, even their kids, their pets. She has a way of making my shitty days just a little bit better.

She can spot when someone's struggling, and she goes out of her way to lift them up. Last year when my girlfriend Shawna had broken up with me, she noticed I was off. I hadn't told Roland, let alone the staff at the coffee shop, but Finley picked up on it. For weeks, she asked if I was okay. I said I was fine, but she knew better, so she'd slip a muffin in with my Danish and scrawl encouragements on my cup like. "Today's a new day!" and "One day at a time!"

What had been routine became something I looked forward to. *She* was something I looked forward to. And before I knew it, I was out of my funk.

Sure, I've thought about asking her out. But she's not my type. I date women who run companies, who live and breathe million-dollar deals. Finley? She makes lattes. Yeah, I hear how that sounds—pretentious asshole, right? Maybe I am. But I stick to women who speak the same language I do.

Still, I'd be lying if I said I hadn't noticed her laugh, or the way she's genuinely interested in people. Or the way her smile hits me square in the chest. Sometimes I wonder what it would be like if I weren't Alex King, cofounder of Zebra Tech, chasing seven million in venture capital. If I'd chosen something simpler, then I'd be someone who could date someone like Finley.

But that's a fantasy, and a stupid one. Even if I wanted to ask her out, I swore off dating after Shawna. I'm a workaholic with zero work-life balance—which she made abundantly clear. And when things go to hell at the office, I'm an asshole to live with. As Roland likes to remind me, we're married to Zebra Tech. For better or worse, richer or poorer. We were banking on richer, but poorer's always lurking. I don't have the luxury of splitting my focus.

"Hey, Finley," Roland says, oblivious to my existential crisis. He leans over the counter. "Do you like Christmas?"

She looks up from making Fake Aunt Sylvia's drink and smiles—when she does, it's not just with her mouth and eyes. Her whole body radiates with it. "Of course, I do, Roland. Only a scrooge wouldn't like Christmas."

"Have you heard of Hollybrook, Vermont?" he asks. "It's the Christmas capital of the world."

I watch in horror as I realize what he's doing. I need to shut him down, but I can't quite bring myself to do it. The thought of bringing Finley to Hollybrook has short circuited my brain.

Maggie takes the credit card from my hand and taps the screen.

That jars me out of my stupor. "Uh, Maggie? We didn't give our order yet."

"Please..." She rolls her eyes so hard I see nothing by whites. "You order the same thing every day. A large flat white and a cheese Danish. Mister Matchmaker over there orders a medium caramel latte." She hands back my card. "Besides, you could do worse than Finley."

There's no doubt my mother would love her.

When my mother met my first serious girlfriend after college, Patricia had called my parents *provincial,* which I didn't think sounded so bad. Mom told me that she hadn't meant it as a compliment. Mom was right, of course. Days later, I asked Patricia about it, and she'd admitted it—unapologetically—that she thought my parents didn't have enough class, and that once we were married, I'd need to distance myself from them.

We broke up seconds later.

I might not spend as much time with my family as they would like, but I'm not going to let anyone trash talk them either.

Then, when my mother met Shawna two years ago, she told me my girlfriend was only interested in the big payoff I'd get when Roland and I eventually sold our start-up. I was pissed and told my mother she was wrong. But months later, I was eating a huge slice of humble pie. Roland and I had hit a low point. We needed more funding, and we were struggling to find new investors. I poured my heart out to Shawna, and instead of offering encouragement, she dumped me, claiming she'd written a paper about sunk cost fallacy, and that she'd wasted enough time on something that was almost guaranteed to lose.

It was only after she left that I realized she hadn't misspoken when she'd said *something* instead of *someone*.

I haven't dated since.

That doesn't mean I haven't been with a woman. I've slept with several, but relationships? Not until we see Zebra Tech to fruition.

But right now, Roland is still chatting with Finley while she makes our drinks.

"You've really never seen a white Christmas?" he asks in amazement. I can spot Salesman Roland a mile away. He's really pushing this.

"Nope, never." Finley has a wistful look on her face. "I've always wanted to, but..." She shrugs and to my surprise, something flickers in her eyes, a hint of sadness, but then just as quickly it's gone. "Who knows?" she says a little too brightly. "If all this crazy weather keeps up, maybe Atlanta'll start havin' blizzards."

Roland props his arm on the back of the espresso machine partition. "Why wait twenty years to see one when you can go to Hollybrook? Did I mention it's the Christmas capital of the world?" He turns to look at me with an encouraging look. I recognize it from when we tag team potential investors. "What do they have up in Hollybrook, Alex? Candy cane eating contests?"

"No," I said with a laugh, but it feels a little forced. I should walk away and leave this woman alone, but I can't seem to stop myself from saying, "But they have just about everything else. The town's kind of Bavarian-themed and there's always snow at Christmas, so they capitalize on it. They have a gingerbread house decorating contest. Sleigh rides. Outdoor ice skating."

She has a hesitant look, but I see the interest in her eyes, and I can't seem to stop myself from adding, "Hollybrook even has live reindeer, and a Santa with a genuine belly and full white beard." I give her a conspiratorial grin. "His name's Tom Henson. He sells insurance in the off season."

A gleam fills Roland's eyes. I've seen that look whenever he snags a new investor in our start-up. He thinks we've set the hook, now we just need to reel her in.

"Finley, I know you don't have plans for Christmas," Roland says. "A couple of days ago, I heard you tell a customer you were spending the day at home with your cat. Wouldn't you rather have a *real* Christmas?"

Her smile fades. Roland's an ass. Who reminds someone they'll be alone for the holidays? I don't know why she won't be with her family, but it's obviously a sore spot.

Roland turns to me. "What are the dates you'll be gone?"

I resist the urge to cringe, only because I don't want Finley to think I'm rejecting *her*, even if I kind of am. "December twenty-second until January first."

"Eleven whole days in a Christmas paradise." Roland sighs, then swings his attention back to her. "You'll stay in a cozy family home complete with a fireplace and a real Christmas tree, experiencing all the things middle-class families in Hollybrook do at Christmas."

Her eyes narrow. "*Wait*—you two are serious."

"As a heart attack," Roland said solemnly, pressing a hand to his chest.

I wonder what Roland told her before I started paying attention, because she seems to know she'd be going with me.

Her gaze lands on me, full of questions.

This idea's insane. But idiot that I am, I don't hate it. There would be a lot of upsides to someone like Finley coming. First and foremost, I'd get my own room. Second, my mother will adore her and stop lecturing me for picking "materialistic women." Third, Finley's chatty enough to be a good buffer between me and my family. It doesn't hurt that I sort of know her, so it wouldn't be as awkward as dragging home a total stranger.

Am I seriously considering this? It's completely ridiculous, yet I find myself leaning closer and lowering my voice. "It's a long story, but unless I bring a girlfriend home for Christmas, I have to sleep on a sofa bed and the brattiest three kids you ever met will be sharing the room with me."

She makes a face. "It's December seventeenth, Alex. I've never believed in love at first sight, let alone experienced it. So, becoming your girlfriend in five days? Not happening."

I held up my hands. "I know, but I have a solution."

The man next to me loudly clears his throat and says in an angry tone, "Are you gonna to make my gingerbread latte or chat it up with Mr. Good-lookin' all day?" His eyes narrowed. "Because *some* of us have to get to work."

Finley cringes, and I resist the urge to grab the man by his yellow-ringed white collar and shove him against the wall for talking to her like that.

Wait. Where the hell did that come from?

"Sorry. Roger," she says. "You're up next." She holds up his cup to show him, then gives me an apologetic look. "I'm not gonna lie, Alex, it's kind of tempting, but—"

"Hold off on that no and but." Roland holds up his hand. "Don't make a decision until you get more information. How about Alex comes down when you get off work and he can give you more details?"

She shakes her head and hands him his caramel latte. "I have to leave right after work."

"Then how about during your break?" he pushes. When she hesitates, he shoots a glance over to Maggie. "Hey, Maggie. Does Finley get a break?"

"Sure thing," she says with a smug look. "Right about 1:30."

Roland nods, a shit-eating grin spreading across his face. "Okay, Alex'll be down at 1:30. He'll explain the whole situation and then you can decide." When she doesn't answer, he adds, "What can it hurt to listen to what the man has to say?"

Finley hands me my drink. "Okay, I'll listen, but don't expect me to say yes."

"Deal." Roland looks triumphant. "You won't regret it, Finley. Hollybrook snow is the finest snow you've ever experienced and the mountain air..." He shakes his head with a far-off look. "You've never smelled anything so fresh."

Roland's full of shit. He's never stepped foot in Hollybrook, let alone anywhere in the entire state of Vermont.

A doubtful look covers Finley's face, but then she focuses on making Roger's drink. I can't help notice that she's not smiling and something pinches painfully in my chest.

Pissed—and not sure why—I shove Roland to the end of the counter. Bethany, one of the other baristas, hands me my Danish. "Have a good day, Alex." She gives me a wink before she heads off to warm up another pastry.

I head for the exit, fuming. Why am I angry? While it's impulsive, bringing Finley isn't the *worst* idea. She's a sweet, thoughtful girl. She'd fit in *perfectly* with my family. So why do I feel like pond scum?

Maybe because you're using her.

Bottom line: Finley doesn't deserve to be a pawn in my messed-up need to keep my distance from my family.

Once we're in the lobby, Roland shoulder checks me. "I've got the line set, King. It's up to you to reel her in." He winks. "And if you play your cards right, you'll get laid out of the deal."

I shoot him a dark look, but he doesn't notice, likely because he doesn't have eyes in the back of his head. He's already headed for the elevator bank.

If Finley actually agrees to Hollybrook, there will be no sex. Convincing her to come is bad enough. Sleeping with her would be diabolical.

But I'm already burying my self-disgust and convincing myself that this can work. If I'm going to spend eleven days with my family, I should be able to do so without emergency trips to the chiropractor. My family will love Finley, and she'll love them. It'll be nothing but sunshine and candy canes.

If she agrees.

Like any good salesman, I just need to figure out what Finley wants.

A shadow crosses over my heart as I realize: convincing her makes me a stone-cold asshole.

And yet... I'm going to do it anyway.

Chapter Three

Finley

I cast a nervous glance to the clock over the Beans to Go exit. It's the same time it was twenty seconds ago—1:28.

This is beyond ridiculous. Roland was clearly joking. I've known since day one he's a smooth talker who could convince a rooster to lay an egg.

But Alex... he's harder to figure out.

He's quiet, but friendly. Then, several months after he started coming in, he suddenly seemed down. I had no idea why, and I didn't ask. I could see he was hurting, so I did what I always do—I tried to cheer him up. I tried to brighten his day. Only with Alex, it felt different. It took me about a month to figure out why, and when I did, I could have kicked myself. I had a crush on Alex King —the stupidest thing in the world.

Guys like Alex King don't date baristas.

I saw one of his girlfriends a year ago. She wore three-inch, red-bottom heels with a pencil skirt, silky blouse, and bright red lipstick. Her long, blond hair was perfectly styled, and she carried a handbag worth more than a semester of my community college tuition. She'd asked Maggie to validate the parking on her Lexus, then pouted when Maggie said no. Alex hadn't been with her, but she claimed to be his girlfriend and asked if the "savant" who remembered everyone's orders could make his along with hers.

Maybe I should've been flattered she called me a savant, but the disdain in her tone made it sound like she meant Forrest Gump.

"That's me," I'd said.

"Oh." She'd looked me up and down, made a face of pure disapproval, then promptly ignored me.

I'd made their drinks, and she hadn't even said thank you. Instead, she complained about a stain on one of the cups and demanded I remake the drink—not pour it into a fresh cup.

After that, I had a hard time talking to Alex. But then I realized I wasn't being fair. The righteous me would like to think the people we date reflect who we are—but almost every guy I've dated turned out to be a jerk. Does that make me a jerk? Or just someone who attracts them? Eventually I figured out who they really were and kicked them to the curb. Should I have been judged before I figured it out? I'd like to think Alex didn't know the real her, just like I hadn't known the real them.

But meeting his girlfriend made it very clear the type of women Alex dates—and just as clear that I don't fit that mold; I'm Finley O'Brien, barely scraping toward a community college degree after five years of night and online classes. I drive a twelve-year-old car and buy purses at Target when I'm splurging—Goodwill when I'm not. I live in low-income senior housing, with furniture scavenged from thrift stores and street curbs. I work two jobs and live on coffee and protein bars. And I'm not ashamed of any of it. Quite the opposite—I'm damned proud of myself.

But I'm also not delusional enough to believe in Cinderella stories. I'm firmly grounded in reality. When you've lived my life, you don't get a lot of choices in life.

Which is why I'm confused.

I'm not exactly sure what Alex actually wants. Roland said he needs a girlfriend to go home with him for Christmas—so he doesn't have to sleep on a sofa bed—which makes no sense.

I've spent the past two hours replaying every word, and I've decided it was a joke. Alex isn't going to show up. And even if he does, I'd be stupid to listen.

But then again, I'd be stupider not to.

Maggie watches me, hands on her hips. "He'll be here."

"No," I say, my eyes burning. "They were full of shit." The

words sting more than I want to admit. I can see Roland pulling a prank. But Alex...

"I don't think they were," Bethany says. "I heard that conversation, Fin. I think Roland was serious."

"*Roland* was serious," I counter. "Alex is supposedly the one who needs a girlfriend, but Roland's the one who pushed it." All the more reason to believe it was a setup.

"Just hear him out," Maggie pleads. "Every Christmas you say how much you wish you could have a *real* one—snow, a tree and all the trimmings. That place has *sleigh rides*, for Christ's sake. At least hear him out. Especially since it's all expenses paid."

Weirdly, I haven't thought about the cost. Not that it matters. Every penny I earn goes to bills. Maybe someday I'll be able to afford a trip like Hollybrook over the holidays, but not now. Hell, I can't even afford to take the time off work.

I shake my head. "This is insane. There's no way I can do this."

"There he is!" Bethany squeals, clutching her hands to her chest. "He just got off the elevators, and he's headed this way!"

My heart hammers as Alex strides across the lobby. He's wearing the blue button-down and gray tie he had on this morning. His dress trousers cling to his hips, and I know I'm in trouble.

Alex King is too good-looking for his own good. Or mine.

Bethany's eyes go dreamy. "Fin, you could do a hell of a lot worse than Alex King."

Maybe so, but I'm equally sure that I am not the kind of woman he's looking for. Besides, I have a plan for my life, and it doesn't include a boyfriend. If I get the scholarship I applied for, my next two years will be busy with nursing school.

When I'm an RN, *then* I can think about a romantic life. For now, I need to stay focused.

Barb's voice echoes in my head. *But that doesn't mean you can't have a fling.*

Not helping, Barb.

Maggie squeezes my hand. "Fin, just hear him out. The fact that he's here means it's real."

"Unless he's here to say the whole thing was a joke."

She frowns. "That boy would never do that to you. What's the harm in hearing him out?"

I want to ask her how she knows he won't. I'd like to think the man I've gotten to know over the past year and a half wouldn't, but how can I be sure?

"I don't know if I should trust him, Mags." My voice trembles.

"If it was Roland, I'd tell you to run," she says, deadly serious. "But Alex? He'll give it to you straight."

Right then Alex walks through the door, scanning the tables, probably trying to figure out where he should sit.

I should march over there and tell him that I have a life. That I can't just drop everything and pretend to be his girlfriend for his family. Even if he claimed to be interested in me, I wouldn't really be his girlfriend. It would all be a lie.

But Christmas in Hollybrook...

Around noon, when I'd had a spare thirty seconds, I made the mistake of Googling the town.

Huge mistake.

Hollybrook was everything my mother and I had ever dreamed about. Every daydream, every fantasy I'd ever had about Christmas all rolled into one small town. It looked like something out of the Swiss Alps, complete with Bavarian buildings and a Christmas market. Alex hadn't been lying about the reindeer, the sleigh rides, or the gingerbread decorating contest. Add in snow skiing, caroling, and so many shops. And the food! They actually have roasted chestnuts. I had no idea those things were even real. Now I'm desperate to go to a place I hadn't even heard of three hours ago. Even if I know it sounds too good to be true.

"Live a little, Finley" Maggie says, resting her warm hands on my shoulders as she searches my eyes. "If anyone deserves something good, it's you." She gives me a gentle push. "Now go talk to him. If you're still worried, make it a business deal. Tell him what you expect and see what he's willing to give." She shrugs. "He's the one with a ticking clock. Which means you've got the advantage."

She has a point.

"Here." Bethany shoves two ceramic mugs into my hands. "A peppermint mocha for you, and his usual flat white."

"Thanks." I carry them toward the table, suddenly hyper-aware of my appearance. I wish I'd had time to check my hair or touch up my lip gloss. But Maggie's right. I'm not auditioning to be his girlfriend. If I agree to this, it's a business deal. A businessman like Alex will appreciate that.

Alex rises as I approach. "Thanks for agreeing to hear me out." Vulnerability flickers across his face, and for some reason, it eases the knot in my chest.

I set the cups on the table and slide into the chair across from him. His phone sits face down on the table, and I appreciate that. I've been on more than one date where the guy was on his screen more than he was with me.

"Bethany made us drinks." I gesture to his. "Your usual."

He wraps his hand around the cup, lifts it, and glances toward the counter. "Thanks, Bethany."

A giggle drifts from behind me.

So, I'm not the only one with a crush on Alex.

He takes a sip, then lowers the cup with a hesitant look.

I could take offense, but instead I'm relieved. He's nervous too. "I'm not sure—"

"Look, I know—"

We both stop, and I give him a tight smile, folding my hands on the table.

"You go first," he says, gesturing to me.

I nod and take a breath. "Okay. First, is this real or is this a prank?"

Color rises in his cheeks as he shakes his head hard. "I'd never do that to you, Finley."

I nod again.

Good move, Finley. He's going to think you're a bobble head.

I ignore the voice in my head and meet his gaze. "I need to make sure I understand. You want to bring a girlfriend home for Christmas." I pause. "But we've never been on a date, so obviously, I won't be your *actual* girlfriend."

"Right," he says, nodding, still looking nervous. "You'll just pretend." He grins, but it's slightly crooked. "And while we're not a couple, I like you as a person, so that's a good place to start. We're not *total* strangers."

My heart caves in on itself. Hearing the guy you have a crush on say he likes you as a person is like him saying *I think of you like a sister.*

Why is that a surprise, Finley? You already knew he was too good for you.

I should get up and walk away. While my head knows the timing is wrong, I also know he's out of my league. But my stupid heart is slow to catch up. It's been broken too many times in my twenty-five years. Do I really want to risk it again?

Just hear him out.

Because while part of me dies knowing he doesn't want me, the rest of me is leaping at the chance to experience the Christmas Mom and I always dreamed of.

"Okay," I say tightly. "You need someone to fake being your girlfriend, so you don't get stuck sleeping in bunk beds with a bunch of little kids?"

"It's a sofa bed," he corrects, his lips quirking up. "Honestly, bunk beds might be better. I want to enjoy my time with my family, not live in hell every night." He pauses, then explains, "I've got two brothers and a sister. Tyler's the oldest, so he always had his own room, Mallory is the youngest and the only girl, so she got her own room too. And since we lived in a four-bedroom house, Grant and I had to share a room. Whenever we go home, we all stay in our old rooms. Which works great for Tyler and Mallory, but not so great for Grant and me. But for the first time,

Grant's bringing his girlfriend, which means I'm stuck in the rec room with three tiny terrors and bed springs from hell. Unless"—his mouth tips up in a sly grin —"I show up with a girlfriend. And because I'm older, I'll get the room."

"That doesn't seem fair," I say. "Grant's had his girlfriend longer."

"But I'm older," he says, like that settles it. "So, *I* get the room."

I fold my arms over my chest. "Which still seems unfair."

"I didn't make the rules."

"You'd seriously make your brother and his girlfriend sleep with kids on the bed from hell?"

He shrugs. "Grants younger than me and has a better back. He'll survive."

"And his girlfriend?"

For a split second, guilt flashes in his eyes. Then he shrugs again.

I've always suspected there was a ruthless streak in him, and this pretty much confirms it. "Why not stay in a hotel?"

"For one thing, every hotel in a fifty-mile radius is completely booked. But even if I found a room, my mother would have a fit. She insists Christmas isn't the same unless we're all under the same roof. And she's right. We stay up late talking, playing games, and watching movies. Mornings mean my parents cook amazing breakfasts. And then, of course Christmas Day wouldn't feel the same if I was driving in from somewhere else." I'm surprised by the wistfulness in his voice. "It's home."

"Which is why Grant and his poor girlfriend get the broken springs and a pack of wild children."

Alex catches the sympathy in my tone. "Trust me, Finley, he'll be fine. Besides, he deserves it for all the crap he's pulled on me over the years."

My blood turns cold in my veins. "Wait. Am I part of a practical *joke*?" The edge in my voice is sharp enough to cut glass.

"What? No!" His eyes widen, panic flashing across his face.

"It's not like that." My glare lingers until he finally looks sheepish. "You're not a joke, Finley." He exhales. "I'll be honest, when Roland pitched it, I thought he was insane. But the more I considered it, the more it made sense." He leans forward. "You've always wanted a white Christmas, and this is your opportunity to experience it. With all the cliché trimmings."

I cringe. "I don't know about *cliché*."

"Sorry," he says, his hand raised. "I didn't mean it that way. I mean traditional. Honestly, I haven't done any of that stuff in years. My sister Mallory loves Christmas too." His expression softens. "She'll adore *you*. She's usually outnumbered by us boys, so she'll have you for an ally. You'll have an instant friend."

I have to admit it all sounds tempting, except for the tricking people. "But Alex, it's your *family*. You're bringing a stranger home. At least Grant's girlfriend is real."

For the first time, guilt flickers across his face. "I've thought about that. Look, I don't want you to feel trapped. If my family's too much, then you can head off on your own. The house is only a few blocks from downtown, and I'll cover for you if you want space. And if you really hate it..." He shrugs. "I'll send you home early."

I blink, stunned. "That's not what I meant. I meant—how do you think your family will feel about *me*?"

He looks at me like I've grown another head. "They'll *love* you, Finley."

Excitement bubbles up before I can stop it. Then reality smacks me like a snowball to the face.

It won't be real, Finley. It will all just be pretend.

But isn't pretend better than *nothing*?

"Okay," I say slowly, "but if your family hates me—"

"It'll never happen," he says, adamantly.

"For the sake of argument, let's say they do, and I go home early. Then you're stuck with the sofa bed."

He grimaces. "They won't hate you, and I'm counting on *you* to fall in love with the town. But if you feel the need to leave, I'll buy you a ticket home and figure out my sleeping arrangement later." A mischievous grin lights up his face. "But they say possession is nine-tenths of the law, so Grant will have to drag me out."

Which meant once he gets in the room, he has no intention of giving it up.

Walk away.

I should get up and go back to work—to my safe world. But every time he mentions his family or the town it makes me want it more.

What am I doing? I can't believe I'm considering this.

Alex seems nice, but how well do I really know him? He's sweet when he comes into the shop, and I've seen him drop five- and ten-dollar bills into the tip jar. He's confident, but not like the finance bros from Hillman Investments on the fifteenth floor. I cringe every time they swagger in, ordering their drinks with a heaping side of innuendo. If one of *them* had proposed this, I wouldn't be sitting here.

The truth is—I wouldn't do this with anyone else.

Which is what makes this even more dangerous. Sure, I might get the Christmas I've always wanted, with a family that Alex claims will love me—but it'll be with a man who thinks of me as his sister and a family that's not mine. Is the reward worth the potential pain?

Be practical, Fin. Treat this like a business deal.

I clear my throat, aiming for professional. I doubt I'm pulling it off, but it's worth a shot. "We need to talk money. Tickets this close to Christmas won't be cheap."

"Don't worry about that. I'll pay for everything," he says emphatically. "Flights, meals, everything. Consider it an all-expenses-paid vacation."

"That sounds great," I say, wincing. "But I'll be missing a week and a half of work."

His enthusiasm dims as though he hadn't considered that. "Okay, I can cover that. I'm guessing you work forty hours a week?"

"I work thirty-eight here," I admit, grimacing. "They can't give us forty hours or that will make us full time. And if we're full time, the owner has to give us vacation and health insurance."

His mouth drops, then snaps shut. "*Wait.* You don't get vacation or insurance?"

"Nope."

He blinks, baffled, like it never occurred to him that an adult could work without getting benefits. "Yeah, sure. No problem. Tell me how much money you'll lose, and I'll cover it."

"That's great." I feel greedy, but I'm doing him a favor. Why should I feel guilty for missing nearly two weeks of work? "But this isn't my only job."

This time, he doesn't bother hiding his shock. "How many jobs do you have?"

"Regularly, just one more. I'm a part-time phlebotomist at a nearby hospital. But sometimes I pet sit when my neighbors are in the hospital."

He grins like I'm joking. "Your neighbors routinely go to the hospital?"

I release a short laugh. "When the median age in my apartment building is seventy-eight, it happens."

He stares, dumbfounded. "Okay, I'll bite," he finally says, "Why are your neighbors so old?"

"I live in a low-income senior apartment complex," I say with a shrug. "How I got there is a long story about a paperwork snafu, but bottom line? The rent is cheap, and my neighbors are amazing."

His grin turns smug. "Then you can tell me the long story on the plane."

There's that confidence. He thinks I'm hooked, so I arch a brow. "I haven't agreed to go."

"*Yet*," Alex sits taller. "Figure out how much money you'll miss from both jobs and text me the amount." His phone vibrates against the table. He turns it over, frowns at the screen, then turns it back over and gives me his full attention.

"I want a contract," I blurt, surprising myself. But Maggie was right—I need to treat it like a business deal. He's already made it clear there's nothing romantic about this, so if I'm giving up two weeks of wages, I need something legal to hold him to it. Lord knows I've been burned by men who claimed to love me. I'm not about to let someone who doesn't get away with it.

Alex looks taken back, then he gives me an appreciative nod. "That's a good idea. Text me your terms, and we'll get it ironed out." His phone buzzes again, and this time he looks irritated. "Sorry, Finley. I need to take this."

He slips a card from his shirt pocket and sets it on the table. "This has my email address and phone number. Once we've worked out the details, send me the contract. But I need to have it by tomorrow night so I can tell my mom and book your tickets. This close to Christmas, we'll be lucky to get seats on the same flights."

He's already on his feet, answering the call before I can respond. He strides out, his low voice murmuring into his phone.

I watch him go, battling myself. This isn't me. I'm practical. Careful. Not impulsive.

Nothing about this is practical.

Promise me you'll be impulsive. Take risks. Promise me you'll live, Finley.

My mother's voice is so clear it steals my breath. I close my eyes and I'm back in her hospital room. She's lying in her bed. Her hair thin and patchy from chemo. A nasal canula taped to her face. She's so frail, she's almost a skeleton. She clutches my hand, trying to squeeze, though her strength is gone. Tears shimmer as her chin trembles. "I named you Finley *Joy* for a reason." Her chin trembles again. "You've been the joy of my life, Fin. But you can't always play it safe. Sometimes joy isn't in the safe places. Sometimes you have to take risks to find it. You have to be *impulsive*." She squeezed my hand again. "Promise me you'll try."

Through my tears, I nodded. "I promise."

I miss her. I miss her so much it hurts. The holidays are always worse, but this year is harder. Lonelier. I picture Christmas Day in my apartment with Maybelle, eating my sad Christmas dinner, with no presents waiting under my sad, thirty-year-old, artificial tree.

But the truth is, I've broken my promise to Mom. The most impulsive thing I've done since she died was deciding to live alone and signing the lease at the senior housing complex, which wasn't impulsive at all. It was the cheapest, nicest place I could find.

But this…. If I agree to this, not only will I keep my promise to Mom, but I'll get the Christmas we'd dreamed of. It feels like destiny has dropped this in my lap.

When I looked at it that way, how could I refuse?

Chapter Four

Finley

Mirna, my eighty-three-year-old neighbor, does not agree. "You're gonna do *what*?"

After I left my job at Beans to Go, I'd headed to my second job, but all I could think about was Alex's offer, what I should ask for and the looming urgent deadline. I needed advice, and my best friends were the ones to give it to me. So, I'd told my boss I wasn't feeling well, and she sent me home. Now I'm sitting on Barb's sofa while she sits in her recliner, the footrest propped up. Mirna, who was on the sofa, is now pacing.

A dreamy look fills Barb's eyes. "Lighten up, Mirna. Let the girl live a little. She's young. This is when she should be livin' wild and free."

"Wild and free is all well and good until she's *dead*," Mirna says, pointing her finger at Barb. "I've heard all about those sex trafficking rings!" She flings her hand toward the door. "She's gonna fly off with this guy and then he's gonna *sell* her to some Russian mafia gang and ship her off to God only knows where." She throws both hands up in the air.

"First of all," I say, trying not to grin, "The words mafia and gang are redundant. Second, Alex isn't Russian. Third, I asked him to send me proof of his family, and he sent me multiple photos of himself with them." I pull up the images on my phone and handed it to her.

A smug grin lights up Barb's eyes. "Smart girl."

I don't tell her it was Maggie's idea. After Alex left, I'd started to freak out over the whole situation, and she'd suggested I ask for the photos.

Mirna sits down next to me and swipes through the images on my phone, shaking her head in disapproval. "He could have photoshopped these. Or used that AE stuff. They can make people naked with those things, you know." Her lips curl with disapproval.

"It's AI, not AE," I say. "And no one is naked in his photos."

She stops scrolling and pauses on a photo that had been taken outside in Hollybrook during the Christmas season. There's a giant Christmas tree next to an outdoor skating rink. A younger Alex is with a middle-school-aged girl on the rink. Both have huge grins, and their cheeks are flushed. Alex is in a bright blue puffy coat with a red knit hat and scarf wrapped around his neck. The hat looks misshapen like it's homemade, and it's so unlike anything I've ever seen him wear, I had to stop and make sure it was him and not one of his brothers. The girl has a white puffy coat, and a pale blue knit hat with a pompom, and a scarf. It's my favorite photo of all the ones he's sent, and I'm sure he included it on purpose. He's showing me that Hollybrook is a magical Christmas wonderland—everything I could have dreamed of.

It was a smart move. The photo turns the part of me that *wants* to go into a *need*.

"I take it that's him," Mirna says in disgust, stabbing his face on the screen with her long, Got the Blues for Red polished fingernail. It's her signature color. "Look at him! Has he no shame? He's *flaunting* the fact he's trafficking that young girl!"

I suppress a chuckle. "Mirna, that's his younger sister, Mallory. He said that was taken about eight years ago, and she's eight years younger than him."

I've spent a lot of time studying that photo, and not just because I got lost in the fantasy of the background scenery. Alex was probably about nineteen or twenty, which meant he'd been in college. Of course, I'm mesmerized by how relaxed he looks wearing his casual clothing—I've only ever seen him in business attire—but my heart warms as I take in the way his arm is casually slung around Mallory's shoulders. And the way her head is slightly tilted up, staring at him in awe and love.

I don't have siblings. Mom used to say it was me and her against the world. When I was younger, I never wanted a sister or brother. Mom was enough. She was my entire world. It was only after she got sick, during the year and a half she fought the cancer that spread from her breast to the rest of her body, that I wished for a sibling. Someone to help carry the load. Someone to share my fears. Someone who understood.

Someone so I wouldn't be so alone.

Obviously, having siblings isn't all daisies and roses. Part of the reason Alex wants a fake girlfriend is so he can best his brother.

I'm beginning to rethink this whole plan.

Mirna searches my face, like she's looking for proof someone else has taken over my body. "I simply don't understand, Finley. This is all *so* unlike you. Taking off work when you're not ill. Going away with a *stranger*..."

"I know." My guilt over lying to my boss is overwhelming, but we were slower than usual tonight, and I needed to hash this out with people I trust. People who have looked out for me for four years.

Most people would think it strange that I'm best friends with two women old enough to be my grandmothers, but I live a small life. I go to work at Beans to Go, then part time at the hospital. Evening and weekend online classes. And home. My time is either spent working, studying, or sleeping. Any infrequent spare time is spent with Mirna and Barb. They're like the grandmothers I never had.

But I'm also counting on their frankness, and so far, both were playing their roles. I knew I could count on Barb to think this is a great idea, just like I could count on Mirna to play devil's advocate like her life depended on it. Or rather mine.

"I know you don't understand," I say, sounding as exhausted

as I feel. "But I'm just so tired of working all the time, and..." I pushed out a heavy sigh. "I just want to have some fun for once."

"And get laid," Barb blurts out.

"I'm not getting laid," I say sternly. Barb's addicted to romance novels of all genres, and for her, life's a romance waiting to be written. Still, she's going to be sorely disappointed with this one. "Sorry, Barb, but this is a business deal. We're gonna have a contract and everything."

Barb makes a pft sound and waves her hand in dismissal. "Poppycock." She turns to her older friend. "And you're crazy to think Finley's about to become a sex slave. Even she's not *that* stupid."

"Hey!" I protest even though I suspect she meant it as a compliment.

"You know what I mean," she says, waving her hand again. Her eyes grow brighter as her excitement builds. "*Unless* it's like that romance novel I read last week where the woman signed a contract to be a man's sex slave for three months." She fans her face. "And when those three months were up, she begged to sign up again."

"I'm not going to be anyone's sex slave, now or ever," I say, giving her a pointed look. "And I'm pretty sure any contract that requires someone to have sex with someone else would be illegal, considering prostitution is still against the law in Georgia. Which reminds me..." I smile a little too widely at Barb. "Do you think Mr. Horowitz could draw up a contract for me?"

"You want Burt Horowitz to write a sex-slave contract?" Mirna asks, sounding thoroughly scandalized.

Groaning, I say in frustration, "It's not a sex-slave contract. I'll simply be his..." I bit back the words fake girlfriend and end up saying, "Companion."

"Another word for escort," Mirna snaps. "AKA prostitute. AKA *sex slave*."

"We don't say prostitutes anymore, Mirna," I say. "They're sex workers, and as long as they aren't trafficked, they're not slaves. Many of them have the control in those situations."

"And how many sex workers do you actually *know* to know this as a fact?" Mirna asks, her eyes blazing.

It's not worth telling her I wrote a paper on sex workers for one of my sociology classes, because no matter what I say, Mirna will believe what she wants.

"Then why do you need a contract?" Barb asks, looking genuinely curious. "That man in the Shades of Steele novel said he wouldn't have sex until she signed a contract." A grin lights up her eyes. "That book *is* a romance, by the way."

"You can cite your romance novels all you want," I say with a short laugh, "but this is a *business deal*."

"What do *you* get out of it?" Mirna demands. "He apparently gets to sleep in his childhood bed—with you in it, I might add." Her mouth pinches with disgust.

I hadn't thought about the bed situation, but Mirna has a point. I need to make it very clear we won't be sleeping in the same bed. Then again, I can't imagine two boys growing up and sharing a bed. Surely, they had twin beds. Or bunk beds. But there's no way I'm sleeping on the top bunk.

That's going in the contract.

"What I get," I say, feeling sentimental, "is to experience Christmas, just like my mom and I dreamed about. With snow and ice skating and all the magic that Hollybrook has. Mom didn't get to experience it, but I will."

My friends are silent for a moment, then Mirna's face softens. "But you'll experience it with *his* family, Finley. Not yours."

Her words hang heavy in the air.

She and Barb fully understand my loneliness. It's one of the reasons they so readily took me under their wing after I moved in four years ago. They'd barely known me when they declared themselves my grandmas. They, more than anyone, understand, because they're alone too. Except for when their families make them go stay with them for the holidays, mostly so they don't look bad.

But still. It's family.

Tears fill Mirna's eyes. "You'll be an outsider looking in, Finley. You have such a tender heart. I'm worried you'll get hurt."

"I know," I say as I swipe at a tear that's escaped. "But at least I'll get to experience it, even if it's not mine."

"Like a voyeur," Barb says with a knowing nod. "Just like in *All Eyes on Me*."

I can't help bursting out in laughter. Leave it to Barb to turn a serious moment on its head. She'd like us to believe she's oblivious, but Mirna and I know better. "Barb," I say, wiping more tears through my laughter. "I think all eyes on *me* would be the opposite of a voyeur. I think that's an exhibitionist."

"Eh." She shrugs. "Same thing."

It's not, but I keep it to myself.

We fall silent and my smile fades. "Mirna, I know his family Christmas isn't mine, but I want to have this. Just once."

Mirna and Barb exchange looks and I know what they're thinking. Ordinarily, I'd hate their pity, but right now, I just want them to understand.

Mirna pinches her lips then pushes out an aggrieved groan. "Barb, call Burt."

I gasp in shock. I never expected Mirna to cave this quickly. "*What?*"

Her eyes turn shrewd. "In the four years I've known you, you've never *once* wanted anything impractical. You're the most sensible person I know. Barb's right. You need to live a little, and if this is what you want, then we'll get it for you. But"—she points a finger at me—"we're gonna be *smart* about it." She turns to Barb. "What are you waiting for? Why haven't you called Burt?"

Barb cringes. "Burt and I aren't exactly speakin' right now."

Mirna puts both hands on her hips. "Why not?"

"I told him he has a shriveled-up pecker, and he told me my boobs were like cantaloupes on bungee cords."

Burt and Barb have an on-again, off-again relationship. Apparently, we caught them on an off time.

"I don't give a rootie patootie if you two are CIA operatives charged with assassinating one another," Mirna says sternly. "You get that man on that iPad of yours and tell him Finley needs his help."

Barb grumbles under her breath but picks up the tablet resting on the arm of her recliner and Facetimes Burt.

When the tablet stops ringing, I hear him say in a self-righteous tone, "Well, look who came grovelin' back. Missed my shriveled-up pecker, did ya?"

"Hell, no," Barb spits in disgust. "Ira's pecker's bigger than yours and lasts twice as long."

"Bullshit!" Burt shouts.

"Believe it or not," Barb says, trying to act like she doesn't care what he thinks, but I see the gleam in her eyes. She's pretty pleased that she riled him up. "That's not why I called."

"I don't give a rat's ass why you called," Burt snaps. "Goodbye!"

"Wait!" Barb shouts. Her bluster comes crashing down and panic edges her voice. "I'm callin' about Finley."

He's silent for a moment, then says, "What about Finley?" he sounds hesitant, like he thinks she's tricking him into staying on the call.

"She needs legal advice. How soon can you get over here?"

"Is she okay?" he asks, now the one sounding panicked.

"She's fine!" Mirna shouts from across the room. "And we're trying to keep her that way. That's why we need you. ASAP."

He grumbles, then says, "I got a new brace for my dropped foot, so it might take me a few minutes longer to get there than normal."

Barb shakes her head in annoyance. "Then get here when you can." She ends the call and drops the tablet on the arm of her chair.

We all stare at one another, and I feel like a pendulum,

waffling back and forth on this decision. I've spent the last ten minutes convincing my best friend grandmas that I should do this, but now I'm thinking it's the worst idea ever.

"What am I doin'?" I whisper. "This is crazy."

"That's why it's so perfect," Barb says as she claps her hands. "Sometimes the best things in life are the craziest." She leans toward me, stretching so far over the arm of her recliner to pick up my hand from my lap that I'm terrified she's going to lose her balance and fall onto the floor. "You're the oldest person I know, Finley O'Brien, and given that you're only twenty-five, that's plain sad. You need to be young. Make mistakes. *Live.*" She squeezes my hand. "Life is in the mistakes, girl." She holds my gaze. "You deserve good things."

Something in my heart latches onto her words. I want good things, so why do I think I don't deserve them? But it's also hard to take Barb seriously as she wobbles, her hips balanced on the arm of her chair like she's mounted a balance beam.

A rap at the front door draws her gaze from mine, and she frowns as she realizes the precarious position she's in.

Mirna opens the door, and Burt walks in with an exaggerated gait. There's a brace on his right leg that wraps around his calf and shin and disappears into his shoes. It's completely visible due to the fact he's wearing Bermuda shorts and knee-high athletic socks.

"What in the world are you wearin', Burt?" Barb asks while she's flailing around, trying to get back in her recliner.

"I should be askin' what in the hell you're *doin*?" he exclaims as he rushes over to her.

"I'm practicin' a new sex position to try out on Henry."

"I thought you were screwin' Ira," he snaps, gripping her upper right arm as he tries to drag her back into her chair.

"I *am* screwin' Ira," she says breathlessly, now wiggling backward across the wide recliner arm. "But that doesn't mean I can't screw Henry too. We women earned our right to screw whoever we want."

"Not if some people have anything to say about it," but I keep it under my breath. Although I wholeheartedly agree with them, I have no desire to get sidetracked for the next hour when all three of them get worked up over how hard they fought to gain women's rights, just to see them stripped away.

Burt almost has Barb wrangled back into her chair, but I feel badly that he's doing it alone. I stand, but Mirna motions me back down with a satisfied look on her face.

She's playing matchmaker, and I'm on board with this plan.

Burt Horowitz is in his early eighties, but most people guess him to be a good decade younger. He works out at the run-down gym around the corner, and he's popular with all the older ladies. He could have his pick, but he has it bad for Barb and won't give any of the others a chance. Even when he and Barb are in the middle of a break.

Barb claims he can't let her go because she's perfected the art of fellatio, only she pronounces it fillet-a-chato, claiming she has a right to call it that since her technique is like licking a gelato. She's offered to give me pointers, but I've turned her down—multiple times—claiming it would be wasted on me since I don't have a boyfriend.

Lord knows if I ever do get a boyfriend again, I'm waiting until we're engaged to tell her.

Barb's butt finally lands in the chair with a thump, and Burt stands next to her, huffing and puffing. I'm pretty sure they don't have any machines in the exercise room to prepare an eighty-one-year-old man to drag his girlfriend across the arm of a recliner and back into her seat.

Finally, his breathing slows enough for him to wheeze out, "Are you in some kind of legal trouble, Finley?"

"No, nothing like that," I say, then give him a condensed version of what I need as Mirna brings him a kitchen chair to sit in so he can face all of us.

When I finish, he's quiet for several seconds before he says, "Let me get this straight. A sexy customer from Beans to Go—"

"I didn't say he was sexy!" I say insistently.

"*I* said he was sexy," Barb sasses.

I swing my attention to her. "You've never even met him."

She taps her temple. "I've met him in here, where he's sexy as all get out." Then she purrs and gives Burt a long, weighted look.

"You need to lower the dose of your estrogen cream, Barb," Mirna says, disapprovingly.

"Ira disagrees." Barb waggles her eyebrows.

Burt swallows, glancing between the three of us, looking nervous. "Okay, so one of your customers has asked you to spend Christmas with him and his family up in a Christmas town in Vermont..." He makes a face that appears incredulous, then hesitantly says, "so he doesn't have to sleep on a *sofa bed*?"

"That's the gist of it," I say. "But he says he'll pay my missed wages and any trip expenses. And—" I can't stop the excitement bubbling up in me. "I get to spend Christmas in Hollybrook. The town is like a Christmas Hallmark movie come to life!"

He eyes me warily. "And that's a good thing?"

"Have you no Christmas spirit, Burt?" Barb demands.

"You know damn good and well I don't," he shoots back. "I'm Jewish."

That shuts her down, but who knows for how long, so I take advantage of the silence. "I've dreamed of this kind of Christmas since I was a kid. You have no idea how much my mom and I wanted to experience it." I pause, realizing how pathetic this all sounds. I know I should be embarrassed, but I can't seem to summon it. Not with my friends.

Burt is still watching me, as though he's waiting for me to yell, "Prank!" But when I don't, he nods solemnly. "Okay, let's make your Christmas dream come true. What do you need from me?"

"I need a contract. I have some requests—"

"Demands," Burt says. "If this guy is as desperate as you've made him out to be, then I suspect he'll give you pretty much anything you want." He pauses. "I take it we're negotiating the demands?"

"This isn't a divorce, Burt," Barb says in disgust. "Way to take the romance out of it."

"There's no romance involved," I tell her, then turn my attention back to him. "This is *not* romantic. It's a business agreement, but I want it to be amicable. I'm going to be spending nearly two weeks with him and his family. So, maybe we don't call them demands."

"Okay," he says with a frown. "Does he have an attorney we're dealing with?"

"No, he told me to have the contract drawn up, but he needs it by tomorrow night."

His white wooly eyebrows shoot up. "Tomorrow night?"

"We leave on the twenty-second, and he still needs to book my plane tickets."

"Do you have the demands"—he makes a face—"I mean, *requests* ironed out?"

"Mostly, but I wanted to talk to you before I addressed some of them." I shrug. "I've never done anything like this before."

"I should hope not," Mirna scoffs.

"You need to do it more often," Barb says with a sharp nod.

Burt ignores them both. "While it's unconventional, to be sure, it's nothing we can't have done by your deadline, presuming you have everything ironed out by tomorrow morning."

"I think I can do that."

He gets out of his chair, then holds out his hand. "I need you to pay me a retainer before we get started."

"You're gonna charge her?" Barb shouts in disbelief.

"I have to charge her *something*, otherwise, I won't be held by the attorney-client privilege." He winks. "Even if it's just a dollar."

"Oh," I say, feeling relieved. "I don't have any cash on me. I'll have to run to my apartment."

"Not to worry," Barb says. "*I'll* pay her retainer." Then she begins to tell him in great detail how she plans to sex him up.

"Barb!" I cry out in protest, putting my hands over my ears.

My cheeks are burning, and Mirna looks like she's about to

stroke out, but Burt's tongue is practically hanging out of his mouth, his eyes wide like a cartoon character.

"Well, somebody has to get sex in this contract," she says emphatically. "If it's not gonna be you, then I'll volunteer as tribute." She fans herself. "I can't help it if all this legal talk makes me *hot*."

"You're hot because you have the damn furnace cranked up to eighty!" Mirna complains.

Barb makes a shooing motion. "I need you two to leave within the next three seconds or you're gonna see me paying that retainer."

I run out like my pants are on fire.

Chapter Five

Finley

My apartment is quiet when I walk in, and there's no sign of Maybelle, not that I'm surprised. She likes to hang out in my bedroom, sitting on the pillows at the top of the bed. I'm the first to admit it looks like a Christmas store has exploded in the one-bedroom unit, and while it usually makes me feel closer to my mother, tonight it's like a burning indictment that I've let her down. My seven-foot artificial tree is in the corner, missing a good portion of its needles. As scrawny as it looks, it's lovingly decorated with all the ornaments my mother and I collected over the years. There's a vintage Nativity underneath that we purchased at a garage sale when I was ten, and I'm happy to see that Maybelle hasn't absconded with one of the figures and hidden it somewhere. I love a good scavenger hunt, but I'm not in the mood tonight.

My usual routine when I come home is to grab a quick snack, but I'm home hours earlier than usual and I ate a prepacked sandwich after I left Beans to Go. Besides, I'm too anxious to eat. Instead, I fill a juice glass from my box wine in the fridge and take a sip before preparing Maybelle's dinner. Her special food costs more than I'd like to spend, but after her bout with bladder stones a few months ago, I do what I need to do for my cranky baby.

She hears the kibble as it clicks into her bowl and slinks around the open doorway to the bedroom, giving me the side-eye like she doesn't trust my motives.

"Sorry," I say in a sweet tone. "I know it's not your favorite, but it's better than having bladder stones."

I never thought it was possible for a cat to look down their nose at someone from one foot off the floor, but Maybelle somehow makes it work. I set her bowl down next to her water fountain and she slowly pads over, like she's sure it's a trap, then sniffs and looks up at me.

"I know. Sorry."

She glares at me a second longer then finally eats.

I take my glass of wine to the sofa and give myself a moment to decompress.

This whole thing is crazy. I can't believe I've actually agreed to go on a trip with a guy I'm not even dating, let alone stay with his family.

I open the photos on my phone again, and scan through the images. His family looks nice, but then again, I doubt he'd send me photos that would make them look like a family of Hannibal Lectors. I open my Instagram app and pull up Alex's account.

Okay, I'm a stalker. I looked him up after he left the coffee shop, but I'm not stupid enough to follow him. He doesn't post much, and there are only two photos of his family. One is an image of him and his two brothers and sister from when they were little. In fact, infant Mallory is sitting on the oldest brother's lap. The three brothers are wearing the same blue-button up, short-sleeved shirts, and jeans. Mallory is wearing a pink dress with lots of ruffles. She has a big pink headband around her bald head. The brothers are all smiling, but the youngest—Grant—has an ornery look in his eyes. Tyler looks like he's taking his responsibility of holding his baby sister seriously. And Alex is grinning, like he's happy to be there, sandwiched between his brothers.

The next photo is of him and his mother and was posted on Mother's Day a year and a half ago. They're standing outside, and he's got his arm around her. He looks happy. She looks like she's in her early fifties, but barely. She has shorter, blond hair, and she's also smiling. It's her eyes that draw me in—they're full of happiness, like she's ecstatic to be hugging her son.

I feel a pinch in my heart, and now I'm missing my own

mother even more than before. I pull up photos I have of her before she got sick, stopping on a selfie of the two of us. We're sitting on a blanket at an outdoor concert. She was so vibrant and full of life. It's still hard to believe that less than six months after we snapped that photo, she was diagnosed with cancer. Tears burn my eyes, and I wonder if this trip is a good idea. Sure, I'll get to live the dream my mother and I had for years, but I'll be doing it without her. And if Alex's family is as nice as they look, will being around them over Christmas and a week before the anniversary of her death make it even harder?

Be smart, Finley. This is so impractical.

But it's the impracticality that's convincing me to do it. My mother's request has haunted me for the past six years. I've found so many reasons to ignore it, but it's time to say yes. It's time to take a chance and do something crazy. And once it's done, I can go back to steady, practical Finley O'Brien.

Maybelle jumps onto the sofa beside me, and rubs herself against my leg, her sign that she's granting me permission to pet her. As I run my hand over her soft fur, I realize the impractical Finley has already screwed up. Who's going to take care of Maybelle?

I send a text to Mirna and Barb in our group chat.

I can't go. It's too late to find someone to take care of Maybelle.

Mirna's name appears with three dots, letting me know she's typing. The dots appear and disappear for nearly thirty seconds, and I wonder if she's writing an essay, but then her text appears.

We'll take care of her.

I frown, then send:

I thought you were going to Chattanooga to spend the week with your daughter's family for Christmas

My phone rings and I'm not surprised to see Mirna's name. She hates texting.

"Why aren't you going to your daughter's?" I ask as soon as I answer.

"I'm going, but just for the day." She makes a sound that

sounds like a grunt, but Mirna's too ladylike to do such a thing. "She's inviting Todd's *family* too." Her disgust is palpable.

Mirna's daughter is in her late fifties, and she got remarried a couple of years ago. While Mirna likes her daughter's new husband well enough, it's a different matter when it comes to his mother. "You *really* should try to get along with Vera."

"Why shouldn't *she* try to get along with *me*?"

She has a point.

"In any case," she says in a prim and proper tone that makes it clear we're done discussing Vera, "I'm going up on Christmas Eve and coming back the night of Christmas Day. I can feed her in the morning before I go, and we can get Burt to feed her that night and the next morning. You know he's not doing anything for Christmas."

It's not a bad plan.

When I don't argue, she says triumphantly, "So *there*. Maybelle is settled and I'll even hang out in your apartment and watch those silly dating shows you love to watch, just to make her feel like you're there."

I know Mirna secretly loves watching those dating shows, so it isn't exactly a hardship.

"Don't spoil anything for me," I tease. "I'm two weeks behind."

"As if," she says stiffly.

We're silent for a moment before I ask, "Are you sure?"

"Watching those dating shows will be a hardship, but I'll muster through," she says, sounding resigned.

I nearly laugh. "I'm talking about feeding Maybelle. And cleaning her litter box. I'll be gone for nearly two weeks."

"Your baby will be taken very well care of," she says, her tone softening. "I'll even ask my granddaughters to teach me how to text photos so you can see her."

Tears sting my eyes again, this time for a happy reason. "Why are you going out of your way to help me? I know you don't want me to go, even if you gave your blessing."

She's silent for a moment. "You're a good girl, Finley, and life has been too hard for you. You need to have fun. Barb's right—you need an *adventure*." She pauses again. "I had a chance to go off with a young man in my youth, but I was too scared. I played it safe, and I've always regretted it." She's quieter when she says, "I've always wondered what my life would have been like if I'd just taken the chance."

I gasp in shock. I know she and her husband had celebrated their fifty-third wedding anniversary weeks before he passed away from a stroke. She moved here not long after, mere months before I moved in. When she speaks of him, it's always with fondness, which is why I'm surprised there was someone else before him. "Oh, Mirna…"

"In any case," she says, sounding sterner. "I think you should go, but if you run into *any* trouble at all, you call me, and I'll book you the first flight home. The last thing I want you to worry about is whether you can afford it or not."

"Mirna," I protest. "I can't ask you to do that."

"I'm sorry, Finley, but that's the only way I'll agree to watch Maybelle."

A lump fills my throat. Part of me wishes I was spending Christmas with Mirna and Barb, but they have their own families—their real families. Still, they're the closest thing to family I have, and it's nice to know they feel the same way. Besides, I don't anticipate needing to come home early—if I did, I wouldn't be going. "Okay. Deal."

"Good," she says, and I can practically hear her dusting her hands. "Now that that's settled, you should work out the details of your trip so Burt can get started on your contract after Barb finishes paying your retainer."

I blush and want to bleach my brain at the same time, but she has a point. We hang up and after I take a breath to settle my nerves, I send Alex a text.

Chapter Six

December 17

Finley 8:10 pm

I've hired an attorney who is willing to have a contract by tomorrow night, but there's a few things we need to iron out first. I've sent a spreadsheet of my wages to your email address for your review

Alex 8:13 pm

I opened your spreadsheet and was impressed at how thorough and exact you are. I realize you're missing work to do this, so I'm more than happy to round up the 93.7 hours you'll be missing from both jobs up to 100 hours

8:15 pm

What else do we need to iron out?

8:18

This next part is embarrassing, but I have to ask anyway

8:21

I don't expect anything sexually, so put your mind at ease. That's not why I'm bringing you

8:25

Thanks for the clarification. My friend Mirna will be thrilled to hear that since she's concerned you're working for a "Russian mafia gang" and plan to ship me overseas as a sex slave

8:26

Mafia gang? 😂

Don't ask

8:27

Would your friend Mirna feel better if I met her and assure her that I don't work for the Russian "mafia gang" or any other mafia gang?

If I introduce you to Mirna, then I'll have to introduce you to Barb and since I really want to go to Hollybrook, I don't want to scare you off

8:28

I realize the first rule of negotiation is to never let the other side know how much you want what they have. Please delete that last text

8:29

Consider it deleted 🙃

8:30

Also, I realize telling you I didn't want Barb to scare you off makes it sound like I think this is a real relationship, which we both know it's not

I don't want you to think I'm some kind of crazy psycho who thinks this is real

Um…now I realize I doubly sound like a crazy psycho, because a crazy psycho would claim she wasn't

8:31

If I thought you were a crazy psycho, I wouldn't have asked you to help me. You come with very good references 🙃

You checked references? Who did you ask?

8:31

Well, I don't want everyone to know I'm only pretending to be your girlfriend, so I guess I'm hiding THAT. Not that I'm trying to actually become your girlfriend

Now you really think I'm a psycho 

8:32

Finley, relax. I want to keep this arrangement quiet as well. Maggie and Bethany are your references, so it was kind of a joke, albeit a bad one..

Would you like me to delete ALL of our texts after the last one I deleted?

8:33

Yes, please

So have you changed your mind about bringing me now? I think it's too late to get my retainer back from my attorney, but I understand if I've scared you off

8:34

You haven't scared me off. But it just now occurs to me that you're paying for an attorney to have this contract drawn up. Please let me repay you for the retainer and any other legal expenses

8:35

A friend paid the retainer for me, and trust me, you do NOT want to repay her. My attorney is a friend of a friend, so after the retainer, I don't owe him anything. But that does remind me of the last thing I need to know

8:38

And that would be...?

8:40

Since you and your brother shared a room, I'm presuming you didn't share a bed...?

8:43

My brother and I slept in twin beds on opposite sides of the room.

Oh, good, because my only demand was that if you had bunk beds, I refuse to sleep on top

(My attorney wanted to call them all demands, but I insisted on requests.)

8:44

I consider your refusal to sleep on the top bunk a reasonable demand.

Not to worry, Grant and I begged for bunk beds for years, but Mom said she wasn't climbing on top to change the sheets every week, so no bunk beds for us. I've never gotten over the disappointment

8:50

Have you considered therapy to get over your tragic loss?

8:51

You're not the first person to suggest therapy, but so far I've suffered with my tragedies in silence 😌

8:52

I just relayed my requests to my attorney. He's not answering at the moment, but as soon as Barb finishes paying my retainer, I'm sure he'll check his email

I'm suddenly curious how Barb paid your retainer

8:53

Trust me. You don't want to know 🙁

🕵 Consider my curiosity piqued…

9:37

My attorney would like to know when and how you plan to pay me for lost wages?

I just realized that makes it sound like I don't think you'll pay me. I'm not insinuating that.

9:38

How about I pay half before we go, and the other half the day after we get back? Does that seem fair?

9:39

More than fair

9:41

If your attorney thinks of anything else, feel free to text. I'll be up until at least midnight

9:52

I told my attorney that you've given me the option to leave early. He wants to know if you prefer to prorate the days. (He's insisting I get at least half the money no matter how long I stay since I've made the effort to come.)

9:53

I agree to those terms

9:57

Is there anything else?

10:08

No, I think that's it.

Thank you

10:09

Don't thank me yet. You haven't met my family

Chapter Seven

I'm pacing the tiny Hartwell airport like an expectant father in the waiting room after his wife's been in labor for what feels like three days straight.

Mom picked me up from the airport earlier and drove me home, chattering about everything happening with the family and around Hollybrook. Her enthusiasm over Finley's arrival is cautious, but I expect that'll change the moment she meets her.

Traffic into Hollybrook was brutal, so it took longer to get home than it took for the flight from Boston to Hartwell. I had barely dropped my suitcase in the entryway and ate the snack Mom insisted on feeding me, before she shoved the Wagoneer keys into my hand and sent me back to the airport. Dad was at work, and Mom said Tyler and Mallory were finishing some last-minute Christmas shopping, but everyone will be home when I arrive with Finley. Everyone except Grant and Eloise, who won't be arriving until late afternoon on Christmas Eve.

I'm suddenly having major second thoughts, but I keep telling myself I'll feel better once she gets here and the introductions are over.

Finley's arriving several hours after me. I couldn't get her on any of my flights, and I was lucky to snag her the last available seat out of Atlanta today, but it arrives three hours later than mine. My original plan had been to meet her at Boston Logan so we could take the commuter flight together to Vermont. But her flight got in too late to make my connection, and when I checked the two remaining flights to Hartwell, each only had one seat available.

She texted that she made it to Boston okay, then followed up that her commuter flight was delayed thirty minutes. I've probably asked the airport manager over a dozen times for status updates. He's clearly annoyed, but my anxiety keeps ratcheting higher. I'm not ordinarily anxious, and it's been six years since I've felt this out of control. I didn't handle it well back then, so I never learned any tricks I could use for handling it now.

I'm just about to ask again when the manager gives me a weary look. "The plane's landing now." Then he points to the window overlooking the two-runway tarmac.

The aircraft touches down then rolls to the terminal. A gentle snow is falling, and my first thought is how much Finley will love it.

The thought catches me off guard. Sure, part of our bargain is that I make sure she gets her full dose of Hollybrook Christmas magic, but once she's here, it technically isn't my job to guarantee she has a good time. And yet, ever since I've landed in Vermont, I've been looking at everything through her eyes. I keep having flickers of excitement at how she'll react, and I'm not sure how to feel about that.

But we *are* friends. And friends want the best for each other. That's all. That's enough.

There's no security at this airport, so I walk up to the glass to watch for Finley. The plane door swings open, the steps are rolled into place, and passengers begin filing out. Enough people get off that I wonder if Finley changed her mind and caught a flight back to Atlanta. Just when I'm about to text her—what, I don't know, because *did you change your mind?* doesn't seem like the brightest idea—she appears at the top of the steps.

She freezes, glancing around the snowy tarmac, and her whole face lights up with wonder. Something swells in my chest, stealing my breath.

What the hell is *that*?

Probably relief? She's here, and she looks happy and excited. That's a solid start. The happier she is, the more likely she'll want to stay.

A man practically twice her size exits the plane behind her, barreling down the steps. When they hit the asphalt at nearly the same time, he shoves her aside in his hurry.

I see red—not just because he laid a hand on her, but because that sparkle in her expression dims.

Passengers file into the building, but the guy charges for the exit. On impulse, I block his path.

"What the hell, man?" he snaps.

"You just shoved my girlfriend when you were getting off the plane," I bite out.

"She was too damn slow. I've got places to be."

"It's her first time here. She's never seen snow like this." My fists clench at my sides. "Your rudeness might have ruined it for her."

Even as the words leave my mouth, I know how ridiculous they sound. What the hell is wrong with me? I'd blame it on jetlag, but Vermont is in the same time zone as Atlanta.

To my surprise, the man's face softens.

"Sorry, man. My kid's sick. I need to get to the hospital."

Now I feel like an ass. "Sorry," I mutter, but he's already running for the exit.

I'm about to examine why I felt the need to accost the guy, when I turn and see Finley coming through the door. Snowflakes cling to her long, dark waves, and the ivory cardigan she's wrapped in makes her hair look even darker. It throws me off since she always wears it up at the coffee shop. Her cheeks are flushed from the cold, and her eyes bright as she scans the tiny lobby.

The second she spots me, a huge smile breaks across her face. My stomach drops like I've just gone over the edge of a roller-coaster.

Okay, now what the hell is that?

Nerves. Just nerves. Relief that she's here and not shaken by that jerk. But I know in my gut that's not the only reason.

Finley's breathtakingly, intoxicatingly, agonizingly beautiful.

I don't have the first clue what to do with that. She's made it *very* clear this is platonic. But there's no time to figure it out, because she's already walking toward me.

Get yourself under control, Alex. Act normal.

"How was your flight?" I ask like I'm a chauffeur making polite conversation rather than a guy greeting his fake girlfriend. I mentally pat myself on the back for keeping it professional. And platonic.

"Good," she says, some of the shine fades from her eyes, and I know immediately that my stiff tone is to blame. The last thing I want to do is steal her joy. I need to shove these feelings down. It shouldn't be that hard. I've got six years of practice, shoving feelings into the cellar of my heart.

Only now the hinges are starting to bulge.

This whole thing is a huge mistake.

Maybe I've built up this attraction. I've been rereading our text exchange from the night we hashed out the details. Finley's more charming—and funnier—than I realized. That, combined with how beautiful she is, mixed in with my shaky nerves over being home... I've probably just latched onto the thought of her being my girlfriend. I need to remember this isn't real.

But seeing the look on her face now, I want to rewind the past minute and try again.

Too late for that now, asshole.

She glances around the lobby. "Do you know where I get my luggage?"

Disappointment hits me like a baseball to the chest. Maybe she hadn't been scanning the room for me. She'd been looking for a luggage carousel.

"Yeah," I glance toward the door to the tarmac. "Give me a second, and I'll get it for you."

"You don't have to—" But I'm out the door before she can

finish. Partially because I don't want to argue, but mostly because I need a second to get my head on straight.

I hurry over to the plane where two men are unloading bags. I recognize one of them from when I was waiting, and he gives me a smirk. "You must really be in a hurry to get your girlfriend home."

His innuendo gets under my skin, but I shove it aside. "Yeah. Something like that."

As they snicker and get back to tossing bags, I realize I have no idea what her suitcase looks like.

I'm an idiot.

I pull my phone out of my coat pocket and see that she's already sent a text.

Green suitcase with a pink ribbon

I scan the pile and freeze. *There's no way...*

An avocado-green, hard-shell suitcase stands off to the side, perched on metal feet instead of wheels, like it's been dropped out of a black-and-white film. A pink ribbon dangles from the handle, as though she'd confuse it in a sea of black roller bags. I check the luggage tag anyway and confirm it's hers. Samsonite is stamped on the metal under the handle.

Where did she even get this thing? From one of her elderly neighbors? Her mother?

At first glance, it seems impractical, but from what I know of Finley, she isn't. The contradiction gives me pause, because the case feels like something she would carry.

Why do I feel like there's a story here? Just like there's a story about her attorney's retainer.

And more importantly, why do I want to know it?

Once I'm inside, she hurries toward me, reaching for her suitcase. "I can take it from here."

Like hell I'm letting her. I shift the bag out of reach. "What kind of boyfriend would I be to let you carry your bag?" I mean it as a joke, but it comes out rougher than I intended.

Her lips part. "But I'm not—" She stops, her light dimming. "I guess it's time to play my part."

Something twists in my chest. She makes it sound like pretending to be with me is a burden. Maybe we should have spent some time together before this. I thought our banter in the coffee shop and the text messages would be enough, but obviously I didn't think this through. I didn't think *any* of this through, and now a woman I barely know has flown to Vermont to pretend to be my girlfriend.

What the hell was I thinking?

I force a smile. "You don't have to look so distraught about the idea of me being your boyfriend."

Her eyes widen. "Oh, no—that's not it!" A flush creeps up her cheeks. "Any woman would be lucky to have you as a boyfriend. I'm just worried I'll mess up."

I shouldn't feel so relieved, and my fifth appendage shouldn't be so excited. But then I realize she didn't say *she'd* be lucky. Just *any woman*.

"You'll be fine," I manage, though my voice feels tight. Then, like an idiot, I blurt, "You don't have a boyfriend, do you?"

She jerks back, scandalized. "What? No!"

"Right." I drag my hand through my hair. Great. *Keep digging, Alex.* "I should've asked earlier."

Her mouth tightens. "If I had a boyfriend, I wouldn't be here." Her words are clipped, and it's clear I've insulted her.

You'd think I have a shovel in my pocket the way I keep digging myself deeper.

"Sorry, Finley. I didn't mean to insult your character. I'm just...nervous." I regret the words as soon as they're out. I'm supposed to be strong, confident—and I usually am that guy. Which is why this feels so unnerving. I don't recognize myself right now.

Her expression softens. "You're nervous too?"

It's too late to deny it now. "Yeah, but not because I think you'll screw up." I stop there because there's no way in hell I can admit the real reason. I'm too aware of her—the curve of her smile, the way her hair spills around her shoulder like it was made to, the faint scent of vanilla and coffee that clings to her. It's distracting. Dangerous. It's throwing me off balance.

I knew she was cute and charming before I invited her to come with me—hell, it's part of the reason I invited her. Then what is going on with my feelings now?

I heft the suitcase into my left hand, partly because it's heavy, partly so I can rest my right palm against the small of her back as I guide her to the door. The move feels automatic, natural. Too natural.

I'm supposed to sell the part. Just a boyfriend gesture, right? But the warmth of her through her sweater makes me wonder if I'm the one falling for it.

We reach my parents' old Jeep Wagoneer and her face lights up. "I thought these only existed in movies. This is amazing!"

The bite of the cold air helps clear my head which lets me sound normal again. "You'll have to tell my dad. He bought this thing new back in '85. He swore it could get him anywhere in any weather. My mother tried for years to make him trade it in, and he finally caved a few years back and bought a new car, but my brother Tyler convinced her to keep this one. Mostly after we all begged and Tyler promised to maintain it."

"He must be handy. Is he a mechanic?"

"He's an engineer," I say with a laugh. "Growing up, he tore apart everything he could get his hands on. He drove Mom crazy. She started buying toasters and blenders at garage sales just so he'd leave the working ones alone."

Finley laughs, the sound carrying into the still night. It's... nice. Warmer than it should be in this weather. I tell myself that's all it is—just the sound of home, mixing with the cold air and the season. Nothing more.

I open the back hatch, lift her suitcase inside, then move to the passenger door. I unlock it with the key and hold it open.

"Very old school," she teases as she slides onto the seat.

"My mother raised me to open car doors."

She chuckles. "I meant the part where you need a key."

Heat creeps up my neck. "Right. That too."

I get in and start the engine. Cold air blows out of the vents, and she shivers. I turn the fan down until it warms. "Are you hungry? Mom made a pot of chili, but we can stop somewhere if you want."

"I can wait."

I pull out of the lot and head toward Hollybrook. "We should come up with a story of how we met."

"Good idea," she says. "Along with a few other things that a couple should know."

"Yeah," I say, "So for how we met, I thought we could say we met at a networking event."

Her shoulders go rigid. "Why not tell them the truth?"

"You think we should tell my family I'm paying you to be my girlfriend?" I ask in disbelief.

"Let's get one thing clear," she says, her voice icy. "You're not *paying* me to be your girlfriend. You're making up for my lost wages and for me to get here, but I'm here of my own free will. I'm not some paid escort."

If I'm paying for her lost wages, isn't that the same thing as paying her to be my girlfriend? But it's obviously important to her to think otherwise, and I'm smart enough to let it go. "Sorry, that's not what I meant."

"And I'm not *stupid*. I'm not going to tell them that. But the fact you want to change the location of where we actually met means you're embarrassed I work at Beans to Go."

"That's not it," I say quickly. "It's just... my brothers probably won't believe I'm dating a woman who works in a coffee shop."

Her eyes narrow, sharp as glass. "Because it means I'm beneath you?" The iciness in her voice makes my gut tighten.

"I didn't say that," I shoot back, defensive.

"Then why wouldn't they believe it?" She pins me with a look that dares me to lie.

I scramble for words that won't sound worse than the truth. Before I can manage it, she cuts in.

"Because you don't date women who work in coffee shops," she says flatly, daring me to deny it.

"It's just that—"

"Your other girlfriends have all had degrees and careers, not jobs, right?"

"That's *not* what I said."

"No," she shoots back, her gaze unrelenting. "You didn't have to."

Her words sting because they're too close to the truth. Since college, every woman I've dated has been some version of polished, ambitious, impressive on paper. Finance, law, PR.

And now I'm sitting next to Finley, who doesn't fit any of those boxes. The way she's glaring at me—cheeks flushed, posture rigid—it should make me irritated. Instead, something hot curls low in my gut.

"I'm not sure this is going to work," she says softly.

Panic spikes in my chest. "Why not? Because we don't agree on the story of how we met?"

"No," she says, her voice edged with hurt. "Because you obviously don't respect me as a person."

The words knock the breath out of me. "That's not true."

"Isn't it?" She turns fully toward me, her eyes sharp. "You just admitted that your brothers would never believe you'd date a woman who works at a coffee shop."

I clench the wheel, biting back a curse. Maybe she's right. Maybe I wouldn't have dated her in real life. But hearing her say it pisses me off, and I don't know why.

My shoulders square. "It's a little late to be having second thoughts."

"You're right," she snaps. "You've gone to the expense of bringing me here, so I'll live up to my end of the bargain."

"Don't sound so thrilled," I mutter.

She's quiet for a moment, then her tone is calmer. Cooler. "In hindsight, we should have worked out the story before we signed the contract."

The unspoken *and I wouldn't have signed* lands heavy between us.

"I'm not going to lie about where we met," she says firmly. "I'll let them believe we've been dating, but I won't lie about me or my life. We met at the coffee shop, and if that embarrasses you, then *tough. shit.*"

Despite myself, my lips twitch. She's angry and absolutely unyielding—and damn if it isn't hot. A woman standing her ground, refusing to let me bulldoze her, refusing to shrink. I should be pissed. Instead, I can't stop noticing the fire in her eyes. And she's right. She has nothing to be ashamed of. So why the hell should I be?

"You have a point," I concede, trying to sound cool even as my pulse is hammering. "We need to stick to the truth as much as possible, otherwise it'll get too complicated."

Her eyes go wide, incredulous. "*That's* what you got out of that?"

"No, it's just—"

"Forget it," she cuts me off. "Here's what we tell them—we met at the coffee shop. Three months ago, you saw that I was sad and asked if I was okay. I told you my cat was sick, and you asked if I needed to talk. So, we met after I got off work—on one of my days off from the hospital. I told you how scared I was that my cat wouldn't make it, and you were supportive. You asked me out again, and the rest is history."

If my brothers won't buy that I'd ask my barista out, they definitely won't buy me noticing she was sad. But the kicker? She's not making this up. The thing is, I *did* notice she was off a few months ago. But I never asked about it. I was too damn self-absorbed to do for her what she once did for me.

I really *am* an asshole.

"Yeah," I say, though it comes out distracted, like I'm scrambling to justify why I never asked if she was okay back then. "That works."

Her eyes narrow. "Does it really?"

I hesitate, then force myself to sound blasé, "My mom and sister will buy it. If my brothers don't, that's their problem." Then, because asking about cats is safer than admitting I'm a coward... "*Do* you have a cat?"

Her jaw ticks. "Of course I have a cat."

"And was she really sick?"

"Yes. She nearly died, but she's back to her same grumpy, hell-raising ways." We're quiet for nearly a minute. I keep trying to figure out where this all went wrong, when she asks, her voice less brittle and challenging, "Do you have any pets?"

I bark out a laugh. "I can barely take care of myself, let alone keep another living creature alive."

The silence between us charges the air, prickling my skin. And I know it's my fault, and it only makes me more anxious. If she can't fake liking me, my family will see right through us.

Practicality kicks in.

"Look, I know we signed a contract," I say, trying to keep my voice neutral, reasonable, "but if you want out, I'll get you the first flight out, but it will have to be tomorrow. I overheard the airport manager tell someone else the flights for tonight are full."

Her chin lifts. "No," she says firmly. "We made a deal, and I want to see Hollybrook." Then her voice softens. "I'll do my best to pretend I'm into you."

The words are meant to reassure me, but instead they cut my ego like a knife. I can't remember the last time I was into a woman who didn't like me back. Middle school? Maybe this is what I deserve, a kick to my ego. But the sting is sharp—and stupid, because I shouldn't be into her at all.

For several minutes, the only sound is the steady beat of the windshield wipers, brushing away the lightly falling snow. I feel shitty. How did we start off so great and arrive at her probably wanting to leave within fifteen minutes?

You're what happened. You acted like an asshole.

I have to fix this, but I'm not sure how.

I glance over at her, and she's looking out the windows now, but the tension of her face has softened. She's not glaring at the glass like it wronged her. Her mouth is parted, and her eyes are round with awe.

This is why she's here. She's not doing this as a favor to me. She hardly knows me. Sure, I could tell myself that she's here because I'm generously reimbursing the salary she's losing by being here, but her expression right now is why she's really here, and I'm ruining it for her.

My anger bleeds out of me, and something else settles in: responsibility. We have a contract. And while I might be feeling attracted to her, acting on it would be crossing the line. The boundary's there for a reason, and I need to respect it. *And* her.

The thing is, I *do* respect her. I respect the hell out of her. As shitty as her life sounds, she's one of the most positive, upbeat people I know. Why should it matter where she works?

"Can we start over?" I ask hesitantly.

She stiffens, then lets out a grudging, "Sure."

It's not full forgiveness, but it's an opening, and I'll take it.

I'd like to patch this up before we get to my parents' house, but I bite my tongue. Everything I've said during this drive has replaced my shovel with a backhoe, and the hole I've been digging is halfway to China. The best thing I can do right now is to shut up.

So, I clamp my jaw and make a private vow: I'll let Finley have her Hollybrook Christmas. I'll keep my hands—and my feelings—reined in. I'll be the solid, non-threatening "boyfriend" my family and Finley expect.

That's what we agreed to, right?

Chapter Eight

Finley

This is a mistake.

I'd never flown before, but I wasn't nervous until Mirna filled my head with all the terrible things that could happen on an airplane. The airports were crowded; the guy next to me on my flight to Atlanta was manspreading as though airing out his junk; and the second plane was so small, I was sure we were going to crash into the side of a mountain.

As soon as the plane landed, I was beyond relieved I'd made it to Vermont alive. And then when I stepped out and saw the snow, I stopped in my tracks.

It was beautiful.

All my apprehension about coming here momentarily faded as I took in the snow-covered landscape and the falling snow. Sure, the view of the airport wasn't breathtaking, but it still felt magical. Full of promise.

And then I saw Alex and it was like the magic had swept into the airport terminal too. He stood in the middle of the lobby, watching me with an intensity I felt to my marrow.

And for a few seconds, this felt real. Like I was really his girl-friend, and he was taking me to meet his family.

Until reality hit.

He would never date me? Because I work in a coffee shop? What?

I can see that he's nervous about what we're doing, but it never occurred to me that part of the reason he's nervous is because he's embarrassed about who I am. Or rather who I'm not.

I'm nothing like the woman who came in that day to get his coffee. I'm not super-model beautiful, and I don't have a high-power career, but I'm damned proud of who I am and what I've accomplished despite my circumstances.

How dare he think less of me because of my *job*?

I nearly told him to turn around and send me home, but he claims there aren't any flights until tomorrow. Which means I'm here tonight anyway, and since he told me days ago there aren't any available hotel rooms, I'm stuck with him for the night.

But I can't get over my overwhelming disappointment in him. I thought he was a decent person. Turns out he's more like his ex-girlfriend than I thought.

Some of my disappointment fades as we drive into town, though. The streets are clear, despite the continuing snowfall, but the ground is covered with multiple inches of fluffy snow sparkling in the glow of the streetlights. Houses line the two-lane road, every one of them lit up with Christmas lights and explosions of decorations. Most are older, in Bavarian- or Tudor-themed architecture, along with some Victorian and Cape Code thrown in for good measure. They're all freshly painted and so well taken care of that it looks like a movie set and not a real town.

But as I take it in, my heart wrenches. Mom would have loved this place.

Alex drives several blocks and then turns onto another street of older homes, these larger than the ones we just passed. After he goes several more blocks, he pulls into the driveway of a two-story Victorian. There's a wraparound porch and even a turret with a small window at the top.

I'm completely enchanted. White lights line the porch and roof lines. Evergreen swags are wrapped around the porch railings, and there are two evergreen wreaths with red ribbons and white lights hanging on the double glass front doors. Several animated reindeer are in the front yard, also covered in white lights.

I gape at the house in wonder. I've spent the last few days

imagining what Alex's house looks like, and while I suspected it was older and charming, this exceeds my expectations.

A new fear hits me. If his family can own a house like this, then maybe they're as snobbish as he's insinuated.

Alex pulls behind a Honda Accord, turns off the engine, then he turns to face me with a sad smile. "I'm really sorry, Finley," he says looking sincere. "Can we try to start over again?"

I turn to him, my resolve softening, but I'm still hurt and disappointed. "I'm not going to lie about who I am, Alex."

He shakes his head. "I know I've insulted you. That wasn't my intention. It's just the women I've dated—"

I groan in frustration. I don't need a reminder that I fall short of the other women he's introduced to them. I level my gaze and say stiffly, "If you're uncomfortable introducing the real me to them, then we should plan on me leaving tomorrow. We'll just get through tonight."

His eyes fly wide. "No! They're going to love you. Trust me on that."

I've trusted him enough to come here, but now I'm not sure my trust was well placed. "Well, I'm here, so I guess we'll see how it goes."

He starts to say something then stops. I'm sure he's worried about how this is going to go. I can't say I blame him. I'm not feeling overly fond of him at the moment.

"I'll be fine," I say, hoping it's true. "Let's pretend this never happened and make the best of it."

He studies me for a second longer than necessary, still looking undecided, but then he opens his door and gets out.

I step out onto the snowy driveway, and my feet slip out from under me on the thin, slick layer of fresh snow. I grab the car door and right myself, realizing I don't have appropriate footwear for this kind of weather. Holding onto the side of the car, I make my way to the back and see Alex holding my suitcase about to close the hatch.

He takes one look at me and frowns. "Do you have any snow-shoes or boots?"

"I live in Atlanta, Georgia," I say with more attitude than I intended.

He takes in my cardigan. "What about a winter coat?"

"Again, I live in Atlanta. We don't exactly need winter coats there." I'm not sure why I find his question so offensive. It's not an unreasonable question.

"Yeah, but..." he says with a frown, "I've seen lots of people in Atlanta wear winter coats."

"Well, not me. I'll be fine. Let's just go inside."

I'm irritated that I'm irritated again, and he looks like he's given up on our truce and is irritated himself. Not that I blame him. He wasn't being confrontational, but I came at him guns blazing.

Get it together, Finley.

He closes the hatch and I'm about to apologize when he gives me a pleading look. "Look, there's a good chance my family is watching out the window. If they see you fall when I could be helping, I'll get nothing but grief. Will you let me help you?"

His gentle tone eases the hurt in my heart, but I can't help wondering if he's only being kind because he feels like he has to. "Yeah," I say more grudgingly than I intend.

Alex takes my arm to balance me, and we make our way up the snow-covered walk until we reach the front porch. Alex drops my arm, and as I stomp my feet to get the snow off, Alex walks over to a mat that looks like a doormat with rough bristles. He wipes the snow off the bottom of his shoes, then opens the heavy wooden and glass front door and gestures for me to go in.

I'm nervous, so I take a deep breath and walk through, not prepared for the greeting party waiting in the foyer. Thanks to Alex's photos, I recognize them all. His parents are side by side in the center of the entryway. His father in jeans and a flannel shirt, and his mother in navy dress pants and light blue, button-down blouse. Mallory is standing next to her mother, wearing jeans and an ivory sweater. Tyler, next to his father, is also just wearing jeans with a black Henley. His brother Grant is missing, and obviously so is Eloise.

His mother and sister take me in, their expressions transforming from neutral to beaming. My worry that they would be arrogant and snobbish fly right out the window.

"Oh, my goodness, look at you! How was your trip?" his mom asks, then doesn't give me time to respond before she says, "We're so excited that you're here!

"*So* excited!" Mallory says, looking like she genuinely means it. "I'll have another girl in the midst of all these boys."

"What about *me*?" Mrs. King asks with a laugh. "Last time I checked, I'm still a girl."

"I meant someone close to my own age," Mallory says, bumping her shoulder into her mother's.

Alex sets my suitcase down on the black and white marble floor. "You and Grant said Eloise was coming," he says carefully.

Mrs. King rolls her eyes. "Of course she is, but you know how she and Mallory get along."

I give Mallory a questioning look and she makes a face. "Eloise can be a bit... temperamental."

Alex hadn't told me that part. Now I'm worried she'll be upset that Alex and I stole her and Grant's beds.

"Don't worry about Eloise," Mallory says. "She's a lot of bark and no bite."

If that was meant to ease my concerns, it only made them worse.

Alex wraps an arm loosely around my back. "As you all figured out, this is Finley." He gestures to the group, starting on the left and working his way around their half-circle. "Finley, this is my brother Tyler, my dad, my mom, and my sister Mallory. Grant and Eloise will be here on Christmas Eve."

I try to hide my relief that his younger brother and his girlfriend aren't here yet. If I decide not to leave, at least I'll have a couple of days' reprieve until the drama starts. "Mr. and Mrs.

King, thank you so much for letting me stay in your home," I say. "You have no idea how much this means to me."

Mrs. King's eyes widen, then she's smiling again. "We're delighted to have you, and please, none of this Mrs. King stuff. Call me Valerie. Please, and this is Bob, or Dr. Bob as a lot of the people around town call him."

I had no idea Alex's father was a doctor, and I give Alex a questioning look.

"It's because Dad takes care of so many of the town's animals," Alex says.

So, he's a vet. Why didn't I ask him these important questions in the car instead of getting pissed?

"You'll have to forgive us for being so fascinated by you," Valerie says as she ushers me to the opening at the back of the entryway. "We didn't even know you existed until Alex told us you were coming, but we're delighted you're here."

"Thank you. You have a lovely home," I say, glancing back at the wood staircase.

She smiles. "Thank you. It's been in the family for three generations. We do the best we can to keep it up."

We enter a large kitchen with white cabinets and white marble and butcher block counters. It's not new or fancy. It's older, but in a classic way. Based on the clutter on the counter, it's definitely not a show kitchen. There's a stack of papers at one end and an assortment of Christmas tins on another section. A large pot is on the large gas range, and multiple containers sit next to the stove. The kitchen looks lived in, and I instantly feel at home.

"Come in," she says enthusiastically. "You must be *starving* after flying all day. I have a pot of chili on the stove. We were just waiting for you two to get here." She stops and gives me a questioning glance. "Oh, dear. I realize I didn't ask Alex if you liked chili."

Alex grunts like he disagrees with what she said. Does he think she purposely didn't ask him? Or maybe he doesn't like chili, and he's upset she made it.

But she's still looking at me, waiting for an answer.

"I *love* chili," I say enthusiastically. "I often make a big pot and portion it out so I can bring it to work to eat during the week."

"You bring your own lunch to work?" Mrs. King asks in amazement, and I can't help wondering if this is a test. "What do you do for work?"

I prepare myself for the derision or disdain that's sure to come. I try not to look defensive when I say, "I'm a barista at a coffee shop in the mornings and early afternoons, and then I work as a phlebotomist in the late afternoons and evenings. I usually bring food to eat either during my breaks or between my shifts."

Both women look at me like I just announced I'm an alien. I'm already planning to excuse myself to look up the next flight out of here when both of them break out into the brightest smiles I've ever seen. They're practically giddy.

"Well, aren't *you* a delight!" his mother says, closing the space between us and pulling me into a hug.

I'm briefly stunned before hugging her back. At least *she* doesn't think I'm beneath her. But that still doesn't explain their enthusiasm. Maybe they're just thrilled to have a barista in the house?

"Are you wanting a coffee hookup?" I ask with a laugh as she pulls away. "Because even without an espresso machine, I can make just about any coffee drink you'd like."

Mallory looks excited at that prospect, then points at me. "I'm *definitely* going to take you up on that. In fact, tomorrow morning we're going to get whatever you need. But first," she looks at her mother, then back at me, "we have to know how in the world you ended up dating Alex."

Alex is standing in the doorway talking to his brother, but I catch him glancing at me with an anxious look. He doesn't think his brothers will buy it, but I'm still going with the story I'd proposed. I won't pretend to be someone I'm not.

"Alex is a regular customer at my coffee shop. It's on the first floor of his office building, so we see each other every day. A few months ago, my cat got sick, and Alex noticed that I was feeling kind of down and invited me to meet him after I got off work and tell him what was going on. So, I told him about my cat, and..." I end with a shrug as though it's no big deal. "The rest is history."

They stare at me in silence for several seconds, and then his mother glances toward Alex, flushing with pride, and mutters under her breath, "Thank God you finally came to your senses."

I'm lightheaded with relief. His mother and sister don't care that I don't have an MBA or a business suit. The jury's still out on his dad and brother, but I'll take what I can get.

Valerie takes my hand and squeezes. "Aren't you a blessing?"

While I'm relieved they don't think I'm beneath them or their son, I now feel guilty she thinks we're really dating.

"You're laying it on a little thick, aren't you, Mom?" Alex asks dryly, giving her a look I can't read.

"You hush," his mother says, as she picks up a large wooden spoon on the counter to stir the chili in the pot. "Let me bask in the moment."

"Don't embarrass, Finley," he says, still sounding unamused.

"I'm not embarrassed," I say, partially to irritate Alex, but mostly because I don't want his mother to hold back on how she feels. I've never believed in love at first sight, but I've spent less than five minutes with Alex's mother and sister and I'm head over heels in love with them.

"When Alex said he was bringing his girlfriend home..." Mallory's voice fades, "Well, you're not at all what we expected."

"Thanks," I say, feeling a bit smug. Alex may be embarrassed by my job, it's obvious the women in his family haven't been too fond of his previous girlfriends. Still, I have an opportunity to downplay our relationship. Now that I adore them, I really hate deceiving them. "I'm not sure if Alex is ready to make our relationship that official. We're still pretty new."

"But he invited you for Christmas," Mallory says. "He's *never* invited *anyone* for Christmas."

A chill washes over me. Why hasn't he invited his previous girlfriends for the holidays? Then again, maybe they wanted to spend Christmas with their own families. For all I know, Alex spent it with them.

Alex must feel the need to convince his mom and sister we're involved because he walks over and wraps an arm around my shoulder. "Finley didn't have anywhere else to go, so I took pity on her."

His mother and sister stare at him in horror.

I want to elbow him in the ribs, but instead I shake his arm. "Yep," I say, keeping my tone playful despite my humiliation. I glance up at him, "That's me—your lonely, holiday pity case."

Something flickers in his eyes, I think I see an apology, but my eyes burn, and his face turns blurry.

Valerie releases a horrified gasp and pulls me into another hug. "Oh, you poor dear." She grabs my shoulders and pulls back, looking deep into my eyes. "Don't you *dare* call yourself a pity case. You're very welcome in our home." She casts a frown at her son, then graces me with a bright smile. "Now, you must be starving, so let's get you that chili. How do you like it? We have all the fixings—cheese, corn chips, sour cream, anything you'd like on top, onions? We even have cornbread."

"We heard that cornbread is a big thing in the South," Mallory says.

I laugh. "Isn't cornbread a big thing everywhere? And yes, please."

Mallory and her mother exchange glances, then she turns back to me. "*We* like cornbread, but some of Alex's *other* girlfriends—"

Then it hits me why Alex was irritated about the chili. It was a test, and I suspect his previous girlfriends didn't pass.

"How about we not bring any of my previous girlfriends into this," Alex says, his voice tight. "We all know that no woman wants to hear about her boyfriend's previous girlfriends."

"Oh, that's okay," I say sweetly, placing a hand on his arm. "I don't mind hearing about your ex-girlfriends. I'm not the *least* bit threatened, because I know my worth." I might be laying it on thick, but I want to make it clear I'm not embarrassed that I'm not one of polished women he usually dates.

Mrs. King shakes her head. "Mallory, you could take a lesson from Finley."

"I know, right," Mallory says, then sighs. "His last girlfriend was ridiculously jealous of everyone and everything. One time she thought Mom was looking at Alex a little too long, and she wrapped her claws—I mean hands—around his arm and hung on the rest of the time they were with us. She was practically claiming Alex as her property."

There's a teasing tone to her voice, but I can also tell that she's irritated with him. I think about the photo I saw of her and Alex taken at the skating rink several years ago. She'd been staring up at him with adoration and awe. I don't see any of that now.

What happened?

Mrs. King scoops some chili into a bowl and then asks if I want cheddar cheese and sour cream. She seems pleased when I say yes to both, then hands me the bowl and a small plate of corn bread. Mallory ushers me to the kitchen table in the attached breakfast room and gets me settled, then volunteers to get me a glass of water.

After everyone else serves themselves, then join me at the six-person table. Valerie and Dr. Bob sit at the ends. The boys flank their dad, and Mallory and I sit on either side of their mother. Alex is sitting next to me.

"So, Finley," Dr. Bob asks, "were you born and raised in Atlanta?" This is the first time he's said anything other than hello to me. Then again, Valerie hasn't let him get a word in.

I nod. "My mom was from Atlanta, or at least a town outside of Atlanta."

"And your father?" he asks.

"My father was from Florida, but his parents weren't the greatest, so he went no contact before he met my mother."

"So, your father moved to Atlanta too?"

"Yes, but not for long. He joined the military and was killed in the service when I was a baby."

He frowns. "I'm so sorry."

"That's okay," I say. "I obviously don't remember him, but I have several photos. My mother never remarried so she raised me as a single mother. We didn't have a lot of money, but she always found a way to make the most of everything."

"She sounds like a special woman," Valerie says.

"Yeah." My voice catches. "In any case, we lived in the suburbs until she got sick. Our car died not long after that, so we moved into the city and used public transportation."

"Is your mother better now?" his mother asks gently.

I'm furious with myself for bringing this up so early, but they're going to wonder why I'm not spending Christmas with my own family. Still, I hate that Alex made me look like a pity case.

Valerie's eyes widen as it dawns on her. "Oh," she says softly. "I just realized what Alex meant when he said you didn't have anywhere else to go."

"My mother passed away," I admit, giving her a reassuring smile. "But it was six years ago, so water under the bridge."

When I tell people it's been years, they seem to think the pain is gone. While it's not as fresh as it was after she first died, grief still sometimes catches me randomly by surprise.

But the empathy in Valerie's eyes tells me she understands grief. "My own mother died a few years ago, and while I had her much longer than you had your own mother, even with the passage of time, you're never over it."

I nod, unable to push words past the lump in my throat.

She tilts her head, still holding my gaze. "So, Alex wasn't being dramatic when he said you were spending Christmas alone?"

"No, but it's fine. I'm used to it," I say dismissively. "Still, Alex felt guilty leaving me, and insisted I come. He had to convince me. I didn't want to be an imposition."

"An imposition?" his mother asks in disbelief. "Of course not!

You have no idea how excited we are that you're here." The look on her face persuades me that she means it. "We want you to feel at home."

Tears sting my eyes. "Thank you." I already feel that way, but I have to remind myself this isn't real. I don't actually belong here. I have a part to play, and in return, I get the Christmas I always wanted.

Still, on the rare occasions I've daydreamed about having a decent boyfriend and what that might entail, I'd be lying if I said the picture didn't include a warm, welcoming family like this.

We're all silent for several seconds, before Valerie says, "Is there anything specific you'd like for meals, Finley? Any dietary concerns?" She nods to my bowl. "I'm guessing you're not vegan since you're eating chili with beef topped with cheese and sour cream."

I chuckle. "No, no concerns and I'm definitely an omnivore. I'm just grateful to be here and experience Christmas with your family, especially here in Hollybrook. My mother always dreamed of spending Christmas somewhere like this." I glance over at Dr. Bob. "You have no idea how much it means to me that y'all are so welcoming." I turn back to Valerie. "Not many families would be."

I'm thinking about Barb's and Mirna's families and how both women had tried for several years to get their families to agree to let me come, but even if they'd said yes, I wouldn't go. I never want to be where I'm not wanted, but my worries that Alex's family might have resented my presence have fled.

"Don't be silly," Valerie says, waving her spoon. "We have an open-door policy in this house. Anyone is welcome." She gives me a broad smile. "Especially a friend of Alex's."

I'm glad she's only called me his friend, it makes me feel less like a fraud, even though Alex and I aren't even friends.

I thought we could be, but now I'm not so sure.

Chapter Nine

While I'm relieved Mom and Mallory like Finley so much, I'm irritated that Mom had several tests for her. Like clutter on the kitchen counters. She wouldn't dream of having a cluttered kitchen with company. And the chili. Mom knows that Shawna hated chili, and my girlfriend before her had turned her nose up at meatloaf. Mom made chili on purpose to see if Finley was a food snob.

I scoop another bite out of my bowl and glance up to see Tyler watching Finley with suspicion. I'm not surprised given she's the polar opposite of my previous girlfriends, but hopefully, Mom and my sister can help keep him in line.

Mom's pleased when Finley gets a second bowl, and when she finishes that, Mom brings out a half-eaten peppermint chocolate cake on a cake stand.

Another test to see if Finley is offended. The only pleasure I'm getting out of this is knowing my mother is probably dying inside having to serve a half-eaten cake to a first-time guest.

"Sorry it's already been cut into," Mom says as she sets it on the table. "But I hate to see it go to waste."

"Are you kidding?" Finley says in awe. "It looks delicious!"

The smile on my mother's face makes it obvious Finley has not only passed but gotten extra credit.

"I suppose you get lots of baked goods working at a coffee shop," Mallory says.

"Their cheese Danishes are really good," I say, realizing I've hardly said anything during dinner.

Finley looks surprised, then says, "Alex would know about the cheese Danishes since they're his favorite, but we don't make them in the store. They're prepackaged and we heat them up. And while I love all kinds of baked goods, the shop only has breakfast foods, so this is amazing."

"You don't bake?" Mom asks nonchalantly as she slips the knife into the cake.

Another test, which gets under my skin. Even if Finley doesn't bake, it doesn't make her a failure. Not all women cook and bake.

But if Finley realizes she's being tested, she doesn't let on. "I do, but I don't have much free time, and besides, it's just me and my cat. Anything I make would go to waste."

"You don't bake for Alex?" Mom asks innocently, keeping her eye on her task.

Finley gives me a panicked look, and I say, "She would if I wanted her to, but she knows I've been watching my sugar intake, so she doesn't give me the temptation."

"But you eat Danishes at her coffee shop," Mallory says.

"It's kind of our thing," Finley says with a soft smile. "When he first started coming in, he couldn't decide what to order, and I suggested a Danish." She gives a small shrug. "He's been getting them ever since."

Mallory clasps her hands to her chest, a dreamy look filling her eyes. "That is *so* romantic."

Tyler's eyes narrow, but he stays silent.

I rack my brain, trying to remember why I even started ordering Danishes. I never ate them before Beans to Go. Did she really suggest it? I come up blank, but I suspect it's true. Finley has a memory like a steel trap, and she said she wouldn't lie.

Mom sets a plate with a slice of cake in front of Finley. "Guests first."

"Thank you," Finley says, smiling at the plate. She's more excited than a person should be over a piece of cake.

"Did I hear you say you have two jobs?" Dad asks as Mom hands him a plate. "That's very ambitious of you."

"Yeah," she says as she picks up a fork. "My mother acquired some medical debt I had to pay off, and I also take college courses part time."

My mouth drops open. I had no idea about the debt or that she was taking college courses.

"Why do you look so surprised?" Tyler asks dryly.

He finally speaks, and of course, it's to point out something that will prove I'm a liar.

I shake it off. "Why would I be shocked? This is me being proud."

And I am, although I don't have a right to be. I had no idea she was going to school in addition to working two jobs.

"How do you have time to see Alex?" Mom asks, her gaze on me.

"We have the weekends," I say. "Plus, you know the start-up takes a lot of my time. Finley's okay with it because she's so busy herself."

Mom shakes her head as she places another slice of cake on a plate and hands it to me. "You work too much."

"We're close to finishing," I say, taking the plate.

Her mouth purses. "You missed Christmas last year because you were close."

"We hit a few snags," I admit. "But I'm here now."

She stops cutting, mid slice, and looks up at me. "Yes, and I'm so glad you are."

The softness on her face makes my heart melt. I've missed being home, and I miss my mother even more.

After everyone is served, we all take a bite and Finley moans with pleasure.

The sound shoots straight through me, and I can't help but imagine what it would be like to be the reason she makes it.

Shit. This is not good. I cannot be reacting like this with my parents sitting less than three feet on either side. Hell, I shouldn't be reacting at all. This is strictly platonic.

Finley gushes to my mother, "If this isn't a treasured family recipe, I'm not leaving here without it."

Mom laughs. "No family recipe. This was actually an experiment. Mallory and I combined two recipes."

"Obviously a successful one," Finley says before she slips her fork into her mouth with another bite.

I'm mesmerized by the sight of her lips wrapping around the tines, and my brain short-circuits like a blown fuse. Every rational thought I've ever had packs its bags and leaves town.

Think of something else. Anything else. Like old witches and scary elves.

Where is this coming from? Sure, she's cute—no, calling Finley cute is like saying the Sistine Chapel is a nice paint job. She's beautiful. I don't know how I missed it before, but I've seen other beautiful women and kept my cool.

Maybe it's some kind of reverse transference thing. She's doing me a favor and charming my family, and my brain's confusing gratitude for attraction.

Yeah, nice try. Most of me knows that's a lie, but the small part of me that wants it to be true is screaming the loudest.

I cannot be attracted to Finley O'Brien for a whole slew of reasons, starting with the fact she's not my type. At. All.

Right?

But the conversation's continuing without me, and I realize Mom's talking to Finley. "Mallory and I are doing some Christmas baking tomorrow if you'd like to help."

Finley's eyes light up. "I'd love to."

"Maybe not the *entire* day," I say, placing my hand over Finley's on the table. "I plan to take her to the Christmas market."

I have no idea where this thought came from, only that I think she'll like it. It has nothing to do with wanting to spend the afternoon with her—because that would be a terrible idea. I just don't want her going to the Christmas market on her own. I mean, I should probably at least show her around the town before setting her loose.

"Oh, you *have* to go to the market," Mallory says. "They have so many amazing things there."

"How about we plan on baking in the morning, and you two can go to the market after lunch?" Mom suggests.

Finley looks at me, and I see that she really wants to do both, not that I'm surprised. She wants the full Christmas experience, and I suppose baking is part of that. "If that works for Finley, it works for me."

Her face lights up with excitement, and a warm feeling builds in my chest. I'm positive if my mother had suggested baking to my previous two girlfriends, they'd be looking for excuses to get out of it. Is that why I've got this warm, glowy feeling? I'd like to blame it on alcohol, but I haven't had a drink in days.

"Val, I think you've lost track of time," Dad says. "Don't you need to leave soon?"

My mother gasps and jumps to her feet. "Oh, my goodness, you're right!" She picks up her plate with her half-eaten slice of cake and takes another bite as she walks to the sink. "The group's smaller this year, so every person counts." She turns her attention to Finley. "The historical society goes caroling every year."

"Christmas caroling?" Finley asks, practically bouncing in her seat.

"Yes."

"We'll join you." I say before I can talk myself out of it. Finley wants all that Hollybrook has to offer, and you can't get much more Christmasy than caroling.

My mother stares at me in shock.

Finley can barely contain her excitement as she turns to face me, clutching my arm. "Really? We can go caroling?"

How can something this simple make her so happy? Then I realize I *like* seeing her so happy. That's probably why I offered to come. Plus, it could go a long way toward getting back into her good graces. "Full Christmas experience, right?"

She throws her arms around me and gives me a sideways hug.

Mallory jumps to her feet. "Well, if you two are going, then I'm going too."

"What the hell is going on?" Tyler asks, staring at me like I've had a lobotomy. "You *hate* Christmas caroling."

Finley loosens her hold on me, her smile crumpling.

I glare at my brother, then kick him under the table. "My girl's never had a Hollybrook Christmas and I plan to give her the full experience, which includes caroling." I turn to her and tuck a strand of hair behind her ear, trying not to let the fact it's soft as silk distract me. "You'll need a coat though." I glance up at Mallory. "Do you have a spare coat Fin can wear? She doesn't have one. And maybe some boots?"

"Got you covered," she says, then reaches for Finley's arm. "Come up to my room and we'll get you dressed warm enough. We'll be outside for a couple of hours, and we don't want our Georgia peach to freeze!"

If Finley's offended that my sister called her a Georgia peach, she doesn't let on. She picks up her bowl and plate and starts to stand.

I reach over and take them from her. "You go get ready. I'll take care of this."

Gratitude fills her eyes and then she follows Mallory to the back staircase next to the kitchen.

As their footsteps fade, Tyler turns to me. "What the hell is up with you?"

I shot him a look of challenge. "What are you talking about?"

"Since when do you go caroling? You fought Mom for years to get out of it."

"I was a kid," I say, eating the last bite of cake, then slide Finley's plate closer and take a bite of her unfinished piece.

"The last time she asked you were twenty-five."

"Look," I say, exasperated. "Finley's wanted a Christmas like Hollybrook's her whole life. Part of the reason she came with me is to finally have it."

His brow shoots up. "So... the only reason she's here is for a real Christmas?"

"No, it's *part* of the reason, like I just said." I flick a glance over my shoulder, checking if Mom's within earshot, but she's gone—probably upstairs getting ready. When I turn back, Tyler's still watching me, one eyebrow arched, waiting for me to slip. "Finley told you guys that we're still pretty new."

"So why bring her home?" he asks, still in interrogation mode.

My dad watches us both, listening.

"Because she would have spent Christmas alone," I say, the words catching in my throat. The image of Finley spending Christmas Day alone with her cat twists something in my chest. "And I knew Mom and Mallory would love her."

He studies me for a long beat, then says flatly, "Right."

"You don't believe me?" I ask my voice harder than I intend.

He shrugs, pulling a face. "What's not to believe?"

"For what it's worth," Dad says, "she seems to be a lovely girl. Even if it's new, I'm glad you brought her. You'd have felt terrible knowing she was alone."

Tyler coughs into his fist, then pats his chest. "Went down the wrong pipe."

Dad buys it, but I don't. Tyler's convinced I'm too self-centered to care about anyone else. He's accused me of it before, and no matter how many examples I throw at him that I'm not, he always walks away unconvinced.

Maybe because part of me knows he's not wrong.

"Do you need to change?" Dad asks.

"I should be good." I'm wearing jeans and a sweater, and my parka, hat, and gloves are hanging in the mudroom.

"I put your suitcase in your room," Dad says. "And I'll take Finley's up too."

"Thanks, Dad," I say.

"And Tyler will help clean up the kitchen."

Tyler shoots him a blank look, turns back to me. "Is this why you're going caroling? To get out of helping with the dishes?"

"Of course not," I balk. "I'm going to make my girlfriend happy."

His brow ticks up. "Your barista girlfriend."

"That's right." I lift my chin, pressure building in my chest. Like hell am I letting him take a shot at her for what she does. Yeah, the irony isn't lost on me, but rational thinking left the building the moment Finley walked off the plane. "Do you have a problem with what my girlfriend does for a living?"

"*I* don't."

The insinuation that I do hangs in the air.

"People are more than their profession," Dad says gently. "It's what's in their hearts that matters."

I force a laugh. "You love her because she has a cat."

"You can often tell a person's heart by how they treat animals," Dad says. "I suppose she's close to hers?"

"She is. She was a wreck when it got sick."

"And you noticed she was upset," Tyler says in a challenge, not a question.

"Yes, actually," I reply, smug. "I did. Finley's one of the sweetest, most outgoing people I know, and she was unusually quiet. The first day, I figured it was just an off day. By the second, I knew something was wrong, so I asked if she was okay. She told me her cat was sick and might not make it."

Guilt twists in my gut. While it's true I noticed, I forgot about her as soon as I walked out the door that day. Why didn't I ask if she was okay? Especially after she asked me, just nine months earlier.

Tyler lifts his hands in mock surrender. "Okay. I stand corrected. But you have to admit that's not typical for you."

I scowl and stack Finley's now empty plate on mine.

"I thought you were cutting back on sugar," Tyler needles, refusing to let this go.

"It's Christmas, Ty. Everyone eats sugar at Christmas."

"He's right," Dad says, patting his belly.

"You always eat sugar," Tyler says with a laugh. "Especially when Mom's not looking."

Dad grins and points his fork at my brother. "What your mom doesn't know, doesn't always hurt her."

"What don't I know?" Mom asks as she enters the kitchen, wearing a red sweater over jeans.

Dad's face softens when he sees her. They've been married for thirty-three years and are still each other's best friends. The magic is still there—I see the way they sometimes look at each other, like they're the only two in the world.

It hits me that none of the relationships I've had have even come close to what they have. Is it because love like theirs is so rare it's almost unattainable? Or have I been picking the wrong women?

I don't like the answer, mostly because I know it's true.

Dad's eyes now gleam with mischief. "What I got you for Christmas."

"I don't buy that for a second." She makes a face at him as she walks over to the sink but then she's grinning at him like he's incorrigible.

"You step away from those dirty dishes," Dad says as he gets to his feet. "Tyler and I have it covered."

I grab the plates and bowls and head over the island while Mom gives me a speculative look. "What?" I ask defensively.

"I'm just surprised that you want to go caroling."

Do I *want* to go caroling? Not even a little. I'd rather smash my hand with a hammer. In hindsight, I should have suggested Finley go with them while I stayed behind to clean. But Mom's glowing and Finley's beaming—maybe I can survive fifteen minutes then slip away.

And yet I can't ignore the tiny spark of excitement brewing inside me. I actually want to see her reaction when she's singing carols.

That's how I know I've really lost it. Maybe my plane lost cabin pressure and I'm suffering from slow-onset brain damage.

"I knew Finley would like it," I set the dishes on the counter and lower my voice. "Coming here means a lot to her. Hollybrook's like a dream come true, and I want her to have every bit of it."

Mom studies me then lifts a hand to my cheek, tears filling her eyes. "Alex, you have no idea how happy I am to hear you say that."

I narrow my eyes in confusion. "What are you talking about?"

She makes a face and drops her hand. "Well, you have a habit of—"

"Only thinking about yourself," Tyler finishes as he walks behind me.

"I think about other people," I snap.

"Bullshit," Tyler scoffs. "Ever since you left for college, it's all about you and how everything fits into your perfect life plans."

My anger spikes. "What are you talking about?"

He stands up, a dirty bowl in his hand, and meets my glare. "You really want me to spell it out? I thought you were the genius with an MBA."

Where the hell is this genius stuff coming from? He's the one with the advanced engineering degree.

I open my mouth to tell him to shove it, but Mom steps between us, one hand on my chest, the other on his arm.

"That's enough, boys," Mom says wearily. "Can you at least wait a couple of days before you start in on each other?"

I bristle. *Start in on each other?* That makes it sound like we're twelve arguing over the remote. But what lingers is Tyler calling me self-centered. Because as much as I want to deny it, he's not entirely wrong.

I could make excuses—the charities I've donated to. The money I send every month to...

No. That's not generosity. That's guilt. And no one here can ever know.

It's been easier to shut myself off from everyone—my family included. It's easier not to get too close, not to feel. Because feeling too much has the power to destroy me. It damn near did six years ago.

I could claim I came home for Mom, but the truth is I need them. I need my family, even if I feel like I'm always walking into a minefield.

And if I'm being really honest, that's part of why I brought Finley. I'm hoping she'll soften the explosions, or maybe even disarm them.

I force the knot in my throat down and turn to my Mom. "In any case," I say, forcing calm into my voice, "thank you for inviting her to bake. It means a lot to her."

"Of course," she says warmly. "She's delightful."

"Better than any other girlfriend you've bothered to bring around," Tyler mutters as he loads the dishwasher.

"Tyler," Mom warns. "You need to rinse those off."

"Actually, you don't," he says, sliding bowls into the slots. "Dishwashers are designed to handle dirty dishes. In fact, the detergent works better that way."

"Look at you, all domesticated," I mock.

He shoots me a smug look. "I'm an engineer, dumbass. I know these things."

"A *domestic* engineer?"

"Alex," Mom sighs, exasperated.

"Sorry, Mom," I say, but I'm still glaring at my brother when footsteps echo on the back staircase.

Mallory appears first, bundled in a pale blue ski parka, knit hat, scarf and mittens. A second later, Finley follows and I'm stunned.

She's wearing a red wool coat that hits mid-thigh, the reindeer pin from the day I invited her is fastened to the lapel. A white scarf is wrapped loosely around her neck, and a white knit stocking hat is pulled low over her head, leaving her dark hair spilling over her shoulders. The crisp white against the bold red and her dark hair makes her eyes brighter and her cheeks flushed.

I've always thought she was pretty. At the airport, I thought she was beautiful. But now—layered up and glowing—she steals the breath from my lungs.

She's wearing more fabric than I've ever seen her wear, yet something about her stirs a hollow ache inside me. A longing for... what? There's no question she's the cause, but it can't be a longing for *her*.

Right?

Maybe I'm getting to the age where settling down doesn't sound so bad. My parents were married right after college—Dad was in veterinary school—and they've made it work for over thirty years. The start-up's almost ready to launch, and I'm already wondering what comes next. Is a real relationship part of that?

If so, then why has that thought never crossed my mind until now?

This is way too many deep thoughts hitting me all at once. It's only because I haven't been home in over a year. I'm too damn young to be having a midlife crisis.

"We're ready," Mallory says, looping her arm through Finley's.

Finley beams, practically bouncing.

"Get your coat, Alex," Mom says. "We're already running late."

I drag my eyes away and stalk to the mudroom, pissed at myself. Finley's clearly not interested in me, which makes me doubly irritated. With myself, for caring. With her, for... looking like that.

I'm not supposed to be interested in someone like her. I mean, she's an amazing person, but she'd never fit into my world.

Still, I'm irrationally irritated that she's not interested in me. Why? Seriously. She could do worse. I bet she *has* done worse.

I shove my arms into my coat, grumbling under my breath. Maybe that's why caroling sounds doubly like hell—because standing next to her, pretending I don't want something I can't have, is torture.

Still, I've boxed myself in. Tyler already suspects me of being a selfish bastard, and a good boyfriend would go caroling with his girlfriend, right?

So, here's the plan: I spend twenty minutes, max. Then I bow out gracefully. Or, better yet, Finley gets cold, and I swoop in as the gallant boyfriend who "selflessly" takes her home. Two birds, one stone.

Honestly, maybe Tyler's right. Maybe I *am* a genius.

If my family sees how attentive I am, maybe they'll stop saying I only think of myself. And if I happen to get something out of it too? That's not selfish. That's *efficient multitasking*.

Chapter Ten

Finley

I feel like I've stepped straight into a Hallmark movie—the *old* ones, where the plot was sweet and centered on orphans or old people—not the newer ones full of cheesy love stories. Not that I'm bashing cheesy romance—I love a good one (don't tell Barb) —but that's not what I'm here for. I'm literally living my dream.

"You've really never been caroling?" Mallory asks from the front seat of her mom's SUV.

"Nope," I say from the backseat, seated next to Alex. There'd been a brief scuffle getting in—Mallory insisting I sit up front for the better view, while Alex insisted he wanted to sit with his girlfriend—before dramatically opening the back door for me.

I slid in dutifully, a little confused at first. But then it hit me— he was trying to sell us as a couple. His mom might be convinced, but his brother was too quiet over dinner, watching me a little too closely. Alex probably thinks sitting beside me, and even suggesting caroling, is all part of the act.

The disappointment that settles over me takes me by surprise. I thought he actually wanted to come. Is it all part of the act? How am I supposed to know what's real and what's pretend?

You don't, Finley. Just assume it's all pretend.

I turn toward the window, watching the snow blur past, and try not to wonder which version of Alex I'm sitting next to.

When Mallory and I had gone upstairs to change, she'd been practically buzzing. "This is *huge*," she said breathlessly as she dug through her closet. "Alex *hates* Christmas caroling."

Guilt prickled at my neck. He was doing something he

hated... for me. "He's just being nice. He knows how much this stuff means to me."

"That's just it!" she said, spinning toward me. "My brother is a lot of things, but being nice for the sake of it isn't one of them." Her smile faltered. "At least, not anymore." She hesitated, then, like someone had flipped a switch, her excitement came roaring back. "So, if he's going caroling just because *you* want to...." Her eyes went dreamy. "He must really love you."

Panic shot through me, and I threw up my hands. "No, Mallory. I promise, he doesn't love me. We're too new."

She tossed a pair of leggings at me. "Here. Put these on under your jeans. I'll find you a coat." She turned toward the closet.

I unbuttoned my jeans, figuring she'd see more of me in a bathing suit. I was wearing perfectly innocent underwear which had more coverage than the bikini bottoms I'd worn at the apartment pool last summer.

"How long have you two been dating?" she asked, still rummaging.

"Not long,"

"You said that already," She flicked another hanger across the rod. "*How* long?"

"We started out as friends so... it's hard to say," I hedged. Technically, true. Ish.

"A few months, then?"

"My cat got sick in September," I had said, like that answered anything. At least it was true. The real problem? Alex and I hadn't exactly compared notes. Dating timeline, first-date story, favorite couple activities—basic things a fake couple should probably get straight. But I've been too starry-eyed about spending Christmas here, and then we'd fought and well, here we were.

Mallory spun around holding a hanger with a tan puffy coat like she was Vanna White. I was perched on the bed, tugging on the fuzzy-lined leggings she'd thrown at me.

"Nope," she declared, tossing the coat into a chair. "We need something that makes you *radiate*." She flipped through more hangers as though on a mission. Then she let out a triumphant gasp. "This one!" She held up a short, bright red dress coat. "It's perfect with your dark hair and pale complexion."

"Thank both my parents' Irish blood for that." I said, slipping off my cardigan and leaving just my black long-sleeve T-shirt.

Mallory smiled when her gaze drops. "I love your pin!"

I glanced down at the reindeer pin. "It was my mother's."

Her face softened. "Even better. We'll put it on your coat so it's not hiding."

By the time she was done layering and accessorizing me like her personal Barbie doll, I was swaddled in a sweater, jeans, the red coat, scarf, hat, and the shiny reindeer pin.

"You look so festive for your first time caroling," Mallory announced, beaming like she'd just won Project Runway.

I couldn't stop smiling.

When we'd gone downstairs, Alex had stared at me for several uncomfortable seconds, and my heart had sunk. His face was completely blank, and I couldn't read a thing. Was he upset I was wearing his sister's coat? He'd known I was borrowing one. He'd been the one to suggest it.

Now, sitting beside him, he keeps a careful few inches of space between us. I'm relieved he's not pushing the touchy-feely act. We had agreed no kissing unless it was absolutely necessary, but we never talked about the rest of it. Would he expect handholding? He doesn't strike me as a hand-holder. More like *an arm draped around his girlfriend* kind of guy. Like when he ushered me out of the airport with his hand on the small of my back, or when he slung his arm over my shoulders in his parents' kitchen.

Funny how different my reactions had been. At the airport, I'd felt a flutter in my stomach and told myself to chill out. Maybe I had a crush, but I couldn't act on it. In the kitchen though? I'd been pissed. I hadn't wanted him anywhere near me.

So how do I feel now?

Confused.

I glance up at him, and his gaze holds mine for a few seconds.

I swear I see a hint of wistfulness before he turns back toward the window.

What am I supposed to make of that? Is he feeling bad about the way he treated me on the ride from the airport? Is his offering to go caroling and to the market tomorrow his way of extending an olive branch? If so, I'll take it—but that doesn't mean I can forget I'm not his ideal woman.

You're just being butt hurt. At least he told you the truth instead of leading you on like most of the guys you've dated in the past.

People have types, and who am I to judge what Alex wants in a woman?

But I'd be lying if I said it didn't sting. Badly.

"Looks like the Kramers painted their house," he says to the front of the car.

"No," his mother says thoughtfully. "I don't think they did."

"Huh. Must look different in the dark."

Mallory twists around in her seat. "Okay, Alex. Spill the details about Finley."

He cocks a brow. "She's sitting right here. You could ask her. Besides, I figured you'd grilled her upstairs."

"She was cagey," Mallory says with a pout.

He shoots me a questioning look.

"She asked how long we've been dating," I admit, "and I told her it was hard to say since we started out as friends. But my cat got sick in September... so we've been friends since then."

He studies me a moment, then turns to his sister. "That's right."

"When did you realize she was more than a friend?" she presses, leaning farther into the gap between the seats.

Alex exhales. "It's hard to say."

Mallory groans. "Come on, Alex. It's not hard. You have to know when you started liking her."

He pauses and something in him softens. "Believe it or not, over a year ago. Right after Shawna broke up with me. Finley noticed I was down and tried to cheer me up for a couple of weeks. I'd seen her in the shop before, but that was the first time I really saw her."

"Oh, my God, that's so romantic," she sighs. "Why didn't you ask her out sooner?"

"I didn't want to come across as creepy," he said, his voice low and steady. "I've seen the finance bros hit on her. They treat her like a game. I even heard they've got a pool going to see who can get her to say yes first."

The blood rushes from my head as I whip my head toward him. "They *do*?"

"Yeah." His mouth twists as he catches my eye. "They're assholes. I knew you were too smart to fall for it, but I worried you'd lump me in with them."

The way he says it—earnest, almost protective—sends a flutter racing through my chest before I can stop it. For a second, I want to believe him.

And that terrifies me.

Because Alex is good. Too good. Roland once told me he was in sales, pitching their start-up to investors. Of course he'd know how to spin words, how to make things sound better than they are. But if he's *this* convincing, it only proves I can't know what's real—especially when we're in front of his family.

I force a smile to cover the hitch in my pulse. "I have a strict no-dating-the-customers policy. Even if I hadn't already pegged them as assholes—which I had, because I'm not a *pushover*."

Irritation flickers in his eyes. So, he did get my call out.

"Wait," Mallory says. "You mean you *had* a no-dating policy, because you're dating Alex and he's still customer."

A smug look spreads across Alex's face. "*Obviously*, I won her over."

His answer pricks my pride, and I roll my eyes. "I had a moment of weakness."

I'm annoyed and I'm not sure why. Is it because he implied I'm easily swayed? Or because he insinuated that his personality is just that charming?

Both. Definitely both.

"We're here," Valerie announces as she pulls into a small lot labeled *Hollybrook Historical Society Private Parking* beside an old house.

"Valerie, how are you connected to the historical society?" I ask as the car stops.

She swivels to look at me like I've grown an extra head. "Didn't Alex tell you?"

Heat creeps up my neck. Great. Now I look like the world's worst girlfriend for not asking Alex. I shoot him a look, and he grimaces.

"Sorry, Mom. With Finley's busy schedule, we don't get a lot of time together, so it hasn't come up."

She sighs. "I work parttime as an archivist for the museum. Though, I don't know how much longer I'll have my job with all the government budget cuts." She pushes her door open before anyone can respond.

The air in the car dips. It's clearly a touchy subject, and guilt knots in my stomach.

"Mom's position has been paid for by grants," Mallory says softly. "She *loves* her job, so it's been hard for her to process."

I can't imagine her losing a job she loves right before Christmas. "I'm so sorry I brought it up," I whisper, sinking lower in my seat.

"Alex would know," Mallory snaps, "if he called her more than a few times a year. Texting doesn't count, Alex." With that, she gets out too.

The car is suddenly too quiet. Alex and I are still in the back. He reaches for his door handle, but I grab his arm. "Alex."

He stops, eyes on me, waiting.

"I feel terrible. If I'd known about her job, I never would have mentioned it."

His jaw tightens. "A fact I would have known if I'd called her. I know. No need to rub it in."

I hadn't meant to hurt him, but maybe if he *had* called her, he would've known and warned me.

He starts to pull away, but I hold tight. "I didn't mean it like that. I promise. Despite what happened earlier between us, I intend to make this as believable as possible." When he doesn't say anything, I add softly. "I just wanted you to know I'm sorry."

His expression softens. "It's not your fault, and it wasn't fair of me to take it out on you. You're doing great, Finley. Trust me." A faint grin curves his mouth. "Let's not let it spoil caroling." Then he opens the door and slides out. Great. Now he's being nice again, which means I'll spend the rest of the night overanalyzing every word.

I'll make it easy for you, Finley: pretend.

Sighing, I climb out, I give Valerie an apologetic smile. "I'm so sorry if I upset you. I didn't mean to stir anything up."

Surprise flashes in her eyes. "Oh, my goodness, stop. I'm fine. You had no way of knowing. We're not going to let this bring us down. We've got some caroling to do!"

The parking lot sits beside the historical society building at the edge of the square. I want to take it all in, but Valerie's already gone inside, and I feel like I've caused enough trouble for one night. I'll see it all soon enough.

The cold air nips at my cheeks as I cross the short distance to the door, the faint hum of voices drifting from inside. Warm light spills through the frosted windows, and I draw in a steadying breath before following her in.

Inside the historical society foyer, about ten people are gathered. One of the men perks up when he sees Alex. "Oh, you brought another male voice, Valerie! Tenor or bass?"

"Tenor," she says with a teasing look.

An older woman with snow-white hair scowls. "And you brought a few more people. I didn't bring enough hot chocolate for three more people."

"You don't have to worry about me," Alex says. "I'll skip the hot chocolate."

"Not me," Mallory says. "Is it homemade or the packets with the rock-hard marshmallows, Anita?"

"As though I'd use those abominations," Anita says in disgust.

Mallory smirks. "Yep, I'm not giving up my hot chocolate. Sorry."

"Anita, don't worry," Valerie says. "We Kings can wait until we get home."

"Even better," Mallory whispers in my ear. "Mom's is the best."

Now I'm excited about post-caroling cocoa.

Another woman circulates with pamphlets. "You all know the drill. We walk around the town square, sing in front of the hotels, then back here for hot chocolate. Any questions for the newcomers?" She grins at Alex and offers him a pamphlet. "Or the old-comers who haven't joined us in nearly twenty years?"

"None," Alex grumps, shoving his hands deeper in his pockets. "I don't need a song book. I'll share with my girlfriend."

The group turns to me. It takes me a beat to remember *I'm* his girlfriend. I raise my hand awkwardly. "Hi, I'm Finley. I've never been caroling before, so thanks for including me."

Anita groans. "You've got to be kidding me. The girl's never caroled before? *I'm* not showing her the ropes."

To my surprise, Alex wraps an arm around my shoulders. "It's not like this is rocket science. I'll show her."

"If it is like rocket science," one of the men cracks, "then maybe your brother the engineer should be teaching her."

Alex's arm tightens around me. "I think I've got it," he says flatly.

I take the pamphlet, relieved to see the songs are printed inside. I recognize every single one—even the obscure ones—but keep it just in case.

"Okay, everyone," pamphlet lady says, "Let's head out!"

"Autobots unite!" Mallory cries and Alex snickers.

"I heard that," an older man mutters as he passes with a glare.

"I meant you to," she says sweetly, then he cracks a smile despite himself.

"I'm sure there's an inside joke there," I whisper, holding back a laugh.

"Years ago, they used to dress up in themes," Alex says, lighter than I've heard him since the airport. "One year, Fred over there —" he gestures toward the man "showed up as a Transformer and yelled that. It stuck." His eyes are bright, and his laugh is easy. And for a second, I just stare. I've never seen him look happier.

There's no doubt he's handsome, but when he smiles like that, he seems more approachable. More real.

Which is ridiculous. How can someone look *more* real? It's not like he's a robot. Maybe what I mean is that, for the first time, he looks like someone I could have something in common with.

"Did you dress up?" I ask, my guard slipping a little.

"Yep. We Kings always did family themes. That year I was Woody and Tyler was Buzz. Mallory and Grant got stuck being the aliens from the claw machine."

Mallory groans. "I'm still bitter about it."

"I'd love to see photos," I say.

"Oh, I'm sure Mom will dig out the albums," Alex warns, grinning.

"Yep," Mallory sighs. "She likes you. You're doomed."

Valerie waves from the door. "Okay, troublemakers. Let's get this show on the road."

We all grin at being called troublemakers, and a mischievous glint sparks in Alex's eyes, like he feels obligated to live up to it.

We spill out into the cold. Mallory giggles ahead of me, and Alex's hand brushes against the small of my back as he guides me through the doorway. Maybe it's the afterglow of seeing him so happy, but I feel a quiet rush of anticipation wash through me. For a few seconds, this feels right—like I'm supposed to be here, with him.

You're being ridiculous. Didn't I just tell myself not to fall for this?

Martha instructs us to pair off and walk two by two toward the center of the square, singing "Silent Night". She starts, and everyone else joins in. Their voices are so perfectly blended, I expect a record executive to appear out of nowhere and offer them a record deal.

But I stop dead in my tracks, my gaze sweeping over the square.

The ground is paved in herringbone-patterned stones that glisten with a dusting of snow. Gas lamps line the sidewalks, each pole decked with wreaths, giant candy canes, Santas and reindeer. To one side, an outdoor skating rink hums with laughter from the dozen or so skaters. At the far end of the square, stands a small shack with a lit-up sign labeled *Santa's Workshop*. If I squint, I swear I see the reindeer Alex told me about in a pen beside it. Near the rink, a towering Christmas tree sparkles with hundreds of twinkling lights as snow drifts softly down.

It's breathtaking. Magical.

"Is it everything you'd hoped it would be?" Alex asks quietly beside me.

I look up at him, tears stinging my eyes. "It's more."

A soft smile lifts the corners of his lips. "Good. You deserve it."

I glance around quickly—the choir, including Mallory and their mother, is a good twenty feet ahead of us. Which means there's no audience to perform for.

"Was that real or pretend?" I ask softly.

Confusion flickers across his face. "What?"

"I know that part of what we're doing for the next ten days is an act, but I need to know what's real."

He stares down at me, his breath misting in the cold "It's real, Finley. You *do* deserve it. I had no idea what your life was like— your mom, the debt, working two jobs, and going to school?" Frustration fills his eyes. "I wish I'd known sooner."

And if he'd known sooner? What difference would it have made? But I don't want to get into that.

"Don't." I shake my head, my voice low. "Don't feel sorry for me."

"Feel sorry for you?" His brows lift, genuinely surprised. "Sure, I feel bad that your life's been hard, but mostly I'm... impressed. In awe, honestly."

I blink up at him, caught off guard.

He draws in a slow breath. "Don't worry. I'm not hitting on you. I just meant what I said. I'm glad you're getting something out of this too."

Warmth and doubt twist inside me. His words feel real—too real—but after everything he said earlier, I can't help wondering if this is just another layer of the act. Maybe he's only trying to smooth things over, damage control after the way he made me feel.

I force a grin and gesture to the group. "I'm pretty sure I just crashed the wrong choir. They're *really* good."

Disappointment flickers in his eyes so quickly, I wonder if I imagined it. "Has it always been your dream to go Christmas caroling?"

I consider lying, but I already feel guilty enough about deceiving his family, and with everything blurring between real and pretend, I'm not adding to the pile. "Yeah."

His face lights up. "Then, you're caroling. You're getting the full Hollybrook experience."

His grin does funny things to my stomach.

But then he keeps looking at me, his smile fading. He lifts his hands, draping them over my shoulders. My breath catches. When he leans in a little more, and my pulse jumps.

Is he going to kiss me?

Am I going to let him?

I should stop him, but I'm frozen—lost in his deep brown eyes, softer than I've ever seen them. They're like a whirlpool, pulling me under.

But I can't forget whirlpools are dangerous.

What is this pull I feel? I shouldn't feel anything. How

pathetic is it to be attracted to a man who thinks he's better than me?

But if he meant what he said...

He leans closer, close enough I can feel his breath across my cheek—and just when I'm about to close my eyes, he reaches up and tugs my knit hat down over my ears.

Heat floods my face.

What am I doing? I'm falling for the Alex King charm.

"Hey!" I swat at one of his hands, trying to salvage a scrap of dignity. Does he realize I thought he was going to kiss me? Worse—does he know I probably would have let him?

He drops his hands to his sides like my hat burned him. "Can't have your ears getting frostbite. It's about ten degrees tonight, and you're a delicate southern flower."

I arch a brow, still feeling like an idiot. "Delicate?"

"Fine, you're a sturdy palm tree. But either way, if you get too cold, we'll head home for hot cocoa. Promise me you'll tell me."

"Yeah," I murmur, glancing up at the choir. They're already near the center of the square. "We better catch up. I don't want to get on Anita's bad side."

He laughs, but it sounds a little forced. "*Everyone* is on Anita's bad side. The best you can hope for is neutral territory."

Still, he slides his arm around my back as we walk toward the group.

It's just for show.

I'm still mortified I thought he was going to kiss me, but I try to focus on the positive—he's being playful. Maybe it's pretend, but it's better than the distance and animosity that's been between us since the car ride to his parents' house. I need to hold onto that.

The choir is gathered in front of a ridiculous bronze statue of two Revolutionary soldiers, frozen in mid-argument—one clutching a musket, the other awkwardly holding a pumpkin. Fresh Christmas wreaths hang around both their necks. I'm sure there's a story there. I plan to ask Valerie about it later. If she's an archivist at the historical society, she seems to be the most likely person to know it.

The carolers are belting out the second verse of "Silent Night" with some amazing harmonizing. Fred scowls as we move to the back of the group.

Alex starts singing and my jaw nearly drops. His voice is rich and strong. I can carry a tune, sure, but no one's inviting me to audition for any girl bands.

By the time we finish "Silent Night" and launch into "O Come, All Ye Faithful", a small crowd has gathered, dropping money into a basket I hadn't noticed.

We carol down the block to a hotel, stopping in front of that hotel, then another, our voices trailing through the streets and echoing off the buildings. Guests crack open their windows to listen, and people gather on the sidewalks. For the first time in ages, warmth bubbles in my chest brighter than the twinkle lights strung across the square.

I can't remember the last time I felt this happy.

And then Alex goes and ruins it.

Chapter Eleven

I can't believe I'm caroling. I hate caroling—wandering around like we're in a Dickens novel, only with phones in our hands instead of warm coals, singing cheesy songs. It sounded like a good idea when I suggested it at home—at least for about two seconds. But then we got here, and I saw how excited Finley was —how in awe of something I always took for granted. Then I noticed the falling snow clinging to her hair—she looked angelic.

I stared at her, awestruck, that I've known this woman for nearly two years, yet I never really noticed her.

And then I almost kissed her.

Thank God I came to my senses and tugged her hat down instead.

What is wrong with me? I've spent the last six years perfecting control and in less than three hours, I'm losing it.

But there's something about her that draws me to her. Is it her wide-eyed wonder? The way she lights up over small things? Whatever it is, it pulled me closer—and I almost kissed her.

That would have been a freaking disaster.

Finley made the platonic line very clear—many, many times. Roland thought she was playing a game of hard to get. "The lady doth protest too much," he'd said with a weaselly smile.

I'd told him if he said it one more time, I was going to punch him in the face.

To my surprise, he believed me.

Even more surprising was that I meant it.

I told myself I was only worried Finley would hear him and

change her mind. I tried to ignore that it was six p.m., we were in our office, the coffee shop was closed, and Finley had probably left for her job at the hospital hours earlier. Unless she had superhero hearing, she'd never know.

But I find myself oddly protective of her, which is totally unlike me. I keep telling myself that even if she gave me the impression she wanted more, I'd turn her down. Finley's the kind of woman who wants forever. Even if she agreed to a fling, I suspect it would end in disaster. And then where would I get my morning coffee?

Maybe the so-called Christmas magic of Hollybrook was trying to sway me, but thank God I came to my senses and tugged her hat down instead.

But it's still troubling.

I'm off my game. That's all. Coming home always messes with me. It's a tug of war: wanting to belong and wanting to run. There's a shadow that lingers here, waiting to drag me under. Only the shadow is my deep, dark shame.

Still, things are better than expected after our rocky start. Finley's turning out to be the perfect distraction. Maybe I can make it through the next ten days without a single emotional catastrophe.

Mallory's already taken to Finley like she's a long-lost friend. She's snapped at least a dozen selfies with her. Grant's going to lose his mind when he shows up with Eloise on Christmas Eve—not only do I get the bedroom, but our sister actually prefers my "girlfriend."

I know it's petty that it makes me ridiculously pleased, but I never claimed to be a saint.

Mallory narrows her eyes at me.

"What? I ask, feigning innocence.

"I know that look, *Alexander*," She drags out my full name because she knows it grates on me. "You're up to something."

I lean closer and whisper in mock outrage, "Why would you say that?"

She shakes her head, not buying it for a second.

Finley glances over at us with a curious look, and I offer her a harmless smile.

She smiles back, her whole face lighting up before turning her attention to the crowd gathered near the hotel.

Her full-bodied enthusiasm gives me pause about enacting my plan, but she *must* be cold. I'm only looking out for her—she's not used to weather like this, and I'd hate for her to get sick on her first day here.

That's when I notice two teenage boys near the curb—hoods up and smirking. One of them has his phone out recording. They whisper something and snicker, and one mouths *this is so lame*.

Something pinches in my chest. Finley looks so damn happy, happier than anyone freezing in ten-degree weather while singing century-old carols should be. I slide a half-step in front of her, angling my body to block their view. I'll be damned if a couple of smart-ass teenagers ruin this for her.

Mallory's still eyeing me suspiciously. That's okay. I'll stay five more minutes, then insist Finley's too cold and needs to rest after her long day. There's no way Tyler can call me out if I bring my tired, freezing girlfriend home.

Look how selfless I really am, Tyler.

We finish a rousing rendition of "Grandma Got Run Over by a Reindeer"—apparently still a hit with the ten-and-under crowd —and move to the next hotel.

Now's as good a time as any to convince Finley to leave.

As she starts to follow the group, I catch her elbow. "How're you doing?" I ask, trying to sound sympathetic.

The corner of her eyes crinkle with confusion. "I'm good."

"Are you sure?" I press. "You look tired."

She shakes her head. "No, I'm fine."

"You look like you're freezing," I counter. "Your cheeks are flushed, and your nose is red. I'm worried you'll catch a cold." (The red nose isn't a lie. Shawna would rather be shot at dawn than be seen like this.)

Confusion fills her eyes. "A red nose never hurt anyone," she says, then adds with a chuckle, "Now if the tip turns black, *then* we have something to worry about."

My brain immediately takes that somewhere it definitely shouldn't—straight to the gutter. Which is more than disturbing, because she's obviously talking about her nose. And yet my body doesn't seem to care.

Mallory notices we've stopped and shoots me an evil eye sharp enough to cut glass.

Shit.

I rub Finley's arm. "Still, hypothermia creeps up on you. I really think we should get you home."

"I'm wearing fuzzy leggings under my jeans, a sweater over my T-shirt, and two pairs of socks," she says, smiling. "I'm okay."

Mallory stops next to us, crossing her arms over her chest. I'm pretty sure she hears Finley listing her layers. "What are you doing, Alex?"

I give her a wan smile. "Finley's cold and tired, so I'm going to take her home."

Finley gasps at my declaration. Mallery's eyes darken, and now she's literally tapping her foot.

Mallory turns to Finley. "Whose idea was it for you to go home?" she demands.

Finley looks torn between loyalty and truth. Her hesitation is all the fuel Mallory needs.

"You *shithead*." Mallory's outrage lands like a slap.

"What?" I say, playing innocent. "What did I do?"

"You don't want to be here and you're trying to convince her to go home so you don't look bad for bailing." Mallory snaps. She turns back to Finley, eyebrows up. "Do you want to go home?"

When Finley looks to me for a cue, Mallory slides in front of me and blocks her view.

"Don't look at him," she orders, in full Momma-Bear mode. "Look at me. Do *you* want to go home?"

Finley hesitates, then asks, "How much longer do you think this will last? Maybe Alex is tired."

Mallory shakes her head and swivels back to me. "Go home. She'll stay with us."

"She's *my* girlfriend, Mallory," I say, the words coming out sharper than I meant. Why do I feel panicked at the idea of leaving her alone. What do I think will happen? A rogue reindeer will charge up the sidewalk? A pack of disgruntled elves will jump out of a snowbank? A gang of teen boys will heckle her?

Mallory's face goes even darker. She jabs her finger at my chest. "Last time I checked, that doesn't make her your *property*. If she wants to stay, she can stay."

No doubt it's going to look bad if I go back without her, but damned if I'm singing carols for another half hour or more. Especially when watching her like this—so open, so happy—is messing with my head.

"It's okay," Finley says, sounding defeated. "We can go back."

Mallory stomps her foot, balling her fists at her side. "Finley," she says through gritted teeth, "are you ready to go home right now? Because there's no reason you need to go back too."

Finley sneaks a glance to me, then says, "I want to stay."

"Then it's settled." Mallory's smug glare lands like a dare. "*Alexander*, why don't you call Dad and get started on making that hot chocolate?"

Dammit. Why didn't *I* come up with that excuse? "Yeah," I say, a bit too bright. "That was my plan. To warm Finley up."

Mallory gives a slow, skeptical nod. "Riiiight." Then she tries to shepherd Finley away, but my girlfriend stays rooted in place, scanning my face as she asks, "Mallory, can you give us a moment?"

My sister looks torn, then says, "Don't let the fun killer change your mind."

"Fun killer?" I vehemently protest. "*You* weren't even planning on coming until Finley did."

Mallory flips me off and moves about ten feet away.

I turn to Finley, expecting to see her guilt-ridden face. Instead, there's a fire in her eyes.

"What is this all about?" she demands.

Oh, shit. She'd warned me she wasn't a pushover. Still, I plan to plead innocent. "What are you talking about?"

"If you want to go home, Alex, you don't need to coerce me into going with you. I'm a grown-ass woman. I can take care of myself, especially since I'm with your mom and sister." She lowers her voice. "Besides, I never expected you to babysit me all week."

I pause. There's no way I'm admitting Tyler will roast me if go back alone, but my hesitation stokes her anger.

"Do you think I'm going to embarrass you if you're not here to keep an eye on me?"

My eyes fly wide. "What? No—why would you say that?"

Something about my delivery does the opposite of convincing her.

"You are!" Tears flood her eyes, but she doesn't look like she's about to sob. She looks furious.

Damn, she's sexy as hell with wisps of hair flirting around her face as she leans toward me like she might attack.

"No, Finley, it's just—"

She shakes her head and takes a step back. "If you don't trust me, then you never should have brought me here, *Alexander.*" Then she spins around and hurries over to my sister.

Mallory loops her arm through Finley's, then puts her free hand behind her back and flips me off again.

"Real mature, Mal," I call after her.

Mallory jabs her finger as though she wants to stab me with it.

I watch them go after the group and I feel a sharp ache in my chest. For a moment, I wonder if the stress is going to do me in, but I'm too young for a heart attack and in too good of shape. It's probably heartburn. I *did* eat two bowls of chili.

I rub my chest over my coat, watching Finley walk away, realizing the bounce is gone from her step.

You did that, you asshole.

The pain in my chest increases.

I didn't mean to upset her. It's not like I was *forcing* her to go home with me.

But you sure tried to guilt her into it.

Now is not the time for my conscience to start lecturing.

I turn around to walk back to the car, because every second I stand here watching the most generous person I've ever met lose her joy makes my guilt bigger.

Pushing out a sigh, I realize I have a new dilemma. I can either walk the mile home or beg my dad for a ride. Neither sounds great, so I pull up my rideshare app, then promptly close it when I see the nearest driver is thirty-five minutes away. There's a chance Mom, Mal, and Finley will beat me home, so I suck it up and call my dad.

I'm not thrilled when Tyler answers.

"You ready to come home, little boy?" he drawls in a baby voice.

"I called Dad, not you."

"He saw your name on the screen, and I eagerly volunteered to answer." His smug tone is like sandpaper on a sunburn.

"Lucky me."

"I'll say. I'm guessing you need a ride?"

I want to tell him to give the phone to Dad so I can ask *him* for a ride, but I know Tyler will just volunteer to do it himself anyway. "Yes," I say, my voice tight. "I need a ride."

"Remember stranger danger, little boy," he says in his mock-serious baby voice. "Your big brother will be there in a few minutes."

"You don't even know where I am," I grunt.

"The town's not that big. I'll pick you up at the park bench by the Santa statue."

He hangs up before I can call him a few choice names, then I shove the phone back into my pocket.

Coming home was a mistake, but it's too late now. I'm here. I need to make the best of it.

Ten minutes later, I see the Wagoneer pull up to the curb. I walk over, steeling myself for the roast Tyler's been saving up.

I get in and shut the door. Tyler pulls away from the curb and heads down the street.

"Why'd you really go caroling?" Tyler asks after about ten seconds.

"And there it is," I say dryly.

"It's a legit question."

"I thought I made it clear I did it for Finley."

"Yeah, I'm not buying that." He shakes his head.

"You think I wouldn't do something for my girlfriend?"

"It's not something you would have done in the past."

I turn in my seat. "How the hell would you even know? You don't know me. Not anymore."

"Exactly." Sadness creeps into his voice. "You don't come around enough for us to know you. Mom had to beg you to come home for Christmas."

"It's a busy time at work."

"How convenient," he says in a snide tone.

"What the hell is that supposed to mean?"

"For someone who claims to be so damn smart, you should be able to figure it out."

"*Claims* to be smart?"

"Mr. I Got Accepted to MIT. You love to lord *that* over us."

"The hell I do!"

"Please," he groans. "You sprinkle that fun fact at every opportunity."

"Are you jealous?" I demand.

"Jealous?" he asks with a sharp laugh. "Of you?" He shakes his head as he pulls into the driveaway, then looks at me with contempt. "I feel *sorry* for you, you asshole." He gets out of the car, slamming his door shut.

I climb out, furious. "You feel sorry for *me*?" I shout after him as he stomps toward the back door. "There is absolutely no reason to feel sorry for *me*!"

No one should feel sorry for me. Disgust? Maybe. Sympathy? Never. I wasn't worthy of sympathy six years ago, and I sure as hell don't deserve it now.

Tyler turns back to me, holding his hands out, and shrugs before he opens the back door and walks inside.

I stand on the driveway, fuming.

I should have never come home.

Chapter Twelve

Finley

"I'm sorry, Finley," Mallory says as we walk toward the group. "He didn't used to be like that."

"Like what?"

She frowns, thinking, then sounds disappointed. "Calculating."

Had he been calculating? He obviously wanted to go home, but it was clear he was trying to convince me that *I* wanted to leave.

A dull headache blooms at my temples. I don't want to analyze Alex's motivations right now. I want to enjoy the rest of my evening with Mallory and her mother, but everything feels tainted now. Why did he come at all? Did he think I wouldn't come without him? I fully expected to do most of this on my own. But he didn't know that until I just told him, and he knew I really wanted to come. What if he suffered in silence until he couldn't stand it anymore?

When we head to the next location, Valerie spots me as she scans the crowd, worry creasing her forehead. "Where's Alex?"

"He got tired and headed back," I said. "I hope it's okay that I stayed."

She gives me a smile, but she looks weary. "Of course it's okay. Are you having fun?"

"I've always wanted to go Christmas caroling. It's more fun than I imagined." I say a little too enthusiastically, then feel my cheeks heat.

Maybe this is exactly why Alex tried to get me to leave. What grown adult is dying to go caroling? But I'm not going to hide my excitement. I won't pretend to be someone I'm not. Not for Alex. Not for anyone.

Valerie laughs. "Finley, you're a delight. When Alex called to say he was bringing you, he said you were eager to experience all the things that Hollybrook has to offer. Don't you worry. We'll make sure you do everything you want before you go home."

Her offer is generous, but I don't want to steal her time from her family. "You don't need to worry about me. I don't want to cause you any unnecessary stress or be a burden."

"Don't be silly," she says with a wave of her hand. "We take all this for granted. It's refreshing to see it through the eyes of someone who's never experienced it before."

She heads after the group, and I follow. Mallory falls into step beside me, shoulder-bumping me and giving me an encouraging look. "Hey, it'll be okay."

I force a smile. "Yeah."

"He used to be happier," she says as we walk side-by-side. "Lighter. Like he was earlier when we were talking about caroling as kids. But after he went to college..." She pauses then says. "No, it started when he came home for Christmas his senior year of college. He was really quiet. Not himself. To be honest, he hasn't been himself since."

"What happened?" I ask.

She shakes her head, sadness washing over her face. "I don't know. I've tried asking him, but he says I'm imagining it. That people change." She turns to me. "How is he with you?"

Guilt burns in my belly. If I were his real girlfriend, I could answer that. Meeting him for coffee and texting him aren't the same as being part of his life. Still, seeing him every morning has to count for something. "When I'm with him... he's been nice, sweet, even." I think about our texts. "Funny, sometimes."

Mallory's eyes flood with tears. "That's how he used to be with us. Maybe he really does hate us," she whispers.

I can't see why he'd hate them. I barely know Mallory and love her already. And his mother reminds me so much of my own that it hurts. His father and brother have been pretty quiet, but I don't get asshole vibes from them. Mallory said he changed when he came home for Christmas of his senior year, so something must have happened. Did he feel slighted by his family? Did he fight with one of his brothers? People don't become cold and hard without a reason. Something must have instigated it.

"He doesn't hate you, Mallory," I say gently, linking my arm with hers. "He showed me photos of your family. One was a picture of the two of you at the ice rink when you were about twelve or thirteen. You both looked happy."

She gives me a sad smile. "He showed you that?"

"Yeah." Sure, he sent them partly to prove he really had a family and wasn't making the whole thing up, but he had them in his possession. That has to mean something. "He loves you, Mallory. I promise."

Tears well in her eyes and she swipes at her cheek with the back of her mitten. "Do you think..." She turns toward me as we walk. "I really hate to ask, but could you find out what happened? You're the first person he's brought home that I felt like I could ask."

The last thing I want to do is get in the middle of a family squabble, but then again, I guess I put myself here. Still, I try to evade the question. "I get the impression y'all didn't like his past girlfriends." But as soon as I've said the words, I regret it. Do I sound jealous?

Mallory jumps on it. "That's an understatement," she says sarcastically. "I think that's why Mom and I were cautiously excited when he called and said he was bringing his new girlfriend home. He's never brought someone home for Christmas, and the ones we've actually met never seemed like they'd want to spend the holidays at our house or Hollybrook. And then you walked in, and I instantly knew you were different." She shakes her head. "I was hoping that meant he'd come to his senses and was himself again." She pushes out a sigh. "We miss him. *I* miss him."

My stomach drops. I hate seeing Mallory so heartbroken. The crazy thing is, I never saw signs of the Alex she's describing until we got to Vermont. He's been nothing but sweet to me. Which means the old Alex is in there. I just have to pull him out.

"If I get a chance, I'll try to talk to him," I say, then instantly regret it.

"You will?" she squeals.

"Don't get *too* excited," I say, trying to keep her expectations in check. "I'll *try*, but I can't promise anything." Especially when I'm probably the last person he wants to confide in.

"Thank you, Finley. Seriously."

We join the rest of the group, and sing several carols, but my heart isn't in it. I'm worried about Alex and his family, and I'm not sure how to help.

When Nancy announces we're finished, I'm more than ready to be done. Not only have I lost the caroling spirit, but my toes are frozen and numb.

Not that I'll ever admit it to Alex.

We all troop back to the historical society, and Valerie tells her friends that we're skipping out and heading home.

One of the older women gives me a snide look and tells her friend loud enough to hear, "Then why did Anita make such a big deal out of the hot chocolate?"

Valerie gives her a tight smile. "Finley's had a long day of travel, so we should get her home."

An older woman with thin red hair that's surely not natural gives Valerie a disapproving glare. "I see Alex left."

Valerie's back stiffens, and her voice is tight as she says, "He was tired too, but he came for a little while because he knew how important caroling was to Finley. See you all after the first of the year. Merry Christmas." Then she turns around and walks past Mallory and me toward the parking lot.

They're all staring at me, so I say, "Thank you all for having me. This was like a dream come true." Then I spin around and follow Alex's mother, Mallory walking next to me.

We're all silent as we get in the car. Valerie turns on the engine but doesn't back out.

Is she mad? Is she trying to carefully choose her words to tell me I need to go home?

I lean forward from the back seat, my heart hammering in my chest. "Valerie. I'm *so* sorry if I caused any trouble by coming tonight."

She twists in her seat to look back at me, outrage on her face.

My heart sinks and I shrink back a bit, but then I'm shocked when she says, "You have absolutely *nothing* to be sorry about. I hope you had fun, despite some of the mean-spirited things you heard tonight."

"I didn't mind. I understand if they planned refreshments for a set number of people and then we showed up. But I loved it. Thank you for including me."

"Of course!" Valerie says. "You even got Alex to come for a little while."

"Yeah, and then he tried to make her go home when he left," Mallory says, sounding pissed again.

Valerie's eyes widened slightly at this, but then she frowns. "I'm sure you misunderstood, Mal. I'm sure he didn't try to *make* her go home."

Mallory shakes her head and crosses her arms over her chest. "There you go again, making excuses for him."

Valerie lets out a long sigh then backs out of the parking space.

I feel awkward and guilty all over again. If I hadn't apologized, Mallory wouldn't be upset with her mother. Valerie wouldn't have to defend her son to her friends, and Alex...

Maybe it was selfish to come with him. I should have asked more questions about his family dynamics. I suppose I only have myself to blame for the mess I'm in, but I feel like my presence might be making things worse.

When Valerie pulls the SUV into the driveway, she opens one of the doors to the detached garage and pulls it in. When she turns off the engine, we all get out and walk toward the back door to the house.

"Finley," Valerie says, stopping in the middle of the sidewalk that leads to the back door. She turns to face me.

I stop in my tracks, my stomach twisting with dread.

She gives me an apologetic look. "I'm terribly sorry that you were made to feel unwelcome at caroling tonight," She holds my gaze with a stricken expression. "And as for our family…" She casts a glance at the house then turns back to face me. "I know we're a bit complicated, and I'm sorry you're having to deal with that. But, for what it's worth, I'm happy you're here. No matter what else is going on around us, I want you to know you are welcome here."

Her words sink deep into my marrow, and I'm overwhelmed with emotion. Other than Mirna and Barb, I haven't felt this wanted since my mother died.

It takes me a second to trust myself to speak. "Thank you," I say past the lump in my throat.

She holds out her arms and when I don't shrink away, she envelopes me into a warm hug. "Thank you for bringing my wayward son home," she whispers into my ear, then gives me a squeeze. She lets me go and hurries into the house before I can respond.

My feet are anchored in place, guilt eating me on the inside like a moth in a closet full of wool. *I* didn't bring her son home. But I can't help wondering why *he* brought *me*. Did he know this would happen? And if so, he should have warned me.

A gust of wind hits me in the face, sending a chill down my back, so I head into the house.

As I'm opening the back door, I hear Alex in the kitchen demand, "Where's Finley?" He sounds slightly panicked.

I hurriedly unbutton my coat in the mudroom alcove, about to call out to him but Mallory beats me to it, and she sounds outraged.

"What? You think we left her there?"

"She's right behind me," Valerie says cheerfully, but I hear the exhaustion in her voice.

"I'm here," I say, stepping into the doorway as I unwrap the scarf from my neck. "I'm just slow."

Alex has changed into sweatpants and a long-sleeve T-shirt, a new look I've never seen him in. But I don't have time to dwell on it. It's the wild look in his eyes that settles when he sees me. He walks over to me and takes over unwrapping my scarf. What in the world? I can't help looking up at him in confusion.

"I can unwrap my scarf, Alex," I say with a forced chuckle.

"I know, but I was worried about you."

I'm still confused, but I keep it to myself since it would probably cause more friction between him and his family.

"Why would you be worried about her?" Mallory asks defensively.

"She's not used to the cold, Mal," Alex says in a short tone. "And she's so nice I suspect she wouldn't tell you if she was ready to go home."

His concern only adds to my confusion, but I don't want them to argue over me, so I say, "Alex, I'm fine. And if I got too cold, I would have texted you to come get me. Okay?"

Something softens on his face as he studies me, then he nods. "Okay. Good to know."

"We're not monsters," Mallory says in disgust.

He turns to face her. "Did you ever ask her if she was too cold?"

A sheepish look washes over her face.

"Y'all," I say, holding up my hands. "I'm fine and I'm not five years old. I'm twenty-five and perfectly capable of taking care of myself. I've done it for the past six years and I'm not only alive but thriving."

We need a change of topic, and fast. I see Valerie pulling a pot out of the cabinet and jump on it. "Valerie, can I help you make the hot chocolate?"

She gives me a grateful look but shakes her head. "I'm fine. I'll have this whipped up in no time. Mal, why don't you get out the cookies Mrs. Baxter brought over."

Mallory still seems to be holding a grudge against her brother. "I thought you came home to make the hot chocolate."

Alex wraps an arm around my back and leads me to the island. "Sorry, Mal. I realized I don't have Mom's secret recipe."

"Secret recipe?" Valerie asks with a laugh as she pulls a container of cocoa powder out of a cabinet. "It's time all of you learn my secret family recipe for hot chocolate." She points to the text on the back of the container. "This is it. Right here." She sounds like she's at her wit's end.

I expect Mallory and Alex to pick at each other again, but to my surprise, they both burst into laughter.

I glance between them, knowing I've missed something but have no idea what.

"You said that recipe was handed down from grandma," Mallory says.

"It was," her mother says as she measures out the cocoa and dumps it into the pot. "And she got it off the cocoa container."

"You always told us it was a special recipe," Alex says, sounding bewildered.

"It was," she says, glancing up at him. "The secret ingredient was *love*." She nods to the cocoa container she's setting on the counter. "You don't see *that* in the recipe."

"You know that that's a cop out, Mom," Mallory says with a huge grin.

"You kids believed it, so...?" she shrugs.

Mallory sets the plate of cookies on the counter while Alex heads over to a cabinet and pulls out mugs.

I'm relieved that they seem to have forgotten their grudge, at least for the moment, but I can't help wanting to patch this up, whatever it is.

Stay out of it, Finley.

I know I should, but they have no idea how incredibly lucky

they are to have each other. I would kill to have a family, let alone one as awesome as theirs. I can't help thinking they can work this out.

A video phone ring comes from my jeans pocket, and I cringe and pull it out as all three of them glance at me. "I'm sure it's my… friends. I was supposed to let them know I made it okay and I forgot."

"You take that," Valerie says then turns to Alex. "Why don't you show her to the study so she has some privacy?"

"Yeah, sure."

I follow him from the kitchen as I decline the call then shoot Barb a quick text.

I'll call back in a moment

Alex leads me to a short hallway behind the front staircase to a paned-glass door. He steps into the dark room, and I hesitate. Then a lamp clicks on and a warm light spills out, and I take in the room. Rich, warm paneling wraps the walls. Two desks face the walls on opposite sides. A lamp on a small table beside a deep leather sofa throws a soft pool of light on a stack of books. The place smells of wood polish and faint coffee.

"You can make your call in here." He sees my gaze shifting between both desks. "My parents share this room. There wasn't room for two offices, and they don't seem to mind."

I nod in acknowledgement.

He takes a step as though he's about to leave, then stops, worry clouding his face. "Are you doing all right? Is my family too much?"

That's a tricky question, but I offer him a warm smile. "No. I love your family."

He lets out a short laugh. "Well, it's early yet. Give it a few days before you come to your final conclusion." He walks toward the door but stops in the doorway, turning as he holds onto the doorjamb. He pauses, as though he wants to say something, then resignation fills his eyes. "Come find us when you're done."

He closes the door softly behind him.

I sit on the sofa, releasing a sigh as I sink into the supple leather, then press the video call button.

Mirna answers on the first ring, a look of desperation in her eyes. "Where have you *been*? You were supposed to call when you got to Vermont!"

I grimace. "I'm sorry. Things have been so busy this is the first chance I had to talk."

Mirna's eyes narrow. "Where are you?" Then horror washes over her face. "Oh my God. You've been kidnapped by pirates."

I shake my head in confusion and laugh. "What are you talking about?"

"I see the paneling on the wall. It looks like a ship captain's room. They're already taking you across the ocean!"

"If only she could be so lucky," I hear Barb say. "Quit hogging the iPad."

"Blink twice if you're okay," Mirna says, the ceiling behind her is moving as though she's pacing.

I blink twice, then for good measure, I throw in a third blink.

"That was three blinks!" Mirna cries in alarm then looks to the side. "What does three blinks mean?"

"It means you're paranoid," Barb snipes off camera.

"I'm *fine*, Mirna," I say with a laugh. "I promise. I'm in Alex's parents' study so I can have some privacy. Why did you answer and not Barb? You hate video calls."

"Because I had to see you for myself."

"She snatched the damn thing out of my hands!" Barb shouts, still out of view.

"As I said, I'm fine. Put the iPad down so I can see both of you while I tell you what I did tonight."

Mirna shoots a dirty look off camera and then sets the iPad on Barb's kitchen table, propping it up on something. Both women sit in chairs, side by side.

"We're waiting," Mirna says primly, both hands on the table, one on top of the other.

"Give the girl a moment to catch her breath," Barb says, lightly smacking Mirna's arm.

I expect the older woman to retaliate in some way, but she's giving me an expectant look.

A big smile spreads across my face. "I went Christmas caroling!" I can barely contain my excitement as I tell them about my evening, leaving out the cranky historical society members and Alex trying to coerce me into leaving.

Barb's face is beaming, but Mirna still looks skeptical.

"You look positively radiant," Barb says as she elbows Mirna. "Doesn't she?"

Mirna's mouth puckers. "I suppose she *does* look happy," she says grudgingly.

"And tomorrow," I say, "I'm baking with Alex's mom and sister, and then Alex is taking me to the Christmas market!"

Barb clasps her hands together, obviously happy for me, while Mirna still looks concerned. "And his family? How are they treating you?"

"They're lovely," I say, my chest warming with gratitude. "They've welcomed me with open arms."

Barb sighs contentedly. "It's just like *Christmas in the Woods.* A woman runs off the road in a snowstorm and gets taken in by four mountain men brothers. They spend a week snowed in their cabin and think of all kinds of creative ways to keep her warm."

Mirna gasps, looking truly scandalized. "That is *nothing* like Finley's situation!"

I laugh, my cheeks flushed. "I have to agree with Mirna on that one."

Barb looks nonplused. "But it *could* be like that. Alex *does* have a couple of brothers, right?"

My stomach revolts as I physically recoil. "Eww, Barb. Please don't ruin this for me. The last thing I want to picture when I look at his brothers is your book."

She shrugs. "You could do worse."

I shudder. "No. Just no. I'm a one-man kind of woman."

"Ha!" Barb scoffs. "You've been a *no man* woman for so long I suspect you don't know what you are anymore."

"Trust me on this," I say, leaning closer to my phone screen and taking a firm tone. "There will be no more talk about your books where the woman sleeps with multiple men."

"They're called *why choose* books," Barb says in a know-it-all tone.

"They should call them *floozy* books," Mirna says in a huff.

I realize why Mallory and Alex's bickering feels so familiar. It's just another version of listening to Mirna and Barb. "Mirna, we don't call women floozies anymore."

Her upper lip curls. "I can't bring myself to call them hoes."

Leaning my head back, I fight a laugh then level my gaze with the screen. "We don't call them hoes either. Women have a right to choose who and how many men they sleep with. Y'all fought for women's rights, and their sexual partners are included in that."

A grudging contrition covers Mirna's face, but she crosses her arms over her chest and says petulantly. "Well, cheating is wrong, and I'm *never* going to condone that."

"You're right," I concede. "I should have said we can't judge what consenting adults of all parties involved agree to."

She gives a sharp nod, and I wonder how I got into a lecture about slut shaming at ten o'clock at night on a video call.

"Listen, I have to go. Alex's mom is currently making us hot cocoa to help us warm up after caroling and I don't want to miss out."

Barb grins. "You go get it, girl."

I shake my head with a laugh. "How do you make drinking hot chocolate sound dirty?"

"It's a talent," she says proudly.

I study them both on the screen, my heart overflowing with love. "Thank you both for caring about me so much. You have no idea how much you two mean to me."

"We know." Mirna's expression softens, then she says, "You're special to us girl, and I hope you get your heart's desire in Vermont."

Tears sting my eyes because I know how hard that was for her to say. "Thank you, Mirna. You and Barb are the best grandmothers a girl could ever have." Then I hang up before I start crying.

I often feel alone in the world, but Mirna and Barb are proof that I'm not. That family is more than blood.

Chapter Thirteen

After I leave Finley and go back into the kitchen, I'm ready for my mother's inquisition.

She looks up coyly from stirring the cocoa. "So, Finley..."

There's no emotion in Mom's voice to tell me what she's really asking. It's an open-ended question, leaving me to fill in the blanks. My back bristles and I go on the defensive. "What about her?"

Mom's never been shy about her dislike for my girlfriends since college. I used to shrug it off. Now I'm on edge in a way I haven't been before. The only logical explanation I can come up with is Finley's sweetness. She's like a baby bird that's fallen out of the nest. Or a baby bunny whose nest has been rooted out by the neighbor's dog. How can I *not* feel protective?

"She's sweet," she says with a soft smile. "I like her."

The relief I feel at her approval is both welcome and irritating.

"Yeah," Mallory says. "I do too." Her eyes narrow with suspicion. "What's up with that?"

I expected this from Tyler and Grant but not my sister. I try to play clueless. "What's up with what?"

"Like Mom said. She's sweet. Nice."

The defensiveness is back. Is she insulting Finley? "What's wrong with nice?"

"Nothing's wrong with nice," she says. "I love nice. I love Finley. But you have to admit that nice doesn't describe your typical girlfriend. Driven. Ruthless. Glamorous is your usual type. Not girl-next-door nice."

I have to admit she's right, but I'm still annoyed. "There's nothing wrong with Finley." Then a new fear hits me. What if she walks in and hears this conversation? The last thing I want is for her to feel like she's being attacked.

Mallory rolls her eyes. "I thought I made it pretty clear I love Finley. It's your previous girlfriends I'm dissing."

Maybe I should defend the honor of my past girlfriends, but I don't see the point. "Those women are in the past. Why are you bringing *them* up?"

"I'm just trying to figure out why you changed your type," she says as she walks over to a cabinet and pulls out a bag of marshmallows.

"What can I say?" I force a smile. "She won me over."

"I can see why," Mom says. She's been strangely quiet during our exchange. "She's a lovely girl, Alex. What happened to her mother?"

I feel a moment of panic, but realize I actually know the answer to this. "Breast cancer."

Mom shakes her head, looking sad. "She said her father died when she was young. She doesn't have any grandparents?"

The panic is back. Why didn't I think to find out these things? Then I remember what she said at dinner. "Her father was estranged with his family."

"And her maternal grandparents?"

"I'm not sure," I say truthfully. "But she currently lives in a low-income apartment complex for senior citizens."

Mallory gapes at me like I announced she eats rocks for snacks.

"What?" I ask, my defensiveness back. "You heard her say she inherited medical debt from her mother. She's been working two jobs to pay it off as well as going to school part time."

Mom shakes her head. "I know. That poor girl."

For the first time, I let Finley's past really sink in. When I was nineteen, I was in a frat, partying without a care in the world, while letting my parents cover whatever scholarships didn't.

Finley had been slogging through minimum wage shifts to pay off medical bills after her mother died. How much debt had she been saddled with? How long had it taken her to pay it off? How much does she still owe?

I can't imagine shouldering medical bills alone after the person you tried to save still died. I've drifted from my family for years, but they'd be there if I needed them—she didn't have that.

The respect I feel for Finley is now mixed with a deep, uncomfortable shame.

"Well," my mother says as though she's the chairman of a board announcing a decision as she reaches for one of the mugs. "We'll make sure Finley has a *wonderful* Christmas."

"Thanks, Mom." I know she'll do everything in her power to make that happen.

Mallory looks up and smiles at the doorway. "Did you check in with your friends?"

I turn around to see Finley walking into the kitchen. She seems lighter than she did when she got home from caroling.

"I did," she says, coming to the island and resting her hands on the edge. "I assured them I wasn't on a pirate ship being shipped off to who knows where." When we give her surprised looks, she laughs. "My friends have very overactive imaginations." Her gaze drops to the pot on the stove. "The hot chocolate smells amazing."

"I was just ladling it up." Mom scoops some into a mug. "Would you like marshmallows? Whipped cream? A candy cane?"

"Or all three," Mallory suggests.

Finley laughs. "Marshmallows are fine."

Mallory dutifully dumps a handful of mini marshmallows into the mug before handing it over. "Mom's secret recipe."

Finley laughs then takes a sip and smiles—truly, genuinely happy. Over hot chocolate.

When was the last time I was that happy over something so small?

How can she have lived through what she's been through and not be jaded and bitter?

Mom serves the rest of us. I'm just about to say no—I haven't had hot chocolate since I was a teenager—but decide to accept. Maybe the secret to happiness is at the bottom of a cup of cocoa. I take a sip, and while it's delicious, I'm not any happier than I was before.

"Alex says you live in an apartment complex with senior citizens," Mom says conversationally.

Finley looks a little surprised. "Yeah. After my mother died, I tried living with roommates, but I seem to be a magnet for bad ones. One stole from me, and another had a boyfriend who liked me a little more than he should have." She makes a face.

Something in me tightens. She's downplaying it—and I want to know who that asshole was and what he did so I can track him down.

Whoa, where the hell did that come from? I've never been a jealous guy, but this isn't jealousy. It's a primal urge to protect her. She's had such a hard life, and I hate that someone made it harder.

Oblivious to my inner turmoil, Finley continues, "So after four disastrous roommate experiences—"

"Four?" Mallory asks incredulously.

Finley's eyes twinkle. "I told you I'm a bad roommate magnet. It made sense to live alone. Apartments are expensive, but I heard about a low-income complex and applied. Thankfully, I was approved."

"Even though it's for senior citizens?" Mom asks.

"I don't know how I slipped through the cracks, they said it was a paperwork mix up, but let me stay. I'm grateful they did. I met two women there who are now my honorary grandmothers." Fondness softens her face. "They were the ones checking on me tonight."

Mom frowns. "Were they worried about you meeting us?"

Finley freezes, then smiles, "No—they're just very overprotective. But I told them how lovely y'all are and about the caroling tonight and baking tomorrow." She cringes at her excitement. "Sorry, this must seem so lame."

"Absolutely not," Mom says firmly, setting her mug on the counter. "I love your enthusiasm. It's refreshing."

Finley lifts her hand to cover her mouth when she releases a big yawn.

"You must be exhausted," Mom says. "Alex, why don't you show Finley to your room?"

"Yeah," I say, sliding off the stool. "Good idea."

Finley drains the rest of her cup and heads around the island to put her cup in the sink, but Mallory intercepts and takes it from her. "I've got this."

"We'll probably get started around eight," Mom says, "You don't have to be here when we start—sleep in if you want and come down when you're ready."

"Oh, no," Finley says, all determination. "I'll see you at eight. Good night."

I lead her up the stairs and stop outside my old bedroom. When I push the door open, I brace for nostalgia. The last time I'd slept here it felt like a time capsule—Grant and my high-school trophies. Twin beds with the same bedding we had a decade ago. Mom hadn't changed a thing.

Only... she has.

The two twin beds have been shoved together and turned sideways into one enormous bed. A California King where my twin bed had been.

"What the hell?" I mutter.

Finley freezes in the doorway, and her whole body stiffens. "Wait. You said we would be sleeping in separate beds," she whispers, stunned.

"I know." I slip past her and shut the door, then gesture helplessly at the monstrous bed. "My mom must have put the beds together. She probably thought she was doing us a favor."

"Well, take them apart," she hisses, whirling on me, furious. "I'm not sleeping with you, Alex!"

I stare at the bed, trying to come up with a solution. "We *can't* take the beds apart. How will we explain it to my mother?"

She presses a hand to her forehead, looking even more tired than she did downstairs. "I don't know. Maybe you can tell her we're so new that we aren't sleeping together yet."

"No one is going to believe that," I say, rolling my eyes. "*Trust* me."

She drops her hand and props it on her hip. "Why? Because you're just so damn irresistible?"

I stepped into that one. "Well," I hedge. "I seem to do okay with women."

The flash in her eyes confirms I just made things worse.

"Well, good for you." She stabs her finger into my chest. "But I must be immune to the Alex charm, because I am *not* sleeping in the same bed with you." She marches over to the bed and grabs a pillow. "I'll sleep somewhere else."

I step in front of her and block her path. "Finley, where do you plan to go?"

She lifts her chin defiantly. "I'll sleep in your parents' office."

"You can't do that. My dad goes in there early. What if he— what will it look like?"

"That's not my problem." Her eyes widen. "Oh, my word! Was this your plan all along?"

"No!" I shout, then lower my voice when I realize my family might hear me. "I had no idea Mom would do this. She never has before."

She clutches the pillow to her chest like it's a shield. "I have a contract that says we do *not* sleep in the same bed." She pivots at the waist and points to the giant mattress. "That is one bed."

She's right. We have a contract, and this is a big problem. "Finley," I say, "let's be reasonable. We're both adults. I'll stay on my side. I promise that *nothing* will happen."

Her eyes go wide, incredulous. "Why? Because there's no way you'd ever touch me?"

Groaning, I press the heel of my hand to my forehead. Is there any right way to answer that? "That's not what I meant. I'm saying I'm not an animal in heat. I can control myself."

Some of her fury cools, but she's still clutching the pillow. "Maybe so, but I'm still not sleeping with you." Her eyelids look even more droopy. I need to figure out a solution. Fast.

But before I can say anything, she drops the pillow at the foot of the bed, squats, and opens her suitcase on the floor. She pulls out a toiletry bag and a pair of cream-colored flannel pajamas, then storms past me toward the door.

Panic hits. "Where are you going?"

She stops with her hand on the doorknob. "I'm going to get ready for bed."

"And where will you sleep?"

She keeps her back to me. "I guess I'll sleep on the floor." She opens the door, crosses the hall to the bathroom, then shuts that door behind her.

I move to the open doorway, guilt gnawing in my gut. I can't let her sleep on the floor, but she can't go downstairs and sleep on the sofa, either. I sit on the edge of the bed and wait for her to come back, feeling worse by the second.

She must think I'm an absolute asshole. I am, but in this instance, I'm trying not to be.

Five minutes later, she comes back in her pajamas dotted with tiny Santas. Her face is freshly washed, and her hair is pulled up into a high ponytail. She closes the door and places her back against it. "Do you have any spare blankets I can use?"

I'm still on the bed, hunched over with my elbows on my thighs. "You're not sleeping on the floor, Finley," I say, trying to sound reasonable. "We can share the same bed, and I swear to God I won't come near you. We can place a mountain of pillows between us."

Her jaw hardens. "We have a contract."

She's right. And we both signed it, but I didn't expect this would become an actual problem.

"Okay," I say in defeat. "I'll sleep on the floor."

She shakes her head, her shoulders sinking. "No. It's your house. Your family. Your bed. The whole point of me coming was so you could sleep in your bed. So, I'll sleep on the floor. Trust me, I've slept in worse places."

A rush of horror hits me. She didn't elaborate on her horrible roommate situations, but I can't imagine what's worse than sleeping on a hardwood floor.

Did she sleep in her car?

But I can't bring myself to ask, and I doubt she'd admit to it anyway. Finley never sounds embarrassed talking about the crap she's been through, but there's a quiet pride underneath it.

She picks up the pillow at the foot of the bed and tosses it on the floor.

I stand and walk to her, gently cradling her upper arm.

"Finley," I say softly. "You're not sleeping on the floor. It's been a long day. You need your rest, and you won't get it on the floor. How about this? I'll go back downstairs for a while and then come back and sleep in the chair." I nod to the overstuffed wingback in the corner. "Then when you get up to bake with Mom and Mal, I'll sleep for a few hours in the bed."

She opens her mouth to argue, but I cut her off. "Nope. It's my house, my rules. The contract doesn't say anything about what to do if two beds aren't available, so as the contractor, it's up to me to make you, the counterparty, comfortable."

Guilt flickers across her face. I try not to think how different she is from the women I used to date. None of them would've batted an eye at kicking me out of the bed. Finley looks torn.

I pull back the comforter and pat the side by the window. "Come on. It's a really soft mattress. Once you lay down, you'll be out in five minutes."

Her mouth tips up, and I know I've won her over. "Do you even know which side was yours?"

"Okay, you have me there," I say. "But we had the same mattress, and if you want, you can play Goldilocks and figure out which one is just right." I pat the spot again.

The corners of her mouth lift up higher. Not a full smile, but at least she doesn't seem pissed anymore. "That's not necessary. I'll sleep here." She sits on the edge of the bed, her movements small, almost uncertain.

She obviously doesn't trust me, not that I blame her. Maybe I should find somewhere else to sleep. Maybe I can sit in Dad's recliner and pretend I fell asleep reading a book or watching TV. "Do you want me to leave?"

Finley hesitates. "It's just weird. We barely know each other, and it's like you're putting me to bed."

Fair point. "Okay, I'll let you get to bed." I take a few steps toward the door.

Her expression tightens with regret. "I'm sorry."

"Finley, it's fine." I force a laugh. "You don't really know me well enough to trust me to sleep next to you, and I get that."

"Thank you," she says softly. "And I'm sorry if I've made things uncomfortable with you and your family."

"God, no," I say with a rough laugh. "My siblings are disappointed in me, and they don't hide it."

"Why would they be disappointed?"

Her question stirs something tight in my chest. I need air. "I'm going for a run. You get some sleep. I'll see you in the morning."

I close the door behind me as I hear her say, "Thanks."

Chapter Fourteen

When I get downstairs, Mom's standing at the kitchen sink, washing out the hot chocolate pot.

"Alex," she says, in surprise, "I thought you'd gone to bed."

I give her a sheepish look. "I mostly said that because I could tell Finley was exhausted, and she's too nice to go to bed without me."

She gives me a warm smile. "That was thoughtful."

Her high opinion of me doesn't sit right. "Thanks," I thumb toward the back door. "I'm going to go for a run."

She looks me up and down. "You're going for a run this late?"

"I'm used to working out late."

"Are you sure it's safe?"

"Hollybrook is probably the safest place on earth." But I know that's not what she means. "I'll be careful."

She studies me for a beat then drops her gaze to the pot as she rinses it. "You have your phone, though, right?"

I pat my side pocket. "Right here."

"Okay, I'll see you in the morning," she says. "I love you, Alex. Thank you for coming home. I've missed you."

I pull her into a hug, holding her for several seconds as I smell her floral shampoo. It's the same one she used when I was a kid. Nostalgia hits me full-force, and I wish for things to be like they were before everything changed. Before—

No, I can't go there.

"I love you too, Mom," I say, softly, then kiss the top of her head. "Sorry I've been gone so long."

She gives me a sad smile. "My prodigal son."

The word tightens the guilt in my chest. "Yeah, I'm here."

If she knew what I'd done, she wouldn't look at me like this.

I take a step back, then leave through the kitchen door and into the cold air. My breath puffs white as I stretch in the driveway, then head toward the street in a slow jog. Once my muscles loosen, I pick up my pace and run the route I used as a teenager home from college. Some houses and yards have changed, but mostly it's the same, and an ache for this place I shouldn't feel settles under my ribs.

By the time I hit downtown, it's close to eleven. Everything is closed, but the neon sign for the St. Nick Tavern still buzzes on the corner—the kind of place that's outlasted half the town. I figure a drink might warm me up and kill some time before I curl up in the chair.

Except I didn't bring my wallet.

I stomp my feet at the door and go inside anyway, holding up my phone as I slide onto a barstool. "Do you take contactless payment?"

"Yeah, sure, man," the bartender says, nodding. "What'll it be?"

I start to order a whiskey or a Manhattan, but there's that damn nostalgia again, and I order a Coors Light. I crack a peanut from the bowl, pop it into my mouth.

The bartender hands me the bottle and brings the cardless reader over. "Want to start a tab?"

"Yeah, sure," I say, holding my phone up to the device.

He walks over to another customer, and I take a long pull, memories of high school washing over me. I'm halfway through my beer when I hear a familiar voice.

"Alex King. Is that you?"

I turn, a grin spreading across my face. Curtis Cunningham, my best friend from high school, is about ten feet away with a couple of guys I don't recognize. He's grinning ear to ear as he walks over to me. "How have you been, man? You look—" He looks me up and down.

"Yeah, don't finish that sentence," I cut in, holding up a hand. "It's been a rough day."

He gestures to the stool next to me with a questioning look.

"Please," I say enthusiastically. "I'd love to catch up."

He waves to his friends and tells them he's going to stick around a little longer. They head out the door as he slides onto the stool.

"On a date?" I ask, my brow lifted.

He laughs. "Two guys would be a little ambitious for me. No, just a few friends."

Phil, the bartender, walks over. "You want something else, Curt?"

"Yeah," Curtis glances at the bottle in my hand. "Thanks, Phil. I'll have what he's having."

"Sure thing," Phil says, heading for the cooler.

"Put it on my tab," I call after him.

Curtis makes a face. "You don't have to do that, Alex."

"Yeah, I know," I say. "Think of it as me buying your company."

He gives me a curious look. "Are you used to buying people's company?"

I laugh. "I suppose I deserve that. No, it's just—for all I know, you had other plans with your friends, and I'm making you stay longer."

"We're good," Curtis says. "I've missed you, man." He pauses and his voice softens. "It sucks we haven't talked in years."

He doesn't outright say I've sucked as a friend, but he doesn't have to. He's been the one who's made all the efforts to keep in contact. I'm the one who's turned away everyone here in Hollybrook. Including him.

"I'm sorry, Curtis. It's not personal. Life just keeps me busy." Before he can call me on my bullshit, I say, "So, how've you been, man? What have you been up to?"

"Believe it or not, I'm teaching high school now," he says with a laugh.

My eyes go wide. "You're kidding! So now you wrangle the same terrorist students we used to be."

He laughs wholeheartedly, and something in me goes hollow with homesickness. Curtis was the loyal one. The guy you could hang with, no drama. I realize I've missed him. Everything I've chased feels superficial. But Curtis is the same guy I've always known. He's genuine and real.

Maybe that's part of why I'm so drawn to Finley—she's real too. No fronts, no artifice. What you see is what you get.

Curtin studies me, concern creasing his brow. "What just happened there? You look kind of sad."

I blink. "What?"

He leans a little closer. "You okay?"

"Yeah," I shrug. "It's weird being home."

"How long has it been since you've been back?" he asked. "I haven't seen you in, what? Four years?"

"Yeah. The last time was when you came to see me in New York City." Guilt edges back in. "It's nothing personal, Curtis. I've been working on a tech start-up in Atlanta the last couple of years, and the hours are insane."

Phil returns with Curtis's beer and Curtis takes a sip. When he lowers the bottle, he says, "You haven't been back to see your parents?"

"I was here for a couple of days for Christmas a few years ago, and for a day or two here and there. Other than that, they've come down to Atlanta to see me."

"What about your brothers and Mallory?"

"I've seen them off and on too," I say, tipping my bottle and shrugging. I drain the bottle and signal to Phil. "Another one, please."

"Sure." Phil disappears and comes back with a fresh bottle.

"So, a start-up? Sounds impressive," Curtis says. "What's it for?"

"A super-secret proprietary tech. We're hoping to go live at the end of January, but it's been a bitch getting all the investors in place. Thank God we're almost to the finish line. It's been pretty intense."

Curtis makes a face. "Sounds awful, if you ask me."

I can't deny it. It *has* been awful, but if this takes off, the last two years will have been worth it.

"Teaching high school can't be much better," I say with a laugh, trying to steer the conversation away from me.

He makes a face and reaches for a peanut. "You'd be surprised. I actually like it." He shrugs and cracks the shell. "I'm young enough to remember all the shit we pulled, so these kids think I've hidden cameras all over the school. I catch them at *everything* they try to do." He pops the peanut into his mouth and laughs. "I'm definitely not going to tell them that we tried it first."

I laugh and lift my bottle. "Well, *we* got away with it."

"Sure did." He bumps his bottle against mine, then we drink.

We're quiet for a moment, before Curtis looks right at me. "We've been through a lot, Alex. I know when you're full of shit, and you're up to your ears in it." His eyes hold mine. "Why have you *really* been staying away?"

A cold sweat breaks out on the back of my neck. If I was going to tell anyone what happened, it would have been Curtis. But it's been too long, and it feels too late to tell him now. Plus, I can't handle seeing the disgust in his eyes when I confess.

"Nothing," I say, squinting at him like he's crazy. "You know how it is. You grow up. Move away. It's the way of the world."

"Is it?" Curtis asks, no sarcasm, just genuine curiosity.

"It is for me." I take a big swig of beer to help swallow the lump in my throat.

Curtis studies me, and I know he doesn't buy it. Still, he sits back and gives me a forgiving smile. "I really have missed you, Alex."

"Me too," I say. Seeing him in front of me makes me realize how much.

"When are you headed back?"

"New Year's Day."

His face brightens. "So, you'll be here a bit. We need to get together. You can meet my new boyfriend."

Some of my gloom fades and I beam at him then glance toward the exit. "Was one of those guys him?"

"Nah. Those guys are in my curling club, and Reggie hates curling."

I snort. "You used to hate curling too."

He shrugs with a grin. "Things change."

I know firsthand that's true. "Tell me about your new boyfriend. He has to be better than Shithead."

Thankfully, Curtis laughs. He wasn't too fond of the nickname I came up with for his boyfriend from college, but I'd told him if the shoe fits... "To be fair," he says, his eyes bright, "that's a pretty low bar."

"True."

"Let's just say, I finally smartened up and kicked him out a couple years ago."

"How long have you been with this new guy?" I ask. "Reggie?"

"Yeah, Reggie. And almost a year." He pauses and his face softens. "It's pretty serious. I'm going to propose after the first of the year."

A rush of warmth fills my chest. "That's amazing, Curtis. I'm so happy for you."

His face flushes. "Yeah, he's pretty great."

"How'd you meet him?"

"At a teachers' conference in Pittsburgh, believe it or not. We got drinks, then dinner, and it turns out he teaches over in Hollister."

"That's like fifteen miles from here," I say in surprise.

He grins. "I know, right? It's like it was meant to be."

I lift my bottle and clink it against his. "Congrats, man," I say, "You deserve the best and more."

"Thanks," Curtis says, and we both take a drink. As he lowers his bottle, he says, "What about you? Any girlfriends?"

I'm about to say no, and then I remember, Finley is asleep in my parents' house right now. Hollybrook is a small town. It's bound to get out that I brought a woman home for Christmas. Especially after taking Finley caroling. "Yeah, but it's pretty new."

Curtis leans in, excited. "Tell me about her."

"Well..." I say, trying to figure out what to tell him. "She's actually back at my parents' house right now."

Curtis's eyes go wide. "What? You're kidding?"

"Nope. She didn't have anywhere else to go for Christmas. She's kind of an orphan." I shrug nonchalantly. "I felt sorry for her, so I brought her home with me."

Curtis does a double take, then shakes his head. "Wait. Back up. You brought a girl you just started dating home because you felt sorry for her?"

My defenses go up. "What's wrong with that?"

"Dude," he says. "That's the *worst* reason to bring a girl home."

"Why?" I ask, staring at him. "She's always wanted to spend Christmas in a place like Hollybrook. She grew up in Atlanta, and she's never seen a white Christmas. It was always something she and her mom wanted to do." Maybe it's the two beers in quick succession that make the words tumble out. "I figured it was a win-win. Grant is bringing his girlfriend home for Christmas, which meant he would get our room and the beds. I would've been sleeping on the sofa bed with Aunt Jean's grandkids." I shudder. "So, instead, we get my room and Finley gets her white Christmas. Like I said, win-win."

Curtis's mouth drops open like a cartoon character. "Let me get this straight. You brought a girl home so you could sleep in your *bed*."

"Don't make it sound so callous," I snap. "The sofa bed's awful, and I'd be miserable for nearly two weeks. And don't forget Aunt Jean's *three* grandchildren sleeping in the rec room with me." I take another swig and stall, regretting how defensive I sound.

He keeps his voice calm. "So, wait—you brought a girl you barely started seeing home for Christmas, so you don't have to sleep on a sofa bed."

"Yeah," I say too quickly. "It's not that big a deal."

"Does she mean anything to you?"

"Of course," I blurt, but it's a little too forced.

Disappointment flashes across his face, and I feel like pond scum.

"Look," I say defensively, "She *wanted* to come. I didn't force her." When he continues to give me a judgmental stare, I add, "My family knows we're new, and they know she was alone." I shrug, trying to convince him it's not a big deal.

Or maybe I'm trying to convince myself.

He studies me, eyes sharp. "You're full of shit."

My heart slams into my ribs, but I force outrage. "What are you talking about?"

"Just like with those high-school kids I teach, I can always tell when you were up to something, and you're definitely up to something now."

My pulse hammers through my temple as he pins me down with that x-ray stare. It takes everything in me not to squirm and force a laugh. "You're paranoid, man."

"No," he says carefully. "I don't think I am."

I take a swig of beer and nearly choke, trying to shove it past the lump of dread in my throat. The fact Curtis could always see through me is why I've kept my distance from him the past six years. Even if missing him felt like losing part of myself.

I was an idiot to forget it.

"You're making too big a deal of this," I grunt.

He lifts a brow. "Am I? You're duping your family. They think she means something to you."

"Like I said, it's not a big deal." I know he's right, but I defend myself anyway. "I break up with girlfriends all the time. We'll go home, and then in a couple of months I'll just tell them we broke up and that'll be the end of it."

"Does she know that you're using *her*?"

Shit. If he thinks this is bad, he's really going to think I'm an asshole if he finds out I have an actual contract with my barista.

"I don't have a great track record with women," I say, trying to sound nonchalant. "Honestly, she'll probably dump me, just like my last few girlfriends did."

"Yeah, 'cause you're such a charming guy," he says with a laugh, but there's nothing sincere about it.

"Are you judging me?" I turn to fully face him.

"Dude, you need to judge yourself." He finishes off his beer.

"I thought you, of all people, would understand," I say. "Look at all the shit we pulled in high school, all the cons we got away with."

He shakes his head. "We were dumb-ass teenagers. But we're not in high school anymore, Alex. This is the real world with real people and real feelings. You're screwing with your family's feelings—and hers. The woman in that bed you wanted so bad." His eyes narrow as a new thought seems to hit him. "Did you sleep with her so you could convince her to come?"

I jerk back, anger flaring. "What's it to you who I sleep with? She's a consenting adult."

Curtis sighs, pulls out his wallet, and slaps $10 on the counter. The sound cracks like a slap. "Yeah, it's been great catching up with you." He slides off the stool.

"I told you I was buying your beer! Where the hell do you think you're going?"

He shakes his head, pity in his eyes. "I don't want you to buy my beer. You've turned into an asshole. If you come to your senses, let me know. I'd love to be your friend again. But this guy?" His gestures to me. "No thanks."

He walks out of the bar as I fight the anger boiling in my chest. But deep down, I know he's right. I'm an asshole, but I'm so deep in this pit of assholery, I'm not sure how to climb out.

Then I think about Finley. How she's so sweet to everyone. When I first started going to Beans to Go, I thought she was fake. That it was a persona for the job. It didn't take long to realize she was genuine.

The way she remembers their names and families. The way she talks about her elderly neighbors. Finley isn't pretending with my family. She's genuine.

Finley is a good person. The kind of person that I'd like to be, but it's too damn late for me, right?

I drain my beer, then motion for Phil to bring me another. Something inside me is broken, and while I'm not stupid enough to think drinking multiple beers is going to fix, at least it will dull the pain.

For now, that's enough.

Chapter Fifteen

Finley

I wake with a start and realize that the bedroom door is open. A faint light spills in, outlining a man in the doorway, gripping the frame like he might collapse. Or charge inside. My heart lurches, and I sit up, ready to scream until I realize it's Alex.

The clock next to the bed reads a little after two a.m. He's still in his running clothes, snow dusting his hair, but he's swaying like a drunk Christmas tree ornament.

"Alex, are you okay?"

He squints at me, words slurred. "Yeah... I don't think so."

I hurry over to him, scanning him for injuries. Then the heavy stench of beer hits me. He's drunk.

Why? For all I know, this is a regular occurrence for him, but I don't think so. This has something to do with his family.

"Come on," I say, taking his arm and guiding him inside. "Let's get you to bed."

He shakes his head in a slow, dramatic wag. "Oh, nooo," he sings, "can't be sleeping in your bed. Might molest you."

I groan and roll my eyes. "Relax, Casanova. I doubt you could molest a doorknob right now."

That earns a lopsided grin, but he still digs in his heels. "Nope. Not safe."

"You're right," I deadpan. "You could dent the floor when you fall over. Just sit down for a moment."

"Okay," he says, his eyelids half shut. "That sounds perfectly weasonable." He pauses and frowns. "Weas—"

"It *is* perfectly reasonable," I say, tugging him to the bed. "That's me. Reasonable Finley."

He lets me guide him, then looks up at me like he's never seen me before. "Just one of your many wonderful attributes."

"Maybe I'll have you make a list," I tease as I flip on the beside lamp. "Then we can go over it in the morning,"

Light floods the room and my stomach drops. One knee of his sweatpants is ripped and dark with blood. His palm is scraped raw.

I kneel in front of him. "Alex. What happened?"

"Oh, there was a hole in the road," he says matter-of-factly. "I think I fell into it when I was running."

"You were running after you'd been drinking? Where'd you get the beer?"

He grins. "How do *you* know I had beer?"

"I'm a mind reader."

He gently tries to tap the end of my nose but misses and his fingertip slides across my cheek. "Wouldn't be surprised. You're good at everything."

A drunken compliment. I can't believe a word he says.

"We'll add it to the list. Did you scrape your knee?" I tug up his pant leg. A gash on his knee is still oozing blood. I look up at him. "We need to clean this. Do you know where your mom keeps her first aid kit?"

He shrugs, loose and sloppy. "Don't know. Don't live here anymore."

"Where did she keep it when you were a kid? The bathroom? Downstairs in the kitchen?"

"Pantry," he whispers like it's top-secret intel, then nods sharply.

"Okay," I say as I get to my feet. "You stay right here. Don't move."

"So I can just stay here on the bed?" He pats the mattress with both hands then quickly jerks his right hand back. "Ow."

"Yes, Alex. Stay on the bed and don't move. I'll be right back."

I head for the door, then turn back. "How many beers did you have?"

"I don't know," he says defensively.

"Take a guess."

He shrugs. "Five. Or maybe six."

"Great. So, you were basically at a frat party."

He perks up. "Where's a frat party?"

Shaking my head, I say, "No more frat parties for you." I add a glass of water to my mental list.

I creep down the stairs. A lamp glows on the kitchen counter, enough to guide me to the pantry. I shut the door before flipping on the light, then dig around until I find rubbing alcohol and bandages, a couple large enough for his knee. But then I grab the whole kit, just in case I missed some of his wounds. Next, I snag a glass of water, some ibuprofen, and a big bowl—insurance against a drunken dash to the bathroom.

When I get back upstairs, Alex is sprawled sideways across the bed, his legs dangling over the side, his arms splayed like a starfish.

I step inside, and his eyes snap open like a horror-movie jump scare. I nearly shriek.

"Finley, be careful," he warns with grave seriousness. "The room is spinning and you might fall off."

"I have gravity shoes," I say with a chuckle. "I'll be okay. But it's good that you laid down."

"I fell backwards and I can't get up." He flails his arms. "I'm like a turtle."

I don't usually find drunk men funny, but there's something so vulnerable about him I can't help laughing. "Well, at least you fell down on the bed instead of denting the floor."

He pats the mattress with both hands. "This must be my bed, 'cause it's really comfortable."

"Yeah, I'm sure that *is* your bed," I say, even though he's patting the middle.

I study him, trying to decide where to start. He's still wearing his shoes, so I start there. I set the supplies on the nightstand, then kneel in front of him to untie his laces.

"What are you doing?" he asks suspiciously. "You going to take advantage of me?"

For a moment I think he's making fun of me for not letting him sleep in the bed, but it's obvious he has no idea what he's saying. "Drunk Alex is funny. Who knew?"

"Taking my shoe off, that's where it starts," he says seriously. "Then you work your way up."

I can't see his face, so I can imagine his expression. "Don't flatter yourself. I stop at the knees."

"I'm not a bad person, Finley," he blurts, voice suddenly raw.

The smile slips off my face. My chest aches. "I never said you were a bad person."

"But you think I am," he says, defeated. "You're just too nice to say it. Everyone thinks it."

"No," I say softly, tugging off his shoe. "I don't think you're a bad person, Alex."

His head pops up and he stares at me on the floor. "Why not?"

I untie his other shoe and slip it off, then perch on the edge of the bed. "If I thought you were a terrible person, I wouldn't have come with you to see your family."

He presses his lips together, considering what I said. "But I tricked you."

I blink, my heart skipping a beat. He's drunk, but his words land heavy. "How did you trick me?"

"Curtis thinks I tricked you into coming with me."

"Who's Curtis?"

"My best friend." His face twists. "Used to be. Now he thinks I'm an asshole."

I gently lift his legs onto the mattress, then scoot him sideways until his head hits the pillow. Out of breath, I sit beside him, staring down at his face.

"You didn't trick me, Alex. I came of my own free will."

"So I could sleep in my bed." His words slur, and he lets out a laugh. "The joke's on me—'cause I still can't sleep in my bed."

The truth stabs me. Because he's right. And I hate that he's right.

He tries to open his eyes wide, but they sink to slits. "I didn't get drunk so I could sleep in my bed."

"I know that," I say softly. "No one's that Machiavellian."

He narrows his eyes. "You know what that word means?"

Irritation sparks, but I shove it down. He's drunk, and I already know that he thinks I'm some country bumpkin. "Yes, Alex," I say, a little sharper than I intend. "I know what Machiavellian means. I'm not *entirely* stupid."

"I never said you were stupid," He frowns, confused.

"But you thought I was uneducated, right?" I scoot back down to the bottom of the bed and roll up his sweatpants leg.

"It's just..." he stumbles over his words. "I don't date women who didn't go to college."

The words sting more than I expect. I already knew that—he pretty much told me so earlier. So why does hearing him say it feel like a slap? Why do I care what this drunk, arrogant man thinks of me?

"That's okay," I say lightly, even though it isn't. "It's not like we're really dating anyway."

I glance up, but his eyes are closed again. I push his pants leg over his knee. The gash is deeper than a scrape, but the jagged edges mean he's not a candidate for stitches.

I grab a wet paper towel from the bowl. "This is gonna hurt a bit." I dab at the wound, and he flinches.

"Ow!" he yelps.

"Shh! You're gonna wake everyone up." If he hasn't already.

"You don't want them to know what a bad person I am?" His eyes are open, earnest and raw.

"Alex." I say again softly, "You're not a bad person. We just don't want to wake the whole house. They need their sleep."

He grumbles something under his breath that I don't understand, then says nothing.

"Okay, round two," I warn, and then dab again.

He flinches, but doesn't speak this time, just tenses as I clean the wound. Tiny bits of gravel cling to the raw skin, and I brush them out with the edge of the paper towel. Then I soak some cotton balls with the rubbing alcohol. "This is really going to hurt, Alex. I'm sorry."

I press the cotton ball to his knee and he jerks, cursing through gritted teeth.

"Sorry," I say quickly. "But you had pieces of the road in there. We don't want an infection."

"Yeah." He exhales, then repeats a softer, "Yeah." The fight drains out of him, leaving him limp.

"The worst is over." I wave my hand over the wound until it dries, then peel open the bandage. "I'll put this on, then check for any other scrapes."

"Are you going to kiss my boo-boo and make it better?"

I snort. "No. That only works in fairy tales."

His right eye cracks open. "You sure this isn't a fairy tale?"

I smooth the bandage over his knee, careful not to stick it to the gash. "I'm pretty sure it's not. Although, I guess you could argue that it sort of is since you're making my dream come true."

He grunts. "A white Christmas is your dream come true? That's just sad, Finley."

He doesn't mean it to be cruel, but the words scrape across something raw inside me. "Yeah, I know. You had a white Christmas every year, so it's nothing to you. But surely there was something that you really wanted as a kid. Something that would have made you happy."

He's quiet for several seconds, then in surprising seriousness, he says, "Yeah, I always wanted to go to a dude ranch."

I blink, startled by how boyish he suddenly looks. "Okay. I can see you at a dude ranch."

His head pops off the pillow, his eyes wide open. "Really?

When I told my last girlfriend, she laughed and laughed and said, 'Yeah, right, Alex.'"

"She sounds like a pretty crappy girlfriend."

"I was a pretty crappy boyfriend, so I guess it evened out."

I try to imagine Alex as a boyfriend and come up short. Before I landed in Vermont, I could have easily conjured the image, but now... now I'm not sure.

"In any case," I say, "I can see you at a dude ranch. Not the professional you who comes into Beans to Go—more the you I see with your family and house you grew up in." I give him a soft smile. "You should go. I'll even help you look some up if you want."

His eyes turn glassy. "Why didn't I meet you ten years ago, Finley?"

My heart does a stupid little flip. He's drunk and drunk people say things they don't mean. I shrug it off with a joke. "Ten years ago, you were at some Hollybrook high school, and I was at Marshall High School in Georgia. Not exactly fate material."

"Yeah, I suppose so." Sadness tugs at his voice and it makes me want to make him feel better.

"But we met *now*," I say. I let the sentence hang for a second. "We can be friends, right? I thought we were friends."

"Yeah, friends," he slurs, his eyes closed.

I roll up his other pant leg—no injuries there. I push up his t-shirt sleeves to his elbows, relieved to find him wound free. The only other scrape is on his right palm, probably from bracing his fall. I dab it with alcohol; it stings, but it's shallow, so no bandage needed.

"That's it," I say.

He's been quiet for so long that I think he's out. But when I move to get up, his left hand shoots out and clamps on my arm. "Where are you going?"

"I need to throw this trash away, but you should sip some water first."

"I need to get up," he mutters, trying to push himself off the bed. "Need to get in the chair."

"You need to get a drink of water first." There's no way I'm letting him out of this bed, but one battle at a time. "Here, let me help." I slip a hand behind his back and ease him upright, then press the glass into his hand. "Drink."

He tilts the glass, and it spills, so I take it back and hold it to his lips. His eyes lift to mine—glassy, heavy-lidded, stubborn, but also vulnerable. It's the vulnerability that makes my chest do a ridiculous little squeeze.

"Not too much," I murmur.

He gulps a few sips, then flops back as I guide him down.

"No," he says, trying again to rise. "I need to get up."

"I'll help you," I say. "But you just lie here while I clean up, and then I'll tell you when it's time to go to the chair."

"Okay," he says, closing his eyes again.

"I put a bowl over here in case you need to throw up," I add.

He lets out a bitter laugh. "I haven't puked from being drunk since high school."

"You probably won't need it, but it's here, just in case." At least I hope he doesn't.

He sinks back into the pillow. "Why are you taking care of me?"

"Because," I say, thinking it's a weird question. It never occurred to me to *not* take care of him. "You need to be taken care of."

"I wouldn't take care of you," he says flatly. "If you were lying here, I wouldn't take care of you."

The words land like a slap. But then I think about Mallory's stories, and the way he is at Beans to Go. *That* person is good. He's real and that man's inside him. Maybe he just doesn't know how to let him out.

"You know what?" I say softly. "I think you would."

"Bullshit," he snaps, pissed. "I would *not*."

"Yeah," I say, and I mean it. "You would." Then I walk out of the room and head to the bathroom to toss the trash.

I stay longer than I need to, gripping the counter until my knuckles ache. Needing the quiet and the privacy to sort out my stupid feelings. Part of me believes he wouldn't help me if our situations were reversed—he's drunk, bitter, and scared. Part of me doesn't believe him at all.

It's either stupidity or instinct, but I have a feeling I'm going to be hurt either way.

Chapter Sixteen

I wake up with a splitting headache that gets worse the second I crack my eyes open. For a couple of seconds, I don't recognize the room. Then it hits me: I'm in my rearranged room, at my parents' house, and Finley is here with me.

Finley.

I roll over, but the other side of the bed is empty. The covers are rumpled, but both pillows look untouched. Why isn't she in bed and why am I sleeping in it?

Groaning, I flop on my back and close my eyes.

Oh. God. What happened last night?

I got drunk off my ass is what happened, then stumbled home like an idiot. Did I crawl into bed with her? Horror seizes me. That last thing I ever wanted was to make her uncomfortable.

But then the stinging in my knee and my palm remind me that I tripped in a pothole in the road. And that Finley patched me up.

I sit up, swing my legs off of the bed, then cradle my face in my hands as my equilibrium settles.

If she hadn't already pegged me as a first-class asshole, then last night sealed it. Did she sleep in the bed with me? Doubtful. Which leaves the chair.

I glance over and see a blanket artfully draped over the back like it belongs there. A blanket that wasn't there when I left last night.

My stomach sinks. Of course she took the chair.

Shame burns through me. Is she ready to bolt? Has she already left? I say a silent prayer of thanks when I see her suitcase on the floor. It's closed, but it's still there.

Sunlight streams through the cracks in the blinds. The clock says 10:12. I haven't slept this late since I was in college.

As bad as I feel, I probably look worse. A shower and a toothbrush should come first, but I can't shake the need to find Finley. I need to know if she's upset with me and if so, how to fix it.

Against my better judgment, I head down the back stairs. Voices float up—bright, happy, and female. I pause when I hear Finley's.

She's telling a story about baking cookies with her mom. About sugar cookies that came out burnt on the edges, but Santa still ate them and left a note saying he preferred them that way.

"That's so sweet," Mallory says.

"My mom was the best. We didn't have much money, but she always found ways to make things special. Like that note from Santa."

My chest warms. I can picture five-year-old Finley, proud of those cookies. My parents had more money, but Mom did the same—turned Christmas into something magical.

I'm strangely proud that Mom and Mallory already adore her. That they're going out of their way to make her feel like part of this family.

Now that I know Finley's happy—even if she's not happy with *me*—I should go back upstairs, shower, and pull myself together.

But her laugh carries through the house, light and easy, and the need to see her with my own eyes nearly drags me into the kitchen.

It's overwhelming. It's also concerning. Why do I want to see her so badly?

It's only because you want to do damage control for last night.

Then let's do some damage control.

I push out a breath of relief at the thought. Yeah, it's damage control. That's all. Feeling more confident, I round the corner into the kitchen, and all eyes turn to me.

"Alex," Mom says with a warm smile. "You're up."

"Yeah." I rake a hand through my hair. "Sorry I overslept."

"You look like you needed it," she says with a concerned look.

Mallory snorts. "You look pretty rough, dude."

But my gaze turns to Finley. She's lifting cut-out cookies from the counter to a baking sheet. She sneaks me a quick smile—soft, almost shy—and something in my chest flutters.

What the hell was that? I shake my head, pain spiking through my skull.

"Want me to make you some breakfast?" Mom asks.

The thought makes my stomach roil. "No, I'm good. I'll just grab a cup of coffee then head up to shower."

Mom cringes. "There isn't any. Finley made me and Mallory mochas, and your father and Tyler Americanos." She laughs. "I don't think they're ever going to go back to the Mr. Coffee coffeemaker after this."

I can't stop a smile. "Well, she *is* a barista." Yesterday I might have cringed to admit it, but now I'm oddly proud.

Finley slides the last cookie onto the tray and carries it to the oven. "Do you want me to make you something?"

"You're not here to wait on me," I say sharper than I intended, but the thought of her waiting on me sits wrong. "And you're not here to do your actual job."

Finley's eyes widen, the hurt flashing before she masks it.

"I should hope not," Mallory snaps.

"Sorry." I rub my forehead. "I have a killer headache and that came out wrong. I meant that she's busy and I don't want to get in her way."

"Well, unfortunately," Mom says as she sifts flour into a ceramic mixing bowl, "as I mentioned, we don't have any brewed coffee."

I grunt in frustration. If Finley's already pissed, that last thing I want is to force her to make me a drink. "I don't need coffee."

I turn around and head toward the staircase. Better to retreat before I say something else I'll regret.

"Alex wait," Finley calls after me.

I turn as she shuts the oven door and sets a timer. "I haven't minded making your family drinks. It's the least I can do after all the hospitality they've shown me." She wrinkles her nose. "Besides, the drinks weren't perfect since I don't have an espresso machine."

"We can get one," Mallory says, her eyes lighting up. "And Finley can teach us before she goes home."

I know what good espresso machines cost, so I doubt Dad will spring for one, but I'm not going to be the one to tell her.

"If you're just wanting a plain cup of coffee," Finley says, still standing in front of the oven. "I can use the French press."

I gape at my mother. "Where did *you* get a French press?"

She waves a hand dismissively. "My friend Jennifer gave it to me a couple of years ago. It's been gathering dust in the cabinet, but Finley showed me how to use it. Isn't she resourceful?"

"Yep. She sure is."

The words feel stiff in my mouth. I don't like the idea of her waiting on me. Especially after she took care of me last night. She already thinks I look down on her—having her serve me like a customer at Beans to Go only reinforces that.

Finley scoops grounds into the press's glass carafe.

"Are you sure you're not hungry?" Mom asks. "I could warm up a muffin."

"No." The thought of food still makes my stomach churn. "Coffee's fine."

I slump onto a stool while Finley works her magic. Mallory is mixing something in a bowl, and she shoots me a sly look. "Where'd you sneak off to last night? I heard you come home pretty late."

Mom's mouth drops open. "How late? Did something

happen on your run?" Her voice rises. "I *knew* you shouldn't have gone out running in the dark."

"Nothing happened," I say, adding a light laugh to calm her down. The last thing she needs to know is that I got plastered. "I ran into Curtis, and we had a drink at St. Nick's."

Her face brightens instantly. Curtis practically lived here growing up. She even called him her fourth son. "How *is* Curtis? I haven't seen him in at least a year."

"He's good," I say, propping my chin on my hand at the counter. "He's teaching at the high school."

The words taste dry, like gravel. Because I know what she doesn't: Curtis doesn't think much of me anymore. Not after last night.

"I'd heard that." She dusts off her hands as she reaches for a measuring spoon. "What's he teaching? Science?"

I realize I never asked. Then again, the whole conversation had gone downhill pretty fast. "I don't know. He just said he's well equipped to handle teenage boys and any tricks they try to pull, since we tried them first."

She rolls her eyes. "You two got into more than your fair share of mischief, so I guess he'd know." She adds a teaspoon of something to the bowl. "I'm pretty sure I heard he's an assistant coach on the middle-school basketball team." She looks up and sees the surprise on my face. "He didn't tell you?"

"No," I say, feeling like a shitty friend. The more questions she asks, the more obvious it will be that we didn't spend hours catching up. "He was too busy telling me about his boyfriend."

A frown creases her forehead. "His last boyfriend was so awful to him. I hope this new one's better."

"Curtis seems pretty happy," I say. "In fact, this isn't public information, but there might be a wedding in their future."

She claps her hands in delight. "Oh! That's wonderful news. His mother will be thrilled."

"I wonder what kind of wedding he'll have," Mallory says.

"I didn't think to ask." Six years ago, he would have asked me to stand up with him at his wedding. Now I'll be lucky to get an invite. Something sharp and heavy knots in my chest.

"Are you two getting together again before you head back to Atlanta?" Mom asks.

That's highly doubtful, but I'm not going to admit to it. "Probably not. I told him I'm here with Finley, so I won't have much free time."

"Maybe you and Finley could meet up with Curtis and his boyfriend," Mom suggests.

Finley swivels her head and gives me an earnest look as she pushes the plunger into the press. "Alex, you know I don't mind if you meet your friends. You probably want to catch up more."

"We caught up last night," I say, then add, "Besides, if I saw him again, I'd bring you with me."

She looks surprised and her cheeks flush before she turns back to her task.

A knot forms in my stomach.

I still need to know where she slept last night. What does she think after I barged into the room, drunk off my ass? She doesn't look mad, but maybe she's keeping up appearances for Mom and Mallory. I want to pull her away and ask, but if she *is* mad, barging in on her baking won't win me any points.

"I don't know how you take your regular coffee," Finley says, pouring steaming liquid into a red mug with a snowman grinning on the side. I'd prefer plain white porcelain, but I'll deal with it.

Mallory stops stirring and gapes at Finley like she's sprouted another head. "Wait. You don't know how Alex takes his coffee?"

Finley freezes like she's a cat burglar caught red-handed, so I blurt out, "I never have regular coffee when I'm with her. She always makes me an espresso drink." Technically true.

"Ah, that makes sense," Mallory says.

I slide off the stool. "I just take some creamer, but I can get it."

Finley's already by the fridge. She pulls out a bottle and a spoon, then hands them to me like it's second nature. Like she belongs here.

I'm amazed that she's so comfortable in my mom's kitchen. None of my other girlfriends would have even considered baking with my mom and sister, let alone learning their way around. It does something to me, something I can't name. It can't be nostalgia—Finley's never been here before yesterday. It feels like yearning, but for what? For her? For this? Either way, it makes no sense.

Finley turns away, but the need to know where she stands gnaws at me. "Are we still on to go to the Christmas market?"

She swivels back with a hesitant look. "I wasn't sure if you'd still want to go."

"Of course I want to go," I insist. "I'm looking forward to it."

Her expression makes it clear she doesn't buy it. Honestly, after last night when I bailed on caroling, I wouldn't believe me either. But strangely, I *am* looking forward to it. If you'd asked me to go last Christmas—or any past Christmas—I would have rather wrestled a wild pig and butchered it for dinner then set foot in the market. But with Finley? I want to see her reaction. Something inside me feels lighter when she's happy.

"Okay," she says slowly, holding my gaze like she's trying to tell if I'm lying. "I'd love to go, but if you changed your mind, Mallory already said she'd take me."

Mallory gives me the stink eye. She doesn't believe I want to go either.

"Of course, I want to go. Why wouldn't I?"

"Well...after your late-night run," Finley says carefully.

"Nope." I stir creamer into my coffee. Hopefully, the caffeine will help with my hangover. "I'm great. Never better." I glance over at my mother. "Mom, what time will you guys wrap this up?"

"We should be done by noon," Mom says. "I plan to reheat the chili for lunch, then you two can head out."

"Sounds good."

I head upstairs with my coffee, still feeling off. Some of it's my hangover, sure, but mostly it's the image of Finley in my mom's kitchen, buzzing around like she belongs there. It unsettles me more than I want to admit.

A long shower helps take the edge off my headache. When I get out, I dry off and redress the bandage on my knee. The cut's deep and throbs, but it's manageable. After I put on jeans and a sweater, I pull my laptop from my bag, sit on the edge of the bed, and check my email.

The first two are from investors. The other three are from Roland, and one is flagged urgent. I open that one first.

Dude, I've been trying to call you all morning. Where the hell are you?

- R

I pat my pocket and realize I haven't seen my phone since I got up, which is highly unlike me. Where is it?

I search the nightstand, the bed, the floor, and sweatpants pocket and come up empty. Did Finley find it and plug it in? If she did, my phone's not in here.

Where could it be? The last place I remember having it was at the bar, shoving it into my pocket after closing my tab. Uncoordinated from the beer, I'd fumbled putting it in my pocket.

Shit. Did I drop it outside the bar? Or maybe when I tripped in the pothole?

I pull up the locator app on my laptop, but it says my phone's battery is at zero, the last time it pinged was at the bar.

Panic floods my head. Everything's backed up in the cloud, but still—my whole life is on that phone. And if some drunk scooped it up...

I take a deep breath. This is not a crisis. If I can't find it, I'll just get a new one. But the closest phone store is in Hartwell, probably an hour away with the Christmas traffic. Not to mention, I'll have to shell out over a grand for a new one.

Worse, two hours I won't have at the Christmas market with Finley. It would be a convenient excuse to get out of it, but I don't want to get out of it. I *want* to go.

I don't spend much time dwelling on why. The answer's

obvious—it's guilt. Besides, I need to deal with Roland. I fire off a quick reply.

Lost my phone and I'm on my laptop. What's up?

Seconds later, a video call request fills my screen. I set the laptop on the dresser, sit on the edge of the bed, and brace myself before accepting.

Roland's face appears, then he recoils. "What the hell happened to you?"

"It's called a hangover," I grumble. "Thanks for the sympathy."

"Jesus, it's nearly eleven. Must've been one hell of a bender."

"Whatever. What's the emergency?"

"Brewster's on me for the report on the response times after the latest upgrade. I don't have it yet."

My irritation spikes. We had this conversation before I left. Twice. "As I told him—and you—the report will be ready on January second. That hasn't changed."

Roland's face darkens. "That's not good enough."

"Well, it has to be. The firm we hired is shut down for the holidays. They'll deliver on the second, just like they promised. You can't rush this."

His jaw sets with frustration. "I said we should've gone with the cheaper guys. They guaranteed December twenty-third." His lip curls. "*And* they cost less."

"We went with the other firm for a reason," I snap. "The cheaper one has a reputation of missing deadlines and cutting corners. Best case with them, we'd get it mid-January. Worst case, we'd get garbage data. You want to hand Brewster garbage?"

"We need results, Alex. Investors don't care about excuses."

"It's December twenty-third," I bite out. "There is no one else. Everyone's gone."

For a second, I'm sure he's about to throw it in my face that I'm gone too, hiding in Vermont with Finley. Instead, he sneers, "The world doesn't stop because of presents and candy canes."

"Roland," I say with forced patience, "If you want to hire

another company, be my guest. But I still stand by the one I chose, and we've got a contract. So, if you can justify to the investors spending a few thousand dollars extra to cover both, go ahead. Otherwise, suck it up and tell Brewster we'll have the report after the first of the year."

Roland leans back with a put-upon sigh. "Well, all right. I guess there's nothing we can do."

"Yeah," I say, forcing myself to unclench my jaw. "Glad you finally see reason."

But I know better. He'll probably circle back tomorrow, same argument, different angle.

Roland's scowl slips into a smirk, that Jekyll-and-Hyde switch I've come to dread. He leans closer to the screen. "So," he says, "did you get Finley to sleep with you yet?"

My chest tightens. For half a second, I want to reach through the screen and throttle him. "You *know* this is platonic."

He scoffs. "*Please.* I haven't met a woman yet who could resist the Alex King charm."

"Hate to break it to you, asshole," I grind out. "But Finley's immune."

Roland clutches his chest in mock offense. "Ouch. That has to sting. You're not used to hearing no, are you?" His grin turns wolfish. "Don't worry. Lay it on thick and she'll fold. They always do."

My stomach turns. It's not just the hangover. It's the way he's talking about her, like she's disposable, like what she wants doesn't even matter.

"She's not my type, okay?" I snap. "You know I prefer sophisticated women."

"Yeah, yeah," he waves me off. "It's not like you're gonna bring her to a business dinner. You screw her, then dump her when you get back. Simple."

The words make my skin crawl. Every muscle in my body coils, ready to launch through the screen. Then I feel a presence behind me.

I twist around.

Finley stands in the doorway, my phone in her hand. Her face is pale but carefully arranged.

Oh. God.

"Sorry to interrupt," she says with a polite smile that doesn't reach her eyes. Her voice is steady—too steady. "Tyler found a phone outside by the back door." She steps in and sets it on the bed, the thunk is loud in the quiet room. "I figured it was yours."

She takes a small step back. "Your mom said to tell you she's heating up the chili."

Her gaze flicks to Roland's face on the screen—just for a second—then she walks out.

"Finley," I call as I lurch to my feet. "*Wait.*"

Roland laughs. "Someone's in trouble."

"Screw you, Roland." I slam the lid shut then hurry after her. She's already at the top of the staircase, one foot poised on the first step. "Finley. Wait. *Please.* Can we talk?"

She hesitates then turns around to face me. Her face is smooth, giving nothing away.

"I don't know what you just heard—" I begin, breathless.

She shakes her head. "I shouldn't have just walked in. I should've knocked. I'm sorry."

"No, it's your room too," I say quickly, trying to sound calm while my panic claws up my throat. If she's still mad about last night—God, if she asks my sister for a ride to the airport—I'm screwed. "Look, about that call—"

"Really, Alex," she says, her expression flat. "You don't have to explain."

"The hell I don't." The words come out louder than I meant, raw with frustration.

Her eyes widen. I rake a hand over my head, forcing myself to breathe. Panicking will only make this worse. "Can you come back to the room so we can sit down? Just for a minute? *Please?*" I'm begging—and I'm not sure I've ever begged a woman for anything. But I don't feel any shame. All I can think about is fixing this.

She looks torn, like she'd prefer to bolt down the stairs, but to my relief, she gives a sharp nod, then walks toward me.

I back up to give her space, then follow and shut the door behind us. She sits in the wingback chair, so I sit on the edge of the bed and take a beat to figure out how to fix this. Seeing her there makes me wonder if she slept in it, but now isn't the time to ask.

"Roland's an asshole," I blurt. "He thinks all men—"

"You don't have to explain, Alex," she says primly. "You made it clear yesterday that you date sophisticated women. Besides, we're not really dating. This is pretend. You get to sleep in a bed, and I get the Christmas I always dreamed of."

She makes it sound so reasonable, and that's what we agreed to, yet it doesn't feel right, and I don't know why. Maybe it's the red Christmas sweater she's wearing, with a snowman with an orange puffball nose. Maybe it's the smudge of flour on her cheek that makes me want to reach out and brush it away. It kills me to think I might have hurt her more than I already have.

"My plan was *not* to bring you here and coerce you into bed," I say, leaning forward, forearms braced on my thighs. "You have to believe me."

She studies me for a moment, then says simply, "I believe you."

The certainty in her tone catches me off guard. "You do?"

"It would be unbelievably stupid to sleep with me in your parents' house, especially this early in the trip," she says dryly. "And besides, if you were trying to coerce me, you could have put in a lot more effort last night. You didn't. You were a perfect gentleman." She gives me a tight smile. "So, yes, I believe that you never intended to try anything." She rises to her feet. "So now that that's cleared up—"

"Wait," Panic flares, though I can't explain why. She just told me she believes me, and she seems to mean it. So why do I feel like the floor's dropping out from under me?

Your behavior last night, moron.

"Wait," I repeat, calmer. "Just one more thing."

She nods then sits down again, folding her hands on her knees. "Can I ask you something?"

"Yes, of course," I say probably a little too eagerly. "Anything."

She exhales, starts, then stops. "This is more than a little embarrassing."

"Is it about last night?" I ask with a grimace.

Surprise flickers across her face before she presses on. "Look, we both know I'm not the type of girl you date. Maybe if you'd had more time, you could have found someone who fits your... profile."

My nausea is back. "Finley, I was out of line—"

"It's *okay*," she says quickly, too quickly, though maybe it's my paranoia. "I wasn't applying to be your real girlfriend, and we just confirmed a few seconds ago that we're both getting what we want out of the deal."

I nod slowly, but the sick feeling in my stomach doesn't ease.

"When you were just a customer at Beans to Go..."

Her voice trails off, and I want to say something—anything—to make this less awkward for her, but I'm the one who caused the awkwardness, and I don't know how to fix it.

"When you were a customer," she says again with a tight smile, "we got along pretty well, right? You seemed to like me as a person."

"Yeah. I did." The understatement feels ridiculous. It's like calling the Mississippi River a stream. "I *do*."

She nods, looks away, then glances back to me. "So maybe we can just agree to be friends. No expectations of anything else. That way you don't have to worry about me getting the wrong idea, and I can relax and not worry you'll try to seduce me. We have to pretend to be involved, so this way we acknowledge it's pretend and not read anything into it."

It takes me a beat to process her words. She's simply restating our agreement—our legal contract—so why does it feel so disconcerting to agree with her? I have to, though. This is what she needs, and it's what I wanted too.

"Yes," I say. "I think that's a good idea. But I'll be honest—I'd like to think we're actually friends, even with just the coffee shop interactions. I don't need to pretend I like you, because I already do." Then I hastily add. "As a friend."

Her face softens into a small smile. "You didn't need to add the 'as a friend.' That's a given at this point."

We sit in a short silence before she says, "You said you wanted to talk about something else?"

"Yeah." I run a hand over my head, unsettled in a way I can't remember feeling around a woman. "I wanted to say I'm sorry about last night," I grimace. "Understatement. I'm sorry for coming in drunk. You were more than kind to help me, especially cleaning up my knee."

Something flickers in her eyes. "You remember that, huh?"

"It's a bit fuzzy, but yeah." I gesture to the bowl still on the nightstand. "You even found the barf bowl."

She laughs, a genuine one, even if it's a little reserved. "You have a barf bowl?"

"No one wanted Mom using a bowl someone puked in for food, so yeah. We had a designated bowl."

"I found it in the pantry. Lucky guess." She hesitates, then says, "I accept your apology. So, if there's nothing else..." She rises, already turning toward the door.

I stand too. "Finley, one more thing."

She pauses.

"Where did you sleep last night?"

Her shoulders ease. "I slept in the chair, which was actually more comfortable than I expected."

"I'm sorry. I shouldn't have put you in that position."

"It's fine," she says, not meeting my gaze. "Don't worry about it."

"It's *not* fine. It won't happen again. I promise." She doesn't answer, and desperation edges my voice. "I don't routinely get drunk, Finley. That was the first time in years, and it was a moment of weakness."

She finally looks up at me. "I'm not judging you, Alex. For any of it."

Then she bolts for the door and heads downstairs.

Chapter Seventeen

Finley

I head down the stairs, feeling sick to my stomach. I held it together in Alex's room, but now that I'm alone, the façade crumbles.

I can't bring myself to face Mallory and her mother just yet, so I sneak out the back door and pace in the snow-packed backyard, pulling in cold air that only makes my chest ache more.

Why are you so upset? You already knew he wasn't interested in dating you. He made that clear yesterday.

I walked into this situation with eyes wide open—this was a platonic, transactional relationship. I'm getting more than my fair share out of the deal, so how can I complain?

But knowing it isn't the same as hearing it. Hearing him tell Roland he'd never sleep with me was one thing. Hearing the disgust in his voice when he said it—like the idea repulsed him— lodges in my chest like a shard of glass.

Tears sting my eyes, and I let them fall, telling myself they're for my mother. I always cry around Christmas, when missing her feels unbearable. That's why I'm sobbing in the backyard. Not because of that jackass upstairs.

Except he's not a jackass. He never once led me on. He made it clear from the start that this was an arrangement, not a relationship. That makes him honest. And sure, he finds the thought of sleeping with me revolting, but he's never been rude about it. He can't help how he feels, right?

Still, my tears won't stop. I swipe furiously at my cheeks with frozen fingers when I hear footsteps crunch on the side of the house.

I look up to see Tyler rounding the back corner of the house with several shopping bags in his hands. He halts when he sees me. I freeze too. Unless he's blind, there's no hiding that I've been crying.

He drops the bags on the sidewalk and takes a few steps closer, uncertain. "Finley, are you okay?" He winces. "Sorry, dumb question. Obviously, you're not." His gaze flicks toward the house. "Do you want me to get Alex?"

My eyes widen in panic. "No!" The last thing I want is for Alex to know I'm out here crying. "I'll be okay. I just need a minute."

He stands in place, shoving his hands in his pockets, then waits a beat before he asks, "Did you give Alex his phone?"

"Yeah." I swipe at my tears again, annoyed they won't stop.

"Did that go okay?" he asks cautiously.

"Yeah," I say, but it comes out shaky. I try forcing a smile. "He was on a call with his partner, so—"

"He was on a call when I found his phone in the snow?" His eyebrows lift.

"A video call." But the thought of the call brings another hot stab of tears.

"Finley," Tyler says softly, taking a step toward me. "You're obviously not okay."

"I will be," I say, trying to assure him, but I'm trying to assure myself too. "I just need a minute."

He hesitates. "Do you want me to get my sister?"

"No." I let out a short laugh. "Please don't. She'll insist on digging into this, and I just need to have a good cry and move on."

He grins, but it doesn't reach his eyes. "You've got her pegged."

"She wears her heart on her sleeve." I wipe more tears from my face. "So, it's not that hard."

"Kind of like you," he says, then looks like he wished he

hadn't said it. "What would help? Do you want me to leave you alone?"

Do I want to be alone? I'm not sure. I spend most of my life alone, even though I'm surrounded by people. Other than Barb and Mirna, this is the first time in years I haven't felt utterly alone—and it's with Alex's family. The irony makes my chest hurt.

"There has to be something I can do," Tyler pleads, sounding helpless. "I don't want to leave you alone like this."

I draw in a deep breath, trying to get ahold of myself. The last thing I need is for someone else to find me like this. I need a distraction, and I know the person to provide it. "I think I'll just call my friend," I say with a small, wavering smile, even as more tears spill.

He nods, uncertain.

"Thanks for stopping and making sure I'm okay," I say, sniffing.

"Of course," he says. "What kind of asshole would I be if I ignored you and went inside?"

I release a short laugh as a tear slides down my cheek. "I'm sure some men would."

He shoots a dark look up at the house, then back at me. "I'm gonna give you my number, okay?"

I narrow my eyes. "Why?"

"Because the fact my brother is upstairs and you're down here crying alone means he's being his usually self-centered—"

"He doesn't know I'm upset," I cut in quickly. The last thing I want is to create a rift between him and Alex. "I'm sure he'd comfort me if he knew I was out here."

"Yeah, but doesn't the fact you're down here crying seem like something a boyfriend should notice?"

I start to protest but stop. He's right. "It's complicated."

"It always is with my brother," he says, disappointment in his tone. "Look," he lifts a shoulder in a half shrug. "My family can get a little overwhelming, especially once Grant and his girlfriend show up tomorrow. If you feel the need to escape, or take a breath, or just have a good cry"—he gives me a soft smile—"all you have to do is text me and I'll create a distraction, okay? I promise I'm not hitting on you. I just want to make sure you're okay."

I consider his offer, then nod. I pull out my phone, add his number as he rattles it off, and send him an empty text so he has mine.

"I'm not planning on using that," I say, holding up my phone.

"I hope you don't need it," he says. "But it's always good to have a backup plan." He studies me for a moment, then picks up the bags and opens the back door.

"Tyler," I say hesitantly.

He turns to look at me.

"I'd appreciate it if you kept my little breakdown to yourself." I grimace. "It's... kind of embarrassing."

"You don't have anything to be embarrassed about," he says gently. "But I understand. Your secret is safe with me." Then he disappears into the house.

I'm alone again, and I shiver, realizing I came outside without a coat. The sun's shining, but it's probably in the twenties and I'm not used to this kind of cold. Still, I need a few more minutes, so it's not so obvious I've been outside crying.

And I really do want to hear Barb's voice. I call her, and she answers on the first ring with a perky, "How goes it in Christmasland?"

A laugh slips out of me, shaky but real. "It's Hollybrook."

"Same difference," she says dismissively.

My plan had been to unload everything that just happened, but now that I hear her voice, I realize I just need the comfort of it. "I baked sugar cookies this morning. And a yule log."

"Are you going to burn the yule log in the fireplace or a bonfire?"

That pulls a laugh out of me. "Neither. We're going to eat it."

"Are you stayin' with a family of beavers? I thought a yule log was a piece of wood stuffed with crap."

"Maybe it is, but in this family, it's a chocolate cake baked on a sheet pan, then rolled up with a cream filling."

"That sounds more like *my* kind of yule log," she says.

"Mine too," I admit, feeling a surprising surge of home-sickness.

"What's wrong, Fin?" she asks softly.

"What makes you think something's wrong?"

"You sound stuffy—like you've been crying or came down with a cold."

"Maybe I caught something from caroling last night."

"Not likely." She's silent for a moment. "Is Alex treating you, okay?"

"Yeah." Because he is. I was the one who overheard his conversation. He hadn't meant for me to hear.

"And his family?"

"Sooo nice," I say. "Almost unbelievably so."

"Then what's wrong, Fin?"

Tears sting my eyes again, but I can't make the words come.

"Sometimes we think we want something and then when we get it, we realize it's not what we imagined."

I turn that over. She's implying I built this trip up into a dream that couldn't live up to expectations. But the opposite is true. It's better than I imagined—at least until I overheard Alex. But if I tell her, she'll be furious with him and insist I come home. For some reason, I want her to still like him.

"Maybe," I say instead. "I'm also missing Mom."

"That's only natural," she says gently. "You and your mom planned something like this for years. Now you're doing it without her. Of course there's guilt mixed in."

"Yeah." I swallow, realizing she's right, though only a little. Because I know Mom would be thrilled that I'm living our dream. "Right before she died, she told me to take risks. But maybe this one was too big. Maybe I should've started smaller."

"Nah," she says with certainty. "This seems like exactly the kind of risk she wanted you to take."

I'd thought so too, but now I'm not so sure.

"They aren't called risks for nothin'. Sometimes risks don't pan out, but sometimes they do. But if you play it safe your whole life, you'll miss out on some amazing adventures, so look at this like one—a story to tell your kids in twenty years."

"Yeah," I say with a sniff, wiping my cheeks again. "I like that."

"Try to enjoy the ride, Fin. And if it's not worth staying, come home. Don't worry about askin' Alex for a plane ticket, just call me and I'll buy one for you."

"Mirna offered the same thing." I laugh. "Not that I'd ask either one of you."

"Of course you wouldn't," she says with a chuckle. "But I'll do it anyway. Promise me if it's all too much that you'll let me know, and I'll get you home."

It's a sting to my pride but I say, "Okay. I promise, but I don't expect to be coming home early."

"I hope you don't either, but it's always nice to have a backup plan."

Tyler said the same thing, and I realize I've probably been out here too long. Valerie was heating up lunch when I took Alex his phone. They're going to wonder where I've been.

"Barb, I should go," I say, wiping one cheek then the other. "We're about to eat lunch then we're going to the Christmas market. It's supposed to be like the German ones."

"That sounds fun," she says, then her voice lowers. "Are you sure you're okay?"

"Yeah, I just miss you."

She's quiet for a moment. "I miss you too. I'll call and check on you later, okay?"

"Yeah."

"Love you." But she hangs up before I can say it back.

I stuff my phone in my jeans pocket, take several deep breaths, then paste on a smile and head inside.

Everyone is in the kitchen except for Alex's dad, who's still at the clinic. Everyone looks up when I walk in, and I drop my gaze, hoping they don't notice my red eyes.

"There you are," Valerie says. "I wondered where you'd gone off too."

"I told Mom you and Alex were probably spending some time alone," Mallory says in a knowing voice.

My face heats with embarrassment twice over. First, that she thought we were having sex, and second, because Alex is probably gagging at the thought.

"But then Alex came down without you," Valerie says. "Then we really wondered where you got off to, but then Tyler said you were outside talking to your friend." She pauses. "You didn't have to go outside, Finley. You're welcome to use the office anytime you like."

"Thanks," I say, walking over to the island where everyone's dishing up their bowls. "It sure smells good."

"Help yourself," she says.

I grab a bowl and add a scoop. I can feel Alex's gaze on me, but I ignore him as I add some cheese to my chili then sit down at the table.

Alex tries to sit by me at the table. Maybe he thinks he needs to be the dutiful boyfriend, but Mallory slips into the chair beside me with a laugh before he can take a seat. "Sorry," she says, sounding anything but. "You get her all the time. It's my turn."

Mallory and Valerie keep the conversation flowing, with Alex and Tyler chiming in only when prompted. Or when Alex aims something directly at me. I answer, hoping I'm coming across as normal. I need to get over this irrational hurt, or this won't work. But I need more time.

Once we finish lunch, we start cleaning up, but Valerie shoos us away. "Alex, you and Finley take off for the market. Since it's her first time, she'll probably want the whole afternoon."

The thought of being alone with Alex makes my stomach knot, so I blurt out, "Mallory, would you like to come with us?"

Her eyes light up, but then she glances at her brother. "I don't want to be the third wheel on your date."

"It's not a date," I say before Alex can respond. "We're just shopping."

She brightens again, though more cautiously. "Are you sure?"

"Of course." I glance over at Alex. "Right?"

"Yeah," he says evenly. He doesn't look upset, but he doesn't look happy, either.

"You know what?" Tyler cuts in, eyes locked with his brother. "I think I'll come too."

Valerie, Alex, and Mallory all start talking at once.

"What?" Valerie exclaims.

"When was the last time you went to the Christmas market?" Mallory demands.

"Why?" Alex growls, eyes blazing.

Tyler shrugs, looking his brother directly in the eye. "You all said caroling was fun last night, so I figure I might as well try the market this afternoon."

The blood drains from my head. Is Tyler coming because he found me crying? Because he knows Alex ditched caroling?

"I think we should drive separate cars," Alex says flatly. "In case you want to leave before Finley's done shopping."

"Sure." Tyler locks eyes with Alex like they're in a staring contest. "I'm good with separate cars. I suspect I'll be ready to leave in an hour or so."

Mallory snorts. "As if you'll last *that* long. You hate shopping."

He shrugs, unfazed. "Things change." Then he heads for the stairs. "Give me five minutes to go change clothes."

Fair enough since he's wearing a pair of black sweatpants and a long-sleeve T-shirt.

"If we're driving separately, we can just meet you there," Alex calls after him, as he bounds up the stairs.

"It won't hurt to wait," Valerie says.

"Ten seconds ago, you were telling us to leave cleaning up the kitchen to you so we could get going," he grumbles.

"Oh, Alex," she says with a disappointed sigh. "He's making an effort. Can you say the same?"

Alex clams up. Mallory drops her gaze, clearly wanting no part in this round.

What is going on with these two? I know about Alex's rivalry with his younger brother, but he never mentioned problems with Tyler. They seemed okay last night. But I can't ignore that Tyler assumed Alex was the reason I was crying.

I pitch in with the cleanup while we wait, but there's barely a mess. By the time we're done, Tyler appears in jeans and a black puffy coat.

"Ready."

Mallory insists I wear her coat again, so we grab our outwear off the pegs in the mudroom. Tyler beelines toward the Jeep Wagoneer, and Alex stops on the driveway. "What do you think you're doing?"

"Dude." Tyler opens the driver's door. "You know I call dibs on the Wagoneer when I'm home."

"Mom gave it to me to drive last night to pick up Finley."

"That was last night," Tyler says slowly, like Alex might not be the brightest bulb. "You can borrow Mom's car." He slides in behind the wheel. "Or ride with Mal."

Mallory is already in the Honda parked in front of the Jeep, engine rumbling.

Alex looks ready to call the whole thing off, but instead, he presses his palm to the small of my back and guides me over to Mallory's car. When he opens the front passenger door, I say, "Alex, you can sit in front."

"Nope." His voice is firm but gentle. "You ride with my sister, and I'll hop in with Tyler. We need to talk. But first..."

He crooks a finger under my chin, tipping my face up until our eyes lock. His voice drops. "Are we okay?"

My breath catches, traitorous, even though he practically gags at the thought of me. I force myself to sound casual. "Why wouldn't we be?"

He lifts a brow. When I don't answer, he leans closer. "Tell me what I need to do to make this less awkward."

The easy answer would be *nothing's awkward*, but we both know that's a lie. "I'll be fine. I just need some time."

He looks like he's about to press, but I slip free and climb into Mallory's car. I expect him to get in the back seat. Instead, he strides to the Jeep, yanks open the passenger door, and hops in.

He barely shuts the door before the arguing begins.

"What's happening?" I blurt before I think better of it.

"Your guess is as good as mine," Mallory says, a spark of excitement in her voice as she watches them in the rearview mirror.

Based on my chat with Tyler, I can only imagine what they're arguing about. But there's a good chance this has nothing to do with me and everything to do with some old sibling grudge. "Are they in the middle of some kind of fight?"

"They're not exactly besties," she says, still watching. "But last I knew, they weren't mid-battle either."

I can't see much through the side mirror, so I throw subtlety out the window and turn around to watch outright.

"I know Alex has a rivalry with Grant," I say carefully. "He told me Grant was supposed to get their room, but we'd be sleeping in there instead."

She releases a short laugh. "Yeah, and Tyler's convinced that's the *real* reason Alex brought you."

My stomach lurches. "What?"

"Oh, don't worry." She gives me a reassuring smile. "Mom and I don't buy it."

"What about your dad?"

She shrugs. "Who knows? He rarely weighs in on family things like that."

Is that what Alex and Tyler are arguing so heatedly about in the car behind us?

Mallory pulls forward toward the detached garage, then backs down the opposite side of the driveway. She flashes me a grin. "No reason to sit here while they duke it out. Otherwise, we'd be parked all day."

Alex cuts the argument short, his gaze locking on us as Mallory backs past. Mallory wiggles her fingers in a mocking wave. "Bye!" Even if he can't hear her, it's not that hard to lip read.

"Maybe I should wait for Alex," I say.

"Pleasssse," she drawls. "It's not like the town's big. They'll find us."

We head toward the square, then turn to the right. Cars are parked all along the street, but she finds a spot in a big lot after circling for a few minutes. "I suppose we could have walked from the house," she says. "But then we wouldn't have gotten to watch my two brothers arguing."

She's clearly amused, but my stomach's in knots. What if the truth about Alex and me comes out?

"Don't look so worried," Mallory says as she kills the engine. "They'll show up in two minutes acting like nothing happened."

Only, when they appear, just as we're about to step onto the street lined with canopies and tents, it's obvious they are not in a joking around mood. Both look stormy.

"There you are," Mallory says brightly, as if she hasn't noticed. "We thought you might have gotten lost."

"We would have made it sooner if—" Alex cuts himself off and I see Mallory giving him a glare that could rival any mother's *look*. "We're here."

"So you are." She beams. "And we're going to have a *wonderful* time, because little Finley loves all things Christmas. And we're not going to ruin it for her, *are we*?"

To my surprise, they both mumble, "No."

Hoping to break the tension, I say, "How can you call me little Finley when I'm five years older than you?"

"You're about an inch shorter," she counters, holding her

hand level with my forehead. "Which makes you little. Or I can go with Wee Little Finley if you prefer."

I can't help laughing. "As long as I get to check out the Christmas market, I'll answer to whatever you want."

Mallory shoots her brothers a satisfied look. "See? Finley's being cooperative. You two should give it a try." She loops her arm through mine and marches us straight into the main aisle between the booths.

Mallory might be determined to spread Christmas cheer, but judging by the glares at my back, peace on earth is still up for debate.

Chapter Eighteen

The second I climb into the Jeep, Tyler wastes no time telling me exactly how he feels.

"It's disgusting how you're using that woman," he snaps, eyes blazing.

"What the hell are you talking about?"

"I know you only brought her here so you wouldn't have to sleep on the sofa bed."

"How can you suggest that?" I demand.

"Please." His lip curls. "I know how you operate."

I should come up with some cutting comeback, but nothing pops into my head.

"What happened to you, Alex?" His anger eases, replaced with something sharper.

My guard instantly rises. "Nothing happened to me."

"Bullshit. You changed your senior year of college. You were always on the narcissistic side, but after that year? It's like you stopped giving a damn about any of us."

"I grew up, Tyler," I say through gritted teeth.

"Funny. I grew up before you, and I didn't cut my family off."

"I didn't cut you off," I lie.

"Bullshit. I can't even remember the last time we saw each other outside a family function."

I remember. It was four years ago, when I was at a conference in Boston. We met for dinner, and it hadn't gone well. I was still too raw and ashamed, and terrified Tyler, who had always been the noblest of the King boys, would see what I'd done written all over my face. He'd seen my behavior as aloof and arrogant. He'd left before we'd finished the meal, saying I was a stuck-up asshole who thought I was too good for my family.

He had no idea that the opposite was true, and that was why I stayed away.

But Tyler doesn't know about the mess brewing inside me and takes my silence as further proof I didn't give a damn.

"Don't be so dramatic," I say. "I'm here, aren't I?"

"Only because you must care a little about Mom. She begged you to come home."

He's not wrong.

"What did we ever do to you?" he asks, shaking his head.

"Nothing. This isn't about you." I flinch. I've already given him too much.

"If it's not about us, then what's it about?"

I refuse to answer. We drive the rest of the way in silence. When he finds a spot and turns off the engine, he turns to me, all business. "If I find out you are using Finley for your own selfish gain, I will be the first in line to bash your face in."

"Why the hell do *you* care about Finley?" I snap.

"Because she's too good for you."

It lands like a punch. I want to tell him she *isn't* too good for me, that she's not even up to the catalog of my usual requirements. She works two part-time jobs, lives in a low-income apartment, and probably drives a piece of shit car. Tyler already knows that—she told them last night. I've been closed-minded about the women I've dated, expecting them to check off the boxes of my required attributes like they're applying for a job.

And yet—and painfully obvious even to me—Finley is a better person than any of them. Better than all of them combined.

He jabs a finger into my chest, hard enough it probably leaves a bruise. "If you screw with her, I swear to God, Alex, I will screw with you."

I don't argue with him. Part of me is quietly relieved he's being protective of her. She's been mostly alone for the last six years, other than her adopted grandmothers, and she needs *someone* in her corner. So, I say nothing, and hope that if I somehow *do* screw her over, he'll hold true to his word.

When I see her with Mallory, all I feel is shame, because I *am* using her.

Worse, I'm pretty sure she heard enough of my conversation with Roland to think I find the idea of sleeping with her revolting. The thought turns my stomach.

The irony is that the opposite is true, and there's not a damn thing I can do about it.

Chapter Nineteen

Finley

I'm instantly captivated by vendors. The first stall on the right glitters with rows of candles in glass jars. Mallory tugs me inside, then abandons me to pick up jar after jar, sniffing like she's a bloodhound looking for a hidden treat.

"Does Finley like candles, Alex?" Tyler's voice comes from behind me, laced with challenge.

I turn around and see Alex leaning in the entrance, arms crossed, while Tyler scans the shelf of Christmas scents.

"What woman doesn't like candles?" Alex answers, deadpan.

"I wasn't asking about *any* woman," Tyler's eyes flicks to me. "I was asking about Finley."

"Of course I love candles." I stride over and grab Alex's arm, tugging him into the stall before he can object. My stomach dips, but at least he didn't recoil from my touch. Tyler already caught me crying earlier, and the last thing I need is to fuel his suspicions. Alex and I agreed to be friends. Friends can touch, right? Plus, I'm sure he wants to sell this as much as I do.

"In fact," I add, forcing a bright tone, "Alex is going to help me pick out one for my apartment."

"Good idea," Alex says smoothly. "Especially since the pine scented candle in your living room is almost gone."

He stops in front of a display, lifts a jar, and scowls at the label. "Burnt sugar cookie?" He shoots me a questioning look. "Who actually wants their house to smell like *burnt* cookies?"

"Hey, Santa loved my burnt sugar cookies when I was little." I laugh as I take it from him, then lift it to my nose and sniff.

"Besides, this smells *nothing* like my cookies. This is cookie dough mixed in with a campfire." Then I hold it up for him to smell.

"Weird combination." Alex leans closer and inhales, before making a face. "A poor substitute for how the kitchen smelled this morning."

"You're right." I set the jar back on the shelf.

"Whenever I want to smell baked goods," Alex says, "I'll just ask you to bake something."

"I thought Finley didn't have time to bake," Tyler cuts in, now standing next to Alex and eyeing the candles like they personally offended him.

I smile up at him. "While I'd love to bake everything from scratch like your mom, sometimes it's box brownies and refriger-ated cookie dough."

"Which," Alex says with the confidence of a man defending a hill he's willing to die on, "is surprisingly good straight out of the tube."

I blink at him, trying to picture buttoned-up Alex sneaking cookie dough out of a plastic tube. "Maybe it's time you learn to bake too," I say. "Asking me to do it is a little chauvinistic, don't you think?"

Alex's eyes widen slightly, but if we were a real couple, I wouldn't be at his beck and call to bake. It's the twenty-first century. He's just as capable of dropping tube cookie dough on a sheet and sticking it in an oven. And as far as me coming across as contrary, real couples bicker. It'll add more authenticity to our situation.

And maybe, I'm still a little salty. Not that I'll admit it.

"Yeah," Alex says, looking properly chastised. "You have a point. I'll bake next time."

Tyler grunts something unintelligible and stalks off to the other side of the tent.

When I'm sure Tyler's out of earshot, and Mallory's engrossed in a candle, I lower my voice and look up at Alex. "What did you and Tyler argue about in the Jeep?"

His face darkens. "You caught that, did you?"

"I'd have to be blind not to."

He moves to a new display and lifts a candle, and I follow him. I think he's not going to answer, but he says, "He was being an asshole big brother."

"Were you fighting about me?"

He looks startled. "Sort of. But it was more about me. Tyler's always been..." He makes a face and shakes it off. "Don't worry about Tyler. He's not upset with you."

"Mallory said Tyler thinks you brought me here to get Grant's bed."

He frowns. "I wish she hadn't told you that."

"But it's true," I whisper.

"Finley," he says, and the smile that follows warms something in my chest. "My family adores you, so don't worry about them. *I'm* more worried about *you*."

My heart skips a beat. Did Tyler tell him he found me crying out back? "Why?"

"That call with Roland." He pauses and my breath sticks in my chest. "Finley, I don't know—"

I shove down my rising panic. "We already discussed that," I say as serenely as possible. "That subject is closed."

"Why do I feel like it's not?" A storm brews in his eyes, and it pulls me in, which is so irritating. What kind of woman is attracted to a man who thinks she's beneath him? I need to get more self-respect.

I flash a sharp smile. "That sounds like a you problem."

He startles. "But—"

I'm not sticking around to listen to him try and pacify me. It would be even more humiliating than overhearing his conversation, so I head out of the tent, leaving him to chase after me.

Tyler's standing in the middle of the crowd, people parting around him like he's a boulder in a stream. I stop about five feet from him.

"I thought you wanted a candle," Alex says in a worried tone as he catches up.

I paste on a sweet smile. "What kind of shopper would I be if I bought something in the first place I stopped in?"

"Looks like Mallory isn't following the same philosophy," Tyler says dryly from behind us.

I turn to see their sister emerge with a shopping bag. "Okay," she says, bright-eyed and beaming. "Next."

As I follow Mallory into the next tent, I wonder how I can pull off the plan I came up with this morning to buy presents for the King family without any of them noticing. It stands to reason I'll have to include Alex, but I'm still too unsettled to talk to him. I need to get over myself. My hurt pride is dampening my joy of experiencing the market.

We visit a few more vendors, and Alex accompanies me like a dutiful boyfriend. Part of me feels sorry for him. I'm sure he'd rather be anywhere than here, so why did he come? Probably to convince Tyler. I'm sure that's why he came caroling, although he didn't look as miserable last night as he does now.

My irritation softens. Sure, he's a snob about who he dates, but I also get it. Roland's right—I don't belong at their business dinners, and honestly, I wouldn't want to go. Alex needs a woman who fits in his world, and that's not me. Why should I hold that against him?

Still, it takes another fifteen minutes before I'm ready to talk to him. We're about to go into a space that sells kitchenware, but I grab Alex's arm to keep him from following his siblings inside. The eager look on his face catches me by surprise, but then again, I've been giving him the cold shoulder, and it's obvious his siblings have noticed.

I take a deep breath, torn between apologizing or not. But an apology will open the door to our earlier conversation, and I'd rather walk back to Georgia than bring it up again, so I dive right in. "I want to get your family Christmas presents."

Surprise fills his eyes, but then he shakes his head. "You don't have to. Finley. They don't expect that."

"I know," I say. "But I like giving gifts, and it's part of the Christmas experience, right?"

He studies me for a moment. "Yeah, I guess you're right."

"The problem is I don't know what they like. What did *you* get them?"

"Gift cards."

I blink, hoping I heard him wrong. "Did you say gift cards?"

He frowns. "What's wrong with gift cards?"

It takes me a beat to realize he's serious. "Alex," I say in dismay. "Gift cards are what you get your dentist or your kids' teachers. It's not what you give your *family*."

Irritation flickers on his face. "It's what I've gotten my family for the past four years, and no one's complained yet."

"Anyone with any tact isn't going to complain." I roll my eyes. "So, as your friend, I'm telling you that you need to get them gifts too."

He considers it and says, "Okay. But what about the gift cards?"

"You can put them in their stockings."

His forehead creases. "What stockings?"

It's my turn to be surprised. "You don't have stockings?"

"We haven't had stockings since I was a kid."

I push out an exaggerated sigh. "We'll add that to the list too."

"What are you two doing over here, looking so intense?" Mallory asks, coming out of another tent, but this time without a new bag.

"Scheming," I say with a grin.

"Well, if *you're* involved then I'm going to presume it's not Alex's usual scheming," Tyler says, following Mallory out.

"That was high school," Alex grunts, but his eyes are twinkling. "I've grown up."

"Debatable," Tyler mutters.

"Well, in this instance," I chime in. "You're right about us scheming good things." I shoot Alex a sarcastic grin. "Probably because I'm the one scheming and dragging Alex along with the plan."

Alex wraps an arm around my back, his hand settling on my hip. "She didn't have to drag me anywhere. All she has to do is bat those big, brown eyes and I'm following like a lost puppy."

My reaction to his touch is immediate. My pulse races, my breath catches.

Mallory's shoulders relax, clearly relieved that we're over our conflict. Tyler's gaze drops to Alex's hand on my hip, and some of his suspicion seems to fade.

Alex smiles down at me, and for one split second, I believe that this is all real. I'm here with my boyfriend and his amazing siblings, having the best Christmas ever. But, ever pragmatic, I remind myself it's not.

Don't fall for the fantasy, Finley.

I don't really want Alex. I like the *idea* of him.

Only someone needs to tell my body that, because there are flutters in my stomach and my heart is racing as he looks down at me with a warm smile. I look away before he notices my reaction, but his breath hits my cheek, sending a shiver down my back. He must think I'm cold because he pulls me closer. "I think we need to get my Georgia peach something warm to drink."

"You call her that too?" Mallory asks, practically squealing with excitement.

"How can I not?" he asks, then kisses the top of my head.

Technically, it's a fine line on the no kissing rule, but I'm not protesting. Instead, I press myself into his side like I belong there.

"You two are so cute!" Mallory says with a dreamy look. "I wish I could find a boyfriend who's that nice to me."

"You don't need a boyfriend," Alex says in a protective tone, while Tyler grunts, "Boys your age are dogs. You need to wait until you're thirty to date."

"Give me a break," Mallory says with a dramatic eyeroll. "You both were on your third or fourth girlfriend by the time you were a senior in college. Hell, Mom and Dad got married the June after they graduated." Then she glances at me, her eyes dancing. "See what I have to put up with?"

"They just love their little sister," I say with a warm smile, and wrap my arm around Alex's back. I do it without thinking, as though it's the most natural thing in the world.

Just friends.

But when I pull away, Alex tugs me back.

"I wish my brothers didn't love me *quite* so much," Mallory says. "Which is why I rarely tell them when I'm dating someone."

Tyler's face goes rigid. "Are you dating anyone now?"

"No," she says smugly.

"Would you tell me if you were?" he asks.

An impish look covers her face. "No."

"Mallory!"

"Are *you* dating anyone?" she asks, propping a hand on her hip.

He lifts his chin. "I plead the fifth."

"Yet you expect me to tell you if *I'm* dating someone," she protests.

"I don't see you drilling Alex," Tyler says.

She gestures toward us. "That's because it would be pretty hard for him to deny he's dating Finley when the evidence is in front of us."

Tyler scrutinizes us for several seconds, but it's not as intense as when we first got here. Like he not only believes we're a couple, but that Alex isn't a nightmare boyfriend.

"I thought we were getting some spiked coffee," Mallory says.

"I never said spiked coffee," Alex counters. "And you're too young for spiked coffee."

She props a hand on her hip. "I'm a month away from being twenty-one, so if you think we're getting non-spiked coffee from St. Nick's coffee stand, then you've lost your mind."

Alex lifts a brow. "The jury's out on where my mind has gone, but we're"—he gestures between me and him—"getting spiked coffee anyway. *You're* getting regular coffee."

"We'll see about that," she says, then turns around in a flounce and heads away from us.

Caught in the glow of Alex and his family, I realize I have two choices. I can keep my guard up and worry about Tyler watching us like a hawk over the next ten days, or I fall into the illusion that Alex is my boyfriend and his family is mine, like it's a ten-day long cosplay. The safe choice is obvious. The risky one is tempting.

I hear my mother's voice in my head, see the pleading in her eyes. *Take risks.*

I suppose you can't get much riskier than this, only my life isn't on the line, it's my heart. But no one's ever died of a broken heart, right?

Look at my heart walking a tightrope without a net.

It's either commit to this or not, but it's not really a choice. For once, I'm going to let my heart lead me. I'll just deal with the fallout when I get home.

I suspect it'll be one hell of a crash.

Chapter Twenty

I'm still not sure what I did to piss Finley off. Was it me bringing up my conversation with Roland again? Or suggesting I'd ask her to bake me cookies? Maybe both? Finley's right. She's not the pushover I thought, although I never thought of it as an insult. More that she'd be a go-with-the-flow kind of woman. Not that I'll ever cop to that either. I'm not *entirely* stupid when it comes to women. The jury's out on the percentage of stupidity though.

When I slipped my arm around Finley, I half-expected her to slap it away. But it was the perfect chance to convince Tyler our relationship is real. We were already "scheming"—her word, not mine—so holding her close as a show of unity felt like a natural step.

I've never been big on public displays with my past girlfriends, but with Finley it feels... weirdly right. And when she slid her arm around me, a warmth spread through me like drinking a fine whiskey in front of a fire. I attribute it to the civil conversation I was having with my brother and sister, the first in years. But I'd be lying if I said Finley wasn't part of it too.

We've been at the market for an hour, but we only got our spiked coffees about ten minutes ago—delayed every few feet by something Finley wanted to check out. And Mallory won out in the end when Tyler got her a spiked coffee, much to her delight.

Now we're sitting at a picnic table, sipping our drinks while she peppers Tyler and Mallory with questions about their hobbies, our parents, even Grant. She makes it seem like causal curiosity, but I know she's compiling a mental list of "perfect gifts." Then it hits me—she does the same thing with the customers at Beans to Go, asking about their lives and actually remembering all the little details. Is that calculated—just good customer service—or does she really care?

Finley takes a sip of her spiked peppermint mocha and says, "So, tell me about Eloise."

Mallory and Tyler go conspicuously silent.

Finley winces. "Sorry if that was out of line. Maybe you haven't had a chance to get to know her very well."

Mallory glances at Tyler. He gives her a questioning look, then shrugs.

"You weren't out of line," Mallory finally says. "It's more like we're trying to be nice."

Finley's eyes widen. "Oh. I didn't mean to start something."

"Don't apologize," Mallory says. "*We're* sorry Grant has shitty taste in women."

"To be fair," Tyler says, setting his coffee cup on the table, "so did Alex until Finley showed up."

"Hey!" I protest, but strangely, I'm not insulted.

"Finley must have picked you for some unknown reason," Tyler goes on dryly. "Because I know you picked the others. And they were—" He cuts himself off, seems to consider his words, then says, "Let's just say they were as bad as Eloise."

"What makes Eloise so bad?" Finley asks, ignoring that he lumped my exes in with Grant's girlfriend. Out of loyalty or because she really doesn't care? I suspect the latter—especially since she's insistent this remain platonic.

Maybe I assume the latter because I don't expect loyalty unless it's demanded by a legal contract. Finley and I *do* have a contract, but there aren't any clauses about loyalty. Then again, I doubt Finley would knowingly be mean to anyone, me included. Maybe she thinks bringing up my exes could be painful.

Is it weird that it isn't?

Mallory turns to Tyler. "If we're going to tell her about Eloise, where do we start?"

"We could start with the complaining," he says with a look of distaste. "I don't think *anything* makes her happy."

"I think *complaining* makes her happy," Mallory counters.

Tyler tips his cup to her. "Fair point."

"She even complains about Mom's cooking," Mallory adds.

"*What?*" Finley cries out in horror. "No!"

Mallory smirks at me. "So did one of Alex's exes. What was her name?" She turns to me. "The girl you dated your last couple years of college?"

My heart slams into my ribcage and a cold sweat breaks out at the nape of my neck.

"Debbie," Tyler says.

"That's not it," Mallory dismisses the name with a wave.

I tell myself to calm down. That they don't know anything about what happened, and Deidre *did* complain about Mom's cooking.

"*Come on*, Alex," Mallory presses. "What was her name?"

"Deidre," I force out, pretending to be disgusted. But my stomach is churning, and it's not from my lingering hangover.

I've buried all that shit in the past, yet the mere mention of her name is enough to rattle me. To be fair, I've been skirting around *the incident*, as my dad calls it, ever since I got here.

"Okay, enough about Alex's exes," Finley says, slipping her hand around my arm and giving it a squeeze. "No girl wants to know the ugly details about the women who preceded her."

"*I* do," Mallory says.

Finley laughs. "That doesn't surprise me in the least. But I still don't know what to expect from Eloise other than she probably won't be happy."

"Isn't that enough?" Tyler deadpans. "Just stay out of her way and don't make eye contact and you should be fine."

Finley shakes her head, smiling. "Surely there's something redeeming about her otherwise, or why else would your brother be dating her?"

"Sex," Tyler says flatly. "Grant claims he's never had better."

He cuts me a dry look. "I always figured the same about your exes."

My back stiffens, and that protectiveness returns. Especially after Finley overheard that video call with Roland. I don't want her forced to sit through a talk about my sexual history.

"Hey!" I snap. "That's enough. Finley already said she doesn't want to hear about my exes."

A sheepish look covers Tyler's face. "Sorry, Finley. He's right."

I stare at him. Genuine apologies don't come easily to my older brother, and there's no doubt this one is sincere.

"It's fine. I'm not naive enough to think Alex walked into my life a virgin," Finley says with a smile. But I'm learning Finley O'Brien's body language, and I know this smile is forced.

"I'll say," Mallory mutters with a fake cough.

Finley shakes her head and I'm relieved when her smile becomes more natural.

"Maybe we should start shopping again," I suggest. "We've only seen half the market and Mallory has at least a dozen more purchases in her before she begs Tyler or me to carry her bags."

Finley looks up at me, her eyes twinkling. "If you were a *good* brother, she wouldn't need to ask."

I laugh and clutch my chest in mock injury. "Ouch."

"Oh!" Mallory declares. "That cinched it. I *love* her."

Tyler grumbles under his breath, but as we stand, he quietly grabs a couple of Mallory's bags. Finley gives me a pointed look, and I reach across the table and wiggle my fingers at my sister.

Mallory laughs and hands me a large bag, satisfaction written all over her face.

"Why are you only giving him one?" Tyler asks.

"Finley still hasn't gotten anything yet," she says with an impish gleam. "I need to make sure Alex has a free hand to hold her bags when she does."

Tyler lifts a brow. "Maybe Finley's just looking and not planning to buy anything."

"Oh, I'm definitely buying," Finley says. "But I want to see everything first, then go back and get what I want."

She's not kidding. She's already spotted gifts for everyone in my family with the exception of Eloise and my father, and she's helped me come up with ideas for mine. She's also plotting stockings and stocking stuffers to make my gift cards less pathetic.

"Well, thank goodness," Mallory says, pretending to wipe sweat from her brow. "I need you to start buying things soon or I'm going to look like a shopaholic."

"If the shoe fits..." Tyler says dryly.

"Hey!" Mallory shoots back, jabbing a finger at him. "I'll have you know I haven't bought *any* shoes."

He gives her a look. "It wasn't literal."

She flips him off, then snags Finley's arm and drags her away from us to the next stall, the two of them laughing like they've been friends for years.

Tyler and I follow. The tension between us is less strained, but he's still on edge.

The girls duck into a handblown glass ornament booth. Mallory drops her hold on Finley's arm and is asking the vendor a question about how they're made.

I hang back, watching Finley like a stalker as she studies the glass ornaments covering a three-foot-tall Christmas tree on a table. I can't seem to help myself. There's something so pure about her that has me mesmerized. I'm enthralled by the look of delight on her face as she lightly touches the ornaments. A feeling I don't understand sweeps over me. There's nothing sexual about it—she's looking at reindeer and Santas and snowmen—yet I'm filled with yearning.

But for what?

Finley?

I've already acknowledged she's beautiful, but this isn't about her physical beauty. Finley isn't a fun roll in the sheets. She's end game. The kind of woman you build a life with.

But not for someone like me.

Funny how yesterday I thought I was too good for her. Now I realize she's too good for me.

The realization fills me with sadness and regret.

I'm about to turn away, but she suddenly stills. The joy bleeds from her face as she lifts a Santa-head ornament from the tree. Her fingertip gently traces the features. Longing fills her eyes, and her chin trembles. She flips over the price tag, and her face pales. Her eyes flood with tears and she carefully puts it back.

What just happened?

She turns and finds me already in her path. The devastation in her eyes nearly brings me to my knees, and the urge to fix this for her is overwhelming.

"What just happened?" I ask quietly, my throat tight. But I already know. It's out of her budget. Still, why does she want it so badly?

She blinks up at me in surprise. "What?"

I don't want to embarrass her, so I need to tread carefully. I gently turn her toward the tree and lift the Santa ornament from the branch. "You looked at this one longer than the others. What makes it special?"

She draws in a deep breath, her shoulders brushing my chest. I want to rest a hand on her hip, to let her know I'm here, but it feels too intimate—more than the "show" we've put on for my siblings. Still, her sadness leaves me empty and helpless. Empty I know; helpless isn't familiar. And I hate it.

"Finley," I whisper in her ear. "Help me understand."

She shivers. I can't help myself—I don't want her sad and cold. I wrap my arms around her, pulling her back against me to share my warmth.

"My mom..." Her voice is so faint I almost miss it.

"Did she like Santas?" I prod gently when she doesn't continue. I need to know what she's thinking, what she's feeling. I've never taken an interest in other women like this, but it must be because we're friends, not lovers. Friends care about each other's feelings.

She leans into me, and I tighten my hold. Having her against me feels too natural. Too right. But I shove down my feelings and concentrate on hers.

"Yeah," she finally says, and even though I can't see her face, I hear the sad smile in her voice. "But there was one she loved the most. Her grandmother gave it to her when she was a kid. She adored her grandmother, so it was really special to her. She wrapped it in tissue paper every year and placed it in a special box. She kept it in her dresser, not with the other ornaments."

"Do you have it on the tree in your apartment?"

She turns and looks up at me. "What makes you think I have a tree in my apartment?"

Somehow, I know she's deflecting, which tells me—along with the way she was looking at this one—that it's gone.

An ache twists in my chest. Finley's already lost so much. It kills me that she lost that ornament. It feels unbearable.

"It looked almost exactly like this one," she whispers, her voice cracking.

I don't care how much it costs; I'm not leaving without it. I'll take out a second mortgage on my condo if I have to.

My chest feels like a hundred-pound anvil is pressing on it. "What happened to your mother's ornament, Finley?"

She draws a shaky breath. "One of my crappy roommates." Then she slips out of my arm and hurries from the tent.

I turn to watch her leave, torn between chasing her and taking the time to buy the ornament. Tyler's standing a few feet away, watching me with a dark look that says he thinks I screwed this up.

I turn back to the ornament and lift the price tag, my eyes nearly popping out. No wonder she got upset. The price is astronomical.

I reach over to take it off the tree, but then stop. If I just buy it and give it to her, she'll think I did it out of pity.

Isn't it?

The ache in my chest throbs, stealing my breath. It's killing me she lost something so precious, but it isn't pity that makes me want to buy it. Finley's always so full of life—I can't stand seeing her so broken.

Is that pity?

Or me being selfish? Only desperate to fix her sadness so my afternoon isn't ruined?

I glance outside the tent but there's no sign of her. Every moment I spend in here is another moment she's alone. The thought of her being sad and alone makes the ache worse.

And then the answer hits me. I can buy the ornament as a gift. A gift isn't pity, right? She's planning to spend God knows how much on my family's gifts and stockings, and that's not pity.

Oh, God.

My stomach drops to my feet. The budget she set for gifts could cover the cost of this ornament. Instead of buying the one thing she clearly wants, she's choosing to buy presents for my family.

If I was forced to choose between something I really wanted and doing something that was right—what would I choose?

You already made that choice six years ago.

Why does that choice suddenly feel wrong?

There's still no sign of her, and my worry grows to panic. I need to make sure she's okay. Once I find her, I'll come back and get it.

I snap a photo of the ornament with my phone, then dash outside.

Tyler is standing in the middle of the street, his arms stiff at his side as he stares at something farther down. He turns to give me a dark look.

"What did you say to her?" he asks.

"I asked her why she wanted that ornament so much, and she said her mother used to have one just like it," I bite out, getting pissed. I should be finding Finley, not justifying myself with him. "But she won't get it because it costs too much."

His gaze drops to my empty hands, then his scowl darkens before he stalks off.

I know he's judging me, but right now, I don't give a shit. I need to find Finley. And then I realize what Tyler had been watching.

Finley is standing to the side of the crowd, between booths, and she's talking to her phone screen. Is she talking to one of her neighbors again?

As though she knows I'm watching, she lifts her gaze to me. She gives me a soft smile and points to her phone.

I smile back and give her a thumbs-up.

"When did you become a thumbs-up guy?" Mallory asks as she approaches with a new bag added to her collection.

"Good question." Since Finley isn't technically alone, I could slip back into the blown glass vendor stall and buy the ornament. But I see Mallory carrying a bag with the vendor's logo. Finley will know I bought something there, and I really want it to be a surprise.

But there's another way.

I pull up the photo on my phone. "See this Santa?"

"Is that some kind of euphemism for showing me porn?" she asks, curling her upper lip in disgust.

I recoil. "What? No! Why would I show my baby sister porn?"

"First of all, I'm not a baby anymore, and second—two words." She pauses and gives me a dead-eyed stare. "Dead possum."

I frown. "That wasn't porn."

"No, it was disgusting roadkill, and you and Grant shoved a photo of it *in my face*."

I roll my eyes. "We were kids."

"You were in middle school, and I couldn't eat red meat for nearly a year."

I scrub my chin with the back of my hand. "Yeah, we were shitty brothers, but it still doesn't explain why you'd think I'd show you porn."

"Roadkill seems appropriate for a thirteen-year-old. Porn seems more appropriate for a man your age." When I give her a blank stare, she shrugs. "I'm just giving you shit. You have to admit you deserve it."

"True," I say, "and deserve even more, but I need you to look at this non-porn Christmas ornament and get it for me. It's a smiling Santa." I hold the phone up so she can see it.

"Most Santas are smiling, Alex," she teases then studies the ornament. "I didn't know you have a thing for Santa ornaments. You seem more like a Rudolph guy."

"It's not for me," I grunt. "It's for Finley. I want to give it to her." Why does admitting that feel so uncomfortable? It's normal to get your girlfriend a gift. But it feels like I'm cutting my chest open and letting Mallory watch my heart beat. "Can you get it for me or not?" I ask defensively.

"Jeez, calm down," she says, looking me over with narrowed eyes. "Of course I will."

"It's insanely expensive," I warn, texting the photo. "I'll Venmo you." I pause. "You do have Venmo, right?"

Her eyes narrow. "Of course I have Venmo. Most thirteen-year-olds have Venmo."

"How do you know the buying habits of thirteen-year-olds?" I ask suspiciously.

"Maybe because I was a camp counselor last summer and bunked with thirteen- and fourteen-year-olds for two months."

Ouch. I should have known that.

Her eyes narrow even more. "Are you getting it for her because you're trying to impress her with your money?"

"What? No!"

But I realize in the past, I've bought my girlfriends gifts based on the dollar amount, not because it meant something. Not like Finley is doing with her gifts.

"Her mother had an ornament like that when she was a kid and Finley inherited it. But one of her jackass roommates did something to it. She really wants it but won't spend that much on herself. So, I...I want to get it for her."

Her eyes go soft. "That's sweet, Alex."

"It's just an ornament," I grunt.

"Obviously it's not just an ornament to Finley."

There's no arguing that point.

She screws up her face. "Why is it so hard for you to admit you want to do something nice for her?"

"What are you talking about?" I scoff. "I just asked you to get the ornament for me."

"Yeah, but you seem..." She shakes her head. "Never mind. I'll get it then send you a Venmo request for payment."

Some of my tension bleeds away. "Thanks. But if you need me to send you money before you get it, let me know."

Her eyes widen. "That much, huh? The one I got for mom was around twenty dollars."

"That's like pocket change compared to this one. But she really wants it." Some of my desperation bleeds into my voice. "Never mind. She's busy talking to her friend. I'll get it myself."

I brush past her, but she puts a hand on my chest. She gives me a strange look, like she's trying to figure me out then gives up. "No, it's okay. I'll get it and hide it in the bag with my others."

I feel like a tightly coiled spring about to be released. "Okay."

"If Finley asks where I am, tell her I saw a friend and wanted to catch up. When I see you two are further down the market, I'll pop in and get it."

I catch sight of Finley again. She's still talking to her friend, and thankfully she doesn't look so sad. "Yeah, the friend story is a good idea."

"Don't sound so surprised. I'm full of them," Mallory says in a sassy tone as she spins around and looks over her shoulder before walking the opposite way.

Chapter Twenty-One

I catch up to Finley, the coil loosening when I see she's smiling at her phone. There's an elderly woman on the screen, and it makes me curious about her neighbors. I walk up behind Finley, lean over her shoulder and smile at the woman.

"Is that him?" she screeches, her eyes wide.

Finley glances over her shoulder at me and gives me an apologetic look. "Sorry. I'll wrap this up."

If her friend is the one who made her happy, then she can stay on the call all afternoon, as far as I'm concerned. "No. I want to meet your friend."

Finley's mouth parts in surprise.

Ignoring her bewilderment, I give my attention to the woman on the screen. "Hi, I'm Alex. I hope you've been assured I'm not a pirate."

Finley giggles, and the sound feels like warm butter on fresh-baked bread. "I think you mean a member of the Russian mafia gang," she says.

"Oh," I say with a huge grin. "That's right. Can't promise I'm not one of *those*."

The woman on the screen laughs. "Oh, Fin, I *like* him."

Finley glances back at me with a soft smile. "Eh. He's okay."

Her comment goes straight to my heart, making it swell.

Jesus, it was a nothing statement, yet it feels like she actually means it. Like maybe I'm not just okay, but worth keeping around.

Where did *that* come from?

Focus.

"You know who I am," I say to Finley's friend, "but I don't know which grandmother you are. You're either Barb or Mirna." I hold up a hand. "Wait. Don't tell me. Let me guess."

The woman giggles.

From what little I knew about her friends, I take a guess based on her laugh, "You're Barb."

"Bingo!" she says exuberantly.

"You should know I'm trying to make sure Finley's having *all* the Christmas experiences," I tell her. "Last night we went caroling. She baked with my mom and sister this morning. We just had boozy Christmas coffee, and now we're Christmas shopping for my family."

Barb is beaming. "She told me."

"I hope she told you she's having a good time," I say, and turn slightly serious, "but if she tells you she's not, I need you to let me know so I can step up my game."

Barb laughs. "She's having a *wonderful* time."

"In case that changes, make sure Finley gives you my number so you can let me know."

She gives me a sly look. "She's already given it to me." Her eyes narrow. "You think I'd let her go over a thousand miles away with a man I've never met with no way to contact you?"

I feel lightly chastised, but I say, "That honestly makes me feel better. I'm glad she has you looking out for her."

She clasps her hand to her chest. "Aren't you a *darling* boy?"

I'm not sure I've ever been called a darling boy before, and for some reason I like it, even if I know I'm not. "Thank you."

"We need to go, Barb," Finley says.

"Alright, but be sure to check in later," Barb says. "You know Mirna wants to talk to you when she gets back." She glances over at me. "And maybe Alex can meet her too."

"We'll see," Finley says. "He might be busy. Love you, Barb. Bye!" She gives a little wave to her phone and Barb blows a kiss just before Finley hangs up.

"She seems sweet," I say.

"She's ornery," Finley says with a laugh as she drops her phone into her coat pocket, then glances around. "Where's Mallory?"

"She said she found a friend and wanted to catch up. She'll find us when she's done." I glance around. "But it seems we lost Tyler."

"He also found a friend," she says, "He said he's had enough shopping and was going to get a beer with a guy from high school at St. Nick's bar." She grins. "Barb called dibs on him if he's not taken."

"He met her too, huh?" I ask, confused by the unsettled feeling in my gut.

Is that *jealousy*? Over my brother? I don't see how. Maybe the coffee isn't sitting well.

"When he came over to let me know he was taking off, he apologized for interrupting. But Barb insisted on meeting him before he left for the bar."

The reminder of St. Nick's fills me with shame over my behavior last night and what Finley overheard this morning. Maybe that's what's causing my unsettled feeling.

We stare at each other for several seconds and a realization hits me. "So, we're alone." The words coming out huskier than I intended.

There's a tiny hint of a smile on her lips, and my gaze lingers there until it lifts to her warm brown eyes, and I lose myself in them.

When I'm with her, I feel calmer. Like she siphons off my stress and replaces it with something I can't name. Like I'm settled, but that's not it either. It's something deeper, something I don't understand, but I *do* know that I like how it feels.

I like *being* with her. I like that there aren't any expectations from either of us. We're just together, having fun. I've never felt that with any of my other girlfriends, but I have to admit, I wasn't friends with any of them.

After a few seconds, she looks away, and says cheerfully, "It would be a good opportunity for us to buy our Christmas presents."

"But we haven't seen everything yet."

She laughs. "There's no way you want to keep checking out homemade oven mitts and candles."

She's right. If someone had told me last week that I'd not only spend several hours at the Christmas market, but do so willingly, I would have laughed in their face. Yet, here I am, and I'm not hating it. "I don't know," I say with a shrug. "I'm having fun."

Finley gives me the side eye, obviously not believing me.

"I am. Now let's start shopping."

We continue to the next booth, but Finley seems less interested in browsing and has now moved into shopping mode.

She says that while they were baking this morning, my mom said she wanted to learn how to bake bread, so she gets her a bread cookbook. I ask what I can get to go with her baking theme, and I get a small jar of wet dough that looks like an underachieving Play-Doh that's apparently sourdough starter, along with instructions on how to "feed" it and a very expensive pot with a lid for her to bake the bread in. The vendor says I can leave the pot there until we finish shopping since it's so heavy.

As we leave the stall, I realize Mallory hasn't sent me a Venmo request for the ornament.

Finley moves to the next stall, so I pull out my phone and see I missed a text.

Alex, I'm so sorry! It's gone!

My heart skips a beat, and I call out to Finley, "I have to make a call. I'll be right there."

"Okay," she says as she disappears into a booth selling knitwear.

Freaking out, I call Mallory and she answers right away. "Oh, my God, Alex. I'm *so* sorry!"

"No. They *have* to have it," I insist. "They *just* had it!"

"I showed them the photo, Alex," she says in a tearful rush, "and the lady said she was pretty sure she'd sold it right before I showed up."

"Did she tell you who bought it?"

"Why?" she asks in disbelief. "Do you plan to track them down and take it from them?"

"Not take it. I'd pay for it."

"Oh, Alex," she sighs, and I can't tell if she thinks I'm stupid or romantic.

"It's important to her, Mal."

"Wow," she says in amazement. "You really love her."

I balk at her suggestion. I definitely don't love her. I barely know her. Still, I can see why she'd think so. This isn't my typical behavior.

"I'm not sure it's love," I say, deciding to use this to my advantage. "But I *really* like her." Not a lie. "Coming to Hollybrook meant a lot to her because it's the kind of Christmas she and her mother always dreamed of. I thought if I could give her that ornament, not only would it be like her mother was with her in spirit, but she'd have something special to help her remember Hollybrook."

"I love that you're trying to give her something to tie her mom to her experience here, but as far as remembering Hollybrook, you can bring her back next year, right?" When I don't answer, she adds, "I mean, you'd be crazy to break up with her."

I pause, unsure what to say. "Maybe she'll break up with me."

"That seems far more likely," she teases.

If this were real, I suspect Finley wouldn't date me at all, so on the off chance we were dating, there's no question she'd be the one to leave me. But this isn't about me. This is about Finley and that Santa ornament.

I feel sick. It's not like she's going to be disappointed I didn't get it for her. She had no idea I was trying. But I've already imagined how happy she'll be when she opens it. The look of pure joy on her face. Even so, it's not like she can be any more disappointed than she already was after losing the first one.

Then why does my failure to get it make me feel like I'm responsible for her pain?

What the hell is wrong with me? I'm not a man ruled by emotion, yet I feel like emotion has ruled me all day.

"I'm really sorry, Alex," Mallory says again.

"It's not your fault," I say, running a hand over my head in defeat while I watch Finley look at a mitten display. "I should have bought it while I was there, then had you hide the package."

"Or I should have gone back there sooner."

"Mal, you did exactly what I asked you to do. I'll just find her something else." But what else could compare? It feels hopeless to even try.

She gasps. "Wait. You haven't gotten her anything yet?"

I cringe, grateful she's not here to see my reaction.

"We agreed not to get each other presents," I say, thinking fast, because I know Finley won't be giving me a gift. But wait—she's getting everyone else in my family gifts. It stands to reason she'll find a way to get me something too.

"Do you need help?" she asks.

I want to say yes, but nothing else can measure up to that stupid ornament. It was my idea, and I want whatever replaces it to be my idea too.

Which is confirmation I've officially lost my mind.

Chapter Thirty-Two

Finley

I'm trying to forget about that ornament. I mean it's just a painted piece of glass, albeit a *very expensive* piece of glass, but it looked so much like Mom's...

But I can't afford it. Not with all the gifts I'm purchasing. And even if I wasn't buying Alex's family gifts, I could never justify the price. Besides, Christmas isn't just about the trimmings of the holiday; it's the spirit of giving, and Alex's family has been so welcoming that I want to give them something in return.

Alex is fully on board with the gift purchasing, but after his phone call, something seems off. I want to ask him if everything's okay, but I'm not sure he'd appreciate me asking. So, we spend the next hour or so buying presents and finding small stocking stuffers. The only thing we haven't found are stockings that fit my meager budget. When Alex realizes what's holding me up, he insists he's paying for them himself.

"I'm the one who came up with the idea. You shouldn't be the one to buy them."

"For God's sake, Finley," he says. "They're my family. Why would I expect you to pay for their stockings?" He pulls stockings from a stack, then realizes there are different styles. "Which ones do you like?"

There isn't much difference between them other than color. "Let's get red for your mom and your sister, and green for you and the guys." I hand him three red to include Eloise, and four green.

He gives me a long look, then grabs another red one and heads to the register.

"Wait. You can't get *me* a stocking," I insist. "I'm not a member of the family."

He frowns in confusion. "But you got one for Grant's girlfriend."

"But she's his actual girlfriend, and she's been around long enough for everyone to know her."

"And you've been around long enough for my entire family to love you," he says with a laugh. "You're more a member of my family than I am at this point. When we 'break up'"—he uses air quotes with his free hand—"I suspect they'll insist on keeping you." When he sees my stricken face, he taps my nose. "Hey, don't look so upset. I'm only partly teasing, and besides, aren't Christmas stockings part of the whole Christmas package? I can't go cheaping out on you now."

"You're not cheaping out on me," I say. "I haven't even been here twenty-four hours and this whole experience is even better than I dreamed of."

His face softens and he studies me for several seconds. "I can't believe you get so excited over this stuff."

I start to take it as an insult, but I realize it's not one. He truly doesn't understand it.

"You lost your spirit of Christmas."

Alex makes a face. "I'm not sure I ever had it to begin with. I just took this place for granted." He stares at me for a few more seconds then takes the stockings up to the register. I feel terrible when I see the total. They cost too much. I should have looked for cheaper ones somewhere else. But he doesn't bat an eye at the price, and when the clerk asks if he wants names embroidered on the cuffs, he shoots me a grin and says, "Well, of course."

"It's too late to get them embroidered today," the woman says apologetically. "But if you don't mind coming back, you can pick them up tomorrow any time after noon, but before we close at five."

Alex glances over at me. "Are we okay with that?"

"Yeah, of course." I lean closer, "But it's too much."

"They have to have names, and I refuse to use glue and glitter." He shudders at the thought.

I lift a brow. "Bad experience with glitter?"

"Let's just say Mallory was addicted to it at one point, and Grant convinced her to glue a bunch of glitter onto something while sitting on *my bed*." He laughs, then tells the vendor how to spell our names.

I watch him, reveling in the moment. I feel guilty that he just spent nearly a couple hundred dollars on stockings, but he doesn't seem to care. In fact, he seems lighter and happier than I've ever seen him. Like, maybe thinking of things to get his family agrees with him?

After the vendor hands him the receipt, we walk out of the stall and search the crowd for Mallory. She caught up with us not too long after my call with Barb, more subdued than she'd been before. When I asked her if she was okay, she said her reunion with her friend hadn't been as cheerful as she'd hoped, but she was better after finding me.

I was worried we'd have a hard time getting the gifts with her around—I don't want her to know we're shopping for her and her family—but she keeps wandering off on her own, giving us plenty of opportunity to make our purchases.

A grin spreads across Alex's face. "I think we need a Christmas market snack."

My stomach rumbles at the mention of snacks. "I wouldn't say no to food."

He sees Mallory and beckons her over.

"Why do you two look like you're up to no good?" She's grinning and studying us as though she can figure it out.

"I wouldn't call getting something to eat being up to no good," Alex says.

She nods in approval. "I'm always on board for food. There's a potato cake booth that way," she says, pointing behind her.

"I have something else in mind," he says, his eyes twinkling. "I think Fin will love it."

"Should we see if Tyler wants to join us?" I ask.

Mallory makes a face. "He sent me a text about ten minutes ago that he left."

"Figures," Alex says with a grunt.

"He doesn't know what he's missing," Mallory says. "Now that you've mentioned food, I'm starving. Lead us to the place you think Fin will love."

Alex transfers the packages to his left hand, then takes my hand in his right and leads me through the crowd.

I nearly stumble, shocked by the contact. We've linked arms and wrapped arms around each other at various times to look like a couple, but we haven't held hands. Maybe because it feels...intimate. Which is ridiculous—they're just hands. Not lips or...other body parts. But then my mind supplies images of what else Alex's hands could do, and I quickly shut it down. Not quickly enough, though. The thought leaves me breathless and tingly.

It's pathetic to lust after a man who has no sexual interest in me. This is all just for show, but my body's reacting as though it's real.

Which makes me wonder if this is smart. But as I fall into step beside him, it strikes me again how right it feels.

It's pretend, Finley.

I shove the thought down deep and decide to stop questioning it all. Mom's deathbed request was for me to take risks. What could be riskier than risking my heart?

Oh, Finley. You're quite the fool.

But I ignore my inner voice and let myself get lost in the moment. Whatever happens, at least I'll have this—a magical day in a winter wonderland. Whether I'll escape with my heart intact remains to be seen.

Alex leads us a couple of blocks to the square where we started caroling last night, then stops in front of a café that looks like it belongs in a Swiss Alps village, not a Vermont town square. Sure, all the buildings here look that way, but this one looks even more authentic with its ancient-looking wooden beams and sidewalk seating. People are sitting outdoors despite the cold, warmed by the gas heaters that are scattered around. Alex finds a table with a good view of the square, close to a heater. He holds out a chair for me, then sits next to me, while Mallory sits next to her brother.

"I thought you might like to people-watch," he says to me, then points across the square. "Especially since the skating rink is right over there."

We hadn't spent much time by the rink last night, so I'd barely registered it, but now I can see people gliding across the ice.

"We should go ice skating tomorrow," Alex says.

I glance back at him, barely containing myself. "Really?"

"Sure, we have to come back to pick up our special project tomorrow anyway." He winks at me. "And it's part of the whole Christmas experience, right?"

My excitement is short-lived. "I don't know how to ice skate. I've never been."

"Don't worry," he says. "I'll teach you." Then he catches the attention of a waitress and beckons her over.

"Alex used to play hockey," Mallory says. "He was the one who taught me how to ice skate. You'll be safe."

Is that why Alex has a photo of the two of them together on the same rink across the square?

When the waitress appears, Alex tells her he already knows what he wants to order, then lists off a bunch of names I don't recognize but that sound German. The only thing I understand is when he orders Nutella and banana crepes and a pretzel.

The waitress writes it all down, then looks at the three of us. "Are you expecting more people?"

Mallory laughs. "No, just us."

The waitress narrows her eyes. "You *do* know this is probably enough to feed at least six or seven people."

"I know," Alex says. "But this is my girlfriend's first time here and I want her to try everything."

My breath catches. I'm still not used to him calling me his girlfriend, but it's the fact that he's ordering so much food that has me flabbergasted. "You don't have to do that, Alex!"

"I know," he says, turning back to smile at me. "I want to."

Shaking her head and muttering something about fools in love, the waitress heads back into the café.

"Are you trying to put her into a food coma?" Mallory asks with a laugh.

He raises his brow. "Maybe I'm trying to put you both into a food coma, so I'll get a moment of peace."

He and Mallory rib each other for several minutes until the waitress returns with three steaming mugs and glasses of water. Once she places them on the table and walks away, Alex picks up the mug in front of him. "Mulled wine. I think you'll like it."

We all take a sip, and as the warm beverage hits my tongue, I can't help the tiny groan of pleasure that escapes.

"If she's that excited about the wine, I can't wait to see her try the gingerbread," Mallory says, then winks at Alex. "And thanks for the wine."

Her frowns. "Don't tell mom."

"Gingerbread?" I ask, more excited than I have a right to be over a baked good.

Alex looks at me like he's in a stupor, but he shakes it off and says, "*German* gingerbread. And plenty of other things too."

The food comes out about ten minutes later, and the dishes cover the table. Alex and Mallory point everything out, using their German names, and then explain what they are in English. I try sausages, and several potato dishes—including potato pancakes, fried apple rings, a pretzel, the crepe, and even corn on the cob, which Mallory insists is a legitimate German Christmas market food. I try some of everything until I'm stuffed.

When we've all eaten our fill, Mallory says, "When Mom gets mad because we barely touch our dinner, I'm blaming you, Alex."

He laughs. "I don't remember anyone forcing you to eat half that pretzel."

"Peer pressure," she says.

"Riiiight."

I've had a full cup of mulled wine, and most of Alex's. He only took a sip or two and gave the rest to me when he saw I'd finished mine. I'm slightly tipsy, and warm inside. "Thank you, both," I say, feeling emotional. "Thank you for making this an amazing Christmas."

"Girl, it's not even Christmas yet," Mallory scoffs, but I can see she's emotional too. "You ain't seen nothing yet."

"I can't wait."

Alex pays the bill, and we gather all our packages—including the leftover food—and walk to Mallory's car. Alex insists I sit in front again, and I wonder if he's about to say he's not riding with us like he did earlier, but he gets in the backseat and is quiet all the way home. Mallory makes up for his silence, telling me about growing up in Hollybrook, and how she worked at the Christmas market when she was a teenager, and during her first two years of college over winter break.

When we walk into the kitchen, Valerie is peeling potatoes in front of the kitchen sink.

"We're having meatloaf and mashed potatoes for dinner," she says as we drop our packages on the floor and take off our coats. "I hope you guys are hungry."

Alex and Mallory laugh, and she narrows her eyes. "What's so funny?"

"Nothing," they mutter, but I say, "Alex took us to a café on the square so I could try a bunch of Christmas market food."

"You took her to the AlpenGlanz Café?" she asks in surprise. I'm worried she's going to be irritated, but she looks pleased. "What did you have, Finley?"

I'm not sure telling her I had a bite of everything is a great idea, so I tell her my favorites. "I loved the mulled wine and potato pancakes. Oh, and gingerbread."

"Good choices," she says, then looks around at the food on the counter. "Maybe I should hold dinner for a bit."

"No need," Alex says. "We'll be hungry by dinner time."

I hand the bags in my hands to Alex. "Can you take these up to our room?"

"Sure," he says, looking confused.

But I'm already halfway to the sink and take the peeler out of Valerie's hand. "Let me do that."

She seems reluctant at first, then hands it over as well as the half-peeled potato in her hand. "If you insist," she says in a teasing tone.

"Alex and I will be down in a few minutes to help," Mallory says, and then they both head upstairs.

"How did you work *that* miracle?" Valerie asks in amazement as she walks to the fridge and pulls out a bottle of white wine.

"What miracle?"

"Getting those two to volunteer to help."

I shrug. "I didn't do anything. Maybe they want to be part of the fun."

She makes a puzzled face, then pours wine into two glasses and sets one on the counter next to the potatoes. "Well, whatever you did, thank you. I haven't seen Mallory and Alex get along like that since..." She frowns as her voice trails off. "Anyway, it's nice to see them getting along."

"Maybe it's the magic of Christmas," I say as I rinse off the potato I've just peeled and set it on a cutting board with the others.

"More like the magic of Finley," she says before taking a sip, lost in thought.

Chapter Twenty-Three

True to Mallory's word, she and Alex come down and help finish dinner. When the meatloaf is in the oven and the green beans and potatoes are on the stove, we sit around the table, sipping wine while they tell stories about Alex and his siblings when they were kids. Tyler joins us after a bit, grabbing a bottle of beer and sitting at the table, but he's reserved and doesn't share much.

Around six-thirty, Alex's dad comes home and apologizes for being late. "Sick cat," he says. "It ate a miniature snowman from a kid's advent calendar, but it's going to be okay."

"What's Finley's cat's name, Alex?" Tyler asks abruptly.

Alex looks like he's been caught red-handed robbing a jewelry store, but then he gets pissed. "What the hell, Tyler? I thought we were over that."

"Boys," Valerie says, sounding more tired than angry. "What are you talking about, Alex?"

Alex starts to say something, then clams up.

"For some reason, Tyler didn't believe Finley was his girlfriend," Mallory says, rolling her eyes. "But anyone with a pair of eyes can see that she is."

"Oh, I believe they're together," Tyler says, "but I have no doubt he only thinks about himself. Which is why I'm asking if he knows the name of her cat."

"Tyler!" his mother chastises. "What has gotten into you?"

"Answer the question, Alex," Tyler taunts. "Can't do it, can you?"

Alex looks at me, maybe because he knows I don't want to lie about my life, and he knows Maybelle is important to me—even if he doesn't know her name. I'm guessing he doesn't want to make one up.

"That's because he doesn't call her by her name," I say, trying to sound light-hearted. "He gave her a nickname the first time he met her, and he's used it ever since."

"Then what do you call her?" Tyler asks.

"Hellfire," Alex says, holding his gaze. "She's grumpy as hell, but when she gets pissed, she brings the fire."

I laugh, because I'm pretty sure I never told him Maybelle's name, but he remembers me talking about her. "It's a pretty accurate description. Especially since she doesn't take to new people very well."

Tyler takes a long pull from his beer.

"You owe Alex an apology, Tyler," Valerie says, still fuming.

"That's okay," Alex says, while giving his brother a long, appraising look. "I think he's just looking out for Finley."

"What does that have to do with Finley?" Valerie asks.

Alex gives her a smile. "Basically, he thinks I'm a first-class asshole and he wants to make sure I'm treating her right."

"Tyler!" his mom protests.

"No," Alex says, "I deserve it. I come by the title naturally, so..." He shrugs.

Valerie inhales deeply and is about to say something, but Tyler gets up and stalks out of the room, taking his beer with him.

Alex's dad is still standing by the mudroom with a dazed expression. "Sounds like I missed an eventful day."

Tyler doesn't come back. He texts his mother that he's meeting friends for dinner and forgot to mention it. I feel terrible, like my presence here has driven Alex's brother out of his own home at Christmas, but I'm not sure what to do about it. Tyler must be perceptive, and the truth is, he's right. It seems unfair that he's being punished for it.

The meatloaf is delicious, but Mallory, Alex, and I are still pretty full from our afternoon smorgasbord, so we don't put much of a dent in the food. At the beginning of dinner, everyone is subdued after Tyler and Alex's confrontation, but soon they get back to the jovial spirit they had earlier, and even the quiet Dr. Bob is more talkative than he was the night before.

We're halfway through the meal when Valerie gasps. "Oh! I almost forgot to tell you! Aunt Jean called this afternoon. She and her grandkids aren't coming for Christmas after all."

"What?" Alex asks in shock. Mallory and Dr. Bob give shouts of gratitude.

I turn to look at Alex, my heart pounding. One of the reasons he invited me was so he didn't have to sleep in the rec room with his younger cousins. If they aren't coming...

"No terror triplets?" Mallory asks hopefully.

Valerie releases a labored sigh. "Mallory, I've told you time and time again not to call them that."

"Yeah, but it's true," she counters.

"But they're not actual triplets," Valerie says. "They were all born separately, even if it was just a year apart."

Mischief dances in Mallory's eyes. "But you're admitting that they're terrors?"

Valerie's eyes widen as though she's been caught. "I never said they were terrors." Then her face scrunches up as she closes her eyes. "But I never said they weren't either."

Mallory bursts out laughing, but I'm looking at Alex, trying to gauge his reaction—the fact that they aren't coming. I already know he thinks they're terrors.

He catches my gaze and smiles. "You're quite the good luck charm, Fin. Your perfect Christmas is giving us one too."

Relief washes through me, and I'm surprised when he reaches over and cups my hand, giving it a reassuring squeeze.

"I'm sure Grant and Eloise will be thrilled to hear it," Alex's dad says. "He was none too happy about sleeping on the sofa bed, let alone with the terror triplets."

"Bob," Valerie gasps. "You too?"

He shrugs and picks up his water glass. "I call 'em as I see 'em, Val."

She shakes her head, then laughs.

We clean up dinner—everyone pitching in. We discuss what to do after dinner and Mallory suggests we watch a Christmas movie. After Alex and his parents agree, they settle on *Christmas Vacation*, in honor of dodging the terror triplets.

When we walk into the living room, I stop short. I haven't been in this room yet, and I gasp when I see the Christmas tree. It's massive, nearly touching the top of the twelve-foot ceiling and more than half as wide. Not only is it huge, but it's also a real tree, and the pine scent fills the room. I'd smelled pine this morning, but I thought it was a candle or a diffuser. The tree is covered in white lights and layers and layers of ornaments. I can't imagine how many boxes it takes to pack them all away.

I walk over to the tree and study the ornaments, admiring the mix of vintage and new.

"A lot of them have been passed down through three generations," Dr. Bob says as he stands next to me. "Val gets the kids a new ornament every year, so the tree is packed."

"Probably too many ornaments," Valerie says as she snuggles onto the sofa with a blanket, a freshly poured glass of wine on the table next to her. "Every year I say I'm going to get a smaller tree, but..." She waves toward the tree. "As you can see, I haven't followed through yet."

"It's beautiful," I say with a sigh.

Alex moves up behind me and places a hand on my shoulder, squeezing gently. Without thinking, I reach up and cover his hand with my own, overwhelmed with emotion. The warmth of his family, today at the market, this moment—it's everything I've ever wanted.

Alex turns me around and pulls me to his chest, engulfing me in a hug.

"I'm sorry about the ornament," he whispers in my ear. "I wish I'd gotten it for you."

I look up at him in surprise, then shake my head. "Alex, no! I didn't expect that."

He tucks a strand of hair behind my ear as he studies me. "I know, but I hate seeing you sad."

Is this for show because his family is watching? It feels real, so I'm going to let myself believe it is. "I'm not sad," I say as a tear falls down my cheek. "I'm happy."

"You cry when you're happy?" he asks in disbelief.

"It's what we girls do," Mallory calls out from across the room.

I bury my face in his chest and release a short laugh of embarrassment.

"Come on, love birds," Mallory says. "You can be all cute and lovey later, but right now, I want to watch a squirrel jump out of a Christmas tree."

Alex gives me a squeeze, then kisses the top of my head before he releases me. To my surprise, he takes my hand and leads me to a love seat. We sit down together, and he wraps an arm around me, tugging me into his side. I curl up next to him as he tosses a blanket over my legs, and I rest my head against his chest, our hips pressed together.

This isn't real. This isn't real.

Alex is not my boyfriend. His family is not my family. This isn't my Christmas. I'm an interloper.

We watch the movie while a fire roars in the fireplace, the only light in the room coming from the tree and the television. It's all so perfect. The family Christmas I've always dreamed of. I push down the fear that I'll be destroyed when it's over. But there's no backing out now. I signed a contract.

When the movie's over, Mallory wants to watch *The Santa Clause.* I'm on board, and Alex agrees, but his parents bid us goodnight and head upstairs.

It's after eleven when the second movie's over. Mallory tells us she's going to bed, leaving the two of us on the love seat.

We sit in silence, watching the fire with the Christmas tree twinkling in the corner. Alex still has his arm around me, and I'm snuggled into his side, our feet next to each other on an ottoman. There's no one to convince right now—it's just us—and I know I should move away from him, but I want to enjoy the illusion for a few minutes more.

Finally, Alex shifts slightly and whispers, "We should discuss the sleeping arrangement for tonight. I can sleep in the chair—"

"*No*," I say quickly. "The whole point of this was so you could sleep in your bed. You gave me a perfect day, the least I can do is give you the bed."

He shifts and looks at me, emotion brewing in his eyes. "Finley, absolutely not. There's no way you're sleeping in the chair again."

"How about this," I say carefully, as I watch for his reaction to what I'm about to suggest. "We can both sleep in the bed." Surprise fills his eyes, and before he thinks that I'm begging him to sleep with me, I add, "Look, we're both adults, perfectly capable of controlling ourselves." I give him a wry grin. "Besides, I know you're not interested in me like that."

Frustration fills his eyes, and he takes my hand. "Finley, I didn't—"

"Alex," I say firmly, squeezing his hand. "It's okay, and honestly, it's actually reassuring. This way there's no confusion."

There's no denying it *could* get messy and complicated, but I can't deny that I'd be open to... *more*. At least to myself. Which is humiliating considering he made it very clear this morning that sleeping with me is the last thing he wants.

But I'm a grown woman, and I'm perfectly capable of controlling myself. Besides, the last thing I'd ever do is throw myself at a man who doesn't want me. I'm not sure I could bear more mortification.

"Yeah," he says, his voice tight. "You're perfectly safe from me taking advantage." He says it in a teasing tone, but his eyes don't sparkle like they have all day when he's joked around.

He slips the blanket off our laps and nudges the ottoman

away with his foot before standing. Then he turns to face me and holds out a hand. "It's time for my Georgia peach to go to bed. We have a full day ahead of us tomorrow."

I reach out, and he pulls me up with a little more strength than I expect. I stumble, and his hands catch my hips, steadying me. Our chests brush, and I look up at him, the firelight flickering on his face.

"I'm not very graceful," I say with a nervous laugh, trying to bury the ache rising in my chest.

"I'm not complaining," he says, his voice low, his gaze locked on mine

The tension between us hums—so real I can almost feel it against my skin. If I hadn't overheard his conversation with Roland this morning, I might think he was about to kiss me. It's ridiculous.

Except...it doesn't feel ridiculous.

Before I can decide what to do, he lets go of my hips and takes my hand instead, leading me to the entryway. When he drops it at the staircase, the loss of contact feels sharper than it should.

What am I doing? The Alex I've gotten to know on this trip is a paradox—snobbish and arrogant one minute, sweet and thoughtful the next. He's a contradiction I can't seem to figure out. And worse, I'm starting to want to.

But the sweet part of him has to be real, right? Still, a part of me is terrified it's just another layer of the act—because it's easier to keep pretending, even when no one's watching, than to turn it on and off. And if it's true, I'll end up looking like a fool for falling for it.

So why do I want to fall for it anyway?

When we walk into the bedroom, I say, "Why don't you get ready for bed first? I suspect you'll be faster than me."

He grabs a pair of sweatpants and a T-shirt out of his bag and heads into the hall, leaving the door open. I pull out my pajamas and stare at the stack of bags in the chair, probably Alex's way of making sure I don't sleep in the chair, as though I couldn't just move them to the floor.

He walks back into the room about five minutes later and says, "All yours."

I go into the bathroom and get ready for bed, and when I return, Alex is sitting up in bed, reading a book that looks like a boring business tome. He glances up and scoots closer to his side of the bed. Not that I have to worry about him encroaching on my side. There's a bulge under the covers—it looks like two pillows lying lengthwise down the middle of the bed.

When he sees my gaze drift there, he says, "I made a wall." He pauses. "Like the Great Wall of China."

"You think you need to keep out an enemy?" I tease, my mouth dry. I'm already nervous about getting in bed with him.

"It's to protect *you*," he says adamantly. "In case I accidentally reach for you in the middle of the night."

I nod, still looking at the bed.

"I can sleep somewhere else," he says, misunderstanding my hesitation. "I don't plan on mauling you. It's in case I don't realize what I'm doing while I'm asleep."

"I'm not worried, but it's a good idea," I say as I walk over to my side of the bed and slip under the covers.

Alex sets his book on the nightstand and turns off the light, plunging the room into darkness. We lie in silence for nearly a minute, and I keep myself plastered to the edge of the bed. Touching Alex came so naturally today. I'm worried I'll try to spoon him in my sleep, pillow wall or not.

"Thank you for a wonderful day," I say softly into the darkness.

He doesn't answer for several seconds, and I wonder if he's one of those people who fall asleep within seconds of their head hitting the pillow, but then he says, "I had fun." He pauses, but then adds, "More than I've had here in a long time, so I feel like I should be thanking *you*."

"We'll just form a mutual gratitude club," I say, then cringe, thankful it's dark, and he can't see my embarrassment.

Mutual gratitude club, Finley? Really?

He chuckles. "Which one of us is president?"

"Me, of course," I say, relief spreading through me that he's playing along. "It *was* my idea."

"Okay, Madam President. Does that make me vice president?"

"Only if you want the title," I say, relaxing. "There *are* other offices to fill."

He laughs, and we fall into silence again, only this time it's more comfortable.

"Good night, Finley," he says, his voice warm and soft.

"Goodnight," I say, smiling to myself. Alex might not be my boyfriend, but I think I can confidently call him my friend. And for now, I call that a win.

Chapter Twenty-Four

I lie awake long after I hear Finley's slow and steady breathing. I can't stop thinking about that Christmas ornament and the way she reacted to Mom's tree. I'm berating myself for taking Mallory's word that the ornament was gone. I should have gone back and checked myself. But tomorrow I'll ask Mallory to keep Finley occupied, and I'll go by the booth and check for myself when I pick up the stockings. If it's really not there, I'll look for something else, because I have to get her *something*. Opening gifts is just as much a part of Christmas as giving them, and I'll be damned if she doesn't have something to open.

But her reaction to the Christmas tree has given me another idea. Finley said she wants to experience as many Christmas activities as possible, so I come up with a plan. We'll have to postpone ice skating, but I suspect she won't complain once she realizes what we're doing.

***

In the morning, I wake up before Finley does. She's curled on her side, facing the pillow fortress, a few strands of hair spread across her cheek. I reach over to brush them away, but just before my fingers graze her skin, I pull back.

What the hell am I doing?

I've never done anything like that for any other woman. I'm not the guy who wakes, wanting to touch someone just to touch them. My relationships have served a purpose, and the women

I've dated fit a profile. They got to be with a man projected to make several million off a start-up, and I got a beautiful, successful woman to bring to business dinners. Fair trade.

Sure, it sounds shallow, but six years ago, I learned the hard way that giving your heart away is dangerous—in the literal sense.

Finley doesn't fit that profile at all.

So, what was I thinking when I almost touched her? There's no audience to convince that we're together. Maybe it's because last night felt a little too believable. Hell, I almost kissed her again when I helped her up from the sofa. Her body so close to mine, the firelight on her face—she's so damn beautiful. And so damn sweet. She's the kind of woman I never thought I'd want, but she brings out the me I used to be. The me I didn't realize I missed.

Still, this isn't real. She's not interested in a relationship with me—especially after what she's seen. She's seen the narcissistic, arrogant side of me here. She'd be crazy to want me too.

God, I *do* want her, don't I?

No, I *can't* want her. I'm just too deep in the role, that's all.

So maybe that's why I planned this morning's surprise. It's part of our deal—she gets the Christmas she's always dreamed of. I'm just making sure she gets what she signed up for.

At least that's the story I'm sticking to.

I slip out of bed and pause at the door. She's still curled up, peaceful, her hair spilling over the pillow. Something twists in my chest—something soft and unfamiliar. Tender. Maybe this is how a guy feels about a girl who's just his friend.

The smell of coffee hits my nose as I walk downstairs to the kitchen. Dad's sitting at the table, reading a newspaper, a cup of coffee on the table in front of him.

He glances up at me and gives me a tired smile. "You're up early."

I head straight for the coffee maker and grab a mug from the cabinet above. "I thought Mom might be up."

"She's still sleeping, but I suspect she'll be down soon."

I fill my mug, then add creamer. After I put the container

back in the fridge, I stand at the counter, my fingers wrapped around the mug, unsure what to do next.

"You can sit with me, Alex," Dad says quietly, sadness softening his voice. "We can talk."

I want to sit. God, I do. But being alone with him.... it's like stepping back into that night six years ago—the night I called him in abject horror and grief.

My chest feels tight, and the walls feel like they're closing in.

Dad must see that I'm about to bolt, because he turns in his chair to face me, his eyes pleading. "I think we need to talk, son. We've gone far too long without discussing—"

I take a step back, a vise clamping my lungs. "I need to take a shower."

Dad's shoulders sag, defeat shadowing his face. "I wish you'd talk to me, Alex." He lifts his chin. "I miss you."

I miss him too. I miss all of them, but Dad is a living reminder of that night—the night I made the worst mistake of my life. I've stayed away all these years out of shame, terrified my family would uncover the truth. Time may have dulled the risk of discovery, but the shame hasn't faded. It's still there, festering.

Tyler thinks I've stayed away because I think I'm too good for them.

The truth is, I'm not good enough—for them or for anyone else

Finley's face flashes in my mind, the way she looked sleeping this morning—soft, peaceful, unguarded. Someone who still believes the world can be good. Someone who deserves good.

And that's not me.

"I wanted to ask mom a question, but I'll ask her later," I spin around to bolt for the stairs, but Mom has just walked into the room.

She stares at me and then at Dad, obviously feeling the tension between us. "Did I interrupt something?"

"Nope," I say, then lift my mug. "Just came down to get a cup of coffee before I hop in the shower."

"Okay," she says, sounding like she's not sure she believes me.

"There is one other thing," I say, lowering my voice, "Do we have any spare Christmas ornaments?"

Her forehead creases in confusion, then her face lights up when I tell her my plan for Finley. "Don't you worry about a thing," she assures me. "Mallory and I will have it under control."

"Don't you have things to do to get ready for tonight and tomorrow?" I ask. Then a new thought occurs to me. "Wait. Do you need me and Finley to stick around and help with anything?"

Her eyes widen slightly. "You're offering to help?"

I wince. "Am I really *that* much of an asshole?"

"You're not an asshole, honey," she says, rubbing my arm. "You're just usually not here long enough to think about offering."

AKA I'm a self-centered asshole, but she's too nice to call me out on it.

"Mom, we can skip this morning, and I can stick around to help."

"Oh, heavens, no!" she exclaims. "Finley will absolutely *love* it. I can't wait to see her face when you get back."

I take a step toward the stairs, then stop. "One more thing," I say. "I need to pick something up at the Christmas market this afternoon. Finley was planning to go with me, but I have another stop to make that I don't want her to know about. Can you and Mal keep her occupied, so she doesn't think I'm up to something?"

"How very mysterious," she says with a laugh. "We have more baking to do, and Finley seemed to enjoy that yesterday, so maybe we can convince her to help us."

My mother's generosity and eagerness to make this special for Finley makes me love her even more. "Thank you for including her. It really means a lot to her," I say, my voice thick.

"We love having her," Mom says. "She's an absolute delight. And as much as she loves Christmas, well, let's just say I'm having fun watching her get excited over everything."

"Yeah." I think about how excited she was yesterday where nothing was too minor. She loved it all. "I am too."

She smiles softly as she pats my cheek. "She's a keeper, Alex. One in a million. Don't let her get away."

I feel a moment of panic, but there's no point freaking out over my family's inevitable reaction when they hear about our *breakup.* I'll deal with it when it happens. "Yeah."

When I go back into my room to get my things to take into the bathroom, Finley's eyes peek open.

"Go back to sleep," I say quietly. "I'm about to take a shower."

Her gaze lands on the mug in my hand. "What do you have there?"

"Coffee," I say, then lift it to my lips and take a sip. "The Mr. Coffee kind. My dad made it."

She sits up and reaches out her arm, wiggling her fingers at me to come closer. I walk to her side of the bed, my heart racing. What does she want?

When I'm next to her, she snatches the mug from my hand and takes a long sip.

Part of me wants to be irritated—that's *my* coffee, dammit—but she's so damn cute I can't seem to muster it up.

I lift a brow. "We're at the coffee-sharing stage of our relationship?"

"Drinks *and* food," she says, her eyes twinkling. "What's yours is mine."

"And you share with me?"

"We haven't reached *that* stage just yet." She takes another sip, then hands the mug to me. "I'll let you know when we do."

I can't help grinning at her.

Good, God. I'm smiling over her saying I have to share my coffee with her, but she doesn't have to share with me? What the hell is wrong with me?

I'm happy—that's what's wrong with me. I don't understand it, yet I am. And if I'm honest, I haven't felt this happy in years.

I'm not sure what to make of it. Maybe it's because this is my first real vacation from work in over two years. Or because I'm home with my family for Christmas.

You're a damn fool if you can't see that a huge part of it is because of Finley.

The hell it is. Other people can't make you happy.

Why is it so hard to accept that maybe she is part of the reason I'm happy?

I walk toward the door, but then I remember I need to tell her about our change of plans. Instead of towering over her, I sit at the foot of the bed so we're at eye level. "I'm switching up the plans for today, but it means we won't be able to go ice skating today."

"That's okay." The momentary disappointment in her eyes feels like a stab in the heart, but then she gives me a reassuring smile. "I hope you know you don't have to entertain me. You're here to be with your family. I can do things on my own."

"I still plan to take you ice skating," I say, ignoring her suggestion she can do things on her own. "Just not today, because I came up with something else that I think you might like better, and it's very time sensitive."

She studies me for a moment. "Wait. You changed your plans for *me*?" She asks it like it's impossible to believe.

"Yeah." I'm feeling uncomfortable. Will she be upset that I'm going to so much effort? Am I doing the wrong thing? I consider my plan again, but it doesn't feel wrong. It feels very, very right. All I can think about is how excited she'll be when she discovers what we're doing. "What kind of boyfriend would I be if I didn't try to make this the most special Christmas ever?"

She's quiet for a moment, and her eyes turn shiny. "Oh, Alex. It already is."

I feel like an asshole, and I don't even know why. Maybe because it takes so little to make her happy. Maybe because this seems like the bare minimum that a real boyfriend would do, and she acts like no one has ever treated her this well before.

It makes me want to track down all her previous boyfriends and beat the shit out of them for not treating her like the treasure she is.

What the hell?

Treasure?

Of course she's a treasure. I mean, come on. Look at her, excited over secret plans. For all she knows, I'm taking her to the dump at the edge of town. She's sweet and adorable. And any man who treated her like shit deserves a beating.

And just because I'm protective of her doesn't mean I want to sleep with her. I'm protective of my sister too.

Comparing Finley to my sister feels revolting, but I'm not going to analyze that thought. I need to focus.

"Well, I'm glad you think your trip has been perfect, but it's about to get even better. I'll shower, then you can get ready. We'll grab a quick breakfast and head out." I get up, but she reaches out and steals my mug again.

She looks impish as she takes a long sip, then hands it back. "Thank you, boyfriend."

I dash out of the room before I do something I'll regret, because for a split second, I wanted her to call me her boyfriend for real.

Chapter Twenty-Five

Finley

Alex still won't tell me where we're going, but from the way he made sure I was bundled up with a sweater, scarf, hat, and gloves, plus a pair of Mallory's insulated snow boots that thankfully fit, I know it has to be outside.

"Are we going sledding?" I ask as we drive out of town in the Wagoneer.

"Nope." He turns and gives me a quick look. "Do you *want* to go sledding?"

"If there's time." But after the last twenty-four hours, I wouldn't put it past him to do a U-turn and find a sledding hill, so I add, "But it's lower on the priority list. Just below a snowball fight."

He grins. "Okay. Good to know."

Now I'll be watching for a surprise snowball attack.

As he concentrates on the road, I study his profile. He didn't shave this morning, and his cheeks and chin are covered in dark stubble. I have a sudden urge to see if it's scratchy, to run my fingertips along his jaw to find out.

What am I thinking?

I hurriedly turn to face the windshield and notice we're heading toward the mountains.

"Are we going skiing?"

"No, but is *that* something you want to do?"

"Below sledding," I say.

He gives a sharp nod. "If you guess where we're going, do you want me to tell you? Or do you want me to keep it from you?"

"I want it to be a surprise." Then I laugh. "But I'll still keep trying to guess."

"Then how about I just shoot down anything you guess, even if you get it right?"

We drive another twenty minutes, before I notice a sign for a Christmas tree farm. My stomach flutters, but I refuse to let myself get excited. Then Alex turns onto a snow-packed narrow road.

He shoots me a look, and I'm dying to ask him, but I don't say anything until the road dead-ends at a snow-packed parking lot that only has two other cars.

I stare out the windshield at a man setting out orange cones next to a building that looks like a gift shop. "Why are we at a Christmas tree farm?"

He puts the car in park and turns to me. "I know you've only had one cup of coffee and half of mine"—a grin stretches across his face—"but I thought you'd be able to figure this one out by now."

I shake my head. "But why? Your parents already have a Christmas tree. A gorgeous one."

"I know," he says, "but I talked to Mom this morning, and we both think it would be great if we got a small one for our room. And then you could go to a Christmas tree farm. Surely that's on your list."

I gasp, certain I heard him wrong. "We're getting a real Christmas tree for *our room*?"

"Yep. Just for us," he says, his smile turning soft. "And we can go to sleep looking at it."

"It's hard to sleep when your eyes are open," I tease.

He taps my nose. "Don't be so literal. Are you ready to cut down a tree?"

I'm already opening the door and hopping out of the car.

Alex goes to the back of the car and opens the hatch. He grabs a thermos and hands it to me. "Mom made hot chocolate."

Then something else hits me. "But it's Christmas Eve, Alex."

"I can read a calendar," he says with a laugh as he pulls out a collapsible wagon. "And Christmas Eve is just in time, right? I told you our task was time sensitive." He drops a saw and a small ax into the wagon, along with a bundle of twine, then closes the hatch. "Let's go find us a tree."

We walk toward the trees, Alex pulling the wagon, me holding the thermos. The wind is cold, and stings my cheeks, but we trek through an already picked-over section. We both agree to be on the lookout for a small tree, about four feet tall. He cracks a joke about *Christmas Vacation*, and that it's my job to make sure there aren't any living creatures burrowed inside.

"Not it." My grin stretches my cheeks. "Isn't it your job as my boyfriend to look for wild creatures?"

"We should make a list of my duties," he teases. "Sharing my coffee and evicting wild creatures are obviously included."

"Those seem like givens. What kind of boyfriend wouldn't save his girlfriend from a wild animal?"

"If a bear jumps out of the woods, I promise to protect you with my life. But if a squirrel attacks." He shoots me an impish grin. "You're on your own."

I arch an eyebrow. "Are you afraid of squirrels, Alex?"

He shrugs. "Superman has his kryptonite. I have squirrels."

I laugh, a full body laugh. "Okay, you protect me from bears, and I'll protect you from squirrels."

His grin softens, and his gaze linger on me with a warmth that makes my stomach tumble. "Deal"

We reach a section of trees that meet our criteria and find one we both approve of.

Alex grabs the ax out of the wagon and kneels on the ground next to the tree, then looks up at me. "You look like you're freezing. You should drink some of the hot chocolate."

I unscrew the top, pour some into the cap, and take a sip. He chops at the trunk. After he whacks it several times, he sits upright and unfastens his coat, tossing it in the wagon.

"You're gonna freeze to death," I protest. It has to be in the upper teens today. The sun makes it feel warmer, but not by much.

"I'll be fine," he says as he chops at the trunk again. "I was getting hot."

He certainly is. The muscles of his back are stretching his black thermal long-sleeve shirt, and I suddenly feel flushed myself. I blame it on the hot chocolate, not the view in front of me. Alex's broad shoulders and well-toned arms are usually hiding under dress shirts, but now they're bulging with each swing of the ax.

Since the tree is small, it doesn't take long for it to fall to the ground. He looks up at me with a grin. "Timber." Alex stands and brushes the snow off his knees, then grabs the twine to wrap up the tree.

"Can I help?" I'm feeling guilty about standing here enjoying the view while he's performing all the physical labor. "We're here because of me, but you're doing everything."

"I'm good," he says, glancing up at me. "Are you warm enough? You still look cold."

"I'm okay." I take another sip of my drink which has already cooled off. "You look like you know what you're doing there." He's already almost finished wrapping up the tree.

"I used to work here," he says.

"What?" I ask in surprise. "Here?"

"Yep, for a couple of years in high school. I got pretty good at both chopping down trees and wrapping them up."

"I'm in the presence of a pro," I tease him. "I should have been taking notes."

"Next time," he says lightly, then seems to realize what he said, and he looks down quickly.

Next time. The words lodge in my chest—a reminder this is my once-in-a-lifetime Christmas. I need to soak in every moment.

And ignore the twist in my heart that there won't be a next time.

He ties off his last string, then tosses the twine into the

wagon. Picking up the tree, he leans it over his shoulder, then grabs the handle of the wagon. "Let's go pay for it."

"I can pull the wagon," I protest.

"I've got it."

I fall into step beside him, trying to memorize the moment before it turns into a memory.

The wind hits us head-on as we walk to the gift shop. Alex props the tree against the side of the building, and we both go inside to pay. The woman at the counter recognizes him and asks what he's been up to. He tells her he's living in Atlanta and home for the week.

I browse the items they have for sale, giving him some privacy, when he surprises me by introducing me as his girlfriend. He stretches out his arm for me to join him.

I walk over next to him, trying not to trip over my own feet.

"Hi," I say, feeling uncharacteristically shy, reminding myself he only introduced me because if his family finds out he didn't, they'll ask why.

The woman gives me an appraising glance, then nods approvingly. "You did good, Alex."

He wraps an arm around my back and smiles down at me, soft and proud. "I know, right?"

My heart flutters.

Not real. Not real.

But I can pretend, right?

His hand brushes my lower back as he reaches for his wallet to pay, and for a second I forget how to breathe. By the time he's finished paying, I've pasted on a smile and convinced myself it's just part of the act.

After we walk out, we head to the Wagoneer. The tree's small enough that it fits in the back. Once we get in the car, Alex turns on the engine to warm it up. I take off my mittens to pour a fresh cup of hot chocolate and hand it to him.

When his fingers brush mine, he frowns. "Your fingers are freezing."

"I'm okay," I say, tucking them between my legs.

He takes a sip of his drink, then sets the cap on the dashboard and gently pulls my hands free, wrapping them between his. There's no center console, and I haven't put my seat belt on yet, so he tugs me a little closer.

"You don't have to do that, Alex," I say, my stomach fluttering.

"I can't have you getting frostbite," he says, his voice low and rough.

The timbre of his voice sends a thrill through my spine, and suddenly the car feels smaller. He's too close and yet not close enough. I'm terrified I might do something stupid, like kiss him.

"Thanks, I'm okay." I ease my hands free and slide over to my side. "We should get back. We still need to go pick up the stockings."

"Yeah," he says, his voice still husky. "Agreed."

We're quiet the entire way home. The air between us feels charged, like the space is holding its breath. I'm not sure what he's thinking, but I'm telling myself to be careful. Unrequited lust is one thing. Acting on it is another. And if I cross that line—if I let myself want what I shouldn't—there's no way I'll be able to stay.

And I really want to stay.

When we get back, I walk through the back door first and find Valerie and Mallory in the kitchen, waiting for us.

"Did you get a tree?" Mallory asks excitedly.

"We did," Alex says as he walks in behind me, the tree over his shoulder.

"We put everything in your room," Valerie says.

My first thought is *thank goodness we made the bed and hid the pillows in the closet*. My second is to ask her what she means by "everything", but Alex is already heading upstairs. When we reach the room, I see several cardboard boxes stacked in front of the dresser, each labeled "Christmas ornaments" in thick black marker. There's also a Christmas tree stand waiting beside them.

Alex makes quick work of getting the tree in the stand. He

grabs several strings of lights and starts to weave them into the tree, but I convince him to turn the lights on first so we can get a better idea about coverage.

"Sounds like you've done this a time or two," Alex says.

"I decorate all the trees at Beans to Go," I say, then tell him how the owner has given me money to add more trees and decorations every year and how I stretch the money by searching thrift stores and yard sales.

Once we get the lights strung, we open the ornament boxes. They've been picked over, and I suspect these are the leftovers from the downstairs tree, but I'm not complaining. Alex picks up ornaments and asks me where to hang them. When I tell him to hang them anywhere, he teases me, saying, "Are you kidding? That's like Picasso telling a middle-school football player to dab some paint on his masterpiece."

I grab an embroidered lumbar pillow that says *To All A Goodnight* in one of the boxes and throw it at him, laughing as I say, "That's what you get for making fun of me."

It smacks him on the side of the head, and he freezes. For a terrifying moment, I'm worried I've gone too far, but then he turns to me, a grin spreading across his face. "Looks like someone's really dying for a snowball fight."

He picks up the pillow and tosses it back to me, but he's thrown it like we're playing catch, and I easily catch it.

"Knock, knock," Mallory says from the open doorway as she raps on the doorjamb. "You two look like you're up to no good."

I turn to her, beaming. "Just decorating our tree."

"I hope you checked it for squirrels," she says, looking it over.

"We checked," Alex says. "Twice."

"Well then, you may have started a new tradition." She smiles her approval. "We all might put trees in our rooms."

"Not this year," Alex says. "This year it's just for Finley."

"Don't be silly," I say with a frown. "Other people can have trees in their rooms if they want."

Mallory walks away, then turns back at the door. "Oh! I

almost forgot. Mom made some beef and barley soup for lunch along with some corn muffins. Hey, Finley, we're going to do more baking this afternoon if you want to help. She wants to get it all done before Grant and Eloise show up around dinnertime."

"You're doing *more* baking?" I ask in surprise. "She said y'all got everything done yesterday."

She shrugs. "She realized she gave most of the Christmas candy to the neighbors and that's Grant's favorite part of Christmas, so... more baking." Her face brightens. "What do you say? Do you want to help?"

I do, but we're supposed to pick up the stockings this afternoon. "Yeah, but..."

"You stay, Fin," Alex says. "There's no need for you to come with me to get the... package."

I feel bad, because it was my idea to get stockings, and now he's stuck picking them up.

But he seems to be able to read my mind—or more likely my face. "Finley," he assures me, "you know you want to bake. You stay here, and I'll take care of it. I really don't mind."

I notice the pile of bags on the floor. "And when you get back, maybe we can wrap presents."

Mallory's mouth drops. "You haven't wrapped your presents yet, dude?"

"Of course not," he says. "They'd just get crushed in the suitcase."

She frowns as she stares at his open carry-on case on the floor. "Your suitcase isn't very big."

"You know what they say about good things coming in small packages," Alex says.

Mallory shrugs. "But some of us like our packages big." Then she flips her hair over her shoulder and flounces off.

"Did my sister just make a sex joke?" he asks with fear in his eyes.

"Yeah," I say with a laugh. "I think she did."

He closes his eyes and shudders. "I think I'm going to need to bleach my brain."

"Don't be so dramatic." I grin, then turn to check out our handiwork.

He studies it too then shoves his hands into his front jeans' pockets. "I should have bought some better ornaments."

I shake my head. "No. It's perfect just as it is." It may be covered with leftover, mismatched ornaments, but it's our tree. And I love it.

"It's missing a star at the top," he says, then walks over to the boxes and shuffles things around.

"It doesn't need a star," I say, mostly because there isn't a tree topper in the boxes. I've already checked three times.

"We can't leave it bare," he says, his brow furrowed.

I walk over and grab his stocking cap off the dresser and put it on top of the tree. "There. Now it has a topper."

He laughs. "I think you got the tree confused with a snowman."

I cross my arms over my chest as I admire our work. "I don't believe in stereotypes."

He watches me with an intense gaze for several seconds, long enough that I feel uncomfortable. It's not a lustful gaze, more like I'm a language he doesn't know how to read, but he's trying.

I'm not sure what I said that could make him so pensive, but I need to lighten the mood again, so I throw the pillow at him and rush for the door.

"What was that for?" he calls after me with a laugh.

"Practicing up for our future snowball fight."

Chapter Twenty-Six

Finley

The afternoon is filled with candy making. Valerie teaches me how to make fudge, peanut brittle, toffee, and a whole assortment of other desserts, but I keep checking the back door, waiting for Alex to return. He's been gone for nearly two hours, and I feel guilty that he's having to pick up the stockings on his own. It was my idea to get them, and I'm sure he has better things to do—especially on Christmas Eve—than running an errand for me.

I'm just about to text him when he walks through the back door. He's carrying several bags, and it's obvious he's picked up more than the stockings.

When he sees my confusion, he grins and lifts one of his hands and mouths, *wrapping paper.*

Somehow in my excitement to help in the kitchen, I'd forgotten we still need to wrap gifts.

Valerie glances over her shoulder in time to see him bound up the steps. "Finley, do you want to go up and check in on Alex?"

I do, but... "We're not done yet."

"All that's left is the clean up," she says dismissively. "And there's not much left since we've been cleaning as we go."

Mallory gives me a mischievous grin. "Plus, you should probably help Alex wrap presents."

Valerie releases a good-natured snort. "It's not hard to wrap a gift card."

"I think he bought actual presents this year," Mallory says with a sly grin. "I'm pretty sure he got them yesterday at the market. Apparently, Finley's a good influence on him."

"Nah." I smile. "He did just fine on his own." I might have shamed him into it, but he came up with most of the ideas, not that I'll rat him out.

Mallory makes a face, clearly unconvinced.

"We have a tradition for wrapping gifts," Valerie says. "Feel free to borrow it if you like."

"You mean, *you* have a tradition," Mallory teases.

Valerie shoots her an ornery grin. "I have no trouble owning it."

"It started when we were little," Mallory says. "Mom would take an afternoon before Christmas, then lock herself in her room with the presents, wrapping paper, and a bottle of wine. She'd refuse to open the door until hours later. Even when we stood outside and pounded on it."

Valerie lifts her chin. "I had three rambunctious sons and a precocious daughter," Valerie says. "I was overwhelmed with everything that needed to be done. A little wine and solitude saved my sanity."

"Sounds like survival to me." I laugh, imagining the chaos.

She crosses to the fridge and pulls out an unopened bottle of rosé. "If you want to continue the tradition, feel free."

"I don't have four rowdy kids," I joke.

"No, but you'll be trapped with three rowdy men and one overzealous woman. The principle still applies." She lifts an eyebrow, still holding the bottle out.

"When in Rome," I say, taking the bottle from her. "Oh, wait. I don't want to take your bottle if you're saving it."

"I've already wrapped," she says with a reassuring nod.

"And she's got five more bottles chilling in the fridge in the basement," Mallory laughs.

"Well, in that case..."

She and her mom load a tray with a bottle opener, two wine glasses, and a plate of assorted Christmas cookies. "Fuel." Valerie says.

"Thank you." I take the tray and head upstairs, surprised to find the bedroom door is locked.

Balancing the trap on my hip, I knock. "Alex, it's me."

"Just a minute." There's a shuffle inside, then about ten seconds later, he opens the door. "Sorry—I locked it in case Mallory came snooping." His gaze drops to the tray then he looks at me, one brow raised.

"Your mom handed me her gift-wrapping tradition—"

"Getting tipsy while wrapping presents," he nods with a grin. "Check."

"And your sister thought we needed fuel to keep us going."

"That tracks."

When I step inside, my eyes widen. Our suitcases are shoved to the side of the bed. At the foot of the bed, he's arranged four rolls of wrapping paper, three different kinds of tape, spools of ribbon, a heap of stick-on-bows, and even two pairs of scissors.

"Wow." I take it all in. "You thought of everything."

Grinning, he takes the tray from me and sets it on the small dresser. "I wasn't sure what you'd like, so I got options. Are they okay?"

I barely glance at them. I'm so giddy he thought to buy wrapping supplies, they could be covered in poop emojis and I'd still be thrilled. "They're perfect."

He narrows his eyes. "Did you even look at them?"

I flash him a guilty smile. "Of course, I did. It's all very... festive."

"First wine." He picks up the bottle and corkscrew, arching a brow. "I suspect she's premedicating you."

"What's that supposed to mean?"

"She's fortifying you for when Grant and Eloise get here."

The reminder drops like an anchor, pulling down my light mood. Somehow, I'd forgotten about that part. "Will he be pissed?"

"He already knows he's sleeping in the rec room," Alex says, twisting the corkscrew into the bottle. "Eloise, though... when she's in a mood, she's a handful."

"What puts her in a mood?"

"Your guess is as good as ours, but it's a pretty safe bet tonight's mood will be about our bed."

I cringe, hating that I'm about to be the spark for family drama.

"Don't you feel bad," he says as the cork pops free. "This isn't about you."

"It has *everything* to do with me."

"I thought *I* was playing the role of the narcissist in this relationship," he teases, pouring wine into one of the glasses.

That makes me cringe. "I never called you a narcissist."

"You didn't have to." He hands me the glass with a smirk. "I earned the title fair and square."

I take it, still watching him, unsettled by the strange dance we're caught in. He's playing the role of attentive boyfriend a little too well—and right now, it isn't for his family's benefit. We're alone. I'm the only audience to his performance.

He pours himself a glass and lifts it towards mine. For a second, his expression makes me think he's about to say something serious, then he deadpans, "May our gifts not look like they were dragged in by the family dog."

Laughing, I click my glass into his. "Speak for yourself. I do a lovely job of wrapping gifts."

"I don't doubt it," he says. "Which is why you should wrap mine too."

"Oh no." I wag a finger at him. "You're a fully grown man, perfectly capable of working with paper and tape."

He gives me a pleading look. "Even if it looks like a kindergartener wrapped them?"

"Especially then." I grin. "All the more fodder for your family to rib you."

We sip some wine, then settle on the floor at the end of the bed. Before long, we're swiping each other's tape and scissors and trading jabs—me mocking the lopsided mess he calls a gift for his father, him accusing me of being a "Christmas overachiever" when my corners come out perfect.

We finish the wine, and I blame my tipsiness on the undeniable pull toward him. He's sitting closer than when we started, but maybe it's just my imagination. We're friends. Friends having fun.

Despite the undercurrent tugging at me, I'm happy. I've had more fun with Alex over the past two days than I've had in ages.

We're about to have a race cutting the wrapping paper for our last gifts—I'll have to sneak away later to wrap his—when the doorbell rings. We both freeze, scissors poised at the edges of the paper.

Alex shoots me a wicked gleam.

"What?" But then the realization hits. It's nearly five. My breath sticks in my chest. "Your brother's here," I whisper.

His merriment fades, replaced by a quiet reassurance. "It'll be okay," he says softly. "I promise."

I glance down at our unfinished wrapping. We were so close to being done. "Should we finish or go down to greet them?"

He looks like he'd rather stay hidden but finally nods. "Let's go down, then come back and finish."

"Okay." It seems like a good compromise.

We throw a blanket over the half-wrapped gifts and head down the front staircase at the other end of the hall. My stomach is in knots as I trail Alex down the steps. He stops at the bottom, watching his family.

Valerie has her arms around her son, while his father and brother linger to the side. Mallory hangs back, glancing at the front door.

"Grant!" Valerie gushes. "I'm so happy you're home!"

"Yeah," he says. "Me too." His tone doesn't match his words. "Sorry I didn't get here earlier."

"Well, you're here now." She hugs him again, then glances

past him. "Is Eloise still in the car? Does she need help with her bags?"

Grant's jaw tightens as he turns, his gaze slicing toward Alex before shifting to me. The look he gives me could pin me to the staircase. "Eloise didn't come."

Alex goes rigid. "Why?"

"We broke up this morning." Grant's voice is tight, his stare locked firmly on his brother. "And it's all your fault."

Chapter Twenty-Seven

I'm still too stunned by his announcement to let his anger sink in.

Eloise didn't come.

I brought Finley for nothing?

Horror flashes across Mom's face. "Grant! You're being rude!"

"Why?" he shoots back sarcastically. "Because I'm calling Alex on his shit?"

Her gaze sharpens, her voice deadly calm. "You're being inexcusably rude to our guest."

Grant's glare swings to Finley, and the hair on the back of my neck stands on end. My fists clench at my sides before I even register the movement. Rationally, I know he'd never lay a hand on her. But reason doesn't matter. Every instinct in me is coiled, ready to step between them without a second thought.

"Aw," Grant says with a grin that doesn't reach his eyes. "The infamous Finley."

"Grant!" Mallory gasps.

I feel Finley shrink behind me. I expected Grant to be pissed, but I never thought he'd go after her. If I'd had any inkling, I would've told her to stay upstairs while I deal with his attitude.

I slide an arm around her waist, snuggling her into my side, and force myself to meet his accusation head-on. "Breaking up with *your* girlfriend has nothing to do with me—or Finley." My voice comes out so tight it scrapes my throat.

"I'll say," Mallory mutters.

Grant whirls on her, pointing a finger. "Don't you start."

"That's enough!" Dad's voice cracks through the entryway, sharp and commanding. We all freeze. "It's Christmas Eve."

My siblings stay silent, Mallory grimaces at the scolding, but Grant still looks defiant.

"Let's get your shit out of the car," Tyler says, striding forward. He slings an arm around Grant's shoulders and all but drags him out the front door.

Mom looks on the verge of tears. She steps toward us. "Finley, I'm so sorry."

"That's okay," Finley says sweetly, forcing a smile. "He's upset about his breakup."

Mom frowns. "It's still no excuse."

"I say good riddance," Mallory mutters in disgust.

"Mallory," Mom warns. "You might not like her, but obviously your brother did."

Mallory makes a face that makes it clear that she thinks Grant's taste in women sucks, but my focus is on Finley, standing so still she looks like she's bracing for another hit.

I tug her closer, my arm tightening at her back, and I wrestle with what to do. Should I take her upstairs, away from this mess, and make sure she's okay? Or stay here and pretend everything's fine? If I knew her better, maybe I'd know which she'd want.

And then it hits me again—Eloise isn't here. Which means Grant and I would be sharing the bedroom if I'd never asked Finley to come. Technically, according to our contract, I could let Finley go home. But not tomorrow—on Christmas Day? That would be heartless. The day after?

My heart stutters. The truth is, I don't want her to leave. At all. I like having her here. She's been fun, and after the grind of this past year, she's been a relief. A distraction I didn't know I needed.

But Mom is still watching Finley, concern etched in her face. "Finley, would you like to help me with dinner?"

Finley glances quickly toward the door, and before she can

answer, I cut in. "Can she come down in a bit? We still have a few more presents to wrap."

"Of course," Mom says. She hesitates, her voice softening. "I just—"

The front door crashes open, and Grant and Tyler come stomping back in. Grant's carrying a duffel bag and a shopping bag, while Tyler hefts a large cardboard box full of wrapped presents.

"I'll just put these presents under the tree." Tyler carries the gifts to the living room.

"And I guess I'll head down to the basement," Grant mutters bitterly, disappearing through the kitchen.

I squeeze Finley's hand, but she doesn't look at me. Her gaze follows my brother instead.

"Let's go finish." I tug her gently toward the stairs. We walk into my room, and she lets my hand fall. I shut the door behind us, then I watch as she takes the blanket off the gifts, sinks to the floor, and picks up her scissors.

Helplessness gnaws at me. Does she want to talk about what just happened? Pretend it never did? Or not talk at all?

"You need to finish your wrapping," she says, trying to sound lighthearted, but it misses.

We should have never gone downstairs. We should have stayed up here and finished wrapping. Then she'd be laughing and teasing me about how bad I am instead of—this. She's not sulking or pouting. She's just... sad. And it's tearing me apart.

Frustration builds in my chest, but I lower myself beside her, grasping for a way back to the easy banter we had before. "You're cheating."

Her head snaps toward me, her eyes huge.

"We were racing before we got interrupted, and you've already started without me."

"Don't tell me you're not above cheating," she says. A grin tugs at her mouth, but it doesn't reach her eyes.

God, I hate this. I have to fix it.

"Finley—"

Her mouth twists, pain flashes in her eyes. She shakes her head once. "Please don't."

"But—"

She leans over and attacks the paper with quick, furious cuts. "I'm gonna beat you."

I watch her for a moment longer, then pick up my scissors. I win, of course. But mine looks like I wadded up some wrapping paper and plastered it in tape. Her gift looks like it's been professionally wrapped.

The irony is, she was wrapping Grant's present.

When she finishes, she starts gathering scraps of wrapping paper.

"Do you want to hang out up here?" I ask.

She turns to me, pale and stricken. "Okay."

My breath catches. *No! That's not what I meant.*

"It was a question, Finley," I say, surprised when it sounds pleading. "I'm not *telling* you to stay up here. I just don't want you to feel any more uncomfortable than you already are."

Her eyes glisten, and she says in a shaky voice, "In light of the current situation, I realize that I'm no longer needed here. I think I should go home tomorrow."

The words gut me because she's right—she doesn't have to be here anymore for my little stick-it-to-Grant charade, but the thought of her leaving fills me with panic.

"You don't have to go," I try to sound casual. "I mean, Grant and Eloise have broken up more times than I can count. Chances are, she'll show up in a day or two, and if you go, then I'll be kicked out."

Her response is a tight smile.

"Do you *want* to go?" I ask, then realize it sounds like a passive aggressive way to tell her to go. "For what it's worth, I want you to stay."

Her eyes widen slightly, then she gives me a grim smile. "Because Eloise might come."

Is that why I want her to stay? The excuse is safer than examining the truth. "Yeah," I say with a casual shrug, then add, "But I understand if you want to leave. I never expected Grant to come at you like that. But I can promise you that Mom won't let it happen again."

Her mouth twists as fresh tears flood her eyes. "I really don't want to cause drama with your family."

"You're not," I say, a sliver of guilt oozing in my chest. *She's* not the cause of this drama—that responsibility falls squarely on me. "Mom and Mallory love you and they'd be crushed if you leave. Especially on Christmas Day." I take a breath, and lower my voice, hoping I come across as reassuring. "But I want you to do what *you* want to do, Finley. If it's too uncomfortable to stay, I'll book the next available flight out of here, but I know Mom and Mal want you to stay." My throat tightens. "And I want you to stay too."

Her gaze drops to the mess on the floor. "In case Eloise shows up," she murmurs.

That's not why but I'm not sure she'd stay for just me. Especially if she knows how I really feel about her. So the Eloise excuse is as good as any.

"I'm going to take the presents down and put them under the tree," I say. "And you can decide what you want to do when I'm done, okay?"

"Yeah." She returns to her task of cleaning up the bits of paper. "Sounds good."

I gather the pile of gifts and leave the room. My hands are full, so I leave the door open behind me and head down the front staircase. After stacking the gifts under the tree, I head into the kitchen and find my family gathered around the island.

"What the hell was that?" I snap at Grant. "How dare you talk to my girlfriend like that?"

"How dare you magically come up with a girlfriend in two days," he shoots back, just as hot.

Mom exhales sharply, and her eyes sink closed.

"Grant." Dad's voice cuts like steel. "You will apologize to Finley the moment you see her."

Grant's jaw sets, but he stays silent.

"Is Finley still upstairs?" Mallory's wearing her worried face and wringing her hands.

"Yeah," I say, weighing how much to say. The last thing I want is to betray Finley's trust, but they need to prepare for the possible fall out. "She's thinking about leaving."

My mother's eyes fly open as Mallory lets out a horrified, "No!"

"I think I've convinced her to stay," I add quickly. "But I also told her it's her choice. The last thing I want is for her to feel unwelcome here."

"Especially on Christmas," Mom says softly.

Grant's shoulders ease, his body losing some of its rigid defiance.

"She doesn't have any other family, you know," Mallory says, shoving Grant's arm. "She's a literal orphan and you're putting her out on the street on Christmas!"

"I'm doing no such thing!" Grant protests. "I didn't tell her to leave!"

"You sure made it so she wouldn't want to stay," Tyler says. The room goes still as we all stare at him in shock. Tyler almost never wades into family disputes, preferring to watch from the sidelines.

Grant's brow practically shoots to his hairline.

Tyler shoves his hand in his front pockets. "She's a sweet woman. She obviously has a serious lack of judgement in men if she's with Alex—"

"Hey!" I cut in.

"—but she's good for him. And you treated her like crap." His gaze could bore holes into Grant.

"How was I supposed to know?" Grant fires back, defensive.

"It's called manners, Grant." Mom sighs. "Honestly, you'd think I raised you kids in a zoo."

"Hey!" Mallory protests.

Mom gives her a gentle smile. "You were raised with the koalas. Sweet and cuddly."

"And stoned on eucalyptus," Grant mutters, and Mal shoots him a glare.

Mom's focus swings back to Grant, her expression hardening. "You *will* be kind to that girl. And if you aren't, we'll take your presents away."

Outrage spreads across Grant's face. "I'm not ten years old, Mom."

"Then stop acting like you are," Mom counters crisply. She turns to me, her face softening. "What can we do to make Finley feel more comfortable? Make Grant eat dinner out in the garage?"

"Hey!" Grant protests, but she ignores him.

"I'm not sure," I admit. "We agreed I'd bring down the gifts, then she'd decide if she's coming down."

"Tell her that I'm making our traditional Christmas Eve dinner," Mom says. "She loves taking part in our traditions."

I want to tell her the reason Finley loves taking part in them is because Mom and Mal have gone out of their way to make her feel welcome—and now that's been threatened. But saying it out loud would just be beating a dead horse. "I'll tell her."

I'm about to head back upstairs, when my phone buzzes in my pocket. I nearly ignore it, desperate to check on Finley, but her name on the screen stops me cold.

I'm going to call my friends. I'll let you know when I'm done

A knot tightens in my gut. Will her honorary grandmothers hire assassins to take me out after letting her get hurt? Or worse—will they convince her to come home? I want to go up and make things right, but Barb and Mirna will likely do a better job of comforting her than I can.

What do I know about comforting women?

I text back:

Tell Barb I said I'm doing everything I can to make this right

Then I send:

Mom's cooking our traditional Christmas Eve dinner, and you'll never guess what it is. So come down when you're done. Or if you want me to come up, just say the word

Her only response is a thumbs-up to my last text.

Funny how a girl I barely knew a week ago suddenly feels like the only thing that matters.

Chapter Twenty-Eight

Finley

After Alex walks out of the room, I shut the door behind him and sink down on the edge of the bed, fighting tears.

Why did I come? Why did I ever think this was a good idea? *Of course* Grant is furious. He has every right to be, especially since this relationship isn't real.

I grab my phone from the bed and pull up a travel site. Tomorrow's flights are astronomical, and the day after isn't much better. My stomach sinks. I don't have that kind of money.

What am I going to do?

Of course, Alex would pay for it. He's already said I could leave if I wanted to. But that would mean breaking our contract. The thought of letting him foot the bill makes me feel even smaller, especially when he's made it clear he wants me to stay.

There's only one other option. Barb and Mirna. But it's Christmas Eve and they're probably busy with their own families.

Still, desperation wins. I text Alex my plan, then call Barb anyway.

To my surprise, she answers right away. Behind her, Christmas music blares, underscored by a child's wail, "I want a candy cane!"

"Merry Christmas Eve, Barb!" I say, but the words catch. Guilt floods my chest. I can't ask this of her or Mirna. I need to suck it up and be a big girl.

Barb's smile vanishes at once. "What's wrong?"

"Who said anything was wrong?" I counter quickly. "Can't I just wish you Merry Christmas?"

"You can, but we both know that's not why you called," she

answers. In the background, another kid shrieks something about a stolen Santa. Barb walks into a room and shuts the door behind her, muting the chaos. "Now tell me what happened, or I'll call Alex and ask him."

Mortification floods me, because I know she's not bluffing. "Alex's brother showed up."

Her eyes light up with interest. "The hot one from yesterday?"

"No, the one whose bed I stole," I say sullenly.

Her lips purse. "You didn't steal his bed. Now tell me what happened."

I grimace. "He was pissed, of course."

I've only seen Barb angry on a couple of occasions, and both times were terrifying—even if her fury wasn't aimed at me. Right now, she looks even scarier. "He was pissed *at you*?"

I'm tempted to lie, afraid of what she'll do if I say yes. But I'm equally afraid of what she'll do if she finds out I lied. "Yeah."

Her eyes bulge and her nostrils flare. "And where was Alex during this?"

"He was standing right in front of me. And for a second, with the way his hands fisted at his sides—I honestly thought he might punch him."

Barb's face softens, dreamy now. "That would be hot. Total alpha-male-claiming-his-mate behavior. Just like the man in *Fighting the Posse for What's Mine*."

I narrow my gaze. "I'm *not* his mate."

Why does the thought send a shiver down my spine? Barb's books must be getting to me through osmosis.

She makes a face. "You said you thought he was going to punch him. What did he do instead?"

"Alex told him not to talk to his girlfriend like that."

"Girlfriend, eh?" she drawls, her eyes widening with exaggerated interest.

I sigh. "He was in front of his family."

She doesn't look convinced. "Where are you now?"

"In our room," I say forlornly. My gaze drifts to the Christmas tree glowing in the corner, the only light in the room now. "Alex took me to a Christmas tree farm this morning. We got a Christmas tree for our bedroom," I switch the view on my phone so she can see.

"Oh." Her expression softens. "That's one pretty tree."

I laugh. "It's full of leftover ornaments, and I put Alex's stocking cap on for a topper. It's not pretty, but that's okay. No, it's more than okay. It's one of the best trees I've ever had."

"Because you got it with Alex," she finishes softly.

I don't acknowledge it, even if it's true. "I want to come home."

Barb's face freezes, then she narrows her eyes. "Turn around the camera. I want to see your face."

I switch it back around.

"*Why* do you want to come home?"

"I'm causing drama with Alex's family. It's not fair to Grant."

Her expression sharpens. "What about his girlfriend?"

"They broke up," I say, my voice low. "Because of me."

"Because of you?" Barb asks, incredulous. "What happened? Did the brother take one look at you, realize you were the only woman for him, and his girlfriend stormed off after slashing his tires, then hopped on the back of a passing motorcycle?"

I laugh despite myself. "That's oddly specific, but no. They broke up before they got here. I think she broke up over the sleeping arrangements."

She narrows her gaze. "Then she must not be much of a girl-friend if a bunk bed was her breaking point." She taps her chin thoughtfully. "Although it worked out for the heroine in *One Man Above Me, One Man Below*."

It's a sofa bed, but I let that go and give her a flat stare.

"What?" she asks in mock innocence. "Margo was very happy at the end. A *very* happy ending."

"I'm talking about Grant, not the woman sandwiched between two men in your book."

Barb's laugh bubbles through the phone. "Two men? Don't limit that poor girl to just two."

I drag in a deep breath. "This isn't a romance novel, Barb. This is real life. And I want to come home."

Her smile falters, then she suddenly starts stabbing the screen with her finger.

"What are you doing?" I ask, half laughing.

"Sending out the distress signal."

"What distress signal?"

She ignores me, still poking, then leans back with a triumphant grin.

"Barb…" I warn.

Her face lights up. "There she is." The screen flickers, goes black, and then a couple of seconds later, Mirna's face pops into a square above Barb's.

"What's the Code Eggnog?" Mirna asks in a panic, flushed and breathless. Behind her, a chorus is butchering *Oh Holy Night*.

"What's a Code Eggnog?" I ask, blinking. "And where are you?"

"It's the code for a Finley emergency," she whispers fiercely, shoving her phone so close I'm staring at her mouth. "And I'm at church."

"Mother," a woman scolds sharply in the background. "Did you really answer that *here*?"

Horror shoots through me. "Wait—you're actually in the sanctuary?"

"Of course I am." Mirna's lip curls. She's so close I can see her mustache hairs growing back after her last wax. "That's where I was when Barb called the Code Eggnog."

"You don't have to stay in the church, you fool," Barb hollers, her voice so loud I'm certain half the congregation just heard.

"Mother!" the woman hisses again. "Get off the phone!"

"This can wait until later," I say quickly, horrified.

"Like hell it can!" Barb bellows—right as the choir stops

singing. The silence is absolute, broken only by a single, distant cough.

I go rigid, certain the entire church just heard Barb curse.

The camera swings upward, giving me a dizzying shot of the painted cathedral ceiling while a storm of angry whispers rise in the background. "Excuse me, excuse me," Mirna mutters as she shoves her way through pews.

The view jerks, heels click on marble until her face reappears—this time farther back. Behind her looms the altar, and a priest in full robes, watching her retreat with a frown that could curdle the communion wine.

I'm mortified but also stunned. If it had been Barb, I'd roll my eyes and chalk it up to another Thursday. But this is prim and proper Mirna.

At last, she pushes through a heavy wooden door and plants herself beside a Christmas tree. "What's the emergency?" she asks as though it's perfectly normal to abandon a Christmas Eve Mass mid-hymn.

I make a face. "Do we want to discuss what just happened?"

"No," Mirna says stiffly. "We will never speak of it again."

"Why did you answer?" Barb cackles. "You could've called me back."

"You said it was a Finley emergency. Of course I answered."

My heart swells with love for these two women. "I'm sorry we disturbed you, but it's not a real emergency."

"Barb!" Mirna hisses through her teeth.

"Don't listen to her," Barb rushes in. "It's *definitely* an emergency. She wants to come home."

Mirna's face goes blank. "What happened?"

"Alex's evil brother showed up," Barb announces, far too gleeful. "He tried to kidnap her, and he and Alex got into a huge fight, and then someone called the police."

Mirna gasps.

"That is *not* what happened!" I protest.

Barb squints. "Well, it *could* have happened."

I give Mirna the short version, ending with the truth—I just want to come home. When I finish, her lips purse. "I thought you were having fun. Has that changed?"

"No," I say carefully. At least not until about fifteen minutes ago.

"Alex took her to cut down a Christmas tree this morning, and they put it up in their room," Barb chimes in.

Mirna's lips pinch tighter. "And what book is that from?"

"That one's actually true," I say quickly. "He thought chopping down a tree at a Christmas tree farm might be on my list." I angle the phone so she can see the little tree glowing in the corner.

Mirna studies it in silence, then asks, "So if you're having fun, why do you want to come home?"

"Because of Grant," I whisper, my heart aching all over again. "He's really upset I'm here."

"Sounds like that's his problem," Mirna says in disgust.

"Everyone's upset," I say. "And I already love Alex's mom and sister so much..." My voice cracks as tears sting my eyes. "This is Grant's family. I'm ruining his Christmas."

They're both quiet for a moment before Mirna asks, "Does Alex know you want to leave? Does he want you to?"

I sniff. "He knows, but he wants me to stay."

A firm look fills her eyes. "Then you stay."

"But he says he wants me to stay in case Eloise shows up."

Mirna arches a brow. "The man who took you to a Christmas tree farm on *Christmas Eve* only wants you there in case his brother's girlfriend shows up?"

A tear slips down my cheek. "I don't know what to believe anymore."

They're both quiet again, then Mirna says, "Well, you can't come home on Christmas Day. You need to stay until at least the day after."

The thought of dragging this tension out makes my stomach churn. But I can stay in our room. Or wander around downtown.

This is a Christmas town—surely something would be open. "Okay."

Mirna offers a tight smile. "See how tonight and tomorrow go. If you still want to come home after that, we'll work something out. Okay?"

Fresh tears spill over. "Thank you, Mirna."

"But for what it's worth," she adds gently. "If Alex wants you to stay, you should stay."

"Mirna..." My voice trembles.

"We love you," she says simply.

"We sure do," Barb chimes in.

Emotion squeezes my chest. "I love you guys too," I manage through my tears. "Thank you."

Maybe they're right. Maybe I should stay. But wanting to and believing I belong here are two different things.

I stare at the phone. I told Alex I'd let him know when I'm done with my call, but I'm scared. Scared he changed his mind about me staying. Scared that his family will resent my presence. But fear never got me anywhere. I could wait for him to come up, or I could take charge and go down on my own.

I chose the latter.

Chapter Twenty-Nine

Mom's roped all of us into making dinner, but the tension's so thick I feel like I'm wading through a swamp.

Grant's still pissed, and I can't shake the thought that most of his anger isn't aimed at Finley—it's at Eloise. I wasn't exaggerating when I told Finley there was a good chance Eloise will show up this week. Grant and Eloise's relationship has always been a revolving door.

I'm setting the table while Tyler and Grant chop vegetables for a salad. Dad sits at the island, nursing a drink, while Mom and Mal bustle around the stove. Finley's been upstairs for more than a half hour, and though I promised her space, I'm two seconds from going upstairs to check on her when she appears in the doorway.

I take a step toward her, then force myself to stop. "Hey," I say carefully. "How was your call with your grandmothers?"

"I thought she didn't have any family," Grant mutters under his breath.

"They're her neighbors, asshole," Tyler snaps before I can.

But the damage is done. The stricken look on Finley's face is like an ice pick to my chest. Without thinking, I set the stack of plates on the table and cross the room, pulling her into a tight hug.

"How'd your call go?" I whisper against her ear.

"Good," she says, then pulls back quickly and plasters on a polite smile that doesn't reach her eyes. "Is there anything I can do to help?"

"We've got it covered," Mom says, casting a long look at her. "You can help Alex finish setting the table, if you like. Dinner's almost ready."

"It smells good," Finley says as she moves toward the table, leaving me to follow.

"Wait until you see what it is," Mallory teases with a chuckle.

Finley sets out the rest of the plates while I lay down the silverware. Just as we finish, Mom announces dinner's ready, and she and Mallory carry over several bowls.

Surprise flashes across Finley's face when she sees what we're having—macaroni and cheese, mashed potatoes, scrambled eggs, Jell-O salad, and a garden salad.

Mom laughs. "I know. Not a traditional Christmas Eve dinner."

"It's all Alex's fault," Mallory says. "He had strep throat one year and could only eat soft food. The boys loved it so much they begged Mom to make the same thing the next year."

"How would you know?" Grant scoffs, setting the salad on the table. "You weren't even born yet, Maleficent."

Mallory glares daggers at him.

"She became part of it," Mom chides gently. "And the tradition's evolved over the years, but the principle's the same."

"Except for the salad," Dad adds with a grin. "That one was my demand."

The table fills with small talk, but tension lingers like smoke. Mom and Mal do their best to keep things light, but Grant's still brooding, and Finley looks wound tight, like one wrong word will snap her in half. My chest knots tighter every second. If she was wavering on whether to stay or go, this dinner is likely to push her to leave.

After we've cleaned up dinner, Dad declares it's time for the second Christmas Eve tradition—game night. We all head to the living room, and Mom brings out a Pictionary box, announcing, "Boys against girls."

Finely and I are sitting on the love seat. Last night, she was curled up against me, but tonight, she's sitting on the edge of the seat, looking anxious.

I lean into her side and whisper into her ear, "We don't have to do this. We can go upstairs and watch a movie or even take a walk downtown."

She looks up at me, her face blank. "But this is a family tradition, Alex," she whispers back.

"So? It doesn't mean we need to do this."

"But you would if I weren't here." It's not a question. We both know it's true. "I'll be fine."

Mom sets out the supplies then declares that the boys can go first since they're obviously at a disadvantage.

Grant's brow furrows with confusion. "But we have four guys while you girls have three."

"Exactly," Mallory says sweetly, then reaches a hand toward Finley. "Come over here with the girls. No fraternizing with the enemy."

Finley obeys and finds herself sandwiched between Mom and my sister on the sofa. I suspect this isn't by accident.

Thankfully, with Mallory's wit and charm and Mom's hospitality, Finley is more relaxed by the time we finish the game. And of course they beat us by a landslide. Tyler and Grant are bickering over the fact neither could guess each other's drawings.

Mallory suggests another game, but it's after ten and Finley looks exhausted. "I think we're gonna call it a night," I say as I get to my feet, then walk over to Finley, reaching out a hand to her.

She looks up at me, and I see a flicker of relief.

"It's still early," Mal protests. "We could play another round."

"And listen to Thing One and Thing Three squabble and draw like preschoolers?" I say, thumbing to my brothers. "Hard pass."

Finley takes my hand, and I pull her to her feet.

"Good night, everyone," she says, as I keep hold of her hand and tug her toward the kitchen.

"Good night," a chorus of voices calls after us. Grant's is noticeably absent.

I continue to hold her hand until we reach our room, then after I close the door behind us, I pull her into a hug.

That's something a friend would do, right?

She leans her cheek against my chest and wraps her arms around my back. I hold her like this for nearly a minute, neither of us saying anything. I soak her in, a sadness brewing inside. She was miserable tonight and it's killing me. She's supposed to be having a magical Christmas, but my shithead brother pricked it like a balloon.

"Don't make a decision tonight," I say softly.

She doesn't answer.

How do I fix this? Panic claws at my chest. I want to kick Grant's ass. I want to shove his face into the snow. I want to force him to apologize and treat her with the respect she deserves.

But none of that will solve any of it. The damage has already been done.

Feeling reckless, I lift a hand to her cheek and gently lift her face to look up at me.

There's sadness in her eyes, but something else too. Something I can't name.

"Do you want to get ready for bed?" I ask.

"We still have to set out the stockings."

After all this, she still wants to give everyone stockings. It only makes my frustration worse.

"Yeah," I say, offhandedly, worried she'll see my frustration and think it's aimed at her. "But everyone's still downstairs. How about we get ready and then put them together and take them down once everyone's gone to bed?"

"Okay."

She pulls away from me, and I miss the warmth of her body as she opens her suitcase and pulls out her pajamas and a toiletry bag. When she goes to the door, I follow her to the opening, watching as she slips into the bathroom like I'm her bodyguard.

I have no idea how long she'll be and standing at the doorway is making me anxious. I'm about to turn back into our room when Mallory comes up the back staircase.

She casts a glance over my shoulder into the empty room that's currently lit by the Christmas tree.

"She's in the bathroom," I say, lowering my voice.

She nods then gives me a sad smile. "I'm sorry about Grant."

I rake a hand through my hair. "Yeah, me too." But I'm still kicking myself for not preparing Finley for his anger, but then again, I expected him to turn the brunt of it on me.

"Do you think she'll go home?" Mal asks, looking distraught.

"Honestly? I don't know. She hasn't asked me to get her a plane ticket home tomorrow, but the day after?" I shrug helplessly.

Determination fills her eyes. "We just have to make tomorrow so wonderful she won't want to leave."

"I promised her a special Christmas." My voice breaks. "I've disappointed her."

Mallory grabs my arm. "No, Alex!" she says in dismay. "This isn't on you!"

But it is, because I brought her here for my own selfish reasons, knowing full well that Grant would be pissed. I was just too narcissistic to think Finley might be a victim in the fallout.

"Tomorrow'll be a better day," she says, and I'm pretty sure she's trying to convince me as much as she's trying to convince herself.

"Yeah," I say, because I'm desperate to believe it.

The bathroom door opens, and Finley walks out, wearing red and green plaid pajamas, and Mallory squeals, "Look at you! You're so cute!"

Finley's face flushes. "Thanks."

"Oh! Next Christmas we should all wear matching pajamas," Mallory decrees with a sharp nod. "Next summer, Finley and I can start looking for some online to order for everyone."

Finley's eyes widen slightly. "Oh, I don't know if I'll be here next Christmas."

"What?" Mallory says in mock outrage. "Of course you will be. My brother would be an absolute idiot to break up with you, and I simply won't allow it."

Finley cracks a small smile. "And what if I break up with him?"

Some of the shine leaves Mallory's eyes. "I can see how that might be a possibility but just remember that the King family is a package deal. You get me thrown in."

Finley laughs, but it's quiet and has a sad note. She won't be here next Christmas. I knew this was the plan, but it doesn't sit right.

"Well, we have things to do," I say, putting my hand on the small of Finley's back and ushering her into the room.

Mallory groans. "Gross. I did *not* need to hear that." Then she goes into the bathroom and shuts the door.

"You sister thinks you're eager to have sex with me," Finley states dryly.

I cringe. "Yeah, sorry about that."

She walks over to the closet and pulls out the bags with the stockings and stuffers. "I thought we could stuff them up here then take the stockings down."

"Good idea."

We sit on the bed and assemble the stockings, inserting my gift cards as well as the candy and other small items we purchased. When we finish, I head downstairs to see if the coast is clear. The living room is empty, but the tree is still lit.

Finley and I hang the stockings from nails already in the mantle to hold up the evergreen swag draped over it.

When we finish, we stand back and examine our handiwork.

"Looks good," I say. "Like when we were kids."

"Good," she says, taking a second longer to view it then heads upstairs, leaving me to follow.

My heart sinks. She may still be physically here, but her heart has already left.

Chapter Thirty

Finley

I wake up to Christmas music drifting through the house. Still half-asleep, I reach for Maybelle, but my hand finds only a pillow. Blinking, I roll over and spot Alex stretched out on the other side of the bed. His eyes are shut, but his face twists in a grimace.

"It's definitely Christmas morning. Mom's blasting carols."

"Is that another tradition?" I ask.

"Yep." He grabs the pillow between us and covers his face.

"Are you trying to smother yourself?" I tease.

"If it saves me from the torture, then yes." His voice mumbles from beneath the pillow.

I tug the pillow away, and he blinks up at me. "Do you want me to suffer?"

"And if I said yes?" I ask playfully.

His eyes crack open in a squint. "Then I probably deserve it."

The weight of reality crashes back—Grant is here, and I'm ruining his Christmas. My smile falters.

Alex's humor vanishes the second he sees it. "Don't," he pleads softly.

"Don't what?"

"Don't go."

My breath catches. I want to stay—so badly. Not just because I love spending time with his family, but because I love spending time with *him*. Once I go home, how do I go back to the superficial banter we had before? Especially when I want so much more. More than he's willing to give.

I sit up, and he does too, turning to face me.

"Just give it today and see how it goes, okay?" he asks. The pleading in his voice catches me off guard. If feels like more than worry over Eloise showing up—but I can't risk reading too much into it. I have to protect my heart.

"Okay." But it's easy to agree because I already promised Barb and Mirna. "So, what does a typical King Christmas look like?" I ask, desperate to change the subject.

"How about I just show you?" A twinkle fills his eyes, and he hops out of bed. "Don't change. Another tradition."

We go downstairs—me in my pajamas, him in his sweatpants and a T-shirt. His parents are already at the island with steaming mugs of coffee—also in their pajamas—and the air smells like sweet and savory heaven.

"Merry Christmas," Valerie says warmly, though her gaze lingers on me.

"Merry Christmas," Alex and I say in unison. He gives me a boyish smile, and my heart flips.

Do not fall for Alex King.

I think it's a little too late for that.

All the more reason to leave tomorrow.

I make everyone espresso drinks as best I can without a machine, and a short bit later, Mallory and Tyler come down, and I make them drinks too. Alex keeps shooting me glances like he's not happy I'm making them, but he doesn't seem mad about it.

A timer dings, and Valerie pulls a bubbling breakfast casserole dish from the oven, followed by a tray of cinnamon rolls. Grant still hasn't come up, but Valerie insists we eat without him. The guilt gnaws at me. Would they have waited if I wasn't here?

We dish up buffet-style and carry our plates to the table. We've barely started eating when Grant shuffles in wearing Santa flannel pajama pants and a gray T-shirt. He has a major case of bedhead and the dark circles under his eyes make him look like he's been on an all-night bender.

If he's annoyed we didn't wait for him, he doesn't let on, but he *does* take offense when he sees the nearly empty coffee pot.

"No coffee?" he demands, giving the pot a shake.

"Your father and I drank most of it," Valerie says smoothly, "but Finley can make you a drink."

"Finley?" His disbelief drips like acid.

"She can make all kinds of coffee drinks," Mallory says. "What do you usually order at a coffee shop?" Mallory asks.

"Coffee," he says dryly, pouring the dregs into his cup. It barely fills it a quarter of the way.

"I can make you an Americano," I offer quickly, getting to my feet. "That's what I make for Tyler and your dad. Or I could use the French press."

Grant's jaw drops. He swivels to me, then to Alex, outraged. "You brought your girlfriend to make everyone coffee? What is she? A barista?"

The room is deadly silent. No one moves.

Grant's eyes go wide. "Oh, my God. She *is* a barista! Did you meet her at your coffee shop?"

Heat floods my face, hot enough to scorch. Is it possible to actually die of embarrassment?

"Grant!" Valerie shouts, harsher than I've ever heard. "Watch your tone!"

"What?" Grant advances, his glare locked on Alex. I suddenly realize Alex has risen too—positioned right behind me.

"You were so desperate for the bed you hired your barista to come to Hollybrook?"

Mass chaos erupts—Valerie and Dr. Bob are shouting at Grant and Tyler physically restrains Alex, who's roaring that Grant's going to pay for insulting his girlfriend.

Mallory watches in horror for two beats before springing into action. She slips an arm around my shoulders and hustles me toward the living room.

"Finley, I am so, so sorry," she gushes. "I have no idea what's gotten into him!"

"He's probably upset about his breakup," I murmur, but I'm drowning in guilt. Because Grant is spot on. Alex *did* bring me so he could sleep in the bed. And technically he *did* hire me since he's paying for my lost wages. We have a contract, for heaven's sake.

"That's no excuse," she says fiercely, her voice breaking.

"I think I should just go," I whisper.

She vigorously shakes her head. "No! Absolutely not. You shouldn't have to leave because Grant's throwing a temper tantrum."

The shouting in the kitchen dulls to a low roar. My stomach twists. Would Alex drive me to an outlying town so I can spend the night and catch a flight tomorrow? Or maybe I can find a flight today. It'll cost a fortune, but I'll find a way to pay Barb and Mirna back.

I pull out my phone and try to call Barb, but it goes to voicemail.

"Who are you calling?" Mallory asks in alarm.

Ignoring her, I end the call and call Mirna, next. It goes to voicemail too.

Of course it does. It's Christmas morning and they're spending it with their families.

"Finley, we don't want you to go," Mallory pleads.

I open our group chat—*Bad Ass Babes* (three guesses who named it)—and type:

Things just took a really bad turn. I need to leave today

"Alex!" Mallory shouts, panic lacing her voice.

Alex storms in, red faced, and wound tighter than a live wire.

"I think she's trying to go home," Mallory blurts.

Alex's face drains of color, and he rushes toward me. "No. We're both going."

"No, Alex," I protest, my tears finally breaking free. "This is *your family*."

"I'm not letting him treat you like that. Not on Christmas." He pulls me into his arms, holding on like he's daring anyone to pry me away.

"No, you can't leave too!" Mallory cries.

"Who's leaving?" Dr. Bob demands from the doorway.

"Alex and Finley!" Mallory sobs.

"No," Valerie gasps, hurrying into the room, her face ashen.

"Alex isn't leaving," I say quickly, wiping my tears. "But *I* am. I think it's for the best. The last thing I want is to cause more trouble between all y'all."

"If you think you're leaving without me, you're crazy," Alex grinds out, his teeth clenched.

I stare up at him, stunned. I'm not his girlfriend. I'm not anything to him. So why is he acting like this is upsetting him enough to make him leave with me? Unless... maybe he just wants an excuse to leave too.

The thought makes me feel even worse.

"No one's leaving," Dr. Bob cuts in, voice like steel, then he stalks out of the room.

Valerie steps close, her hands trembling, eyes shining with tears. "Alex, I know you're upset—and you have *every right* to be —but *please,* don't go. I *just* got you here. And Finley—" her voice breaks. "Finley's such a delight."

The hardness on Alex's face flickers, but only for a second. "I can't let him talk about her like that." He gestures toward me, his fury rising again. "I promised her a sweet family Christmas, and she's crying. On Christmas!" His fists clench, every muscle in his body wound tight, his hands fisted at his side. "He can say what he wants about me, but *not* her."

Valerie lifts her hands, pleading. "I know, I know. We'll fix this. Just... don't make any decisions yet. *Please.*"

He gives a stiff nod, then wraps an arm around my back, tugging me close.

I glance up at him and lower my voice. "Alex, can I speak with you alone?"

He stares down at me, and the worry in his eyes steals my breath. How can he look at me like that? How can he be so worried about me?

Because he's not a monster, Finley. Besides, he's your friend.

He nods, then leads me into his parents' office, shutting the door behind us.

"God, Finley—" he starts, his voice raw.

"Let's just take a deep breath." I do it first, holding his gaze. Inhale. Exhale. I draw another breath, and this time he follows, and a little tension drains from his shoulders.

"Okay," I say, forcing calm, even if it's a struggle to reach it. "I know you don't know me very well, but despite the fact I came on this trip with you, I'm usually very practical."

"I already know that," he says, his forehead creasing. "You can't live the life you've lived without being practical."

My heart gives a ridiculous flutter that he knows that about me, but I shove it aside. "We need to look at this logically. Grant's acting out because he's hurt over his breakup, and I'm the easy scapegoat. I think the most logical—and kindest—solution is for me to go."

He starts to protest, but I close the space between us and press my finger to his mouth. "Alex. You know I'm right."

His eyes flare slightly, and it's like a jolt of electricity sparks from his lips into my fingertip. Does he feel it too—the pull for something more? Does he want me to replace the finger with my lips?

What would it be like to kiss him? Just once. I've never believed in Christmas wishes, but if my Hollybrook Christmas is unraveling, would it be so bad to steal one? This is already ending badly. How much worse could it get?

But before I can act on my impulse, he gently tugs my hand down and lets go. "You leaving isn't being kind to *you*. I promised you a Hollybrook Christmas."

Disappointment washes through me at the lost chance to kiss him, but the truth is, things *could* be worse. I'd rather live in the fantasy of possibility than the reality of rejection. "And I got a Hollybrook Christmas." I manage a crooked, self-deprecating smile. "It just wasn't the Christmas either of us expected."

"No." Fury fills his eyes. "If you go, then I go too."

"And you'll break your mother's heart."

Something wavers in his expression. He knows I'm right.

A knock interrupts us, followed by his father's voice. "When you two finish up here, will you meet us in the living room?"

I stare up at Alex, my chest tight. For a heartbeat, I let myself imagine this is real—someone fighting this hard to keep me. Someone whose arms could be home.

I'm so very tired of being alone.

But this isn't real. It never was.

I turn and walk past him before he can stop me, opening the door. He follows, of course.

When we step into the living room, everyone is already seated. Valerie and Mallory are on the sofa. Dr. Bob is in his recliner. Tyler and Grant are sitting in two armchairs, and Grant's head is lowered.

"Will you please sit?" Valerie asks, gesturing to the empty love seat.

I don't wait for Alex to answer and take a seat. He joins me, taking my hand in his and holding tight.

"We sincerely apologize for the way you've been treated, Finley," Dr. Bob says. "Grant has something to say."

Grant looks up, his eyes red like he's been crying. He swallows. "I'm sorry for my behavior. I'm upset and took it out on you, but it won't happen again." His words sound right, but there's still an air of defiance under the surface. He still resents me being here.

"Thank you," I say simply. "I accept."

"I don't," Alex snaps. "You were out of line."

Grant lifts his chin, meeting Alex's glare head-on.

"Grant apologized," Valerie says firmly, raising her hands. "Let's try to salvage Christmas."

Alex doesn't look appeased, and Grant looks like a pressure cooker that's let out a little steam but is still ready to blow.

"Okay," Mallory says with a forced cheerfulness. "Should we finish breakfast then open presents?"

"That's a good idea," Valerie agrees.

A half-hearted chorus of *not hungrys* ripples through the room.

"Okay," Valerie says, looking a little defeated. "Maybe we should open gifts. Bob, will you get us started?"

Dr. Bob looks like he doesn't think it's the best idea, but he obeys his wife, reaching under the tree and handing a present to Mallory.

She checks the tag and beams. "It's from Alex. And it looks too big to be a gift card."

He gives her a tight smile, then squeezes my hand.

She tears into the paper and squeals. She uncovers a cream-colored leather wallet—the same one Alex and I saw her eyeing at the market. "Thank you, Alex," she gushes, clutching it to her chest. Then she grins at me. "And thank you, Finley."

I smile back, warmth flooding my chest.

Dr. Bob must take that as a good sign because he passes out more gifts to everyone but me, which I expected. Still, I watch with genuine delight as they unwrap each present. Tyler has given his mother a painted portrait of the four kids when they were younger. I recognize it instantly from the photo Alex sent me.

"Tyler, this is... beautiful." Valerie's voice trembles.

"That's not all," he says, a little stiff. "It's been a while since we had a professional family photo. I booked a photographer while we're all here."

"Oh, Tyler!" she exclaims. "Thank you."

He gives a sharp nod.

One by one the gifts are opened, and laughter fills the room, and the earlier heaviness starts to lift. I ooh and ahh with the rest, caught up in their excitement. The unwrapping stretches on for over an hour, each gift shown and admired before moving to the next.

Alex must have tucked my presents for his family in the back, because they don't surface until nearly everything is gone. At last,

Dr. Bob pulls out the last few packages wrapped in paper I recognize.

He hands them around, and everyone looks down at the tags in surprise—everyone except Grant. He hangs his head.

"Finley," Valerie protests. "You didn't have to get us anything."

"I wanted to. Y'all have been so kind." I pause. "I just wanted to say thank you."

They open their gifts, and some of the ache in my heart fills with warmth. I love Alex's family and seeing them happy makes me happy too.

Another reminder of why I need to go.

"Bob," Valerie says, craning her neck to peer around the tree. "There should be at least one more gift under there."

Dr. Bob crouches, then slides out several presents. "Actually, there are three." He checks the tags, then hands them all to me. "For Finley."

My eyes fly wide in surprise. I can't remember the last time I was part of a Christmas morning gift exchange, let alone opened a present meant for me. Barb and Mirna and I exchange gifts, but usually in Barb's apartment with glasses of sherry.

This is different.

My fingers linger on the paper, savoring the moment, then I feel silly for stalling.

I start with the largest, a rectangular box tagged *From the Kings*. Inside is a beautiful knit scarf I'd admired at the market. Tears fill my eyes, as my gaze finds Mallory. "Thank you."

"Of course," she says.

I loop it around my neck, patting the spot where it crosses under my chin. "I love it."

"You've got two more," Mallory urges. "Open them!"

The next is smaller, the wrapping unmistakably Alex's. I grin at him. "The tag only has my name, but it has your handiwork all over it."

He smirks. "You came upstairs just as I was slapping on the

last piece of tape. I barely got your name on before I opened the door."

My heart swells as I tear it open. Inside is a delicate heart locket on a chain.

"Open it," he says.

I snap it open and grin like a fool when I see a tiny photo of our tree inside.

"What's in there?" Mallory asks.

"That's private," Alex cuts in, though his voice is playful. He takes the locket from me, and I lift my hair so he can fasten it around my neck.

When it falls into place, I tug the scarf down so the locket shows. "Thank you," I murmur, meeting his gaze.

His eyes lock on mine, so intense it makes me want to lean in and kiss him. The kiss I'd wanted in the study was sweet; this one burns with heat. Every nerve in my body sparks, aching for him.

My breath catches—until someone clears their throat. Loudly.

Probably Grant.

My cheeks flush as I pull back and look at the last gift. It's featherweight, wrapped in paper I haven't seen on any other package—white with embossed snowflakes. The tag is written in elegant script: *To: Finley. From: Santa.*

I glance up at Alex, my lips tugging into a grin. "Santa?"

His expression gives nothing away.

Curiosity buzzing through me, I peel back the paper and lift the lid of the box. My breath catches and I feel lightheaded.

No. It can't be.

Inside is the Santa glass ornament from the market.

Chapter Thirty-One

What the hell? Where did that come from?

Finley shakes her head, her eyes glassy. "This is too much, Alex."

My heart is racing. "I never said I got it."

"Of course you did." She runs a fingertip over the ornament, reverent. "You're the only one who knew."

I flick a glance to Mallory. She's wide-eyed, shaking her head.

The truth claws at me. I could take the credit—clearly the giver wanted to stay anonymous—but Finley deserves honesty. She insisted on it when I introduced her to my family, and I know her well enough to know she values truth in everything—especially with something as dear to her as this.

"Finley," I say carefully, "I didn't—"

"He didn't do it alone," Tyler cuts in, leaning back in his chair. "He had help so you wouldn't notice."

I freeze, my mouth parting. *Tyler* bought it? Why?

Finley glances at him then turns to Mallory. "Is that what you two were up to?"

"Guilty as charged." Tyler leans back and rests his ankle on the opposite leg. "They say it takes a village."

Why did Tyler buy it? Does he have feelings for Finley? It's not hard to believe. He's been protective of her since the moment she walked in the door—and look at her. Sure, she's gorgeous, but her heart is even more stunning. How could he not feel something?

A hot twist coils in my chest. Is that ... *jealousy*? I've never been a jealous guy, but this white-hot poker in my ribs is just that.

Why would I be jealous?

You know, you idiot.

I glance at Finley. Her face glows with Christmas joy, and it hits me like a baseball to the face.

I know beyond a shadow of a doubt—I want this woman. Not as a friend. Not as someone I'm casually dating. I want her to be my girlfriend.

How a relationship would work, I don't know. Especially after the way I treated her on the drive here, and with everything Grant's thrown at her. But I want her anyway.

Now I just have to convince her to give us a chance.

I mouth *thank you* to Tyler. Whatever his motives, he just saved Finley's Christmas. He gives a short nod. I'll pay him back for it later.

Mom looks puzzled by the exchange, so I explain why the ornament is special to Finley and how it became a group effort. I leave out the part about where Mallory missed buying it in time—better to let Mom glow over the idea of her kids working together for once.

Then I catch Grant's scowl. His gaze snags on the fireplace. "Since when do we have stockings?"

The stockings.

In all the chaos, I forgot about them, and apparently everyone else was too preoccupied to notice them hanging from the mantle. I open my mouth to explain, but Grant barrels on, venom dripping.

"And why does Finley have one—when she's probably just Alex's flavor of the week—and Eloise doesn't."

The color drains from Finley's face. Her joy bleeds away like he stabbed her straight through.

"Grant!" Mom protests.

Finley rises, clutching the ornament box to her chest. Her

voice is steady, sweet—too sweet. "Thank you for my gift and the help you gave Alex to get the ornament. I'm feeling a little tired, so I think I'll go upstairs and lie down."

She heads up the stairs, and I'm about to follow, but Dad says, "Alex, wait."

I glance toward the entryway, then back at him. "I think it's best we leave." I say calmer than I feel.

Mallory points a finger at Grant. "Why are you being such an asshole?"

His face reddens. "I'm not the one—"

"Yeah," Tyler says, his voice tight. "You *are* the one."

"You don't even know what I was going to say," Grant protests.

"Does it matter?" Tyler shoots back. "There's nothing you can say to justify how you've treated Finley."

"I just wanted to know why she had a stocking and Eloise doesn't." He turns to Mom with an accusing look.

She shakes her head. "Don't look at me. I had nothing to do with the stockings."

"Then who did?" Mallory asks, looking around the room.

"Maybe it was *Santa*," Grant says, his voice dripping sarcastically.

"It was Finley," I say flatly. "She has a stocking because I insisted that she have one too. And for the record, Eloise has a stocking upstairs in our room, but we didn't put it up because she's *not here*."

When he starts to argue, I hold up my hand. "And the fact Eloise isn't here has *nothing* to do with Finley. You might think I've got a flavor of the week," I seethe, "but at least I'm not stuck in a toxic relationship."

Grant's jaw works like he's about fire back, then clamps shut.

What am I doing standing here? Finley's upstairs alone—her Christmas ruined—I'm wasting time with this. "I'm going upstairs to pack."

"He'll stay in line," Dad says, narrowing his laser-focused glare on my brother.

I turn back to face him. "No offense, Dad, but you and Mom have been promising Finley she wouldn't be subjected to any more of his bullshit since last night, and yet he keeps dishing it out."

Mom's cheeks flush.

"Hey!" Tyler snaps. "Don't talk to Mom and Dad like that."

"It's okay, Tyler," Mom says quietly. "He's right. We promised it would stop, and it didn't."

To his credit, Grant looks embarrassed.

I start toward the entryway when the doorbell rings.

It's so out of place with the mood that none of us move. Then it rings again. And again. Whoever's out there isn't leaving.

I'm the closest to the door, so I head to the entryway and yank the door open, prepared to send someone packing—only to freeze.

Two older women are standing on the porch, bundled up in so many layers, they look like escapees from an unprepared arctic expedition. Multiple scarves are wrapped around their necks and heads, and oversized purses are slung over their arms. The tall one clutches a pet carrier shrouded in a knit blanket.

"Well, don't just stand there!" the shorter, stockier one barks, her eyes blazing. "Let us in."

Her voice carries so much authority; I don't even question it —I back up and they storm across the threshold like they're staging a raid.

"Where is she?" the shorter woman demands, shooting daggers at me. Her face looks vaguely familiar, but I can't place her. Is she one of the neighbors?

"Who?" I manage, still thrown off.

"Alex," Mom calls from the living room. "Who's at the door?"

The shorter woman stalks a few more steps into the house and bellows, "Finley!"

I blink in shock. Wait, they look just like—

"Where's Finley?" the taller one demands her tone sharp. "We want to see her *immediately*."

"Mirna?" I ask, dumfounded.

"I bet they have her locked in the basement," the short one declares. "Just like in *Buried with the Mob Boss*."

If I take away the hat and the two scarves wrapped around her head, I realize it's Barb.

They flew from Atlanta. On Christmas Day.

"Now is not the time for your silly books," the woman who must be Mirna snaps, then pins me with a glare. "Hello, Alex. Now, *where* is Finley?"

A loud, angry meow erupts from inside the carrier.

"*Mirna?*" Finley calls from the top of the stairs.

"I'm here too!" Barb hollers, making a beeline for the foot of the stairs.

My family has spilled into the entryway, staring at the two older women like a circus act has barged into the house mid-performance.

"Barb?" Finley calls again as she hurries down the stairs. She's changed out of her pajamas into yoga pants and a long-sleeve T-shirt.

My stomach drops to the floor. She wasn't resting. And there's no way she'd change into that casual, unholiday-like outfit to spend Christmas Day with my family. Not even after the disaster of a morning.

She's preparing to leave.

When she called Barb and Mirna last night, did she ask them to come get her?

Hurt slams into me. She didn't have to ask them to rescue her. I would have done it.

But you didn't, did you? You made her stay until tomorrow.

And then things got even worse.

Finley throws her arms around Barb, clinging like she's found solid ground after a shipwreck. Then she turns to Mirna, who has brushed past me to fold her in too.

"What the hell is going on?" Grant asks, dazed.

I start to answer, but I can't get out the words lodged in my throat. I've let her down, and I'm not sure I'll ever forgive myself.

"What are you two doing here?" Finley asks, incredulous.

Mirna's face hardens. "We came to rescue you."

Relief rushes through me—they came on their own. But if they left Atlanta before dawn on Christmas Day, then Finley must have painted a bleak picture last night to make them drop everything.

"Finley," Mom says cautiously behind me, "I take it these are your grandmothers?"

Finley turns to her, giving her a half smile. "Yeah, Barb and Mirna—" she gestures to each of them "—this is Valerie King, Alex's mother."

Barb doesn't bother with niceties, but Mirna takes a step forward and says stiffly, "Thank you for your hospitality, but we're here to take Finley home."

Mom looks close to tears. "I really wish you wouldn't." She glances back at Grant, who, to his credit, actually looks embarrassed. "I realize things have been rough, but I promise they'll smooth out."

Mirna lifts her chin. "There shouldn't be anything to smooth out. Alex brought Finley here, practically guaranteeing her a nice, traditional, family Christmas."

"To be fair," Grant mutters, grimacing. "Disagreements are often part of a traditional family Christmas."

Mirna's glare could turn a mere mortal to stone, and Grant rightfully shrinks. "Disagreements are one thing, young man, making her feel unwelcome is quite another. We would have never let her come if we'd known you were going to treat her this way."

Mom flushes, and even Dad hangs his head. "Again, we're so sorry this has happened and—"

"Stop," Finley cuts in. "Look, I understand why Grant's upset, and I don't blame him for it."

"Finley—" I start, but she raises her hand, silencing me.

"No," she says softly, looking up at me. Tears pool in her eyes. "The last two days were everything I ever dreamed of having with my mom. I never would have had them without you." Her voice trembles. "So, thank you."

I catch her hand, pressing it to my chest. "Please don't go," I whisper, my heart raw.

A tear falls down her cheek. "You know this is best. Just like you know you need to stay." She rises on her toes and brushes a soft kiss against my cheek.

Mirna's voice cuts like steel. "Asking her to stay is selfish. And you know it."

I do. That's the problem. I want her here more than I've wanted anything in a long time. But what she needs isn't me. It's to get out of this house. And the truth lands like a blow to the gut.

I can't ask her to stay. But I don't know how to let her go.

Finley turns to my family. "Thank you for a magical two days. It's more than I could have ever asked for. You've all been so gracious…" Her voice breaks, and it takes everything in me not to pull her into my arms. But I've already failed her, and now her friends are here to do what I couldn't.

"Finley," Mom whispers, tears spilling. She rushes forward, wrapping her in a hug so fierce that I think she might keep her here by sheer force of will. Finally, she pulls back, cupping Finley's cheek. "You are the best thing that ever happened to Alex. I hope you won't hold the last eighteen hours against him."

Finley nods, and my heart sinks. We only had this week. Once we're back in Atlanta, our lives go back to the way they were. Only now, the thought of that feels hollow.

Mallory steps in next, hugging Finley while she cries. "You were the sister I always wanted. Please come back. We'll lock Grant in a barn next time."

Finley releases a choked laugh. "You're the sister I've always wanted too."

Dad embraces her quickly, his voice rough. "Young lady, you brought the magic of Christmas back to this family, and you brought home our wayward son. For that, I'll always be grateful. And as my wife said, I hope you give us another chance, but I understand if you don't."

She manages a tight smile. "Thank you."

Tyler hugs her next. "You deserve the best, Finley. Sorry we didn't give it to you."

Grant lingers, shame etched across his face. Finally, he mutters, "Sorry, Finley. I was out of line. I promise to do better. You don't have to go."

"Thank you for your apology," she says, brushing at a tear. "But we both know I need to."

He nods, hanging his head again.

Mirna steps forward, resting a hand on Finley's arm. "Are you sure this is what you want?"

Finley looks at Mom, then scans the room—her gaze lingering on Grant. "I think it's for the best."

"Then go get your things."

Finley holds her eyes for a beat, then nods and heads upstairs.

We all stand in awkward silence for a few seconds before Mom says, "You ladies traveled all this way. Would you like to stay a little while? We have breakfast casserole and cinnamon rolls."

Barb perks up immediately. "I could eat."

Mirna lifts an arm to block her. "You can wait until we get to the Airbnb."

My heart stutters. "You're ... not leaving today?"

"No," Mirna says, her gaze cool. "We didn't know how long this would take, and besides..." She pauses. "Why should Finley not get the winter holiday in Hollybrook she was promised?"

"Does that mean you're not leaving tomorrow either?" My voice cracks with how desperate I feel.

Her gaze turns arctic. "I don't think that's up to me to say."

A loud, indignant meow comes from the pet carrier.

"Do you happen to have a litter box?" Barb asks. "Maybelle's been holding it since Boston."

I glance at the pet carrier—Finley's cat is inside!—and then at Dad. He makes a face. "We've got some sand in the garage."

"Yeah," I say quickly. "I can take her out there." I reach for the handle.

"Don't try any funny business, young man," Barb warns. "The villain in *Goat's on You* stole the heroine's goat and tried to blackmail her into sleeping with him to get it back."

I cringe. I've been reduced to the villain of the story. And the worst part? I probably deserve it.

I carry the pet carrier to the garage out back, going through the side door and shutting it behind me. Dad's got a stack of sandbags in the back corner, so I pour some onto the concrete floor, and hope it will do. We had a few dogs when I was a kid, but never any cats.

Crouching in front of the carrier, I tug the blanket off. A white, fluffy cat with large grey eyes glares at me like she's trying to suck out my soul.

"Your mom's not very happy with me right now," I say. "But you and I can still be friends. I hear you've gotta go, so I'm gonna let you out, okay?"

She doesn't blink—just keeps giving me the death stare—before prancing out like she's royalty. She struts to the sand pile and takes the nastiest dump I've ever seen or smelled.

Gagging, I wave a hand in front of my face. "Good God, Maybelle. What have Barb and Mirna been feeding you?"

"I thought you called her Hellfire," Tyler says behind me. His voice is sharp. His suspicion is back.

I don't turn around, keeping my eye on Finley's cat. I know how important Maybelle is to her. The last thing I want to do is lose her. "Yeah. I usually do, but..." I'm not sure how to finish the thought and don't even try.

"How is it you didn't recognize her grandmothers?"

"We told you we were pretty new."

"How new?" he presses. "Since last fall? As close as she is to them, you'd think you'd have met them by now."

I straighten, finally facing him. He's not accusing me of lying about our relationship. He's accusing me of being a crappy boyfriend.

"Neither one of us have a lot of free time," I bite out.

He just stares at me, waiting for me to crack.

"You bought her that ornament," I fire back, my tone a challenge. "Why?"

"Because any fool could see it meant something to her, and you'd already been an asshole to her, so I figured I'd try to make up for it."

I narrow my eyes. "When was I an asshole to her?"

"I found her crying in the backyard two days ago. I offered to get you, but she practically begged me not to. Which told me you'd already upset her."

I searched my memory in panic, but it only takes a second to realize when it was—after she overheard my call with Roland.

Dammit. I made her cry. The thought cuts like a knife.

"You know she's too good for you," he says flatly.

I do, but I'll never admit it. "Why? Are you planning to go after her instead? You sure act protective enough."

"Somebody has to," he grunts.

"I was going to get the ornament," I snap, my anger sparking. "But she's too proud to let me just get it for her, so I asked Mal to go back for it. You can ask her yourself if you don't believe me."

The fire in his eyes flickers, easing a fraction.

That's when I glance down and notice the sand pile. Maybelle's buried her mess, but she's vanished.

"Where the hell's Maybelle?"

He scans the garage. "She's somewhere unfamiliar so she's probably hiding."

We start searching, and I finally spot her perched on Dad's

workbench, crouched behind a toolbox like a white ball of judgment.

"Come here, Maybelle," I coax, stretching a hand toward her. "Let's get you back in your carrier."

She hisses and swats, leaving a deep scratch across my knuckles. Then she launches at me, claws sinking into my chest.

I yelp but, thank God, I have the sense to grab her body instead of swatting her away. Holding her at arm's length with my hands tightly around her chest, I hurry to the carrier. She's screeching like a banshee, back claws raking my arms.

To his credit, Tyler grabs the carrier and holds it open. I shove Maybelle inside, earning a few more scratches before Tyler slams the door shut. He gives me an appraising look, some of his animosity easing.

"You've got a few war wounds, dude."

They sting like hell, but I grit my teeth. "I couldn't lose her cat too."

He nods, and we head back into the house.

Finley's in the entryway with her suitcase and wearing the heavy sweater she had on when she first arrived.

Her eyes go wide when she sees me. "Alex!"

"Maybelle's done her business and all in one piece," I say, pretending blood's not running down my arm.

"Same can't be said for you," Grant says under his breath.

Finley takes the carrier with one hand, her suitcase in the other, and looks me over. "You didn't try to pick her up, did you?" she asks, alarm flashing in her eyes.

I shrug, not wanting to talk about my war wounds. Because right now, all I can think about is the fact that she's about to walk away from me—maybe forever—and the thought rips through me harder than Maybelle's claws ever could.

"Thanks for everything," she says hesitantly. "Despite it all, I'm still glad I came."

That damn lump's back in my throat. I try to clear it, failing miserably. Instead, I shake my head.

She gives me one last glance before turning and walking out the door. Mirna and Barb follow, but at the threshold, Barb looks back, disappointment etched in her eyes.

"You're a disappointment, young man. I was sure this was going to turn out just like the couple in *Holiday Fake Out*." She shakes her head and marches out the door.

And Finley takes my heart with her.

Chapter Thirty-Two

"What are you two doing here?" I ask, walking down the sidewalk toward a car I don't recognize parked at the end of the driveway.

"Wait until we're in the rental car, dear," Mirna says, circling to the trunk.

I set the pet carrier on the ground and heft my suitcase in, but it takes a bit of maneuvering to fit it in with their two giant bags. "Why did you pack so much?"

"Because we're not going home," Mirna says matter-of-factly. "We're staying in Hollybrook for the rest of the week."

I gape at her. "What?"

"We know how much this meant to you," she says. "So, if Alex can't give you the Christmas you want, we will."

"But how did you find a place?" I ask, still stunned. "Alex said everything's booked solid this time of year."

"We found an Airbnb with a last-minute cancellation," Barb says proudly. "And we grabbed it. Now we're having a winter holiday with you."

Tears sting my eyes, as I hug Barb. "But what about your families? It's Christmas Day."

"Pft," Mirna snorts. "My daughter is still furious about the church service fiasco—she wouldn't even speak to me. And you know how I feel about Todd's mother. I called Barb and said I was coming to Hollybrook, with or without her."

"And I couldn't let her go without me," Barb says, as though the idea is absurd. "Besides, my sons were working my last nerve. So…" She shrugs.

"But how did you get here? It's barely noon."

"We caught the first flight out," Mirna says like it's the most logical thing in the world. "And I didn't trust anyone else with Maybelle, so we brought her along." She softens, adding, "Plus, I thought you might need her." Her gaze flicks toward the house. "We have an audience. Let's finish this in the car."

I glance back. Alex, Mallory, Tyler, and Valerie are framed in the doorway, their faces pressed to the glass like we're a scene on TV. My stomach drops. Alex is watching me leave, blood dripping down his arm from my cat's claws, and he didn't even flinch. I picture patching up his knee two nights ago, and the memory makes my throat ache.

I slide into the backseat with Maybelle, blinking hard against tears. The carrier rattles beside me, but I feel the phantom press of Alex's hand in mine.

Mirna gets in the driver's seat—thank God, because Barb behind the wheel would terrify me—and backs out of the driveway. Barb lifts her hand and in a cheery wave.

"Don't do that," Mirna scolds. "They're the enemy."

"They're not the enemy," I say softly, my heart cracking wide open. "They did the best they could under the circumstances."

"Alex dragged you into that mess," Mirna says, all steel. "And you texted this morning that you couldn't stay."

"I know," I admit, my voice cracking. "But Grant is Valerie's son. He just broke up with his girlfriend—partially because she was going to have to sleep on the sofa bed. Because of me. I couldn't make Valerie choose between us. It's Christmas. He needs his family."

"Blaming you is asinine," Mirna fires back.

Her words sting, because she's right. Deep down, I tell myself this isn't my fault, but isn't it? I knew what I was getting myself into when I accepted Alex's offer. We lied to Alex's family, so maybe this is exactly what I deserve. Besides, our lie wasn't without victims. Alex's mom cried when she hugged me. Mallory said I was the sister she always wanted. I hurt other people too.

I can still see Alex's face, like me leaving broke him. But that was just guilt, right? He only felt bad because I'm so upset.

"I know blaming me is wrong," I whisper, my heart heavy. "But Grant's hurting."

The car falls silent until we reach the square, and when Mirna pulls into the driveway of a tiny cottage, it feels like the end of something I barely got to begin.

"This is where we're staying?" I ask, dumbfounded. From the porch, I can see the ice rink and the Christmas tree glittering on the square.

"It's like it's meant to be," Barb says proudly. "We got it on the cheap for the rest of the week, so you can take your original flight home if you want."

Is Alex on the same flight? Were we supposed to sit together? Should I change it?

We haul our luggage up to the front porch. Mirna punches a code into a keypad, and when the door clicks open, I step inside—and stop cold.

It looks like Buddy the Elf was on a sugar high and decorated the place in one night.

The entire house is Christmas themed from the red sofa and chairs, the artificial tree in the corner, the garland and lights strung across the ceiling, and—oh, God—the animatronic elves and reindeer jerking at the foot of the stairs.

"What the...?" Mirna mutters.

"It sure is festive," Barb offers cheerfully.

Festive. That's one word for it. I walk deeper into the room, my throat tightening. A week ago, this would have been my dream —an explosion of Christmas spirit everywhere, no empty spaces. But now, all I can do is compare it to the King's house. Their decorations had been warm, elegant, alive with memories. This feels more like a theme park—loud and hollow.

"Well, it's something," Mirna says, abandoning her suitcase near the door and heading into the kitchen. I follow, still holding Maybelle's carrier, the garish holiday cheer pressing in on me.

The kitchen's no better. A round table for four is in the breakfast nook, a two-foot ceramic snowman with multiple smaller snowmen crowded around him sits in the center. A painting of Santa outside a snow-drenched building hangs on the wall next to a picture of a Hanukkah menorah. Even the dish towels are imprinted with holiday sayings like *Santa, I Was Framed* and *My Bells Don't Jingle Without Coffee*.

It's everything I thought I wanted. So why does it feel so wrong without Alex?

We poke our heads into a bedroom off the kitchen—a king-sized bed, dresser, and bathroom—every square inch smothered in Christmas cheer.

Upstairs, tucked into the attic, we find another bedroom with a full-size bed and the tiniest ensuite bathroom I've ever seen. Corner sink, cramped toilet, and a shower that looks only slightly bigger than a waterslide tube. The decorations up here are toned down, with a red and green quilt on the bed, and a throw pillow that says, *Ho Ho Snow*.

"Well, obviously, Finley gets this room," Barb says.

"No way," I say. "There are only two bedrooms. I'll sleep on the sofa."

"Neither one of us wants to climb these stairs," Mirna says sensibly. "There's a king-size bed downstairs. We'll share."

I don't argue, not when my throat feels raw from holding back tears. I set the carrier down, then perch on the edge of the bed, still in shock that they're actually here, that they came all this way because I couldn't handle staying.

"We still need to rustle up food for Christmas dinner," Mirna says briskly, standing by the door. "Which means we need to find an open market."

The thought of pushing through a crowded store makes me want to collapse. "Don't do that. Let's go out to eat. My treat."

"You're not paying," Barb says immediately. "Absolutely not."

"Alex will pay me everything we agreed to. I can afford it." My voice cracks on his name. I have no doubt he'll follow through, even if we hadn't had a contract.

The two women exchange a glance that feels heavy with unspoken things, then Barb softens. "Alright. Do you want to get settled for now?"

My gaze falls to the pet carrier. Maybelle's quieted down, but she's been in there for hours. "I need to get Maybelle some food and water."

"Already taken care of," Mirna says. "We brought some food with us. It's in my bag. But we don't have any litter or a pan."

"Thank you," I say. "I'll get her some litter soon, but for now, I'll just keep her in here with me." I grimace. "Do you mind if I stay up here for a little while?" My guilt is back in full force. They flew all this way to rescue me, and here I am asking for space. "I need to take a minute to…"

"Process," Mirna finishes gently.

I nod. "Yeah."

Her eyes soften. "We're here for you, Finley. Whatever you need."

"Thanks," I whisper, grateful and empty all at once.

Mirna goes downstairs then comes back with the Ziploc bag of food and two bowls. After they both study me for a long moment, they leave the room, shutting the door behind them.

I take a deep breath, glancing around. A dormer window overlooks the square and drawers are built into the sloped walls beside the bed. It's small, but cozy. And unlike the rest of the house, tasteful. Still my gaze keeps drifting to the empty corner where Alex's tree should be. Will he remember to water it? Will he even want to?

I let Maybelle out of her carrier, and she struts around the room, sniffing like she owns the place, as if deciding whether it meets her standards. After I fill her food and water bowls, I sink into the bed, staring up at the ceiling. My chest is so heavy it feels like I could sink through the mattress, through the floor, all the way into the earth.

How could something that felt so perfect fall apart so fast?

I curl up on my side, and there's a soft thud as Maybelle hops up beside me. She presses against my stomach, her warmth seeping into me. My hand slides over her fur, and her steady purr vibrates against my palm. For such a moody cat, she always seems to know when I need her.

"What are we going to do?" I whisper.

She doesn't need to say anything. I already know the answer I don't want.

Alex will come back to Atlanta in a week. Maybe he'll pretend the last few days never happened. Or maybe he'll stop coming into the shop altogether, so he doesn't have to see me and remember the mistake of bringing me home.

The thought shreds me. I don't know which is worse: being forgotten or being avoided.

Tears slip free, hot and unrelenting. I squeeze my eyes shut and let them fall, wishing—aching—for my mom. When I was small and the world felt too sharp, she'd curl around me and tell me what to do.

What would she tell me now? To fight for Alex? Or let him go?

But how do you let go of someone you never really had?

Chapter Thirty-Three

"Alex, we need to get you cleaned up," Mom says.

I'm still staring out the window, even though their car is long out of sight.

"Come on, big brother." Mallory tugs gently on my arm.

I let her lead me into the kitchen, still in a daze. Just yesterday, Finley and I were chopping down a tree, hanging ornaments, wrapping gifts she convinced me to buy. And now she's gone. She was here less than seventy-two hours, yet her presence lingers everywhere. Without her, everything feels wrong.

Mallory nudges me onto a stool at the island. She and Mom disinfect my scratches, but all I can think about is Finley tending to my knee. I haven't hurt this much since the incident six years ago. But that was shame and guilt. This is intense loss with some guilt mixed in.

Mallory wraps my hands in gauze until I look like a mummy. When they finish, I murmur a quiet thank you then head up upstairs.

In my room, I stop short. On the bed is a small, wrapped present with a folded note.

Alex,

With everything that happened last night and today, I didn't get a chance to give you your present. Despite everything, I still consider my time here a gift.

Please stay the rest of the week for your mom and try to mend things with your family—even Grant. You're so lucky to have them.

Don't take them for granted. I don't know what happened to drive you away, but they love you. They miss you.

They want the best for you. I do too.

XOXO

Finley

P.S. Now you get your own bed.

My eyes sting and the words are blurry. Typical Finley—always thinking about what's best for everyone at the expense of herself. Because it isn't lost on me that in this whole mess, she's the one who lost the most.

Our Christmas tree glitters in the corner, mocking me with its twinkling lights and the stupid stocking cap perched on top. Frustration boils over, and I start shoving my things in my suitcase.

"What are you doing?" Mallory's voice breaks through, tight with panic from the open doorway.

"I'm not leaving," I grunt, keeping my back to her. "Grant wants his damn bed so much, he can have it."

"I'm sorry," she whispers.

I snap the zipper closed hard enough to make my fingers sting. I'm so damn tired of everyone saying they're sorry. Sorry doesn't fix anything. Sorry doesn't bring Finley back. Sorry doesn't take her pain away.

I grab the note and gift off the bed, stuff them into my bag, then head for the door. Mallory's still planted there, watching me with wide, uncertain eyes. There's something in her expression, something that tells me this isn't just about Finley leaving.

"What?" I bark, sharper than I mean to.

She flinches, but she doesn't back down. Instead, she shuts the door behind her and squares her shoulders. "I read *Holiday Fake Out.*"

I shake my head in confusion. "What the hell are you talking about?"

"The book Finley's friend mentioned when she left."

My jaw tightened. The morning's a blur of chaos, and I barely remember anything beyond Finley's face as she walked away. "And?"

Mallory's voice trembles, but she pushes forward anyway. "Barb said she thought you were like the guy in that book." She hesitates, then blurts, "Alex—that book was about a man who hires a woman to pretend to be his girlfriend at Christmas parties."

The blood drains from my face.

Her eyes search mine, glassy and hurt. "Alex, is Tyler right? Did you hire Finley to pretend to be your girlfriend so you didn't have to sleep on the sofa bed?"

I drop my bag on the floor and sink onto the edge of the bed, my gaze landing on the tree in the corner. "What do *you* think?"

Mallory shifts uneasily. "Honestly? I want to believe she's real, but...she's not your type. At all. And yeah, I saw you hold her hand and have your arm around her—but I never once saw you kiss her. *Still...*" She takes a breath. "You did things with her that you never would have done for any of your previous girlfriends, let alone someone you'd hired. Plus, you're genuinely upset about the way Grant was treating her. And you were gutted she left. That's not something you can fake." Her shoulders sag. "Sorry, I don't know what I was thinking. Sorry I asked."

I could keep lying, keep the walls up. Maybe it's Finley's influence, or maybe it's my exhaustion of hiding things from my family. Either way, I chose the truth. Come what may.

"It's true," I say quietly.

Mallory frowns. "What's true? That I was rude to ask?"

I swivel my head to look up at her. "That she's not my girlfriend. Grant was right. She's the barista at my coffee shop." The words taste like glass. "Grant texted me while I was in line with Roland. He floated the idea, and the more I thought about it, the more I liked it."

Her eyes widen in horror. "You *tricked* Finley?"

"No," I protest, then grimace. "Maybe. I don't know what's real anymore." I drag a hand over my face. "But Finley—she never lied. Except for when we started dating. Everything else is true. She insisted on it." A reluctant smile tugs at my lips. "When I told her no one would believe I was dating a barista, she said if I couldn't take her as she was, she was calling the whole thing off."

Mallory sinks down beside me, her voice shaking. "You tricked us, Alex. You made us love her and it wasn't even real."

I swallow hard. "But I want it to be."

Her head snaps toward me, her eyes shining. "What did you just say?"

I turn to face her. "I want it to be real. I want her to be my girlfriend. Tyler was right. She *is* the best thing that's ever happened to me."

Her whole face lights up. "Then you have to win her back."

A bitter laugh escapes me. "I never had her, Mal. You can't win back someone you never had."

"I saw the way she looked at you," she insists. "She wants you too."

"I've hurt her, Mal. Badly."

"No. *Grant* hurt her."

I could argue that Grant's fury was sparked by my lie, by me springing a fake girlfriend on the family, but that would be beating a dead horse.

Mallory leans forward, practically vibrating with excitement. "Let's figure out how to win her back."

"You're going to help me?" I ask, stunned.

She smacks my arm. "Of course! Do you think you can do this on your own?"

I snort. "Mallory, I'm in the middle of building a multi-million-dollar tech company. I think I can handle this."

She arches a brow. "You might be a brilliant businessperson, but you're a disaster at love. Exhibit A: your sucky previous girl-friends."

I shrug. She has a point.

"She's still here in town, right?" she presses, practically bouncing on the bed.

"Yeah, but I have no idea where."

She gives me a pointed look. "This is Hollybrook. People here can't keep a secret for ten minutes. How hard can it be to track down two Valkyrie old women dressed like they raided a thrift store and wore everything out, and a gorgeous younger woman with them."

I consider it, but it doesn't take long. "We'll have to get Mom in on it."

"Well, duh!" she says like I'm an idiot. "You know she'll be all over this."

"Yeah." But suddenly, doubt creeps in. This is what I want—but what about what Finley wants? Here in Hollybrook, being with her feels easy, natural. But what happens when we get back to Atlanta?

My professional life is chaos and will be for few months. I try picturing her at a business dinner with investors' wives, and the image falls apart. She wouldn't belong there—not because she isn't educated or sophisticated enough, but because she's too damn genuine. Too real. She's above all the pretense and posturing.

The thing is, I've dated polished, sophisticated women. None of them have made me feel half of what I feel for Finley.

But what does that mean for us? How would she fit into my world? And more terrifying—how would I fit into hers? She barely has any time to breathe. Would she want to spend it on me?

"What happened?" Mallory asks, studying me. "Where'd you just go?"

"This is what *I* want," I admit. "But is it what's best for Finley?"

Her glare could cut steel. "She's a grown woman, Alex. Maybe let her decide what's best for her instead of deciding for her."

I give her a self-deprecating smile. "Yeah, I guess I deserve that."

"Damn right," she says with a laugh. "Now, how about we find Mom before she drinks all the wine in the house? She's got at least five bottles in the basement fridge, so you'll be saving her from herself."

"Okay," I say, my chest tightening with equal parts excitement and terror. But another thought hits me—one that makes cold sweat prickle down my spine "But if I'm doing this...really doing it...I need to come clean. About everything."

Her smile quickly fades. "Grant's gonna lose his mind. And Tyler..."

I shrug, forcing a rueful smile. "I know. But if Finley gives me a chance, I don't want any more lies."

Her worry lingers, but she finally nods. "Okay. Then let's go get everyone."

Chapter Thirty-Four

Five minutes later, we're gathered around the kitchen table. Mom's topping off her wine glass from a half-empty bottle, and Dad's nursing another cup of coffee. Tyler looks bored and Grant won't meet my eyes.

"Thanks for agreeing to sit in on this," I begin, my voice rougher than I intend. I'm at the head of the table, flanked by Mom and Mallory. "I have a few things I need to tell you, but I think I'll start with the biggest—why I've stayed away for so long. Why I've been ashamed to face you."

"Oh, Alex." Mom clasps my hand, her voice breaking. "What are you talking about?"

I look down the table at Dad. His expression is grim, but he nods.

It's time.

My throat is as dry as sandpaper. "Six years ago, my senior year of college, I went to a party with my girlfriend, Deidre. We'd both been drinking, but I was wasted—celebrating passing my fall midterms. When it was time to leave, she drove. We'd taken her car anyway, since I'd planned to party. And even though part of me knew she wasn't safe to drive, I was too drunk to stop her." My mouth twists into a grimace. "The fact is, she got behind the wheel, and she never should have."

My chest squeezes so tight I can barely breath. Every instinct tells me to shut up, but I force the words out.

Dad's voice cuts in, strong and steady. "It's okay, Alex. You're right. Telling them is long past due. Go on."

Mom jerks her gaze to him. "Bob, you knew?"

Dad gives a slow nod. The guilt slices deeper. I should have thought about how coming clean would drag him into this too. Will Mom resent him for keeping my secret? Will this blow up my family the same way I blew up everything else? Maybe I really am a narcissist who ruins everything he touches.

But Dad must see the panic on my face, because he says firmly, "It's okay, Alex. Secrets fester inside us, and this one is eating you alive. It's time we both let it go."

I suck in a shaky breath. Everything is spinning out of control. I already lost Finley—what if this costs me my family too?

Mom pats my hand, her voice fierce. "Alex, there's nothing you can say that will make me stop loving you." I turn to look at her, and her eyes are fierce. "*Nothing.*"

I turn to my brothers. Tyler smirks. "Don't look at me, man. Moms are required to love their kids unconditionally. Brothers on the other hand..." He shrugs like it's no big deal, but his grin softens the jab. He's giving me an out, a lifeline.

Grant though—Grant won't even look at me. His silence burns more than any insult.

"Go on, Alex," Mallory urges, her eyes kind. "We'll still love you. Just say it."

I draw in a jagged breath. Time to jump off the cliff.

"What happened in the car is blurry. I was half-passed out, but I remember Deidre swerving over the center line—then the impact."

Mom's whole body goes rigid beside me, her hand crushing mine.

"When I came to, the airbags had blown. Deidre was screaming. It took me a second to understand what happened—we'd hit a minivan. Head-on." My throat burns. "I forced my door open and stumbled onto the road. That's when I saw it—the wreckage."

"Was Deidre okay?" Mallory asks.

I nod. "Mostly. A broken leg and a few stitches in her cheek and her hand. All things considered, she was lucky."

Tyler leans forward. "What about the passengers in the other car?"

I hold his gaze. "There was only one passenger—a married father with three kids. He was unconscious with blood streaming down his face. Thank God, I had the sense to call 911, because we were the only cars on the road. But while I was talking to the dispatcher, smoke started coming out from under his hood. Within seconds there were flames."

Mom and Mallory gasp. My brothers sit frozen. Dad gives me a soft, steady look, urging me on.

"I screamed at Deidre to get out of the car. She managed to stumble away, but the other guy was still passed out. I tried to open his door, but it was crushed. So, I circled around to the passenger side, opened the door, and crawled inside. When he wouldn't wake up, I unbuckled his seat belt, then dragged him over the passenger seat, onto the pavement, away from the fire."

Mom presses a hand to her mouth. "Oh, Alex! You could have been killed!"

"I was fine." But I wasn't. I'm still not. Sometimes I can still smell the acrid smoke. I still hear Deidre's screams. Still see my hands slick with his blood. It replays like a broken record at three in the morning, or in the middle of a business meeting, or when I'm driving down the road. The only way I've learned to cope is shove it down so deep I can pretend it never happened. But burying it didn't just kill the guilt. It smothered everything else too.

Grant finally looks up, his face unreadable. "What happened to the man?"

"He lived. He spent weeks in the hospital and even longer in rehab." My voice splinters. "He'd broken his back in the accident and when I dragged him out..." I inhale sharply. "He's paralyzed from the waist down."

Mom and Mallory gasp. Dad just keeps his warm eyes on

mine. "And what did the hospital staff tell you?" he asks gently. "That if you hadn't pulled him out, he would have died. By the time emergency services arrived, the van was fully engulfed. You saved his life."

I shake my head, because no matter how many times someone says it, his life should never have been in danger to begin with.

"I send him money every month," I blurt out, instantly regretting it.

Tyler's brows shoot up. "Wait—what?"

"They started a fundraiser for him. It was still open when I graduated, so I began donating under another name. I still do, more now that I can afford it. He doesn't know it's me. I never want him to." I swallow. "I've never told anyone before. You guys are the first."

Mom's eyes shine with tears. "Alex, that's incredibly thoughtful."

I shake my head, my voice rough. "No. It's not thoughtful. It's penance."

Grant leans forward, his voice firm. "You weren't driving, Alex. Deidre was. And yeah, maybe pulling him made the injury worse, but at least he's alive. His kids still have a dad."

"Do you know if he's doing okay?" Mallory asks, her face pale.

I nod. "Yeah, I've done some light social media stalking. He's a software engineer. Still married. His oldest kid's in high school. The youngest is in middle school."

"So, he has a full life," Mom says.

I've tried to tell myself that a thousand times, but the weight on my chest hasn't budged.

"You need therapy," Tyler says quietly. I blink at him, surprised. "You lived through a trauma, Alex. You've been punishing yourself for years. You need help." Then his mouth tilts into a crooked smile. "And maybe you can work on that narcissism while you're at it. Only a narcissist would manage to take credit for paralyzing a guy while saving his life."

A half-laugh escapes. "Maybe you're right."

"That's why you've stayed away?" Mom asks, her voice breaking. "Because you were ashamed?"

"Yeah." I rake my hand through my hair. "I don't know. It's complicated." The words feel like gravel in my mouth. "I was scared of what you would think of me if you knew, but maybe..." My voice falters. "Maybe I also thought I didn't deserve to have you...?" The realization hits me as I'm saying it.

"Therapy," Tyler says, leaning back with a knowing look. "Trust me."

I stare at him, stunned. Has Tyler been in therapy? When he talks about trauma, it sounds like he's speaking from personal experience. When did he suffer through his own trauma? Does he have secrets of his own?

"Bob," Mom says, turning her gaze to my father. "How did you find out about all of this?"

"Alex called me from the crash site," Dad says quietly. "After the police and EMS got there. I told him to let me know where they were taking him, and I left and met him there."

"He was hours away," Mom says in disbelief. "How did you even get away?"

"Remember when I told you my sister Sylvia was having trouble with her second husband and needed my help?" She nods. "That was then."

"You were gone for days."

"Alex had a concussion, so I stayed to make sure he was okay." He gives me an apologetic smile. "Maybe I didn't stay long enough."

"And you didn't tell me?" Mom demands, her voice sharp now.

"The only way Alex would tell me what was going on was if I promised not to tell anyone—especially you. I've tried to get him to release me from the promise, but..."

"There's one thing you can always count on," I say softly, "and that's that Dr. Robert King is a man of his word." Guilt spears through me as I realize how much damage forcing him to keep my secret has caused. "I'm sorry, Dad."

He nods, his eyes glassy.

Tyler sits back in his chair. "Wow. You really do suck at asking for help, huh?" His tone is light. There's no malice behind it—just brotherly love.

"Did Deidre get in trouble?" Mallory asks.

"She was charged with DUI and a couple of misdemeanors. She ended up with probation, but we broke up because she tried to claim the crash wasn't her fault—that it had nothing to do with her .08 blood alcohol level. I couldn't stomach her lack of guilt when I was drowning in mine, so I ended it."

Silence hangs heavy for several seconds before I take another breath. "And since we're on the subject of confessions, I've got one more."

All eyes swing to me.

"There's no way to ease into this, so I'm just going to come out and say it: Grant, you were right. Finley is the barista at my coffee shop. I hired her to play my girlfriend, so I wouldn't have to sleep on the sofa bed."

Chaos detonates. Everyone starts talking at once.

Tyler blows up first. "So, what—her whole orphan act was fake? Tell me she was at least paid extra for the tragic backstory."

Grant pumps his fist. "I knew it! Pay up, Tyler!"

Mom bursts into tears. "You used that poor, sweet girl—on Christmas, no less. How *could* you?"

Dad doesn't say a word. He just stares at me, the disappointment on his face louder than any words could be.

Mallory shoots to her feet and lets out a piercing wolf whistle. Everyone freezes, mid-yell, like kids caught by their teacher.

"Thank you for your attention," she says matter-of-factly.

I cut straight to Tyler, since he's the only one questioning Finley's integrity. "Her backstory is real. The only thing we faked was the timing—when we told you we started dating after Maybelle got sick last fall." I hold up my hand to stop Tyler's imminent protest. "And yes, Maybelle really did have bladder stones."

Mallory jumps in before anyone else can pile on. "Good. Now that that's cleared up—what Alex hasn't said yet is that he's realized what they have *is* real. He needs to win her back. And *we* are going to help him."

"Say what?" Grant sputters, his eyes wide.

"You heard me. And everyone else saw it, am I right?" She sweeps the table with a pointed glare. "Who liked the Alex we saw with Finley?"

Hands shoot up—everyone except Grant.

He shrugs at the glares. "What? I hardly saw him with her. But..." He makes a face. "I'll admit, he was pretty defensive of a woman who supposedly isn't his girlfriend."

"Exactly." Mallory grins, triumphant. "We know Finley and her grannies are somewhere in Hollybrook. We just have to find them."

"And then what?" Tyler asks, skeptical.

Mallory turns to face me. "That part's up to Alex."

Tyler and Grant groan, but Mom's ready to springing into action. When the King family is determined to do something, we make it happen.

Right now, it's not *if* we find Finley—it's *when*. The terrifying part is what happens if she doesn't want me.

Chapter Thirty-Five

Finley

To my frustration, when I wake, I realize I slept the entire afternoon away.

Mom always told me that when I was little, my defense mechanism for overwhelm was sleep. Some things don't change. Only now, I don't feel rested—I feel hollow. I miss Alex, which is stupid. How can you miss someone so much after only three days?

Maybe staying in Hollybrook is a mistake. This is his town and everything will remind me of him. Maybe we should just go home.

When I start down the stairs, I find a pan of kitty litter in front of the door. After I set it in the bathroom, I shut Maybelle inside and go down. The smell of something warm and savory hits me, pulling me toward the kitchen. Mirna and Barb are bustling around in a way I've never seen before—working together, no bickering—and it stabs me with a memory of the past two days in the King kitchen.

A lump rises in my throat.

Stop thinking about Alex's family. They're not yours.

Mirna glances over and sees me in the doorway. "Well, look who's up."

"What are y'all doing?" I ask, even though it's obvious— they're cooking dinner. The sky outside is already dimming toward dusk.

"We found an open market to get kitty litter and decided since we were there, we might as well get stuff to make dinner," she says with a smile. "You can treat us to a meal another night. I trust you found the litter pan?"

"I did, and whatever you're making smells delicious. Sorry I slept so long."

"Poppycock." She waves me off. "You needed it."

"What's on the menu?"

"Ham, scalloped potatoes, green beans, and sweet rolls," Barb says. "And we even got a chocolate cake for dessert."

"Can I help?"

The two women exchange a glance before looking back at me.

"We've got everything under control," Mirna says. "You've got some free time. What would you like to do? Watch a movie? Read a book?"

"I've got several books in my suitcase you might enjoy," Barb says excitedly. "I can go grab them if you want."

I give her a weak smile. "No offense, Barb, but the last thing I want to read is a romance."

Her smile falters. "Yeah, I suppose I can see that."

"You really liked this boy?" Mirna asks.

I nearly laugh at her calling Alex a boy. "Yeah," I say with a sigh. Foolish heart.

Mirna turns back to chopping an onion. "He looked pretty devastated when you left. More devastated than a man ought to be over losing rights to a bed."

I know she's right. But in my mind, I twist it into something smaller. He was upset because of how badly Grant treated me. He felt responsible. That's all.

And yet, there's a tiny sliver of hope growing in my heart. I'm torn between coaxing it to life or stomping on it before it takes root.

"How about I just sit in here with you guys while you cook?"

"Whatever you want, dear," Mirna says.

"So, how mad were your families when you took off to rescue me in Vermont?" I ask with a laugh.

They dive into stories about the fallout—angry kids, annoyed daughters-in-law, and guilt trips galore. And for a little while, their voices are enough to pull me out of my spiral. The ache in my chest softens, if only for a moment.

A half hour later, they announce dinner is ready. I set the table with Christmas dishes from the cabinet and glasses with painted Santa faces. We've just started eating when there's a knock at the front door.

We all freeze, glancing at one another.

"Who on earth could that be?" Mirna asks.

"Maybe it's the landlord," Barb says. "Just like in—"

Mirna shoots her a glare sharp enough to cut glass, and Barb clamps her lips shut.

"I'll get it," I say, pushing away from the table. A grin tugs at my mouth. "Maybe it's the owner, only hopefully not here to do whatever depraved things Barb was about to suggest."

Barb's eyes sparkle with mischief. "Speak for yourself."

I cross the living room and pull open the door. Snow is falling again, a fresh layer already dusting the sidewalks and street. No one is on the porch, but a small group stands on the sidewalk, holding candles. As soon as they see me, they start to sing *Let it Snow, Let it Snow, Let it Snow.*

Carolers.

A week ago, I would've been bouncing with delight. Tonight, their voices and the song only make me ache. Alex should be here, listening to them with me, or out there singing with them.

"Who's at the door?" Barb calls out.

"Christmas carolers," I answer, my voice flatter than I intend.

"Well, *that's* a pity," Barb grumbles, appearing behind me.

"Where did that snowman come from?" Mirna asks as she steps into the doorway next to me.

I follow her gaze. Sure enough, a small snowman—three feet tall, at most—stands at the edge of the yard. I'm certain it wasn't there when we arrived. At first glance, it looks like any snowman: charcoal eyes, a carrot for the nose, a stocking cap, and a knit scarf.

But then my breath catches.

Because I know that hat. And that scarf.

They're Alex's.

My heart skips a beat.

Jingling bells cut through the night, growing louder. I step onto the porch just as a horse pulling a sleigh appears at the end of the street, trotting toward the house. An older man is sitting on the front bench, holding the reins.

"Is that... a *sleigh*?" Mirna asks, sounding dazed.

The sleigh stops in front of our house and my breath catches.

Alex is sitting in the back.

He stands and hops out, never looking away from me as he walks closer.

Behind him, another group appears on the sidewalk—candles glowing as they join the other carolers. It takes me a second to recognize them.

The King family.

I gasp as tears sting my eyes.

Alex stops at the bottom of the steps. His hands flex uselessly at his sides, like he doesn't know what to do with them. His jaw is tight, his shoulders tense, but his eyes—his rich brown eyes—are locked on me, pleading.

"What is this?" I ask, my gaze darting from his smiling mother and sister to his decidedly less-enthusiastic brothers.

Barb leans forward, her voice dry but amused. "Why, isn't it obvious? He's wooing you."

I gasp, my heart stuttering in my chest, unwilling to believe. I glance back at Mirna.

She gives me a small, knowing smile. "For once, I think Barb might be right."

Alex extends his hand. "Would you like to go on a sleigh ride?"

My chin trembles. "It depends."

Fear flickers in his eyes. "On what?"

"On whether you're asking me as your friend or..."

"Girlfriend?" he finishes, then swallows hard. "What if my

answer is—I *want* you to be my girlfriend. But if all I can get is friend, I'll take it and hope you'll let me prove I'm trustworthy."

I take a step toward him, sure I've misheard. "And if I said I'd like to be more than friends?"

His mouth curves, soft and unguarded. "Then that would be the best Christmas present I've ever gotten in my life."

"Hey!" Grant shouts. "It can't be better than the year I got you *Call of Duty.*"

Mallory elbows him hard enough to make him grunt and stumble.

Alex flashes a grin at his brother. "Sorry, asshole. This would be a million times better." Then he turns back to me, everything else falling away. "So... what do you say? Want to go on a sleigh ride?"

I try for a joke, my voice wobbling. "Isn't the line 'wanna build a snowman?'"

He gestures to the snowman in the yard. "Already built one for you. But we can build one together if you want. We can do *all* the Christmas things—I want to go sledding, have a snowball fight, and teach you how to ice skate. We can make gingerbread houses or paint Santas on ceramic plates and anything else you want to do."

"You actually want to do all that?"

He steps onto the lowest porch step, closing the space between us. "I want to do them with *you*, Finley."

I swallow hard. "But why?" My voice is barely a whisper. "I was only supposed to pretend to be your girlfriend. You don't have to do any of that with me."

He lifts his hand to my cheek. His fingers are cold, but his touch sends a thrill through me. "Because I *want* to be with you, Finley. I want *you*. I've been miserable since you left."

"I've only been gone about six hours," I murmur, stunned.

"The longest six hours of my life."

"It's true!" Mallory shouts behind him. "He's been moping around like a sad sack."

"Finley hasn't been much better," Barb calls from behind me.

"Barb!" Mirna snaps. "No helping the enemy."

"I just call 'em as I see 'em. And he's not her enemy—he wants to be her lover. Although enemies-to-lovers is always a satisfying trope."

My cheeks burn.

"How about we take it one step at a time?" Alex's eyes twinkle. "We could start with a kiss."

My breath hitches. "That seems like a reasonable place to start."

He grins. "How do you feel about public displays of affection?"

I grin back. "Depends. Are we in public right now?"

Still smiling, he lowers his mouth, his lips brushing gently against mine. I press into him, kissing him back, soft but certain. It's a tender kiss, but under the surface is the promise of so much more.

It's perfect.

When he pulls away, his gaze is full of wonder. "So... about that sleigh ride?"

I arch a brow. "Will it take us somewhere less public?"

His answering grin is pure mischief. "That can be arranged."

"Then why are we still standing here?"

Laughing, he sweeps me up into his arms and carries me to the sleigh.

"She doesn't have a coat!" Mirna calls after us.

"Her coat's in the sleigh!" Mallory calls out.

Sure enough, Alex sets me down in the sleigh, and under a blanket is Mallory's red coat and the scarf she got me for Christmas.

"You left it behind," Alex says.

He helps me into my coat, adjusts the scarf around my neck, and slips a hat and mittens on me, then he settles beside me and draws fake-fur blankets over us until I'm warm and cocooned.

"Okay, Jerry," he says to the driver. "We're ready."

Jerry snaps the reins, and the horse plods down the snow-covered street. Mirna and Barb wave, and Barb calls out, "Don't do anything I wouldn't do!"

"Why do I get the impression there isn't much Barb wouldn't do?" Alex asks with a laugh.

"Because it's an accurate assessment."

His family waves as we pass. Mallory is literally jumping up and down.

"Why do I think Mallory was instrumental in setting all this up?"

He grimaces. "Would it ruin it if she was?"

"No. It's like getting her blessing."

"You have my whole family's blessing," he says quietly. "I told them everything. That you weren't my girlfriend—but I want you to be."

My happiness falters. "Do they hate me?"

"Do you think they'd be out here caroling if they did? My brothers *hate* caroling." He tucks a piece of my hair behind my ears. "But they like you."

I stare up at him, sure this is a dream, and I'll wake up and find myself back in Atlanta. Alone.

"How did you find me?"

He laughs. "The joys of living in a small town. Everyone knows everyone's business. It took Mom about ten minutes and that was because she got stuck on the phone with Mrs. Hamilton for about seven of them."

I can't stop smiling.

"Do you think this is less public enough?" His gaze pins me. "Because I'm not sure how much longer I can wait to kiss you the way I've been wanting to kiss you for days."

"Yes." The word slips out, breathless.

His palm slides up the side of my neck, his thumb grazing my pulse as he tilts my head back. Then his mouth is on mine—hotter, hungrier than before. Every ounce of restraint we've been clinging to shatters like ice. My hands fist in his coat as I kiss him back, just as needy, just as desperate.

He kisses me like a drowning man searching for air—and I'm his only breath. When he finally pulls away, I'm dizzy, my lips tingling, my heart pounding against my ribs. "Is this real?" The words tumble out before I can stop them.

His thumb sweeps across my cheekbone, anchoring me. "Yes."

"How are we gonna make this work, Alex? We live completely different lives."

His thumb strokes my jaw, slow and deliberate. "I don't know, Fin. But I *do* know I was miserable without you. I don't want to feel like that again, so we'll figure it out—whatever it takes."

He lowers his mouth to mine again. This kiss is slower but no less intense, a promise in every brush of his lips. By the time he lifts his head, I believe him.

"Will you come back to my parents' house?" he asks softly.

For the first time, I glance away. "I don't think that's a good idea."

His face falls.

"But Barb and Mirna have the house for the rest of the week," I add quickly. "So maybe we could... date?"

His smile blooms, warm enough to melt the snow around us. "I would love to date you, Finley O'Brien."

The sleigh glides forward, the bells jingling in time with my racing heart, and as Alex's hand finds mine under the blanket, I know this is just the beginning of our story.

Epilogue

Finley

One Week Later

When I walk into Beans to Go on January second, I'm prepared for an inquisition. Maggie and Bethany texted me all week, demanding updates. But I kept things vague—just the holiday activities, nothing personal.

To be honest, I'm exhausted, but in the best possible way. Alex kept me busy every day, especially after Mirna and Barb went home a few days before New Year's Eve. Things were going well between us, and since he'd given Grant the bed in their room and moved to the sofa bed, he started staying in the cottage with me.

Not that I'm complaining.

Still, I'm nervous about being home. Hollybrook was like a fantasy—snow, sleigh rides, and Christmas village magic. But today's our first day in the real world, and I'm not sure how this version of us will hold up.

I unlock the door to the shop and walk inside. Maggie and Bethany are already behind the counter, prepping to open the shop. Maggie looks up, and her face lights up.

"Finley! Tell us everything!"

Bethany rushes over to join her. "Was it everything you hoped it would be?"

My face flushes. "That and more."

Maggie lets out an ear-piercing squeal. "Oh, my God, girl! You slept with him!"

My eyes fly wide. "Maggie! Shh! The whole office building's going to hear you!"

"Tell us everything!" Maggie insists.

"*Everything*!" Bethany echoes, grinning like a kid on Christmas.

"I don't think there's enough time before we open to tell you *everything*," I say, laughing. "But let's just condense it: the first two days were magical, Christmas Eve night and Day were awful, and everything after that was a dream."

Maggie narrows her eyes. "You never said a word about your Christmas being awful."

"I didn't want to worry you, but it all worked out in the end." I glance around the shop. "How were things here?"

"As I predicted," Maggie says in a smug tone, "We were slow. Everyone here takes off between Christmas and New Year's and we handled everything just fine."

"It's true," Bethany says. "So back to you and Alex—was this a holiday fling or an *actual* relationship?"

Heat creeps up my neck. "We're definitely going to try to make it work."

They both squeal and I cringe, laughing. "Why are you both so invested in my love life?"

"Because you deserve good things, girl," Maggie says. "And if that man has a lick of sense in his head, he'll make sure this works."

"Now give us more details!" Bethany demands. "We've about fifteen minutes until we open. You can talk while we work."

So while I set up the espresso machine, I give them the highlights—Christmas caroling, the Christmas market, and how Alex surprised me and took me to a Christmas tree farm to cut down a tree for our room.

"And then Grant showed up, and it all went to hell," I say, wincing. I tell them how furious he was, how he blamed me for his girlfriend breaking up with him. Then I tell them about Mirna and Barb swooping in to rescue me—renting a cottage across from the square and insisting I stay with them so I can still have my white Christmas. Until Alex showed up in a sleigh like something out of a Hallmark movie.

"Are you kidding me right now?" Maggie demands. "An honest-to-God sleigh?"

"With a horse and everything." My cheeks heat again. "He asked me to go back to his parents' house, but I told him I couldn't—and asked if we could date instead."

"You went on dates with the man who hired you to pretend to be his girlfriend?" Bethany asks in disbelief. "And he was okay with that?"

"Yeah," I say softly. "He was."

The truth is that week was magical. We *did* go on dates, sometimes all-day long dates that left me so exhausted I fell asleep the second my head hit the pillow. He taught me how to ice skate. We made snowmen, went sledding, and even had a snowball fight with his entire family—where I got sweet revenge by accidentally plastering Grant right in the face. We made a gingerbread house that collapsed five minutes after we finished and laughed until we cried.

Things went so well that on December twenty-eighth, Mirna and Barn announced they had to get back to Atlanta. The next morning, I stood on the front porch, waving goodbye as they drove away. I thought I'd feel sad, finding myself alone again, but I wasn't. I knew they'd come back in a heartbeat if I needed them. Besides, I had Alex. And his family.

After another fun-filled day—complete with visiting Santa and his reindeer—Alex took me to a festival in the square. A live band was playing, and when the music swelled, he held out his hand. He didn't say a word, just gave me a look I'd become addicted to over the past few days—a slow, mischievous grin.

I took his hand, and he pulled me to my feet. We danced under the twinkling lights while snowflakes drifted down around us. There were people everywhere, but it felt like we were the only two people in the world.

And when Alex took me home that night, I asked him to stay. And he did.

Last night was the first night I'd been alone since leaving for Hollybrook, and now, back in reality, I'm terrified Alex will change his mind. That he'll wake up in his real life and realize this was all a mistake.

But minutes before we're set to open, a knock sounds on the glass door.

"Someone's eager to get their caffeine fix," Maggie mutters, but then she looks up and grins.

I turn, and my breath catches. Alex is standing outside the door.

After seeing him in jeans and sweatpants all week, it's a shock to see him in a suit again—proof that we're back in the real world.

Maggie hurries over to the door and unlocks it. "Come in," she says, opening it wide. "But don't start thinking you can take advantage of dating one of the baristas."

He grins. "I can't make any promises, Maggie."

She laughs. "Well in that case, I suspect I'm not the one you're here to see."

"While I love seeing you, no." His gaze is locked on me.

I step around the counter as he walks toward me, a grin spreading across his face.

"What are you doing here?" I ask, my cheeks warming.

"I know you're not open yet, but I couldn't wait to see you." He pulls me in his arms and lowers his head, brushing his lips over mine in a tender kiss. "And I figured I wouldn't be able to do that once you opened."

I laugh, the last of my fear melting away. "Good thinking."

He leans close, his breath warm against my ear. "I missed you last night."

"I missed you too."

He glances over at Maggie and Bethany. "I take it you two knew our fake-dating situation turned into the real thing?"

"We did," Maggie says, beaming. "And for the record, I knew you two would be perfect together."

"You're a wise woman, Maggie," he says.

"It's about time someone figured that out," she grumbles.

We both laugh.

I grab the lapels of his suit jacket and tug him closer. "Go conquer the world today."

He smiles down at me. "And you keep them caffeinated."

Funny how less than two weeks ago, he would've been embarrassed by my job. Now he accepts it's part of who I am—at least until next August when I start nursing school. I found out I got the scholarship on New Year's Eve. I'll probably keep my phlebotomy job to help cover rent, but my classes will be during the day, which means my Beans to Go days are numbered.

I look up into his eyes, surprised how familiar they already feel. How right *this* feels. With our crazy schedules, it won't be easy, but we'll find a way.

I rise up on my toes and kiss him, still clutching his jacket. When I pull back, he stares down at me, beaming.

"You're sexy as hell when you do that," he says in a low rumble I feel down to my toes.

I kiss him again, wishing we both had the day off, but we don't so I sink back down. "I'm gonna miss you today."

He cups my cheek. "I'll miss you too. But I'll see you tonight when you get off work."

"Tonight," I echo.

He nods, smiling. "Tonight."

I release his lapels then smooth them down. "Okay, you better go now before we give our customers a show they weren't expecting."

"We're not complaining!" Bethany calls out.

Alex laughs, leans in for one last kiss, then he turns and heads for the door. He unlocks it and glances back at me, a smile lighting up his whole face.

The next two years might be tough, but I believe we'll make it.

✳ ✳ ✳ ✳ ✳ ✳

Read a bonus chapter of Finley and Alex's day in Hollybrook the day of the festival.
Go to:

Read Tyler's story, *Snow Hard Feelings.* the second book of the We Three Kings series, releasing October 2026.

Author's Note

The idea for this book was born in the summer of 2025. My kids and I were at the Outer Banks with my son-in-law and his parents. We were having such a great time that we decided we wanted to go back the next year. We found a house we would all fit in, but my currently single second oldest son, Ross, realized he would be relegated to the bunk bed room with his two younger siblings. One of his older sisters said, "You need to get a girlfriend so you can have a bed."

Ross said, "Maybe I'll ask the barista at Starbucks who always flirts with me."

His sisters thought that was a great idea, to which I said, "That sounds like a great romcom book. But what would be the title?"

Ross, who's a witty guy, said, "Bunk beds or Barista."

The conversation moved on, but I kept thinking about it. The next month, we were back home, and I texted my kids, "I think I'm going to write that book, only it's going to be Christmas instead of the beach, and bunkbeds instead of a sofa bed."

My kids weren't all that impressed, but I'm used to it. LOL

Honestly, they could care less what I write. Especially since they rarely read my books.

But I digress...

For readers who know the trouble I've had with creativity and writing, I'd only written one book this year, so this seemed like a *terrible* idea. I needed to write more mysteries. I needed to keep up the momentum.

But here's the thing—I was *really* excited about it. And I really needed excitement and some fun. So I threw caution to the wind and started writing that same day.

And I absolutely loved it.

Readers who know me, also know I'm a pantser, not a plotter. I had a few ideas about what I wanted to happen, but let's just say the story got away from me and turned into something completely different.

Let's just say I hadn't planned on writing a no-door romance. LOL But that's the way the story worked. The whole premise played on the the "does he/she really like me?" Anything sooner than the first kiss would give it all away.

As I started to get my ducks in a row to publish this book, three very knowledgeable, respected people in the world of self-publishing told me they thought I should write it under a pen name. Let's just say I balked at the idea until the very last moment —when the cover designer put my name on the cover and the narrators asked for the author name.

And thus, Rachel Thorne was born.

So for those of you who mostly read my mysteries and read this book: thank you for indulging me. And for those of you who are new readers, thank you for giving me a chance. I have multiple other romcoms under my Denise Grover Swank—some closed door, some a little spicy.

Thank you to Ross, Julia, and Jenna for helping birth this idea.

Thank you to my other children, Trace, Ryan, and Emma for supporting my and my career, especially as I've suffered and whined my way through writer's block over the last year.

And thank you to my readers, especially the ones who have been with me since the beginning.

About the Author

Rachel Thorne is the pen name of bestselling author Denise Grover Swank. While Denise now focuses mostly on mysteries, Rachel writes sweet, feel-good romcoms filled with heart, humor, and happily ever afters.

Rachel—okay, fine, Denise—is a single mom to three French bulldogs and one half–Golden Retriever. She also has six human children, all technically adults, though the jury's still out on a few of them.

She lives at the Lake of the Ozarks in the middle of Missouri. Yes, that Lake of the Ozarks—like the show Ozark—although not exactly like the show. She's yet to see Marty Byrde or anyone else from the series, and for the record, the lake isn't that wide, and the shoreline is absolutely packed with docks. (Those scenes were filmed in Georgia. False advertising much?)

Rachel's hobbies include reading, wasting massive amounts of time on Facebook and Reddit's AITA threads, deck gardening (poorly), and learning how to drive her new used boat—which keeps breaking down. (It's not her fault. She swears.)

Rachel hopes you love her books—and if you do, she'd love for you to leave a review. Denise, meanwhile, is busy cleaning up after the dogs.

www.ingramcontent.com/pod-product-compliance
Lightning Source LLC
Chambersburg PA
CBHW030532190726
48283CB00006B/1873